JOHN DALTO
STREET

y's Church
dden Gem

Pump House
Museum

GRAMPIAN
HOUSE

HEADPRESS 20
"Are you travelling BACK
through TIME?"

HEADPRESS

Editor
David Kerekes

Layout
David Kerekes & Walt Meaties
Front cover
Tom Brinkmann
Inside front cover photo
Will Youds
Back cover photo
Marie-Luce Giordani
Proofing
Sun Paige

Contributors
Anton Black
William Black
Tom Brinkmann
Mikita Brottman
Gemma Bryden
Jörg Buttgereit
Eugene Carfax
Michael Carlson
Rick Caveney
Simon Collins
Andy Darlington
Mark Deutrom
Progeas Didier
Dogger
Matthew Edwards
Mark Farrelly
Marie-Luce Giordani
David Greenall
Adrian Horrocks
Martin Jones
Brian Krueger
Drew Larson
James Marriott
Sun Paige
Pan Pantziarka
Anthony Petkovich
Rik Rawling
Dee Rimbaud
Jack Sargeant
Stephen Sennitt
Jack Stevenson
John Szpunar
Phil Tonge
Sarah Turner
Joe Scott Wilson
Will Youds

HEADPRESS 20
"Are you travelling BACK through TIME?"
Published in May 2000
by Headpress

Headpress
40 Rossall Avenue
Radcliffe
Manchester
M26 1JD
Great Britain
email: david.headpress@zen.co.uk
official unofficial website: www.headpress.com/

World Rights Reserved

British Library Cataloguing in Publication Data
A catalogue record for this book is available from the British
Library.

ISSN 1353-9760
ISBN 1 900486 09 1

Acknowledgements/Copyright

Adriadne (WW Norton), Hayley Ann (Co-
dex), Darren Arnold, Steve Bickerstaff,
Andrew Blake, Laura Briscall (Taschen),
Allan Brown, Tim Buggie, Mike Butterworth
(Savoy), Marisa Carr, John Carter, Mark
Chapman (Titan), Harvey Fenton (FAB),
Miranda Filbee (Creation), David Gregory/
Jake Shaw/Carl Daft (Exploited), Alex
Heminsley (MacMillan), Dave Huxley, Paul
Imagine, Lesley Kerekes, Stefan Jaworzyn,
Shusuke Kaneko, Jade Marcella, Caroline
Millar (BFI), Andrew Parker, Dave Patrick,
Harvey Pekar, Petra, Steve Puchalski (Shock
Cinema), Chris Reed (BBR), Lisa/Rachel
(The Associates), Roger Sabin, HE Sawyer,
David Slater, Alan Smith, Roy Stuart, Jan/
Eva Švankmajer, Claire Thompson/Joe Prior
(Turnaround), Anna Vallois (Serpent's Tail).

EDITORIAL

It's been a busy year so far for Headpress and our Critical Vision imprint. *See No Evil*, the long-awaited book on British "video nasties" culture is nearing completion and should be out by the time *Headpress 21* hits the shops. Subscribers to *Headpress* will be notified on its publication, and of course are entitled to a 10% discount (as they are on all new Critical Vision books). August will see the release of *Fleshpot*, Jack Stevenson's excellent overview of cinema's sexual myth makers and taboo breakers. It contains plenty of rare and previously unseen images, as well as featuring contributions from George Kuchar and Kenneth Anger, amongst many others.

One Critical Vision publication which has recently come out and already caused an outcry — according to the *Glasgow Sunday Herald* anyway — is *Killer Komix 2*. You can read all about it on page 159, but to fill in a little background information the outcry starts and ends with this particular piece of "exclusive" reportage. Thanks to Douglas Baptie for sending us the clipping.

Well, it's a sunny day and I'm inclined to go for a walk in the park. After that I might even visit the seedier stores of my fair city, before big business and local government squeezes the last of them out for the sake of sporting-bids and brand name coffee houses. Catch you later! DAVID

CONTENTS

ON THE RACK~Magazines & Racks I Knew and Loved, or, Pulp Consumer Consumed by Pulp
Tom Brinkmann   *4*

THE SUCKER PUNCH~A Personal Discourse on Females Slugging It Out In The Ring and The Men Who Like To Watch
Gemma Bryden   *14*

SPLENDOR—AMERICAN STYLE!~An Interview with Harvey Pekar
John Szpunar   *20*

SOCK IT TO EVERYBODY! AT ONCE!~A Brief Interlude with Zeta Magazine
David Kerekes   *34*

ELVIS THE CONCERT
Joe Scott Wilson   *38*

CRIME CALLS... BUT IT DOESN'T PAY
William Black   *40*

THERE AREN'T MANY HIPPIES IN HULL~An Interview with Andy Darlington
David Kerekes   *44*

PLAYING DEVIL'S ADVOCATE~Five Reasons Why The Exorcist Isn't Scary Anymore
Adrian Horrocks   *59*

I SAW HUGE SPIDERS~Meddlesome Christians Flush Your Stash Down the Toilet
Martin Jones   *64*

TO GRILL A CHRISTIAN
Matthew Edwards   *67*

DARKNESS LIGHT DARKNESS~Meeting Jan Švankmajer pt 2
Will Youds   *68*

L'ABÉCÉDAIRE CHIMERIQUE
Progeas Didier   *71*

OH, DR KINSEY!~Swinging Sex and Pseudo Science
Mikita Brottman   *72*

MEN IN RUBBER SUITS~Jörg Buttgereit Talks To Japanese Monster-Film Director Shusuke Kaneko
Jörg Buttgereit   *75*

CAK-WATCH! PRESENTS: The Wicker Bastard
Phil Tonge   *79*

INSIDE THE WICKER MAN~An Interview with Allan Brown
Sun Paige   *85*

BEAUTIFUL LETTUCE PAGES & Rubber Dolls
88

GENERATION XPLOITATION & An Interview with Alan Smith
Simon Collins   *90*

FROM INDONESIA WITH LUST~An Interview With Jade Marcella
Anthony Petkovich   *105*

OF CELLULOID AND SLIME~An Insider Retrospective of the Scandalous 1997 Hamburg Short-Film Festival
Jack Stevenson   *109*

PAUL SCOTT~Artist at Large!
Drew Larson   *115*

THE QUEST FOR THE POETRY GROUPIE
Andy Darlington   *117*

THE HEADPRESS GUIDE TO EXCITING! MODERN! KULTURE
126

MERCHANDISE~Books, T-shirts & Subscriptions
159/160

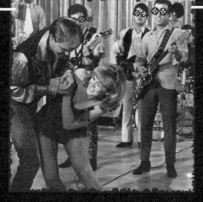

THE GIG FROM HELL

WE WANT YOUR STORIES!

We've all played one (or 200): bad equipment, hostile club owners, preposterous venues, bizarre bookings, substance abuse, ego trips, fights, weird sex, vermin, audience antics and all the rest. Now collecting your true GIG FROM HELL stories for an upcoming anthology. Anyone with stories of any length are welcome to contribute.

Response so far has been morbidly hilarious.

We'll focus mainly on things at the PUB/CLUB LEVEL, for that added air of hopelessness. Remember, what's typical for you is often outrageous to others.

We'll list only first name, city and instrument played (or whatever position/occupation at time of story) but will change or withhold details upon request. All submissions become the property of Headpress/Critical Vision for publication in THE GIG FROM HELL.

Sorry, but we cannot pay for submissions.

Here are the ways you can contribute:

1. Type and mail your story to the PO box below
2. Speak onto a cassette and mail to same
3. Email to: david.headpress@zen.co.uk

Critical Vision, PO Box 26, Manchester, M26 1PQ, Great Britain

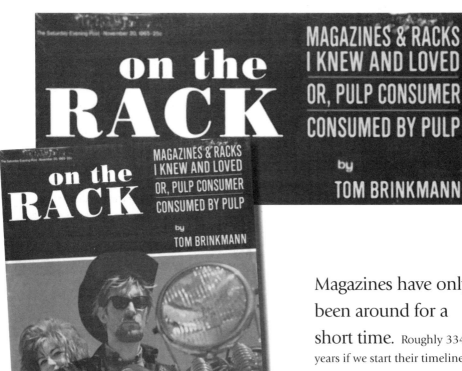

on the RACK

MAGAZINES & RACKS I KNEW AND LOVED OR, PULP CONSUMER CONSUMED BY PULP

by

TOM BRINKMANN

In a **time travelling frame of mind**, putting magazines from future racks onto past newsstands would be considered a subversive act. Randomly and discretely placed supermarket tabloids announcing **the death of Elvis**, placed in the open windows of parked cars in 1999. Putting 1960s **gore tabloids** in the waiting-rooms of doctors! Intergalactic distributors, **vying for shelf space**... bundles of 25 falling from the sky... magazines from other worlds, earthbound, as reported in some future issue of 'The Fortean Times'...

Magazines have only been around for a short time. Roughly 334 years if we start their timeline with what is considered to be the first periodical, the French *Journal des scavans*. The first to actually use the word "magazine" (in the sense of a periodical for entertainment) was reportedly the English monthly *Gentleman's Magazine*. How these early magazines were distributed, I can only guess — hawked them on street corners, probably.

So the news-stands evolved to shelter the early dealers of pulp from the elements. And what of the little bundles of joy themselves? The magazines? Sold to the public; never to be nestled together again in the same space and time; scattered to the wind like pollen or seed, disseminated bits of information, gossip, humour and news.

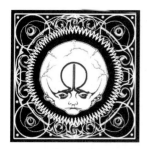

I ENTERED THE TIMELINE of magazines in 1960. I was five-years-old, sitting in my grandfather's library looking at 1940s and Fifties issues of the *National Geographic Magazine*. Not able to read much yet, I was fascinated by the photos and paintings, which would mesmerise me for hours. A few years down the line I had graduated to such things as *Highlights* and *Boy's Life*, to which I subscribed, courtesy of my parents.

The first pulp rack I found myself attracted to was the comic book rack at the local mom & pop grocery store — Millbrook Market. For some reason, they only carried comics with painted covers; all the Gold Key, Dell and Classics Illustrated titles. In 1962 I bought my first comic book, the third issue of *KONA Monarch of Monster Isle*. The cover depicted Kona astride a monstrous shark while plunging his bayonet into it. In the background were the family he was protecting, cowering on a ledge of a cavern. The art on the inside was drawn by Sam Glanzman, and in hindsight looks like a sloppy version of Joe Kubert. But at the time, what did I know or care? I was impressed enough to go home and ask for the 12 cents to purchase it. I was given a quarter. I promptly went back to the store and scooped the comic off the rack, paid for it and walked home while gawking at it like I had discovered some rare alien treasure. (Which in a way I had.) When I got back home my parents asked if I had the change from the quarter. Of course I had, and gave it back… only to be informed that it wasn't the right amount of change! I had to go back and get the right money, which kind of put a damper on my first comic book purchase. As of issue #15, *Kona* stopped using painted covers, and switched over to pen and ink art with four-colour overlay. I was disheartened when in 1967, after 21 issues, it stopped altogether. I wrote a letter to Dell comics asking the reason why. They replied that it wasn't selling well anymore…

AFTER KONA I WENT ON TO OTHER COMICS — also with painted covers of feral-looking heroes battling monsters, dinosaurs and beasts in general. Comics such as *Turok Son of Stone*, *Tarzan* and later on, DC's *Anthro*. I also got hooked by the "dinosaurs attack" covers of DC's *Star Spangled War Stories* where the monsters fought against tanks and soldiers. Later on when it started running its "Enemy Ace" series, this became my favourite comic (and actually *was* drawn by Joe Kubert).

To find these comics — which were not sold at the local mom & pop store — my friends and I had to make excursions on our bikes to other parts of town. This brought us into contact with more exotic and sleazy fare — gems such as *The Police Gazette*, *Monsters To Laugh With*, *Monsters, Unlimited*, *National Enquirer* and the sleazy tabloids of the time. Also we started noticing the girlie magazines, which again were not to be found at our friendly neighbourhood mom & pop. *Mad*, the

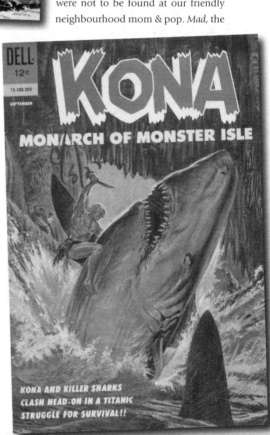

kids' bible back then, was a major fascination to me, but because good ol' mom had seen a copy once and found something inside she considered racy, I wasn't allowed to bring *Mad* into the house. This of course didn't prevent me from reading it, thanks to friends and their older brothers.

In the summer of '65 I turned 10 and the ban on *Mad* was lifted (after much bellyaching from me). The first copy I bought was #96. I eventually subscribed and continued to buy it for the next eight years, along with the paperback reprints of the earlier issues.

About a year later, when visiting relatives on Long Island, mom and I went into New York for the day and one of our stops was the offices of *Mad* magazine on Madison Avenue. The halls were lined with some of the original cover paintings by Kelly Freas and Norman Mingo. We were shown around by the janitor and visited the art department and a few of the offices. He gave me a couple of Alfred E. Neuman promo records, which were, I think, "It's A Gas" and "She Lets Me Watch Her Mom & Pop Fight". In the elevator on the way out we found ourselves with someone who spoke with a heavy foreign accent, and during the conversation he informed us that he was the artist who drew the Spy vs. Spy strip for *Mad*! I didn't know his name because he always signed his strips in Morse Code.

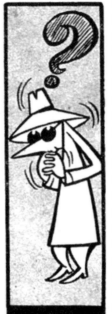

THE FIRST MONSTER MAG I BOUGHT WAS THE August '65 issue of *Famous Monsters of Filmland* which had a painting of Fredrick March's Mr Hyde on its cover. This I found at Britt's Department Store, whose magazine rack was located near the lunch counter. It became my favourite rack at this time. *Famous Monsters* also got my loyalty (along with its sister illustrated horror titles), until the early Seventies when I stopped buying it. Other types of publications that I was reading included UFO/Flying Saucer mags, Pro-Wrestling mags with gory covers of wrestlers' faces covered in blood, and the usual juvenile humour mags in all their many manifestations. Then in the late Sixties puberty set in — around this time Raquel Welch in her *One Million Years BC* costume was turned into countless posters, one of which ended up on my wall. After this my pulp interests were redirected towards the "adult" offerings available.

I discovered *Playboy* sometime in the Sixties — again with a little help from my friends and their older brothers. And on occasion we would raid our parents' drawers for adult pulp goodies. In 1967, during the "Summer of Love", one of my friends' parents went on vacation to San Francisco and took a bus tour of the Haight Ashbury district to see the hippies (who had become a tourist attraction, much to their dismay and amusement, I would guess). They bought

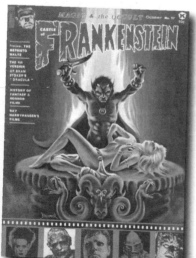

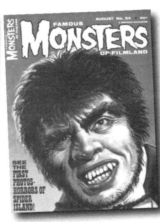

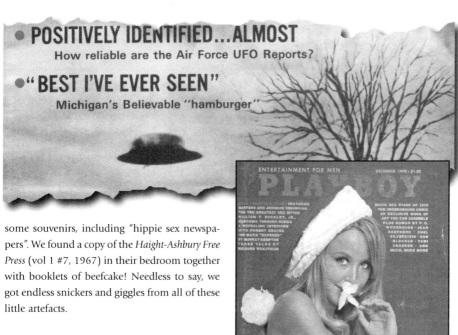

POSITIVELY IDENTIFIED…ALMOST
How reliable are the Air Force UFO Reports?

"BEST I'VE EVER SEEN"
Michigan's Believable "hamburger"

some souvenirs, including "hippie sex newspapers". We found a copy of the *Haight-Ashbury Free Press* (vol 1 #7, 1967) in their bedroom together with booklets of beefcake! Needless to say, we got endless snickers and giggles from all of these little artefacts.

THE EASTMAN GARAGE WAS AN ABANDONED AUTO mechanic shop across the street from Millbrook Market. One day a friend and I decided it would be a good idea to get into the place through a hidden side entrance. We climbed in and wandered around the deserted building, looking at rusty tools, cans with old labels, and some rather large spiders hanging out in the corners. Then we found a stack of old magazines! They were mostly 1940s *American Mercury* and, as I remember, some men's adventure type mags. The *American Mercury* was a digest-sized publication with interesting painted caricatures on the covers (comprising notables of the time). It was founded and, up until 1933, was edited by HL Menken. Given my age at the time, the only things that held my interest were the great covers and political cartoons on the inside. One artist, whose name I don't recall, drew these incredibly detailed caricatures mocking the likes of Hitler, Mussolini and Hirohito. They were extremely ornate, having a Beardsley or Harry Clark quality to them.

One day, while doing who knows what at the age of 13, I stumbled upon the motherlode of all magazine racks! In the middle of town was a store called Super X (no kidding), which primarily sold all the things you would find in a pharmacy, except for prescription goods. Once you got past the front counter and made a left, the magazine rack was staring you in the face. A mass of col-

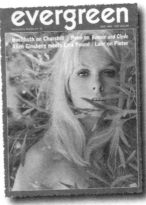

ours, pictures, titles, grabbers and blurbs from the floor upwards, it ran the whole length of the aisle to the back of the store, where it ended in a small jungle of turn-style racks for paperbacks. It seemed as if every magazine published was on this rack, stuff I didn't even know existed. The scales had fallen from my pulp searching eyes! Every sleazy men's adventure magazine was there, alongside detective, girlie, sex humour, UFO, horror, monster, juvenile humour, crime, wrestling, war stories, hot rod and tabloids of the most questionable sort. All resided together on that one wall. I would spend countless hours and dollars there during the next four or five years, trying to avoid the eyes of the dark-haired, cigar chomping, swarthy looking sentinel behind the front counter, and the

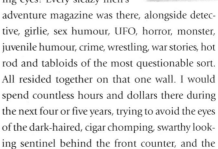

mirror that overlooked the magazine aisle in which he could see everything.

It was from this rack at Super X that I first discovered the *Evergreen Review*. Lured by the blonde beauty on the cover, *Evergreen #55* June '68 opened up a new world, hipper than *Playboy* and far more underground as far as content went. But it was the article on *Bonnie & Clyde* that I bought it for — a small fad that year on account of the movie which had stirred up controversy due to its explicit violence. The killers became resurrected folk heroes overnight. I was completely infected with the B&C bug having gotten in to see the film against my parents wishes and despite the age restriction. I bought all the related paperbacks, crime magazines (also from Super X), and the soundtrack album! A one-shot mag called *Gangland Killers* had a b&w cover with Warren Beatty (as Clyde) in the throws of shooting a tommy-gun, beneath which was a picture of the real killer-couple.

Crime Does Not Pay and *Crime And Punishment* were the two titles that I sought the most, as they often had articles on Bonnie & Clyde and other gangsters from past decades (not to mention a smattering of scantily clad women throughout). Most issues had brightly coloured circus poster-type covers with monotone photos on them, until the last few issues when they changed over to painted covers, one of which depicted a gangster tied to a chair while another guy was burning his face off with a blow torch.

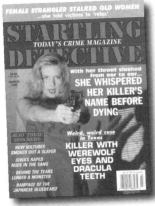

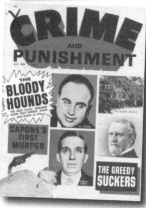

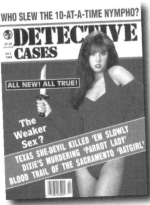

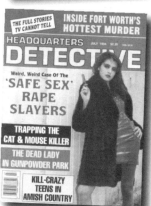

I HAD SEVERAL SUBSCRIPTIONS to comics and magazines over the years: *Mad*, of course, *Metal Men*, *Star Spangled War Stories* and *Showcase*. I was much more a DC fan than Marvel at first, until Marvel came out with *Conan the Barbarian*.[1]

Esquire was another magazine that interested me. It always had very clever and topical covers, so I was a fashionable subscriber in 1968 and '69. Going through a fascination with radical underground Sixties politics and the MC5, I sent in my dollars for a subscription to the *Ann Arbor Argus* — as close as you could get to an official White Panther Party newspaper. It featured The Stooges, Up, SRC, MC5, John Sinclair, Pun Plumandon and all the other WPP cast of characters, with a dash of stars and stripes and a heaped helping of guitars, guns, marijuana leaves and purple ink. Its main house artist went by the name of "Bad Dog", and #26 had a cover by Detroit poster artist Gary Grimshaw.[2]

By 1979 I had collected over 200 underground papers from all over the country, many purchased in Greenwich Village paper ephemera/ nostalgia shops. Everything from the *East Village Other* to the *San Francisco Oracle* was in there, including a stack of *International Times*, which the son of a book store owner had collected in England before moving to the US.

IN 1969, I SAW FOR THE FIRST time several strange little

otherworldly comics at a friend-of-a-friend's house, and was instantly entranced by the colourful covers, bizarre graphics and pants pissing hilarity. These were *Bijou Comix* #2 and #3, and *Zap Comix* #1 and #2 — one of which was drawn by "that guy that did the *Cheap Thrills* album cover" R. Crumb. It was no wonder then, when I first saw the title *Headcomix* staring up at me from the bookstore table, I immediately recognised the artist and bought it. This particular book got my comix toting butt thrown out of Junior High School for a day. I had loaned it to a fellow student, who got caught passing it around his class. It was confiscated by the teacher, who then gave it to the principal. Since I had written my name on the inside front cover (and coloured in many of the panels with coloured pencils) it didn't take Dick Tracy to figure out whose comic it was. I didn't care about my suspension, but I was pissed that I didn't have the book any more! My parents were called, Mom showed up, and with as much drama as he could muster, the principal sat us down and pulled out a manila envelope. "Your son was caught passing this around to other students," he said. Mom took the book, flipped through it quickly and handed it back to me — much to the principal's dismay and my surprise!

What seemed to have offended the principal most was one panel depicting a tunnel of breasts and nipples. I didn't go to school the next day, but I still had my book!

HEAD SHOPS STARTED POPPING UP HERE AND there, all containing new racks and shelves to scour. My friends and I made pilgrimages to college towns to find little hole-in-the-wall head shops with their handfuls of comix and underground newspapers. A couple of early comix finds I remember were *San Francisco Comics* #1 with a great R. Hayes cover, which I got from a head shop called Xanadu in Hampton Beach, NH (it had a bunch of comix on a shelf that you had to dig through while inhaling incense, which could still be smelled on the comix years later), and *Yellow Dog* #9/10, which I found at a head shop called Bull Durham, in Durham, NH. Then, in the December 1970 issue of *Playboy* there was an article on the phenomena of underground comix, which put them into historical perspective and legiti-

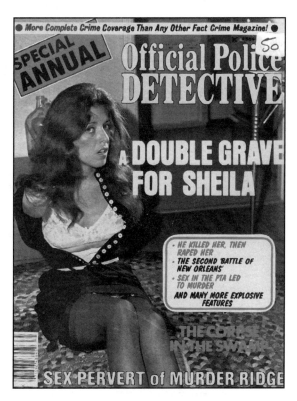

mized them in my mind as something to be avidly collected. I got the addresses of places I could buy them mail order, thereby filling the holes in my collection.[3] Even at that early date some comix were out of print and hard to find. It never occurred to me that people other than myself were trying to complete collections of these comix, and it wasn't until I got to NYC a few years later that I discovered collectors putting together wants lists of underground comix and papers. In seeing these lists, I discovered there were many "regional" type comix that I had never heard of, such as *Gimmeabreak Comix* from Ohio.

ROCK MAGAZINES WERE ANOTHER STAPLE OF MY pulp diet, starting in the late Sixties with titles like *Teenset, Circus, Crawdaddy, Creem,* and *Rolling Stone.* Later on came *Rock Scene,* which covered more of the early glitter/glam/punk bands I was listening to, and the only American rock magazine to put the NY Dolls on the cover (March '74 issue).

One of the stranger magazines in this genre was *Star* (not to be confused with the celebrity tabloid), which came out sometime in the early

Seventies and was — we were to believe — written by, and for, groupies in their early teens. This was the second wave of groupies, giving the original lot — who had become older and maybe wiser — a run for their rock stars. As I remember, the articles were about how to get backstage, into

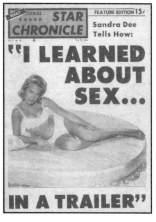

hotels, how to be noticed by certain rock gods and how to foil the wiles of your groupie rivals. Included were photos of young girls dressed in their finest groupie regalia. *Star* didn't last more than a few issues.

MY BASEMENT AT home had turned into a reading room of sorts. Friends would come over and I'd show them this or that weird magazine or comic. For a while I kept my underground comix in an old trunk in a small "bomb shelter" that my parents had built in 1960 at the height of the

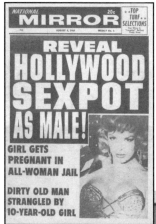

atomic scare. It was no more than a corner of the basement walled off with cinder block, and had a "maze" type doorway leading into it (the theory being that radiation couldn't go around corners or some such nonsense).

RUMFORD PRESS WAS A LARGE PRINTING PLANT in the town where I lived, and was its biggest employer; printing, binding and shipping around the clock, using several, two storey high, web presses. They had printed the Classics Illustrated comics at one point, but had long stopped by the time I got a job there while in High School, working the "graveyard" shift (4pm-12am) in the bindery deptartment. Some of the many titles they did print during my employment were *Analog*, *Alfred Hitchcock's Magazine* and *Sexology*. These provided good reading material when the machines went down or when things got slow.

The early Seventies were a watershed of freshly discovered magazines, comix and offbeat tabloids. I started buying older tabloids, trying to tap into the sleaze and sensationalism vibe from years past[4] as the recent editions had already gone ga-ga over star gossip, specifically related to "Jackie O" and the Kennedy clan.

There were plenty of sleazy sex tabloids, emanating from Canada and sometimes printed on tacky looking pastel pink or green newsprint. These I found on a little wire rack that resided in a small store, dingy on the inside, whose propri-

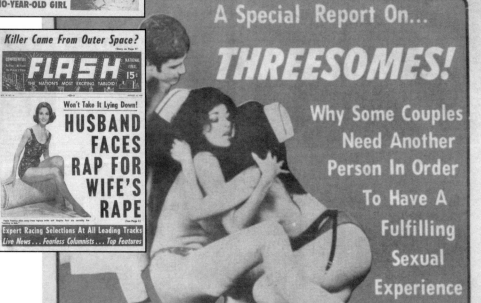

etor always gave the impression of being slightly drunk. He was always happy to sell us cigarettes, beer and tabloids, even though we were underage. These tabloids were the only reading material he sold. I bought the premiere issue of *Star* — b&w except for the red logo — which had Bruce Lee on the cover. Now it's all in colour, and second only to the *Enquirer*.

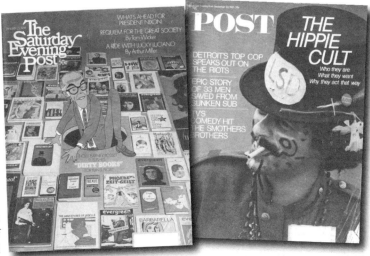

I HAD HEARD ABOUT, BUT NEVER seen a copy of *Castle of Frankenstein*, until one day I walked into a lunch counter which had hitherto escaped my notice. Opposite the counter, there on a shelf that ran along the floor, was a copy of *CofF* #15. This was a great little mag, which didn't contain the run of the mill monster articles. They had ads and reviews of underground comix, fanzines, and some obscure horror movies. I bought other issues as they came out and rounded up the back issues.

On one trip to a head shop in a nearby town, I found the first issue of *High Times*, an interesting and timely publication on the use of drugs! Since I had been using drugs myself for five years, I thoroughly enjoyed this maverick magazine. Sorry to say, the current issues do not stand up very well against their earlier incarnations.

Up until this time, girlie magazines had contained only comparatively tame T&A material. But around 1971, a British mag by the name of *Penthouse* had come to the US, and introduced pubic hair to the waiting masses. All the other adult mags followed its lead. One day, at a truck stop gas station on the edge of town, I noticed a new title nestled between the usual girlie fare: *Hustler*. I picked it up (vol 1 #6 Dec. '74) and flipped through, discovering that the layouts were a little more explicit in the genital dept and the cartoons a lot more scatological. Being the curious, stoned little horn dog I was, I bought it.[5]

OLD ENOUGH TO DRIVE, MY FRIENDS AND I would haul ourselves down to early Seventies Boston, which opened up new vistas of pulp searching heaven. I didn't waste any time finding the joke and porn shops on Tremont Street and in the "Combat Zone", Boston's XXX district.[6]

It was around this time that I started having dreams involving magazine racks. Not your run-of-the-mill racks nor environs, but racks in the open under starry night skies, containing magazines with strange hieroglyphic titles and bizarre covers; mazes of racks; strange people milling around, like in some unknown hybrid painting by Chirico or Magritte, shuffling in trench coats and sunglasses, and flipping through even stranger pages. This was in contrast to other dreams I'd had of a more claustrophobic nature, featuring tight underground staircases dug into

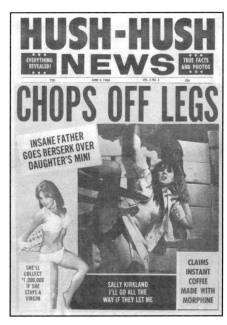

the earth, leading down to root choked libraries of a decidedly ancient nature; aisles with barely room to move, dust and dirt in eyes and lungs; fungi and lichen encrusted books of all dimensions and descriptions, through which earthworms would burrow.

These dreams aren't that odd considering I spent a lot of time around magazine racks and book stores, and of course had read all the Lovecraft I could get my hands on. I had always looked upon comics, magazines and books (amongst other things) as entities unto themselves, which I still believe they are — part of the overall glamour that enhances our lives.

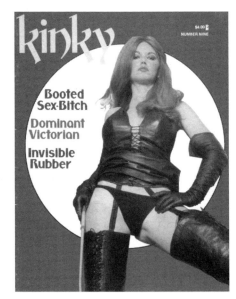

IN 1975 I MOVED TO START SCHOOL IN NYC, whereupon I started to notice these little flyers/ posters which stated, simply, "PUNK is coming". They didn't give much away but did feature a caricature of Lou Reed in a leather jacket. This drawing turned out to be the cover of *Punk* #1, an innovative zine that began as a folded-in-quarters paper before it changed to a magazine format. It was unique in that it was entirely hand lettered, i.e. no type setting at all! *Punk* truly defined the punk mindset, and came from The Bowery in NYC — punk central, home of CBGB's. A few blocks away, in the East Village, there were many little book stores, magazine racks and shops selling new and used pulp, not least of which was the Gem Spa corner news-stand, famed for having the New York Dolls pose in front of it for the back cover of their first album.

The late Seventies and early Eighties were the start of the real boom in alternative and self published magazines and comix, thanks to faster, cheaper and higher quality copiers and printers. I picked up the early issues of *RE/Search* (when it was a tabloid), *Slash* and *Search & Destroy*, along with countless other mags in St Mark's Place.

Back then, hardcore/fetish porn seemed more interesting than it is now — very possibly because it was all new to me. Almost all the fetishes explored in porn magazines in the Sixties and Seventies, became

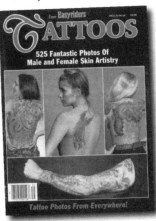

fashion statements in the decades that followed. Tattoo magazines are an interesting case in point.

There were no tattoo magazines sold on newsstands until 1983, when *Easyriders* put out *Tattoos*, the first news-stand magazine solely devoted to the subject. It was a one-shot that filled a vacuum, in spite of the fact that most of the tattoos it featured were of the common and rather crude variety found in the biker magazines. Apart from the occasional article in girlie mags, biker mags had been the only widely available source for tattoo literature; publications like *The Tattoo Advocate* and, later, *Tattootime* were mail order only, for "people in the know".[7] But because of growing demand, *Biker Lifestyle* brought out with *Tattoo*, and a few years later the publishers of *Outlaw Biker* came out with their own *Tattoo Revue*.

WITH TODAY'S LARGE, WELL LIT mega-book stores, comic book department stores and the likes of Tower Records and Virgin dipping their toes in the alternative waters, small shops will either go the way of the head shop, and become nonexistent, or will succumb to collector price fever along with flea markets, where everything is touted as "collectable". The line between comics and comix has been blurred beyond recognition. Nowadays, kids buy comics hermetically sealed in double bags and store them away as "investments".

Ballpoint pen marks, creases, book store stamps, stickers and mailing labels, all act as fingerprints as to where the magazine, comic or paperback has been. But these signs of human perusal and activity may soon be a thing of the past, with multimedia/interactive "magazines" on CD-ROMs perhaps soon becoming the norm. *Totally Mad* from Broderbund/The Learning Company, comprises seven CD-ROMs on which all the issues from 1952-1998 are contained in their entirety. To paraphrase a recent TV commercial for e-business, eventually you will be able to get anything ever published anywhere, in any language, at any time.

Then there are the on-line auction sites, where I can find myself in a bidding war with someone unseen and unknown, for a lot of six copies of *National Enquirer* from 1971. Losing the bid with only seconds to go, I laugh maniacally at the absurdity of it all!

But, if you're lucky, you just might find that little out-of-the-way place you never noticed before. You go in. The floors are wooden and not

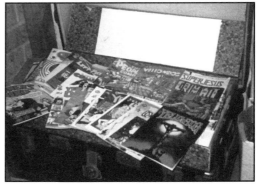

The author's trunk o'comix, circa 1972.

quite level. The place is cramped and dingy. There's a musty smell. The assortment of goods on the shelves serve almost as props, or a good excuse to have a magazine rack. The guy behind the front counter, with the red bleary eyes, doesn't even notice you. Your eyes gaze along the titles in search of *Interstellar Planetoid Daily* vol 45 #469, which is nowhere to be found. They come to rest on a curious title, *Mondo Headpress 3000*. You wonder whether it's a descendant of that mag you read way back in the 21st century. Now *that* was a magazine! But, today you settle for the tabloid on the bottom shelf, *Horizontal Midnight #1*. ✒

1. Barry Smith's version of Conan was a little disorientating after Frazetta's quintessential paintings for the paperback series. It could be my imagination, but Frazetta seems to have fashioned his version after a Jack Palance character from a 1950s sword and sandal movie!

2. Even though my copies are long gone, I kept a list of all the underground newspapers in my collection at the time (the bibliophile in me) and my subscription

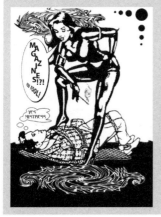

ran from Volume 1 #13 Oct 8-22, 1969 through #33 Nov 12-26, 1970 (17 issues).

3. The Print Mint, Bud Plant (starting out), San Francisco Comic Book Company, Last Gasp and so on. By 1972, many underground comix were stocked at local bookstores, which took the adventure out of searching for them.

4. As in fifth grade when the class had to do oral book reports, and this one kid bases his on a story he had taken out of a *National Enquirer* belonging to his mother! The story involved some husband or wife who had ground up their spouse in a garbage disposal! This same kid had regaled us in the lunchroom with tales of someone adrift in a life raft at sea, who had to drink their own urine to survive. Now we knew his source!

5. Apparently *Hustler* had it's beginnings as a four page, b&w *Hustler Newsletter* in March of '72 — a service to the members of the Hustler Club chain in Ohio. In July '74 the magazine was launched.

6. A good account of one of the Zone's porno theatres (The Pilgrim) can be found in issue #4 of *Vex*.

7. Heavily tattooed and pierced people were mostly considered "underground", notably the sex underground. Who could have known that 10 years later it would be a major fashion with young people!

Benton, Mike. *The Illustrated History of Horror Comics*; Dallas, Tx: Taylor Publishing, 1991
Benton, Mike. *The Illustrated History of Crime Comics*; Dallas, Tx: Taylor Publishing, 1993
Betrock, Alan. *The Illustrated Price Guide to Cult Magazines 1945-1969*; Brooklyn, NY: Shake Books, 1994
Betrock, Alan. *Sleazy Business: A Pictorial History of Exploitation Tabloids 1959-1974*; Brooklyn, NY: Shake Books, 1996
Brackman, Jacob. "The International Comix Conspiracy", *Playboy* v17 #12, Dec 1970
Henkel, David K. *Collectible Magazines Identification & Price Guide*; NY: Avon Books, 1993
Hogshire, Jim. *Grossed-Out Surgeon Vomits Inside Patient!*; Venice, Ca: Feral House, 1997
Kennedy, Jay. *The Official Underground and Newave Comix Price Guide*; Cambridge, Ma: Boatner Norton Press, 1982
Stevenson, Jack. "The Day They Turned the Lights Up", *Vex* #4, Spring/Summer 1999
Watson, Carl. "Lurid Tabloids of the '60s!", *Toxic Horror* #4, June 1990

the Sucker Punch

Gemma Bryden

The blonde stood in her corner, her well toned arms resting lightly on the ropes. She looked over to the blue corner and her opponent who was being talked to by her coach. The other girl was larger, her bare midriff solid and glowing with warm-up sweat. **She looked like she could take a few hits**. It should be a good fight.

The bell rang and almost instantly they were upon each other. As punches and kicks flew, the smell of leather and sweat filled the air. For two minutes the girls embodied fury as punches stung lips and solid kicks invaded taut stomachs. **Their muscular bodies glistened as they worked on each other**; their thighs touching as they reached in close, seeking an entry point and the chance to connect with kidney or temple.

A personal discourse on females slugging it out in the ring and the men who like to watch

Photos this article © Andrew Blake
Art © Gemma Bryden

The bell rang and they retreated to their corners. Sucking in deep breaths, the blonde did not lose eye contact with her opponent for a second. The brunette was breathing hard, a small cut on her brow leaking slightly — but she still had more to give. The blonde stood and stretched her lean, lithe body, drawing in strength for the next round.

The bell rang and once again they were alone in the ring. The second round was not so furious, with fatigue sneaking into their limbs. The brunette feinted low and came up sharply with a crunching upper cut. The blonde reeled for a second grunting in pain, but she gracefully turned and let go with a beautifully executed heel kick. It connected well with the darker girl's mouth, forcing the lower lip to give under the pressure. It was the brunette's turn to waver and the blonde capitalised by continuing with her spin, smashing a back fist into the side of her opponent's face.

The brunette's strong limbs gave way.

She was only out for a second but it was enough. The blonde reached a hand out to her opponent and hauled her to her feet. Breathing hard the two women embraced, relishing the feel of each other.

Did that get you hot boys? Did the idea of two women slugging it out raise a rod? Don't worry, you are not alone. How about another story...

Last November I was scheduled to fight in a charity competition. This was to be an evening event where local businessmen paid for a three course dinner and watched kick boxing bouts as entertainment. Money was raised by the audience 'betting' on the opponents — the supporter of the fighter who lost having to donate more to the charity. All very noble indeed.

However, as the time for the fight drew nearer I was attacked by flu and was not fit to fight. As I had friends who were competing I still attended the event.

The 'suits' were all seated downstairs in the main auditorium. The rest of us — fighters, friends and coaches — were stored upstairs with only a small balcony from which to look down into the ring. Before the first fight my coach (three times world heavyweight kickboxing champion) gave a demonstration to explain the techniques and scoring system. He stressed the abilities of the fighters present, but also pointed out that there would be some novice fights and that full support from the audience would be required.

The first fight was not a great example of the sport: the fighters were mismatched and a young lad I trained with was easily knocked out. The crowd however loved it. The all-male audience bayed and cheered over their fish course and relished the violent spectacle. They were fired up for the next bout, and got even more excited when the two fighters who entered the ring were female. I knew both competitors, having fought both of them before, and it made my blood boil to hear the cat calls and comments directed at the accomplished sportswomen (either of whom could have pasted anyone in that audience). In this situation they were seen as another kind of sport entirely.

But worse was to come.

After a few more bouts there was an interval during which a collection was taken. This was performed by strippers who removed more clothes as more

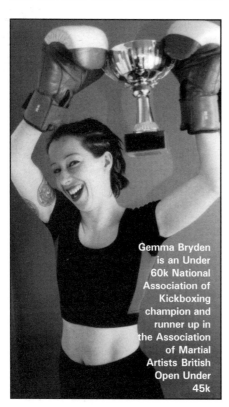

Gemma Bryden is an Under 60k National Association of Kickboxing champion and runner up in the Association of Martial Artists British Open Under 45k

money was contributed. Now this in itself is fine — men and their money are easily parted by a pair of tits and a smile (although it must be said that these were hags and there was a justified look of embarrassment on the faces of a few of the suits). The problem was that while the strippers were still flaunting their tired wares, the women's novice fight was announced. It was just too much for some of the men. On the one hand they are being offered sagging naked flesh, and on the other they are being invited to watch the physical exploits of two well toned girls — not women, these fighters were 14 and 16. As the girls struggled to overcome their nerves at their first fight, wallets were held up and a chorus of "get them out" rang round the auditorium. The girls fought as best they could, the younger girl just about holding back tears throughout, which only provoked the suits more as they thought she was physically hurt. After their bout I talked to all the female competitors, expressing my disgust at their treatment. Everyone was angry and upset at the situation they had been placed in, and all of us went home annoyed.

Now having told that story you probably think I am a sex-hating, man-hating butch fighting machine. Sorry to disappoint, but my real problem was that the more I thought about it, the more I wanted to be in the ring that night. Against everything my noble principles told me, I wanted to be fighting in front of an audience that was sexually charged. I would not have cried, I would have prowled and snarled and jeered at their calls, confident in the knowledge that I was untouchable, protected by the ropes and my own abilities.

In *Kill the Body and the Head Will Fall*, her controversial and brilliant book on female aggression, Rene Denfeld talks about the "climate of fear" in which women find themselves. They cannot walk home alone at night, hemlines are being lengthened and personal alarms are being carried... just in case she "asked for it". I used to feel this climate of fear every day; at just five feet two and 98lbs I felt vulnerable. Tired of being placed in the role of victim, this was one of the reasons I took up boxing, not realising the profound change it would have on my life. I got a real hit just lacing on a pair of steel toe-capped boots, knowing that combined with a spring loaded round house, I was a lethal weapon.

This arsenal carried with it a license that reads

I promise to uphold the true spirit of martial arts and not use the skills I am taught against any person, except for the defence of myself, my family or friends, in the event of danger or unprovoked attack, or in the support of law and order.

Please! How loose do you want to be? Basically I hold a license to kill. The playing field has been levelled, boys.

Often when men find out I am a kickboxer a tell-tale smirk crosses their face, and they *always* ask: "Could you beat me up?" I smile sweetly, cast my eyes down before looking at them squarely, and respond, "Sure." At that point I know they are mine.

The allure of the violent woman is powerful, but a difficult one to understand. In the sexual sense it is very much tied in with sexual power — not so much equality, but the threat and thrill of being beaten by a woman. In the early, rose coloured days of sexual freedom, the idea of a violent woman would probably have been a bizarre fantasy indeed. Not just because they were generally a bunch of tree hugging hippies back then, but simply because there was no space for female aggression.

So, despite your adolescent wank fantasies, maybe you guys are finally ac-

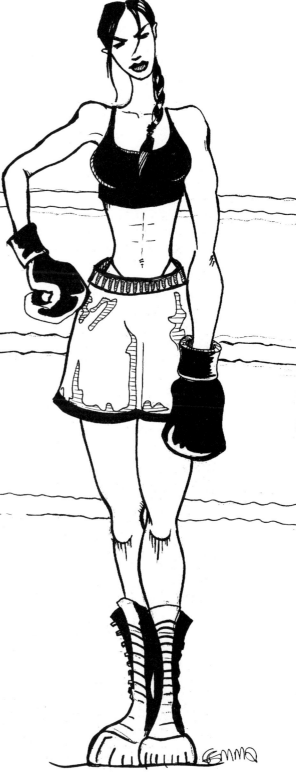

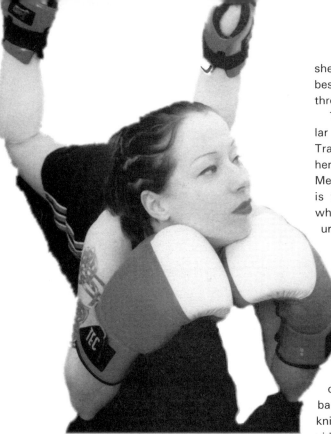

she knows how to use her body to the best advantage and gets what she needs through her physicality.

This can be seen implicitly in the popular *Xena* episode, 'Warrior, Priestess, Tramp'. Here Xena encounters two of her lookalikes: Leah, a Hestian virgin and Meg, a barmaid. The virgin/whore model is thus mapped straight onto Xena, who's already an adolescent fantasy figure. Thankfully it is the warrior who remains the hero of the tale, but it should be noted that both the virgin and the whore get to kick ass too.*

If adolescent popular culture does not get you going and you require more grown-up examples, try looking in your porn collection. Flick past the splayed cuties and check out the ads at the back. Amongst the schoolgirls' soiled knickers you will often find adverts for videos featuring women's boxing. These are not all 'foxy boxing' (a boxing match fought for erotic spectacle, where the participants wear oversize soft gloves so as not to hurt each other) — many are for regular competitions, recorded on home video and sold for around £20.

Cheaper by far is *Playboy* at around the £3 mark. The November '99 edition features Mia St John on the front cover. For those of you pleading innocence (yeah, like you don't all subscribe), Mia St John is the world feather weight boxing champion with an undefeated record. Not having seen her fight I cannot comment on her fighting skills, but she certainly looks good in a pair of boxing gloves and not much else.

In the September '99 issue of *Bizarre* they ran a wrestling special, a large portion of which was devoted to 'catfighting' (their term — cat fights tend to be far more dignified affairs in real life). Providing a reasonably comprehensive history of the fighting femme in popular culture, the whole package was

cepting women as sexual equals. Certain so-called feminists (friends and otherwise) will probably be disgusted with me for suggesting such a thing. Partly because they still believe in the great feminist in the sky who despises all that is male, i.e. violence, and have chucked their lot in with the right wing anti-abortion, anti-porn (and indeed, anti- most things I enjoy) brigade.

In the next section of this article I would like to further explore *why* the fascination is there, but more importantly I would like to open the topic for debate.

From Amy Fisher to *Xena, Warrior Princess*, the violent woman has in recent years filled the gap between virgin and whore. Like the virgin she is untouchable, not because she is 'morally opposed' but because she would kick your head in if you made an improper advance. Like the whore,

*Although not directly related, I simply couldn't resist sneaking in my favourite Xena quote: "The way to a mans heart is through his rib cage."

presented with a salacious voyeurism and a front cover that featured Playboy TV presenters Emma and Chrissy in mock wrestling scenes. My main problem with *Bizarre* was that the emphasis seemed to be on no-talent brawling. Their rather simplistic take is that men like women who fight (preferably over them), but ultimately the woman must not represent a real threat to the man. This is sometimes the case, but does not accommodate the breed I have personally encountered. Nor does it afford space to the popularity of *Xena* or *Buffy The Vampire Slayer*.

More recently a *Playboy* special has hit the shelves devoted to Rena Mero, aka Sable of wrestling fame. So undoubtedly the idea of two women slugging it out does raise... interest. Again: Why?

Perhaps it is the same as watching lesbian sex, and just another form of girl-on-girl action? Maybe you like the idea that women have similar appetites to men; that they are not prudish or reserved? Ah, maybe now we are getting somewhere... If a woman can get in the ring and slug it out in front of an audience (that perhaps she gets off on), then she is not going to be reserved in the sexual arena. Undoubtedly the very physicality of violence is important: to hit someone you have to invade their personal space, you have to make contact, and in a sport like boxing or kickboxing you often find yourself closer to someone than in a lovers embrace.

I suppose another very obvious point is that a woman who can kick some distance above her own head is going to bring certain qualities to a relationship not found in a regular girl.

While researching this piece I discussed with several people the ideas I was exploring, and one phrase kept getting thrown into to the ring: "the crisis of masculinity." I do not want to spend a great deal of our time on the intricacies of male neuroses (if you are interested, try Susan Faludi's new book

Stiffed). However, the notion of a masculine consciousness under fire may help us to understand the desirability of the aggressive woman. Men have been placed in the big bad wolf role for so long that many are now feeling they have to repress certain attributes, one of these being the "aggressor". The violent woman relieves him of this role. She is not someone who will break if he touches her, she is not a victim and she is not scared of him. The rather pathetic theory that all men are rapists is not important to my kind of woman. Once the climate of fear is eradicated the pressure eases all round. The transgressional role of the aggressive woman releases the male from any masculine behavioural traits he may feel forced upon him.

Or maybe there is no crisis of masculinity? You are all as shallow as ever and there is nothing going on behind the physical. In which case, do me a favour — next time you a get a rod on watching Buffy kick someone in the head, ask yourself why before wanking yourself stupid.

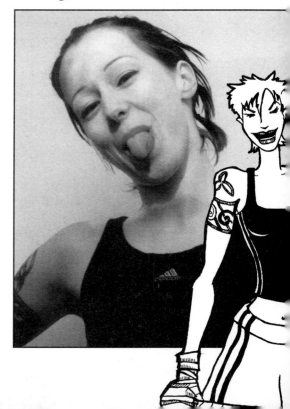

*From off the
streets of
Cleveland comes...*

SPLENDOR
★AMERICAN STYLE!★

*An interview with
Harvey Pekar*

John Szpunar

I arrived in Cleveland an hour early. I wanted to give myself time to get my bearings. About a half hour outside of town, I had stopped for something to eat in a suburban strip-mall. It was a little early for lunch, but I wanted to check out the map one more time. And to go over my questions again.

Ohio is a hellish place to drive through. Miles and miles of flat, green land and not much else. A quick search through the FM stations revealed a painfully large selection of religious programs on the radio. "Children in India, China, Japan know what to wear because Jesus is there." I pointed the car east and kept going.

I pulled up to the VA hospital with time to spare. I decided to check it out so I'd know where to go. I followed the signs through a maze that lead to Admittance. Then went out and had a smoke. In 45 minutes, I would meet Harvey Pekar. Harvey Pekar works as a file clerk in a Cleveland VA hospital. He's also the man behind **American Splendor**, a comic book that is, quite frankly, one of the greatest mirrors to be held up to the face of America in a very long time. Pekar doesn't do the artwork, he just does the writing. Eccentric, opinionated and very gifted, he's been writing about his life in Cleveland for over 25 years. It's an ordinary life. Driving to work, going grocery

shopping, listening to jazz. In the wrong hands, virtually all of the subjects that Harvey writes about would be instantly forgettable. But Pekar's work has such a rhythm, honesty and truth to it that it makes even the most mundane events seem dramatic.

Over the years, Pekar has collaborated with such comics luminaries as Robert Crumb, Spain Rodriguez, Drew Friedman, and Alan Moore. Almost in spite of the talent involved, his work is still relatively unknown. What would Harvey be like in person? I wasn't sure. The day before I drove down to meet him, he called me at home and asked if I was interested in buying some big band and R&B 78s. It seemed typical. I was reminded of a story of his where his future wife first met him face to face. As she sat on the plane, flying toward Cleveland, her mind conjured up different images of Harvey. Each image was illustrated in a different artist's style. This was how I knew Harvey Pekar, through the pages of **American Splendor**. Now, I'd get my chance to meet him face to face. In the VA hospital. In his world. I crushed out my cigarette and decided to have a look around town. The area

seemed nice enough. A five minute walk in any direction soon dashed that idea. I stood for a while opposite a shack that promised me 'The Best Roast Beef in Cleveland'. Then I turned around and made my way back. Back through the maze and into Admittance. The room was very crowded. People spread out on vinyl chairs and couches scanned each other's feet through narrow eyes. I could almost read their thoughts. I paused for a moment and then walked further down the hall into a larger room. I leaned up

against the wall and checked my watch. It was about that time.

From around the corner, a figure lurched toward me. Plaid shirt tucked into black jeans. Mismatched socks and untied shoes. Wide, intense eyes staring at me from across the room. He stooped for a moment as if to collect his thoughts and then slowly made his way through the sea of faces to me. Extended his hand and smiled. Then the eyes narrowed and burned into me. Ladies and gentlemen, this is Harvey Pekar.

*The Harvey Pekar
Name Story*
Text © Harvey Pekar
Art © R. Crumb
Bob & Harv's Comics
(Four Walls Eight
Windows)

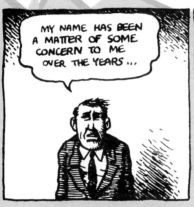
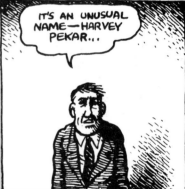

HEADPRESS **Do you have any idea what kind of audience reads AMERICAN SPLENDOR?**

HARVEY PEKAR I get the impression that the ordinary comic book fans are not at all interested in my work. I mean, they might even really hate it. Well, maybe hate is too strong of a word. But they're into the idealisation of characters and escapism. I'm my protagonist; I'm definitely not into idealising myself. I don't know that I'm particularly modest, but I think that if you brag about yourself when you're writing autobiography, you turn people off.

The book has a perfect title. Well, you know, the title AMERICAN SPLENDOR is meant ironically. And I think that ordinary comic book fans want to really read about what *they* consider splendour: Superman, Batman, fighting aliens, or some stuff like that. To me that's kid stuff.

The title is ironic, but most Americans are leading lives like yours. I get the feeling that your book could reach a wider audience, it's just that the people who'd read it don't even know it exists. Exactly. A lot of people who I've heard from over the years who

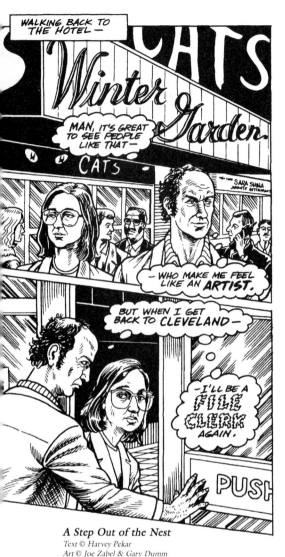

A Step Out of the Nest
Text © Harvey Pekar
Art © Joe Zabel & Gary Dumm
American Splendor Special
(Dark Horse Comics)

read the book are intellectuals. They really read. They tend to be into prose fiction or politics or something like that, rather than comics. And unfortunately, it's extremely difficult for them to find my work, *period*. I guess the first place that someone would look would be in a comic book store. And not even they are carrying it now.

It's difficult to find. Even some of the anthologies are starting to disappear. Yeah.

You know, I think that almost anything can function as escapism. Well, I mean, in the first place, I'm just talking about people who read about the exploits of some super hero and imagine themselves to be that guy instead of the 97 pound weakling in the Charles Atlas ad. But, there *are* people who my work might have the same effect on because they read it and think, "Wow, there's somebody else out there who's like me, going through the same stuff that I am." And it can be comforting to them. Maybe it gives them a good feeling, the same as escapism would give a good feeling to a kid reading Superman down in the basement in his mother's house. Obviously, I think that there's a place for fantasy. I mean, in terms of escapism, I think that there's a place for even kind of lightweight escapism in a person's life. I look at cartoons on TV, you know, or any number of trashy things from time to time. They have their place, but I think that there's more to art than that. Most of the stuff that I read or look at, I'd like to be stimulating and challenging.

Let's back up. Where were you born and raised? Here, in Cleveland. I've been here all my life.

Your parents were from Poland. Can you tell me a little bit about them? Yeah, sure. They were Jewish, and they came from an area in Eastern Poland. My father was really religious. His father died when he was 10-years-old and he had to go to work. He drove a horse and wagon over there; he would pick up grain for farmers and take it into the city. He'd sell it to the people who made flour. My mother's father was a butcher. She had more education than my father. My father hardly had any public education. My mother didn't finish high school, but she had some public schooling. And while my father was very religious, she was like a Communist. I don't know if she was ever a party member, but she was a Communist sympathiser. She was idealistic; we're talking now in the Twenties and Thirties when a lot of people were left-leaning. There was like this war going on between labour and capital here. She was very much, at one time, pro-Soviet. I remember that we used to subscribe to this paper called THE DAILY WORKER.

That must have left a lasting impression on you. Well, I've written about this in a story called 'Red Baited'. In 1948, my mother supported the candidacy of Henry Wallace for President. His was a progressive party that was like a left-wing splinter group off the Democrats. Wallace was supported by the Communist Party. He had been vice-president under Roosevelt. His platform involved trying to make peace with the USSR. He thought it was possible. So, those were my parents.

Did they have big families? Well, my mother had a lot of sisters and brothers. What happened was that the oldest brother came over to Cleveland. First he went to South America and then he came up here. He worked and gradually saved the money to get them here one after another.

How close did they come to being caught up in the Holocaust? In my mother's immediate family, they all got out before the Second World War. It was kind of close. The last members got out in 1937. A lot of my relatives that weren't in that immediate family were killed. Practically my father's whole family was wiped out. But, that's the way it went down. They came over a little at a time. And over here, it was like, my mother's brother-in-law owned a neighbourhood Mom & Pop type grocery store. My father worked for him and when the guy went to do something else, my father bought the business. So he just had this little grocery store from the mid-Thirties until he retired in 1970.

Where'd you go to school? In Cleveland. Public school.

How about college? I went to college for about a year-and-a-half.

What kind of a student were you? I was a good student. I was kind of indifferent early on, but I was pretty good. I had a really good memory, so there were some courses that I could just ace, like history and geography. And I was really interested in that stuff too. I was a good student in college. But by that time, being a good student became a big deal to me. I freaked out because I was putting so much emphasis on it; I was obsessing about it. I worried about grades to the point where I couldn't even function. I mean, I thought that was what would happen to me if I went to college so I didn't go right away. I worked and everything and it was only as a last resort that I went to college. You know, I had a whole bunch of lousy jobs, one after another. I got to the point to where I just couldn't take it. I thought, "OK, I need a rest from this crap." So I went to college and at first I had a high grade point average. But, like I said, I freaked out. So, I quit school, got married and had a series of flunky jobs.

How long have you worked here? I got this job when I was like 25. So I've been with the federal government for close to 35 years. I mean this is kind of a flunky job, but it's a steady job. It's got benefits; this is probably the best I could have hoped for. At that time.

Do you recall the first writer who had a major impact on you? Yes, I do. That's funny, because there was a writer who had a major impact on me as a kid. Her name was Eleanor Estes. She wrote a series of books about a family. It was a single-parent family, the father had died. The mother was like a seamstress. Estes started writing them in the early Forties, but they were about when she was a kid in the first World War. I started reading them as a kid. Before I read her, I was reading the typical kind of kids books. Adventure stories and stuff. And when I read *this* stuff, I was kind of astounded by how observant she was and how realistic the stuff was. I later found out that she was a very highly regarded writer. But that had a big impact on me.

Anyone else? There's a guy that's very underappreciated by the name of George Ade. Ade was very popular at one time, but he doesn't get anything like his props. He might have ruined his reputation by sort of selling out. In other words, he wrote some tremendous things for a short period of time. But he lived a long time, so he got into repeating himself and stuff. Maybe he shot his wad, I don't know. But anyway, he became like this really popular journalist. The majority of his work isn't very good, and people tend to forget or discount his earlier stuff. He went through a few generations of readers; at the last stage, people probably thought that he was some kind of old hack. But he was a great writer.

Another guy is Daniel Fuchs, who wrote those stories about Brooklyn in the 1930s. And then James Joyce. He's an important writer that I admire. Those are a few guys.

When did you first attempt to write? When I was 19 I wrote a short story. I found it years later, and was kind of surprised to find how similar it was to my comic book writing. In fact, I wrote a comic book story from the experience. But, I just sort of drifted into writing. When I was a kid, I read a lot, but I was kind of directionless. I was a really big jazz fan. When I was 19, I was corresponding with a guy who was a really good jazz critic. He told me about some magazine that had just started up, and said, "Why don't you send them some of your

This page: The Man Who Came To Dinner –
And Lunch and Breakfast
Text © Harvey Pekar
Art © Carole Sobocinski
American Splendor #15
(Harvey Pekar)

Next page: A Tribute
to Bill Marks
Text © Harvey Pekar
Art © Chester Brown
American Splendor #15
(Harvey Pekar)

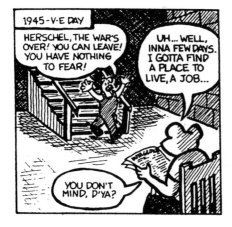

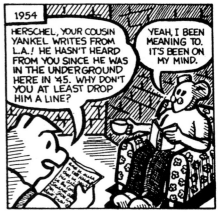

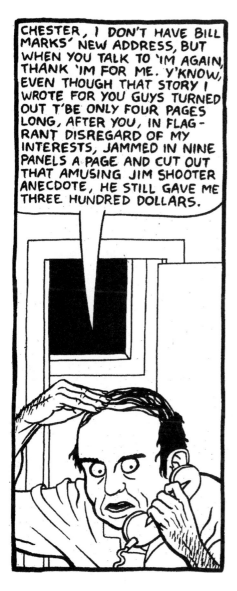

CHESTER, I DON'T HAVE BILL MARKS' NEW ADDRESS, BUT WHEN YOU TALK TO 'IM AGAIN, THANK 'IM FOR ME. Y'KNOW, EVEN THOUGH THAT STORY I WROTE FOR YOU GUYS TURNED OUT T'BE ONLY FOUR PAGES LONG, AFTER YOU, IN FLAGRANT DISREGARD OF MY INTERESTS, JAMMED IN NINE PANELS A PAGE AND CUT OUT THAT AMUSING JIM SHOOTER ANECDOTE, HE STILL GAVE ME THREE HUNDRED DOLLARS.

the music. That really wasn't a popular way to write about it. So I found that I only got so far. I could write record reviews, but these magazines didn't want me to write too many feature articles. Well, I could write feature articles if I wanted to work for nothing. A lot of these publications didn't pay. But that got to be a real drag, it got frustrating. I was learning more and more and I thought my work was getting better and better. I wasn't making any more money, I didn't think that editors respected me enough.

How did this lead to comics? I got into comics — you've probably read about that in 'The Young Crumb Story'. There was a batch of stories that I wrote in 1972. Crumb was a friend of mine and he visited me. I had been theorising about comics and about how they were really an underused form. About how you can do anything in comics. When Crumb came to visit and crashed with me in 1972, another guy named Robert Armstrong was with him; he was a really good cartoonist. I wrote down some stories for them. Crumb took one and it was published that same year. He just illustrated it right away and it came out in THE PEOPLE'S COMICS or something like that. And Armstrong did some of my stuff and a few of those got published. There was this guy named Willie Murphy. He contacted me in 1974. He was a very good cartoonist. He died at 40. Anyway, Willie illustrated some of my work and that came out. By that time, I was sick of writing about jazz. I didn't think I was getting my props. But I was starting to get a nice reaction to my comic work. So, I just put down the jazz stuff. I said, "To hell with this. I'm not going to be knocking myself out for nothing." At the end there, I was just doing it because I felt like it differentiated me from other file clerks. It was for self respect. But it wasn't fun. It wasn't fun at all.

work?" There were some real knowledgeable people writing for that paper and I thought there was no way they were going to take my work. But, I sent a long letter to the editor about some topic and the guy wrote me back. He said, "This is the best thing we've seen on this guy. Why don't you make an article out of it." So that's how I got started, writing about jazz. I wrote for DOWN BEAT and several jazz magazines in the Sixties through about 1976. At first I was thrilled. But I didn't write pop-criticism, I took my work very seriously. And I used musical terms and stuff. I was interested in close analysis of

What was your first reaction to the Undergrounds when they came around? Well, you know, I liked them. The thing is, I met Crumb in 1962 when he came to Cleveland as a kid. So I followed his development. At that time I wasn't so much into comics, although I had read them as kid. I collected them for a while, but then I got sick of the superhero stuff and funny animals. I mean there were some that I liked all the way through; I liked MAD. But I got sick of most comic books by the time I was 12. Now when Crumb came along, he showed me the first thing he did, THE BIG YUM YUM BOOK. It was a work in progress when I met him. I was actually tighter with his roommate, Marty Pahls.

What kind of guy was he? He was a strange guy. He was a pack-rat kind of guy. He was sort of an intellectual; he probably *was* an intellectual. He was pretty well read. He was one of these guys who just… lived down in the basement. He just kind of like gave out. I take it you know something about him.

He wrote some great introductions for Fantagraphics' COMPLETE CRUMB series. Yeah. Marty was OK with me, but I don't exactly know what happened to him. He was doing OK for a while. It was funny. He didn't work for a really long time, and then he got a job with an employment agency. I guess he was writing copy. He did really well at it; he migrated from Cleveland to Chicago [laughs]. He was working for the company, and he started doing other stuff. I think he was writing for these tabloid kind of papers, maybe even writing pornographic novels. But the point was that he was making some *money*. We thought, "Well, finally. Pahls is doing something." But then he got… He got diabetes. And everything just totally collapsed for him. I mean, he just went down the tubes. I don't think he ever held any job for any length of time after that. I still don't know how in the hell he died.

He died? Yeah. He moved out to San Francisco and that was that.

Did Terry Zwigoff make any attempt to talk to you about any of this? This was all sort of ignored in Crumb. Yeah, they didn't do anything with that period. Zwigoff wanted me to be in the movie, or at least to interview me. But he couldn't come to Cleveland. He wanted me to fly to New York on my own nickel because he was too broke to do an interview. I couldn't see doing that. I mean, even with the

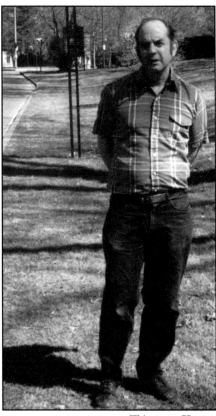

This page: Harvey.
Next page: Where Harvey works.
Photos © Brian Krueger

success of the movie, I don't know if I would do that. Spain Rodriguez was in there, and I don't see where it did him a lot of good.

It's hard to say. Spain's kind of popular, but the core audience for that film was probably already exposed to him. Yeah. But I mean, I've been on THE DAVID LETTERMAN SHOW eight times and you see where I'm still at. I didn't get very much from that.

It gave you some material to write about. What did you gain from that experience? I didn't help my sales any. I guess the best that it did was get me some writing gigs. I mean there are these magazine editors who aren't very informed about anything. It's like, this guy was an English major and he somehow got a job as an editor. God knows why. Some of them saw me on Letterman and they liked what they saw.

And so, when I started writing about jazz again, they'd heard of me. They'd figure like, "Well, hell, I've heard of this guy, how bad can he be? He was on national TV. Let's give him a shot." They didn't know what the hell I was writing about. Ignorant.

How'd you go about self-publishing the first issue of AMERICAN SPLENDOR? Well, I just decided I was going to do it because the business was in such bad shape. So, I found out how much dough it was going to cost to do it and I figured I could save up the money. And I contacted a couple artists. I just gave them stories and they did it Then I found a printer and we just did it. Fortunately, there was some interest left in comics. I mean it was really waning fast. So I sort of caught on at the end.

How was the first issue received? It was received well. I mean, there wasn't a hell of a lot of press about it. This was like the end of the Underground comics. The end of it.

What were you trying to accomplish with AMERICAN SPLENDOR? Well, I'm an autobiographical writer. And I try and write about the 99 per cent of life that people experience and *don't* write about, because they think that nobody's interested. I write about work, and get-

ting by; relationships with other people. The kind of stuff that life is mostly made of. Like I said, it's the stuff that doesn't get written about because it's not spectacular. I try and make my work as accurate as possible so that people can identify with it.

Do you think your work would change if you lived solely off of your writing? I can only write one way, that's the thing. And because I *can't* change it, I can't make more money

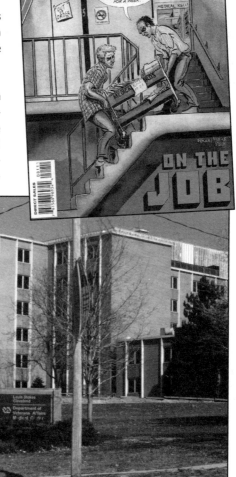

at it. In order to write crap and get a lot of money, it really helps if you like the stuff that you write about. For instance, I read where Jackie Collins said, "The critics put me down, but I don't pay any attention to them because Harold Robbins thinks I'm a really good writer." So, obviously, she thinks that Harold Robbins is some kind of a gifted writer. If you write garbage, it helps if you like garbage. It helps an awful lot. I mean, you think you're doing something great. So you don't have to try and fake the stuff or learn how to write. If you write better stuff than this, if this stuff doesn't come naturally to you, you have to figure out the formula. I haven't really attempted to do that. It's just do much damn time and trouble. And I want to do good work.

IMAGINE MY AMAZEMENT WHEN I REALIZED THAT MOST OF THE PEOPLE RIDING WITH ME WERE MEMBERS OF SUN RA'S BAND, WHO'D FINISHED A GIG IN CHICAGO AND WERE ON THEIR WAY BACK TO PHILLY, WHERE THEY LIVED IN A COMMUNE.

When do you do your writing? Do you have a set routine? Sometimes I write around here, sometimes at home. I'm pretty disciplined and turn out a lot of work. Especially now.

Are there any artists that came from around here that you gave a start to? Well, there were guys who were working here, but no one who's a big name. I've worked with Gary Dumm for a long time. In fact, he illustrated what I'm working on now for AMERICAN SPLENDOR, 'The Terminal Years.' I've been working with Gary for around 25, 26 years.

Do artists approach you to do work for American Splendor? Yeah. There were some guys that approached me, like Drew Friedman

and Frank Stack. Frank wrote me a letter. He had pretty much quit doing comics and then he started to do them again with me.

Do you give artists specific directions on how to do your stories? I'm talking about layout and when to put in silent panels; things like that. Yeah. That's exactly what I do. I storyboard for them. That's what form my scripts are. Only I use stick figures and balloons. I write directions in. I mean, I'm not like—

Harvey Kurtzman? [Laughs] Well, I don't tell them every little detail to put in. They've got, I think, a fair amount of latitude. But, you know, I describe the general scene. And a lot of times I send out photographs. Stuff like that.

It's got to be satisfying to work with such talented people. Yeah. Now, I'm working with some smart guys. And it's a pleasure. But, when I initially started working, I didn't really have much of a choice; I had to pretty much take what I could get. You know, I don't think that anyone has really crossed me up, or totally misinterpreted a story. Still, some of the guys that I used to work with weren't that bright. But now, when you work with someone like Joe Sacco or Frank Stack, you don't have a problem. They know what you want.

Which artist do you think best captures your work? Well, it depends on what kind of stuff I'm looking for.

So do you try and find an artist that best suits the style of a particular story? Yeah. And it also has to do with availability. If you notice, some of the guys that I work with have very realistic styles. Like Gary Shamray, for example. That's probably as realistic as comic book work has ever gotten. And, that's really unusual in comics. Usually, they just want exaggerated super hero kind of stuff. Or cartoony stuff.

Did you like the way Drew Friedman handled your work? Yeah, I thought he did a pretty good job. I don't know what he's doing now. The thing was he used to be kind of limited in what he did. He's probably doing pretty well. He's probably making a lot of money; probably doing a lot of commercial work. But, yeah, I thought the stuff he did for me was pretty good. But there were some things about him — like the way he would draw hands, for example. And there wasn't a lot of variety in the composition of the panels.

I found his work for you distracting because I would ignore the writing and try and look for an imperfection in the artwork. He had his thing going with the stippling, you know, and an almost photographic realism. But then, there'd be some things that were really weird, like a guy with his hand turned in a way that was almost anatomically impossible to do.

Who haven't you worked with that you'd like to? Oh, I imagine that there's probably a lot of guys. But I'm not looking to expand my contacts right now, because I'm working with

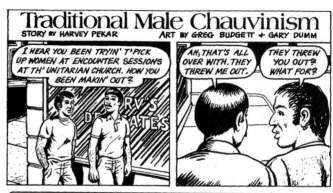

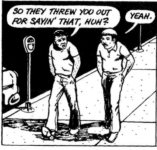
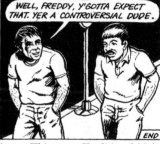

Previous page: Harvey bumps into the Sun Ra Arkestra.
Text © Harvey Pekar
Art © Joe Sacco
American Splendor Music Comics (Dark Horse)

This page: Traditional Male Chauvinism
Text © Harvey Pekar
Art © Greg Budgett & Gary Dumm
The New American Splendor Anthology
(Four Walls Eight Windows)

good people and I don't want to make it too complicated. When you start working with 10 guys, it's like you're juggling. I used to work with 10 or 12 guys on a 60-page comic. If you work with that many people, there's always somebody that you'll have some kind of a problem with. It's too much to keep going. Now I'm doing smaller books. It's not that difficult.

Your writing seems very spontaneous. How do you go about writing a story? Well, something clicks. It's hard to say. I'm sure it can be explained, but I haven't explained it to myself. Maybe, I'll have an experience that at one time I would write about, but at another time, I wouldn't think to write about. I guess it depends

on what I have on my mind and what my priorities and concerns are at the time. I just go through life, and sometimes something will happen to me. I'll have an experience and it almost gets framed for me. The structure takes place; the structure of the experience. I don't usually set out and say, "I'm going to write about this," or "I'm going to write about that." I just live and it comes to me. That's how I do it.

How many stories do you throw away? That happens pretty seldom. I don't count them, but usually, if I see something that I want to do, I'll do it. Some of the stories that I haven't done might be because I just forgot about them. I couldn't write them at the time, and when I

I saw Crumb, portrayed sitting in a separate room (drawing) and described as a "quiet, retiring guy..." I'd always been labelled "SHY" (and ordered to "snap out of it"). I thought if I did what Crumb did... find some kind of 'Bohemian' crowd to join in with, things would start to improve. A social worker had said I'd "missed out on certain key developmental stages"...all I had to do was "get out and socialise"...and I'd soon "catch up." He was wrong, but I tried it...

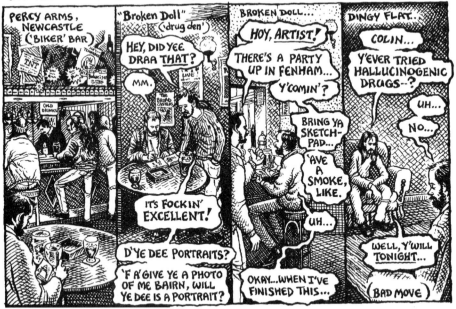

thought about them, I'd forgotten so many of the details. That's when I don't want to try it, because I don't remember enough about the experience. But I don't discard a lot of ideas.

How long does it take you to write an average story? Well, sometimes, just as long as it takes for me to have an experience and to sit down and write it down. Sometimes something will happen, and the whole thing will be a really fast process. I'll just have an experience, go around the corner and sit down with a pencil and paper and write about it. It's not a very time consuming process for me.

How often do you twist around the truth? I try and tell it as straight as possible. If I think that I'm going to hurt somebody's feelings, I'll change their identity. But I try and make it as accurate as possible.

How do you feel about being compared to writers like Raymond Carver and Charles Bukowski? I guess the reason people compare us is because we write about everyday experiences. But I don't like Raymond Carver's work because I think it's kind of affected by his self-conscious. He owes too much to the writing of Earnest Hemmingway, who's another affected self-conscious writer. As far as Bukowski, he's a pretty good writer. I mean, he had a job at a post office and I've got a civil service job, so maybe people find some comparison there. But, I think he made too much out of being a low-life. He comes out of Henry Miller. In fact, I think they corresponded. But he limits himself a lot more than Miller did. I mean, I'm sure that Bukowski was interested in more things than he dealt with in his stories.

Do you mind going into some of the people that you've written about? For in-

Author's note As I transcribed this interview, I couldn't help but laugh at the creaking sounds coming from the vinyl seat that Harvey was sitting in. He has the strange habit of sliding down in his chair — so far down that he literally almost falls off. Just when it seems as if he's going to hit the floor, he pops himself upright. I could trace his progress as the tape wound on. Was he hiding from his supervisor? I don't know. My friend Brian summed it up best as we drove back home: "So that's what living in Cleveland does to you..."

stance, Freddy? Yeah, Freddy. I met him in the Seventies. He was like a Vietnam Vet and he was going to college here. He's from Brooklyn, New York. He is pretty much the way I portrayed him; I wasn't exaggerating at all. I don't know what the hell happened to him. He went back to Brooklyn and sort of dropped out of sight.

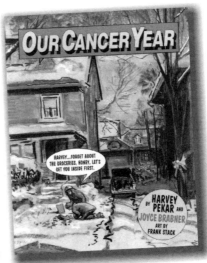

How about Sid from the 'Guerrilla Theatre' and 'On the Corner' stories? Well, Sid actually was... did you ever hear of a popular novelist named Herbert Gould? Sid was his brother. Herbert was like an honours student. He taught on a college level and stuff. And Sid's father came from the Ukraine. He was an immigrant and he really made a lot of money. Herb went through school and was the kind of person that his father hoped he'd be. But Sid quit school when he was 16. He ran away and joined the circus like I wrote in the story; that's all true. He never even got a high school diploma. So, he sort of retired when he was around 31-years-old. That's when I met him, back in around 1960. He never did anything. He just lived off of his parent's money, I guess, in these really seedy apartment buildings in bad neighbourhoods. He'd get up at one o'clock in the morning and hang out all night. He had a stroke and died a couple of years ago. That was Sid.

Previous Page:
Colin Warneford in
Transatlantic Comics
Text & Art © Colin Warneford
American Spendor
(Dark Horse Comics)

This page:
Our Cancer Year
Text © Harvey Pekar &
Joyce Brabner
Art © Frank Stack
(Four Walls Eight Windows)

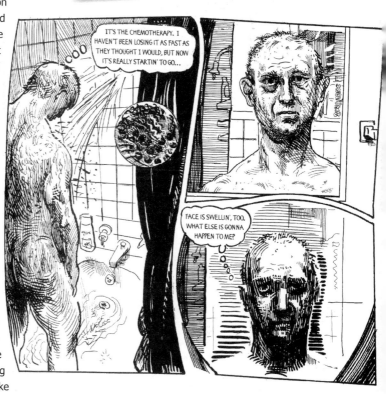

In the latest issue of AMERICAN SPLENDOR, you did some work with an autistic man named Colin Warneford. How'd your collaboration with him come about? He just started to write me. He's a really smart guy and an excellent artist. He sent me some examples of his work, and I thought it would be great to do something with him. He was sending me these extremely long letters, and I edited them into a story within this framing sequence that I set up for myself. It was like a story within a story. Colin's a really bright guy, a really talented guy. I'm very impressed with him and I hope I can do something with him again in the future.

How long did it take to finish that story?

Maybe around 10 months. I was doing other things while that was going on.

Other than your wife Joyce, was that the first time you ever collaborated with someone like that? Yeah. It was a unique experience for me. I saw it as a way to put out a really good comic, and also to help a guy out a little bit. I don't deny that. I thought that maybe Colin would benefit from it. No one was aware of his talent.

What sort of experience was writing OUR CANCER YEAR? The years in which I wrote that were very depressing years for me. My physical problems didn't end until I got a hip replacement. So, for two and a half years, I was limping around. If I had gotten the hip replacement done right away like the doctor said, instead of waiting and trying to gut it out, until I couldn't walk, which is what happened — if I would have gotten that taken care of, I probably would have been fine. As it was, when I was writing the book, I was really bummed out and depressed. That was an awful experience. I was limping around, I didn't know what to do. And it was

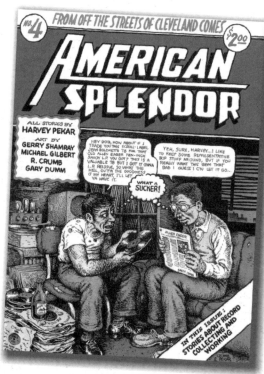

physically very painful for me. I could have avoided all of that.

Do you think that your work is more of a catharsis for you now than it was in the past? I think it's always been that way. I don't know that it's more of a catharsis now.

What was the general reaction to the book? Well, I get very good reactions to it, but it didn't sell very well. People don't want to read about that stuff, I guess.

You've been writing AMERICAN SPLENDOR for a while now. Did you think, that with time, comics would become more canonical? Yeah, I was hoping. I didn't quit my day job, you notice. But I was hoping that things would get better. Things did get better up until the mid or late Eighties. The first couple of collections of my work for Doubleday sold relatively well. And I got an award, and so forth for the first collection. I thought that the movement would keep going.

What do you think it's going to take for comics to be taken more seriously? I don't know. I'm stumped. All I'm doing is keeping on putting my work out. I mean, there's such a stigma attached to them. What they need is people that use them in a variety of ways. Good people. Because right now, there's a lot of good writers and artists who don't think it's possible to do anything in comics. They only see this crap that comes out from Marvel and DC and stuff like that. And they think it's impossible; they don't even take the medium seriously. They leave it to the hacks.

Do you think that Marvel and DC are cutting their own throats? I think things really took a turn for the worse when Marvel and DC started with that exclusive distributorship stuff. The business is in pretty bad shape right now, from what I understand. Maybe I'm wrong, but it seems that sales of every kind are on a decline. Comic book stores are dying. And, naturally, the first books to suffer are the economically marginal ones. I'm just very fortunate.

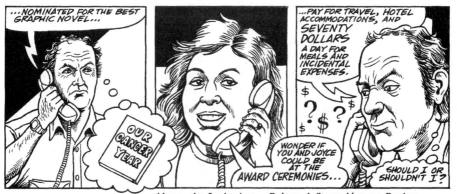

Above: An Invitation.
Text © Harvey Pekar
Art © Joe Zabel & Gary Dumm
American Splendor Comic-Con Comics (Dark Horse)

Below: A Story About a Review.
Text © Harvey Pekar
Art © Joe Sacco
American Splendor Music Comics (Dark Horse)

Are things easier for you now that Dark Horse Comics distributes the book? Yeah. I was putting out my own work, but then I got sick and got cancer. For that one time, I wasn't physically able to do it. And I got a couple of companies to put it out for me. I'm lucky I stuck with Dark Horse. I suppose if worst came to worse, I could still put out a comic book again, but I don't want to be bothered with it.

How did you handle distribution when you self-published? Well, I wasn't sending the book directly to retailers. I sent it to distributors like Capital City. Now Dark Horse does all that. I own the copyright, but they get all the copies and send them out.

I know that you're about to sign an option with a film studio. How do you feel about that? It's good, because I make extra money when I sign an option. I'm on the verge of signing one now with a company called Good Machine. I was just talking to the guy today. I'm not looking at films as a step up the aesthetic ladder, that's for sure. A form is a form.

You've been approached by the studios before. I've signed something like five options now, and nothing's happened. I mean, if you're asking me what I think about Hollywood, this is not a Hollywood studio. Hollywood, that stuff's just crap, commercial crap, for the most part. It's a business. But, I haven't got anything against Hollywood because, it's not like they're crowding anybody out. That's where people are at. They wouldn't go see better movies if there was no Hollywood. They'd just read trashy novels or something, or watch more TV. And if TV got better, people would watch more trashy movies. If people want trash, they'll get it.

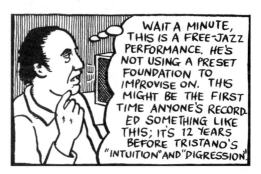

A film could bring you a new audience. Yeah, but more than that is the fact that I'm almost 60. I'll be 60 in October. I'm thinking that I don't want to work here until I drop dead, although it may work out that way. And now I've got this little girl that I'm taking care of, a foster daughter. At least for now. I don't know how that's going to work out. I mean, I've got to support an 11-year-old kid. That takes money. So, if I could make 100 grand, or something like that, I could retire. I've worked here long enough that I can get a pension of 65 per cent of what I make. And then, in couple of years, the social security pension will kick in. I'd be pretty secure financially. But, I don't know what the future's going to hold for me. I don't know. 🦋

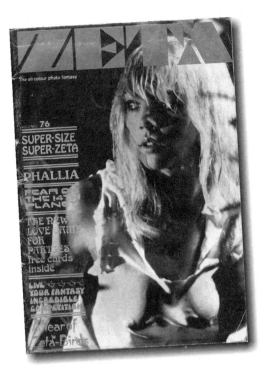

SOCK IT TO EVERYBODY! AT ONCE!

A brief interlude with
ZETA magazine

David Kerekes

ZETA billed itself as '*The all-colour fantasy*', a trippy statement in keeping with the times in which it was printed — the latter half of the 1960s. The format is reminiscent of the photo-story titles that remain so popular on

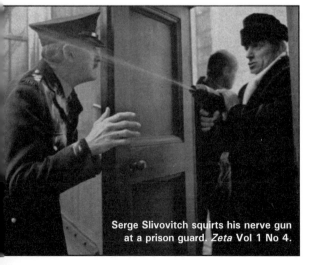

Serge Slivovitch squirts his nerve gun at a prison guard. *Zeta* Vol 1 No 4.

the continent (and with *Viz* readers in Britain), but substituting the typically teen romance-based plot element of those zines with sci-fi and action-adventure aimed specifically at hot-blooded adult males.

The thing that strikes you most with *Zeta* is the fact that publisher Michael Gassman obviously sunk a lot of money into it. The production values are excellent, with glossy paper stock and full-colour throughout. A full production team was also behind the venture, if the credits for business manager, marketing director, production manager and even 'colour consultant' are anything to go by. It's difficult to imagine now how anyone could have imagined a high profile adult photo-story magazine like this would have found a market. But then, the anonymous Gassman was working in a time of rapidly expanding liberties and horizons, where things were swinging and happening like never before. Who could possibly know in which direction

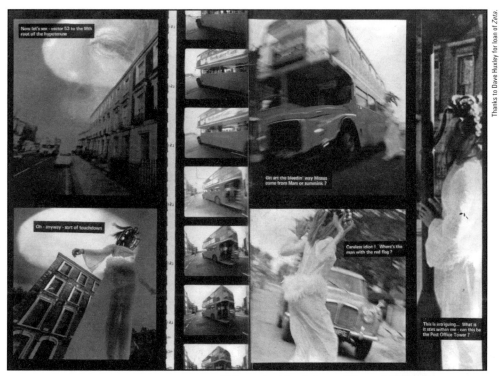

Thanks to Dave Huxley for Ivan of *Zeta*.

"Git art the bleedin' way Missus." Phillia comes down to Earth in *Zeta* Vol 2 No 1.

the younger generation might take off next (apart from perhaps a 'colour consultant')?

Zeta is a valiant literary experiment on the face of the Sixties' acid-laced burgeoning alternative press scene. Mind-expanding permissiveness is very much a part of the two issues discussed below (the only two which this author has ever seen). The latter issue contains little text but plenty of big *Oz*-type photo montages and is abstract in a way that smacks of a last ditch attempt to get on the rapidly accelerating bus.

Vol 1 No 4 Price 5/- February 1968

Divided into lightweight chapters, the story this issue is entitled '*double double trouble*'. The first chapter ('19th Nervous Breakdown') concerns Serge Slivovitch, 'an impotent Russian émigré,' who masterminds a jailbreak utilising a new type of nerve gun on the prison guards. Four pages and approximately 500 words later, the weapon is proved a success and Serge loads his waiting van with escaped cons. I'm not sure what bearing this act has on the rest of the story, or indeed what the story is about exactly other than it involves ex-cons of both sexes, orgies, a proposed raid on Scotland Yard, a blonde woman who assumes a different identity and a black girl who looks uncannily like Sixties singing sensation PP Arnold (whose backing band for a time was The Nice). The following chapter ('England expects...') comes in at a whopping 52 words and reveals James Word, secret agent, having his lovemaking interrupted by a ringing telephone. The miserable James finds consolation in the fact that phones ring at precisely the wrong moment for everybody sometimes, while the accompanying picture shows him with an arm around his red-headed lover and a screwed up expression on his face.

Slivovitch, the impotent Russian émigré, rears his head again before the issue closes, only to fall foul of James, who usurps the villain with his own cherished nerve gun (courtesy of some antiquated photographic trickery).

Why is the Russian impotent? Presumably for the same inexplicable reason that a group of female prisoners sit down to play strip poker amongst themselves (in the chapter 'No hearts and a straight flush') — to add a bit of skin and sexual colour to the tale.

The credits in this edition of *Zeta* extend to the numerous outfitters for the groovy clothing, and an original tattoo design by 'Tattoo Jock'. Also, the winner of the 'Write a *Zeta* Story' competition is announced. Out of more than 300 entrants from as far afield as Holland, Germany and Italy, Mr R. Lewis of London takes the £100 prize, while the editorial staff lament on the number of entries

that were too alike in location, idea and theme. For example, favourite fantasy settings seemed to be, in order of popularity, girls schools, nudist camps, luxury yachts, and Scottish castles and the theme of too many of the stories was the abduction of girls for various nefarious reasons, bullion robbery, or drugs.

Vol 2 No 1 Price 7/6
December 1968
Almost a year separates the above edition and this 'super-size super-*Zeta*' special (there may well have been other issues in between). The format remains full-colour throughout, but the style has changed completely. The esoteric photo-strip concept of *Zeta* is taken to its logical pop art extreme. Some of the characters from the above earlier edition are brought back for a sci-fi opus entitled '*Phallia*' (maybe these characters ran

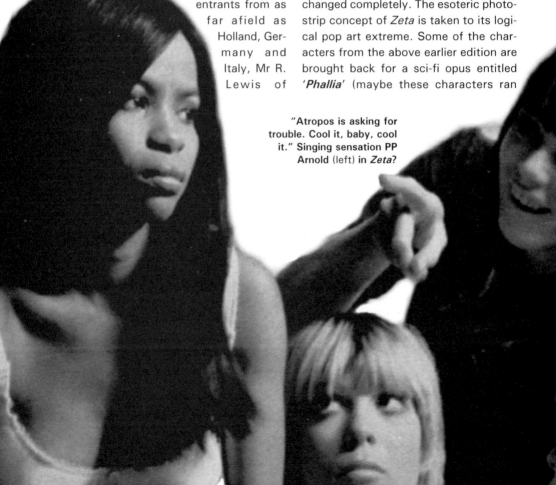

"Atropos is asking for trouble. Cool it, baby, cool it." Singing sensation PP Arnold (left) in *Zeta*?

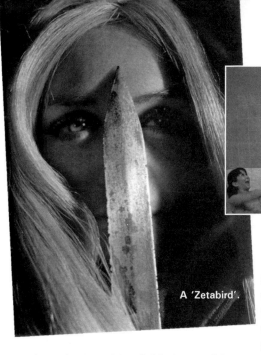

A 'Zetabird'.

Fred gets a bathroom sponge thrown at him by a soon-to-be agent for Phallia and world peace.

through every issue? It's impossible to say). Set in the 'deepest recesses of the Fourth Dimension, beyond the furthest Quasar', it tells of the eponymous Phallia, 'former Queen of Angvia' (an anagram of 'vagina', pop pickers!), who has the thankless task of safeguarding the universe from the Eternal Villains — a rather shadowy bunch who are described simply as 'the Bourdons of this world, and other worlds'. Drifting in blackness, Phallia (in gold paint makeup) turns her attention to planet Earth and laments in typical flower-power agitprop fashion that 'The United States must get out of America', before touching down in front of a London bus. The story is fragmentary to say the least and comprises entirely of clipped hip-speak sentences.

It appears that a milkman by the name of Fred and various nymphets are recruited by Phallia to help overthrow the dastardly world powers that create WAR... but don't quote me on that. ('Violence! VIOLENCE! Now when I was a young girl OTHER things made the world go round.' This statement appears within a double-page montage of a globe in the night sky and cut-up pictures of breasts.) A Most Honourable Chinese leader by the name of Hong Kong Tong is the first to

be successfully seduced into peace by the semi-naked otherworldly femme force. Button pushers of America, Britain and Russia quickly follow suit. World peace is looking good. But a trio of terrorists and dictators residing in a 'secret hideaway, disguised as a normal suburban bomb site' are not so easy influenced. Courtesy of some surreal, double exposed graphics, Cassius von Schirach, Abdul Atavist and Seamus O'Silence espouse radical philosophical musings like 'RAPE FOR PURITY!', 'KILL FOR PEACE!' and 'GENGHIS KHAN WAS RIGHT!' Fortunately for us this is where the tale concludes for now, to be continued the following month we are assured.

The latter part of this *Zeta* comprises of a text story ('Fear on the 14th Planet'), pin-ups from a year of 'Zetabirds', a letters page (with one letter from a reader in Brussels printed in French), and a questionnaire which asks

Is there enough emphasis on sex in *Zeta*? Please tell us briefly what you think of:
(a) the photography in *Zeta*
(b) the birds in *Zeta*

How *Zeta* with its lavish production values could be breaking even, let alone turning a profit, is a mystery. How long did it run? How many issues were produced? Any information would be gratefully appreciated...

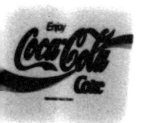

ELVIS
THE CONCERT

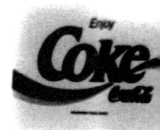

Joe Scott Wilson

Elvis The Concert, 1998–99 World Tour
Wembley Arena, London, January 23 1999

Footage of 'The King' from 20 years ago with a live 16-piece orchestral accompaniment and members of the original Presley musical entourage. The publicity package described ELVIS THE CONCERT as 'the first time that an entertainer who is no longer living has headlined a live concert tour'...

WEMBLEY ARENA WAS HEAVING with people, with plenty more pressed around the bar waiting to be served. An announcement over the PA reminded the throng that refreshments, toilet facilities and merchandising were also available at the less crowded, bottom end of the concourse. Getting nowhere in this queue, I left my place at the bar and followed the advice... only to find a dead-end and a security guard who asked politely where I thought I was going.

Some time later, clutching a drink I sincerely hoped would see me through the evening, I made my way to the auditorium, into my seat and dufully waited for the show to start. The audience consisted almost entirely of an older generation (kind of like LOGAN'S RUN but in reverse) with most men sporting sideburns and DA haircuts, thinning in a manner that characterised every shopsteward I'd ever known. A round of applause and a cheer went up as a jump-suited Elvis lookalike made his way to his seat, but he proved to be the first of many and the welcomes became progressively lacklustre. While almost anyone in a white jump-suit and gaudy sunglasses (gold framed ones being available from the merchandising stand at £12 a pop) bears a passing resemblance to The King at his most rotund (an easy period to replicate), I was certain that at least one of the lookalikes had undergone cosmetic surgery to better facilitate his imagined identity as 'Early Elvis'. He sat not far away and women with Confederacy flags came to take pictures.

Over on the far side of the arena, a group of barely discernible Teddy Boys broke into a tuneless rendition of Love Me Tender. But they were quickly silenced by a steward with a flashlight. I couldn't envisage the jiving in the aisles or destruction of seats my dad had told me about in the days when JAILHOUSE ROCK played the local Roxy.

The show started. With the requisite 'Elvis theme' (Also Sprach Zarathustra from 2001: A SPACE ODYSSEY), a hush of anticipation fell over the darkened auditorium. Suddenly there was an explosion of light, and the band launched into the rock'n'roll riff of See See Rider, setting the video projectors ablaze. And there he was, 100-feet tall in all his world championship-belt finery: Elvis was in the building! This was no lookalike, this was the jump-suited King himself from some TV Special or MGM Concert film, quite literally larger than life; past his best, but not yet obese and still good-looking. The guy to my immediate left could contain himself no longer and shot to his feet with a shriek, flinging his arms into the air. But he wasn't the only one: long-term Elvis fans — finally seeing the idol who had never toured Britain during his lifetime — were jumping to their feet all around the arena. The place was alive with whoops, whistles and flashbulbs.

See See Rider rode straight into Burning Love. When this song reached its multi-vocal coda ("A-hunka hunka burning love!" — "Ooooh!"), no one in the house could fail to have been awed by the technical wizardry that amalgamated live musicians and aged concert footage so seamlessly in real time.

The choice of concert footage was restricted to those films which originally employed multi-track recording, allowing Elvis' vocals to be isolated on the soundtrack and that way facilitate the live musicians present in the arena. Unfortunately this criterion restricted the choice of Elvis performances to those in the last decade of his life (see below) — with the exception of the leather-clad TV special ELVIS, the jump-suited showman years. Still, some fun was to be had with the savage crash-zooms, dramatic air-punching and high-kicks, at their most excessive during Suspicious Minds. Love Me Tender was almost vocal-free as Elvis spends the duration canoodling with the women of the front row. I had to wonder what prompted the cameraman of one Seventies concert film to focus at length on a man in the audience wearing thick-rimmed glasses, in-creasing concern reflected in his expression.

At this point I finally had to ask the woman next to me get back into her seat, the presence of The King and the angle of the seating having extruded her uncomfortably in my direction. I knew she was trouble the moment she sat down, excitedly regaling me with details of the show's premiere in Memphis, effortlessly reeling off the names of all the celebrities present. These included Lisa-Marie, who looked "lovely"...

In spite of some terrible songs, and terrible versions of otherwise tolerable songs, Elvis The Concert was nothing short of astonishing. More than once through the performance it slipped my mind that this event was largely illusion — an entertainer no longer living headlining a live concert tour. Things became even more surreal when the two smaller video screens started to flash images of the live band members, replicating a solo or vocal that they were performing on the main screen in a concert 20 years ago. And the performers who got the biggest response from the audience outside of Elvis were the drummer (understandable, as that's the way it is with drummers) and a flautist, whose solo performance on American Trilogy was greeted so rapturously it was all but obliterated. Picture it: the mellow, refined sound of a flute meeting with a cacophonous cheer and a solitary heartfelt cry of "G'wan, my son!"

Concert performances taken from the following films and TV specials:

Elvis (68)
Elvis, That's the Way It Is (70)
Elvis on Tour (72)
Elvis, The Lost Performances (72, outtake footage)
Elvis: Aloha from Hawaii, via Satellite (73)

Elvis the Concert   39

Crime Calls

...but it doesn't pay

William Black

What follows are the transcripts of tape-recordings made for Crime Calls, a premium-rate phone line service. Simply ring the listed number and you could listen to the chilling but enthralling true-crime stories of mass-murderers, serial killers and rapists.

Bit of a difference from *Hot and Steamy! Ring Me!* and *Sexy, Sultry, Spanking Fine Girl! Ring for two minutes of sexual heaven! Call now!*

Premium phone lines today deal almost exclusively in sexually orientated titbits. But once upon a time they covered a broader spectrum, and you could have found a phone line for information on the coming weather, sports results, stock market prices and travel news. You could have consulted with agony aunts, discovered whether you were suffering from a social disease, cancer or AIDS, and much more. At a

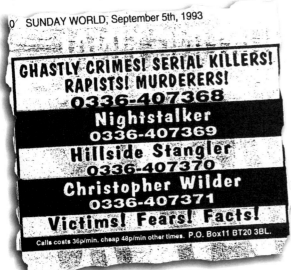

price.

So I got into the market with Crime Calls, short news packed items detailing the activities of some of America's most notorious criminals. Ideas that will create massive interest with the telephone-ringing public are eagerly sought by those in the business. The operator — myself in this case — lives on a percentage of the call fee. I kept the idea for Crime Calls a secret, or so I thought. But a few weeks before I was to launch the scheme a competitor pipped me to the post.

The British tabloid press had a field day with my competitor's new phone line, heightening the alleged sordid nature of the crimes it spoke of. Not long after, he pulled the plug.

I went ahead with Crime Calls. The only newspaper I could afford to advertise the service in was the only one that would take my ad anyway.

It was a local tabloid and not on the British mainland. I sat down and waited for the phone to ring...

I hear there are close on 200,000 people who purchase each month one of the three major British true-crime magazines. Sixty percent of them are supposed to be women; the rest men. If that's the case, I can only assume not one of them can afford to run a phone as I'm still waiting for that first call...

Hold **HEADPRESS** in one hand and your telephone in the other. Now imagine you can hear the soft, sensual voice of a young woman revealing the horrendous violence of depraved sex-killers. It won't cost you a penny. But it cost me plenty.

"*Hallo! Hallo! Is there anyone there? Is there anyone there? Please help me! Help me, please...!*" Click. Bzzzzzzzz...

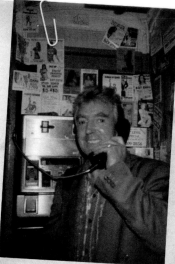

The author minutes before being evicted from his office, his wallet smaller than his ambitions.

CRIME CALLS
Tape One Script

Ghastly Crimes. Serial Killers. Rapists. Murderers The Victims. The Fears. The Facts

Woman's Voice: No! Don't...! (screams)
Man's Voice: Stop struggling. Get down. Get down. I'll kill you. I'll kill you.
Woman's Voice (scream loud to fading): Oh, help me. Help me...

The crimes detailed here will shock and horrify you. Freddie's nightmares are but daydreams when compared to the horrors of real-life crime. You have been warned...

The Hillside Stranglers. The Nightstalker. The Yorkshire Ripper. Christopher Wilder. Ted Bundy. Peter Kurten. Dean Corll. This is an infamous roll call of serial killers from around the world. Some are British. Others are European. Most are American. But all of them are crazed loners out to satisfy blood lust in mutilation and murder.

Woman's Voice: (scream loud to fading)

He stalks dark streets and lonely car parks. He searches through intimate cocktail bars and peers warily from the edge of disco dance-floors. He is confident but cunning. Presentable but paranoid. Masculine, mad and murderous.

He could be the man smiling at you invitingly from across the crowded bar. He could be your workmate or your neighbour, your husband or your son. But this man is different from us all. He is hunting humans. He is a serial killer.

Newspaper headlines scream out murder and mayhem. Television newscasts show bodies uncovered, police with guns drawn, forcing their way into seedy houses and slum apartments. And then a lone struggling handcuffed figure is manhandled into the back of a police car.

It is the end of the killer's reign. Or is it? For shocking as it may seem, a new monarch of murder is poised to gain the throne of blood.

The horrifying fact is that, in America it is believed there are at any one time 50 serial killers, stalking, slashing, strangling and shooting their way across the country" towns and cities/

Fuelled on drink or drugs, greed or lust or simply hatred of mankind, they are psycho killing machines. They take violently what they want when they want it. They lack morals and a sense of right or wrong. And so they rob, rape and kill without a second thought.

Woman's Voice (scream loud to fading)

Among them was The Nightstalker, the 25 year old drifter Richard Ramirez, a grim-eyed lanky six foot Mexican. He ran rampage through the Los Angeles suburbs during 1984 and 85, killing a total of 13 people, and sexually assaulting many more. He looked dangerous but he was worse than he looked.

Ted Bundy, however, had the looks of a movie star, and IQ of 124 and a university education. But he had the morals of an alley cat and sadistic sex instincts. He brutally murdered more than 20 young women he charmed into his arms across six States. Police believe he actually killed 40.

The Hillside Stranglers were Kenneth Bianchi and his cousin Angelo Buono. During a one year period they picked up, raped and murdered ten young girls and dumped their ravaged bodies among the Los Angeles hills.

Woman's Voice: (scream) Let me go… Oh God. (scream loud to fading)

Peter Kurten is the acknowledged depraved king of killers. A German born in Düsseldorf, he committed his first murders, believe it or not, at the age of just nine years old. He spent 20 years of his life in prison for other crimes before becoming a vicious serial killer. His crimes were known by the media as the Vampire Killings and the Werewolf Murders. He was eventually convicted of nine murders and seven attempted murders, all carried out in the most appalling manner.

Dean Allen Corll tortured and killed 23 young men, the numbers of bodies found. However, Corll's two young henchmen told police there were ten other victims. Their bodies were never found.

Englishman Peter Sutcliffe parked his long distance truck in the back streets on North of England cities and picked up prostitutes. He had paid sex or raped them. Then he killed them. During his "cleaning up the streets" campaign innocent women died along with the callgirls.

On the other side of the Atlantic at the same time Christopher Wilder was a rich killer. A dollar millionaire in fact. Born in Australia but domicilised in America he took a brainstorm and over a period of just seven weeks kidnapped, tortured and murdered eight women.

Ghastly crimes indeed. Serial Killers. Rapists. Murderers. For a full insight into serial killing, the murderers, their motives and how they carried out their horrific crimes and lured their victims to a terrible death call Ghastly Crimes… NOW!

CRIME CALLS
The Hillside Stranglers

Woman's Voice: Help me...! Somebody help me...! (scream loud to fading)

Ghastly Crimes! The horrendous story of the Hillside Stranglers.

One November 20th 1977 the naked corpses of three young college students were found in different areas of Los Angeles. They had been tortured and raped. Five days later a fourth girl was abducted and found bound, tortured, raped and murdered. Within another three days yet another female was discovered naked and dead, dumped in the Hollywood hills, her body obscenely exposed, like the others, with the legs spread apart.

The crimes were committed by two cousins, Kenneth Bianchi and Angelo Buono, the infamous Hillside Stranglers. But they were ...

CRIME CALLS
Christopher Wilder

Ghastly Crimes! Serial Killers! Rapists! Murderers!

Christopher Wilder — the millionaire murderer. He had as much money as any man could need. And his wealth drew beautiful women to fawn over him. But Wilder wanted more. He wanted the women on their knees, naked with his knife at their throat...

Woman's Voice: (scream loud to fading)

Eight murders in just seven weeks. Eight young, attractive and naïve women, lured by fast talk, fast cars and his rich playboy image. Wilder played with his victims but the game was one-sided and ended in death.

Christopher Bernard Wilder was bearded, presentable and nearly handsome. With an expen- ... his neck and a portfolio of pictures of glamorous girls in a glossy ... He promised them front-page

CRIME CALLS
The Night Stalker

The Night Stalker. The Satanic serial killer. Ghastly Crime. Rapists! Murderers! The Night Stalker robbed, raped and murdered. He slaughtered the men to get to the women. And he took the women without mercy.

The men died where they slept — shot or stabbed to death. The women young and old were viciously beaten, sexually abused then raped, stabbed or strangled.

Woman's Voice (scream loud to fading): Stop it... Stop... (scream)

The Night Stalker, a depraved creature from society's underbelly, even assaulted children of both sexes, some no more than six years old, raping and sodomising them.

But these were no street attacks. They did not take place in dark alleys or isolated laneways, nor in parking lots or deserted shopping malls. All occurred in what ...

THERE AREN'T MANY HIPPIES IN HULL

An interview with
ANDY DARLINGTON

David Kerekes

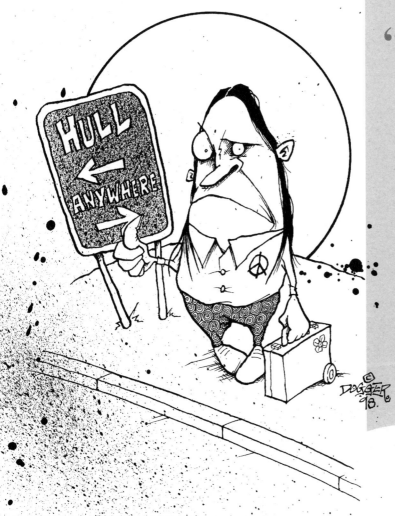

> **The first thing I actually had published was in 1971. I was writing before that — but I was writing without really knowing what to do with it. Stockpiling experiments. But '71 I regard as the start of it, really…**

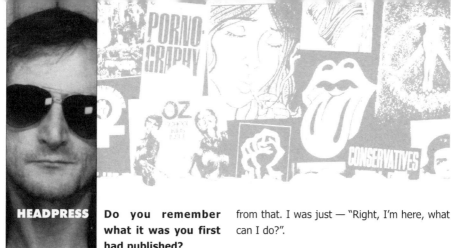

HEADPRESS Do you remember what it was you first had published?

ANDY At the time I was living in this kiosk-sized room in Leeds and I had this beat-up typewriter on which I was churning out this novel that I was adding to forever, which never got to completion. At that time I didn't know how to structure anything — I was just writing whatever came into my head. I was inspired by everything I was reading at the time, and the novel would suddenly swerve off into other directions influenced by William Burroughs, Edgar Rice Burroughs, Jet-Ace Logan*... Whatever I happened to be reading at the time, I was sort of writing this novel in a void; I didn't know how to construct anything, where to send it, or what to do with it. I didn't realise alternative DIY press existed. And then I was in what they used to call a Head Shop, which was like on Hyde Park corner in Leeds. And I saw this mag called SAD TRAFFIC, and that was the first mag I'd seen of its kind. I bought it. I'd written two poems and sent these off to the mag, and to my astonishment they accepted them.[†]

I was so totally overwhelmed by that, I immediately piled everything I owned into the back of the beat-up 15 quid van that I owned at the time. The mag was published in Barnsley, and I travelled down the motorway and moved in with them, literally! They had no choice in the matter — they were publishing this mag; I wanted in!

SAD TRAFFIC is a quote from a poem by Brian Patten, I think.

They were dropped-out, hippie layabout type students, and they started working out ideas for this mag which was to supersede SAD TRAFFIC which was to be STYNG ultimately. So I was in on the launching point for STYNG. And it kind of grew

from that. I was just — "Right, I'm here, what can I do?".

So were you on the STYNG editorial board — if they had such a thing? It was a very loose coalition type thing. There was one guy who was in charge — Roger Hutchinson — and he was like this demonic Aleister Crowley figure who'd manipulate us and set up all these deals with printers, you know. Basically, he'd swindle everybody. He'd say to printers, "We'll pay for issue one with the profits when we sell them all". He was really a Machiavellian guy — a really good character. He was squatting at the centre of this thing. And there were various circles of different hanger-ons, who'd come in and do their various things. I was one of them — I'd write, whenever I got the chance. Bits of layout. STYNG was a tabloid, very similar format to INTERNATIONAL TIMES (IT). Glossy paper; two or three colours on occasion when we could extend to that.

Looking back with what I know now, I could have done far better — lots of opportunities missed and things like that. But, you know, you do what you do at the time and it was good. And I got a lot out of it.

It had quite a large circulation didn't it? Around 7–8,000 I understand. Whenever anyone quotes a circulation figure you ought to half it! That's one of the basic rules of publishing! But it did do well — it was building nicely when we ran out of printers we could con. We

> *A Dan Dare style SF comic strip which ran from 1956–64. Michael Moorcock wrote some of the scripts. Andy wound up writing a Jet-Ace Logan story for an attempted relaunch, which featured artwork by the late Ron Turner, one of the original artists on the strip.
>
> [†]The poem 'Anthem For A Lost Cause' appeared in SAD TRAFFIC No 5 (May 1971).

were owing money to every printer in South Yorkshire.

You got busted didn't you? Oh yeah, there were a couple of busts. There was one particular councillor in Barnsley who pledged to drive this evil publication out of town. It was fun.

You reported on police beating up a tramp and killing him in custody. Was that the catalyst? That wasn't one of mine. I interviewed Genesis P. Orridge from Throbbing Gristle — that was one of the first things that I did. I did stuff like that.

What was he like back then? He's in exile now, following all those pornography busts. A bit unfair, you know, because I've seen some of those videos that he did — they were strange but they were art-porn. Originally I come from Hull, and I knew him when I lived in Hull. He was a very conspicuous character even then. He was always a mover and a shaker in Hull in those days. In fact he had a band called Coum — and the logo for this band was an ejaculating prick. And they used to print this on the letterheads, posters, and it was painted on the side of the band's transit van. Inevitably, as he fully expected and as he fully intended he got busted for that. That was part of his 'master plan'. And I went down to interview him about this particular obscenity bust. I spent a day in court with him. 1972 or '73.

In the late Sixties, there seemed to be a world party going on and I didn't have an invite. Wherever you happen to be, it's always happening somewhere else. I was in Hull and I was desperate for things to happen, you know. And then I saw these beautiful, pre-Raphaelite hippie girls who were in the IT and things like that and I thought, 'I want one of them'.

I wrote this thing for KNAVE* called 'The Quest for the Poetry Groupie',

where I wrote about desperately trying to get laid and it not happening. [*The article is reprinted on page 117.*] Whereas all these poets were going around with all these girls. Allen Ginsberg — he's gay, but all these girls are flocking to him, loving him. Kissing his toes, all this kind of thing. I thought, 'That's the way to do it' — become a poet. At that time it was like a gang of angry young men like Alan Sillitoe, Stan Barstow, people like that, and they were writing about Northern working class lives, and they exactly defined the dissatisfaction and claustrophobia of what it was like to be stuck in that particular situation, but they didn't explain how you get *out* of that situation; whereas the Beat writers — in America particularly — they kind of provided a blue print for escape. This is how you escape. Burroughs provided narcotic routes; Ginsberg defined sexual routes; Kerouac said just get on the motorway with your thumb. Do it. They provided the lifestyle models, and that's what I was doing — just exploring.

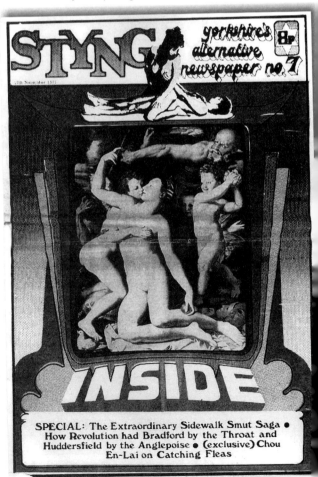

SPECIAL: The Extraordinary Sidewalk Smut Saga • How Revolution had Bradford by the Throat and Huddersfield by the Anglepoise • (exclusive) Chou En-Lai on Catching Fleas

The Angry Young Men always had a catastrophe at the end of the story — someone usually died — usually the young man. Or went back to work, and that was kind of it. Sillitoe — he's still a shit hot writer. Arthur Seaton in SATURDAY NIGHT, SUNDAY MORNING — he's like a rebel; he's stuck in Nottingham in this factory, but he's not gonna get trapped like his father — he's gonna get out and have a good time and shake the world. But by the end of the novel his girlfriend is pregnant, he's gonna end up married, he can see it unfolding — he's gonna end up just like his father. He'll be stuck in one of these council houses with his wife; he'll be working in this factory, you know. First of all it defines; you know exactly how Arthur Seaton feels, that you wanna get out and do something with your life, change the world...

Did you ever read Colin Wilson's THE OUTSIDER at around this time? Oh yes. When I got to STYNG, a lot of the people were university students and I'd never been to university and I was like the token proletarian. I'd worked in a factory and actually got my hands dirty. I read a lot but there were gaps in what I'd read, and Colin Wilson's THE OUTSIDER added a few pointers. Wilson can be pretentious and fascistic on occasion but he influenced me in a lot of directions. I think he'd be a good guy to interview.

Do you think coming from a background in engineering† gave you more of a down-to-earth view? I'd like to think so because a lot of the SF writers I've liked haven't made a living from writing. People like EC Tubb work as traffic wardens, walking round in a uniform in London with a hat with a yellow strip on, booking people, while at the same time his head's full of these universes, space ships and galaxies. Booking people. And I interviewed him and he was telling me about how he was doing this warden job and somebody actually physically assaulted him because he booked some guy, and punched him in the face — *whack!* And he was down there with his nose bleeding, and I thought — "That's EC Tubb who's written all these books; whose nose is bleeding because some guy has docked him for double-parking." But I don't think

it's a bad thing to have your feet grounded in reality. What's that they say, you can lie in the gutter but your eyes are on the stars? I think Shane McGowan said that.

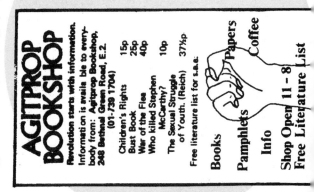

I can't imagine Shane McGowan saying anything much these days. It looks like they just wheel him on whenever he performs. I saw him performing at the Heineken Festival in Leeds. He did that 'Christmas In New York' with Kirsty McColl. And Kirsty McColl came up on stage and they attempted to do a duet together — and he keeps getting the lyrics wrong. He's written this song, and they're his lyrics and he keeps forgetting them! She does her bit and he goes to do his bit — and forgets it. Lost, so she takes over and brings it back into the verse and they do it again, does her bit, setting him up and he's totally out of it. It was touching. He also did 'Baby, Please Don't Go', the Them song — and he sang that three times for no apparent reason! He did it twice in the set and came back to do it for an encore. It was great.

First interview you did? Probably the Genesis P. Orridge one. When STYNG disintegrated and everyone went their separate ways, I started living in a caravan in Denby Dale drying out, a little Pennine village. STYNG was the first place I came across drugs. I was in the STYNG office and Roger Hutchinson was rolling one of these hash pipes, rolling silver paper and all this ritual that goes into it. I was watching it mesmerised. I'd never seen this before — exotic, other worldly. I've never advo-

*KNAVE Vol 1 No 19 (January 1987).

†Printing, actually.

cated drugs because I think it's a dangerous thing to do; I've interviewed people like Peter Green out of Fleetwood Mac and I know all about Syd Barrett and this brain damage stuff — I know there's a bad side to it, but at the same time, this thing about drugs — 'Just say no'... When I saw Roger Hutchinson with that hash pipe, there was just no way on earth I could have said no. Anyway, I was in this caravan, drying out of all this stuff and I got involved with other magazines. Roger Hutchinson moved down to London and did a few things for OZ, and became an editor of IT briefly. It had a revolving number of editors and he was one of them. And he got me in writing for them. One of the things I did for them was interview Mike Butterworth and Dave Britton of Savoy, because they'd just been busted — I think it was for stocking bootlegs in their shop. I say interview — I spent a rambling, incoherent day with Mike Butterworth and Dave Britton, the results of which were published in IT*.

*IT (Frivolous Summer Issue), August 1980.

*HOT PRESS Vol 5 No 4, March 1981.

Simultaneously I was producing this mag called LUDDS MILL. That was a mag I inherited — not my choice of title. My title was Eight Miles High Leisure Industries.

There are a lot of arts mags and poetry mags that have an elitist attitude, but I was looking back at myself when I was trying to start, this socially dysfunctional guy living in this little room in Leeds, not knowing where to go or what to do. I'd come across SAD TRAFFIC and it had opened up this phantasmagoria — which is what I wanted to do for other people; get this mag out and people could stumble across it — not literary types, not people who read poetry; ordinary people, like I considered myself at that time.

I put people like Patti Smith on the cover — put arty things on the covers and arty people buy it, but you put Patti Smith on the cover and Rock fans buy it. It was the time of punk. You put Patti Smith, Tom Verlaine or Burroughs on the cover, the 'right' people buy it. That's a way of infiltrating and getting your name across.

Also when I was doing LUDDS MILL, the DIY record industry was starting up. DIY tapes, DIY records. Years earlier all those big hippie bands who were anti-establishment and revolution for the hell of it — they were all signing to RCA and CBS; Jefferson Airplane and the Grateful Dead signed to Warner Brothers and all that. At the time of punk, people started producing their own cassettes and their own 7" singles, and so I started reviewing them and promoting them. One of the tapes I got for review was by this band called Vice Versa, from Sheffield, and they actually went to the extent of taking out a full-page advert [in LUDDS MILL]. Vice Versa eventually became ABC with Martin Fry. They were play-

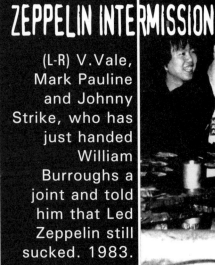
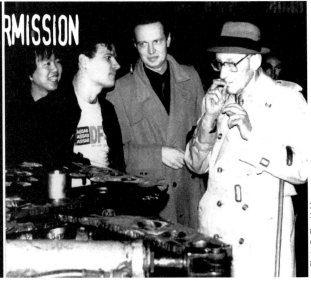

ZEPPELIN INTERMISSION

(L-R) V.Vale, Mark Pauline and Johnny Strike, who has just handed William Burroughs a joint and told him that Led Zeppelin still sucked. 1983.

Photo © Clay Holden

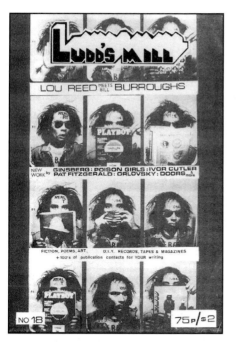

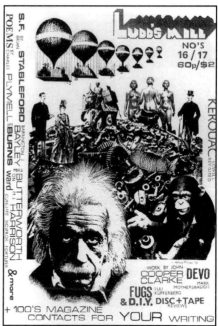

ing synths, drum machines, samples and all this kind of thing. To me it was revolutionary. I interviewed them for this fanzine called WOOL CITY ROCKER which Nick Toczek ran in Bradford and then HOT PRESS took it. They had been big in Ireland and they were trying to expand into the UK and were looking for regional writers, and I happened to be in the right place at the right time with Vice Versa. And they published it.* I actually sent that article to the NME and MELODY MAKER and they rejected it. But six months later they were clamouring for interviews with ABC.

After that I became caught up in that whole Sheffield thing — Cabaret Voltaire, Clock DVA, all those bands.

Why do you think those pockets of similar sounding influential bands erupt at the same time in largely industrial towns?
Perhaps if I'd heard Cabaret Voltaire first, I wouldn't have been so impressed with Vice Versa. They were part of the same group, but Cabaret Voltaire were the people who started it off. Even now I still like all that dance-electronic stuff and I hear Prodigy now and I think 'That's bloody great!'. But Cabaret Voltaire were doing stuff very similar years ago. All this stuff like DJ Sash and Future Sounds of London — you know,

it's brilliant stuff, but it all comes from what people like Cabaret Voltaire were doing at that time. Now it's all samplers but then it was literally taped loops. I can remember going round to Adi Newton, the guy from Clock DVA, down to his flat and he assembled this tape which was initially the Kennedy shooting, cut it up into little bits and stuck it all together with this other — what you call white leaders. And he had this tape going round the tape deck — all these white bits where he'd stuck it all together. It must have took him bloody ages to do all that with scissors. I remember it as being good. It was what Burroughs was doing with words. Why that particular thing happened in Sheffield at that particular time, I don't know.

Dave Davies from the Kinks explained it well when I interviewed him. Back when he was starting off with the Kinks, in '62 or something like that, Elvis Presley was still number one in the charts, and Frank Ifield and all those squeaky clean pop singers, and at the time in Liverpool, there were the Beatles, and all that up in Newcastle The Animals, and in London, The Stones, Alexis Korner and the Kinks, and they were all working in isolation — none of them knew what any of the others were doing. But at the same time they were operating on the same kind of

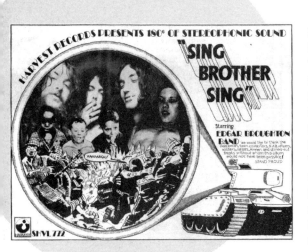

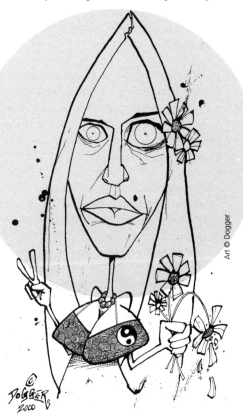

basis — which was American Blues. All working in the same area at the same time. Dave Davies said it was some kind of signal that went out — like a radio signal — connecting in people's minds. That's the way he saw it.

It's kind of an evolutionary process, as Colin [Wilson] would say. People do kind of pick up on the same ideas around the same time.

Can you remember what record, at the beginning of each era or decade, made you stop and think, 'Wow, this is a times-they-are-a-changing thing, you know'? Like the Sixties, what was it there, and what was it in the Seventies? I like energy and violence. I'm not a violent person — not physically violent but I like extremes in art, extremes in music. I've always gone for that. It's always been like, in the Fifties there was Bo Diddley and Little Richard and people like that — the black R&B, rock'n'roll people. And then it was like the Yardbirds, The Who, The Stones, and then it was 'Eight Miles High' — The Byrds. Brilliant record — stopped me in my tracks... I actually interviewed Gene Clark from The Byrds. I told him I was in Hull when 'Mr Tambourine Man', the first Byrds record came out. I was in Hull and I was at school and had enough money to either get the bus home, *or* buy 'Mr Tambourine Man'. So I bought 'Mr Tambourine Man' and walked the ten miles home. I interviewed Gene Clark, long after the event obviously. He was actually playing at a Working Man's Club in

Wakefield. Can you imagine that? The Pussy Cat Club, it was called. It had been called Wakefield Theatre Club. He was playing support to Lindisfarne. People think The Byrds, they think Roger McGuinn, Jim McGuinn, but if you look on those first three Byrds albums, Gene Clark wrote the majority of the stuff — he really was an on-the-ball guy. He actually wrote the original draft to 'Eight Miles High'. I was saying, tell me how you wrote 'Eight Miles High', and he starts off we're in this tour bus, and he starts off with these original lines. And Brian Jones was there, and he comes across and says, oh that's great poetry, and starts putting lines in and developed it from that. He was telling me this story, and from the new music journalism point of view, it was a job, you get paid for it, but at the same time it was a privilege for me to sit with these people. They had shit in their life.

Can you tell us some of the people you have interviewed? It's funny because people always say, oh you interviewed William Burroughs — can I have a copy of your William Burroughs interview and all this kind of thing. Obviously it was great interviewing Burroughs

— it was really good. Some of the ones that I'm proudest of are probably people that aren't so obvious, like Clock DVA. I did some of the best things I'd written inspired by Clock DVA and Cabaret Voltaire. Recently I've done Skunk Anansie, I've done Chumbawamba, I've done Erasure, I've done The Kinks, I've done Deep Purple. I've done Ian Hunter, the guy from Mott the Hoople. I've done Kraftwerk, I've done Can, I've done all the Sheffield bands — Heaven 17, The Human League, and all that lot you know. I've done writers as well — I've done Kurt Vonnegut, I've interviewed him, I've done Ramsey Campbell, Storm Constantine, all these people. Peter Green out of Fleetwood Mac — that was an amazing interview. You're familiar with the story, that he founded Fleetwood Mac? I think he was something of an unstable character to start out with — kind of psychologically unstable and not suited to the pressures of stardom, put it that way. Obviously he was empowered by the music and very much inspired by the music, by the Blues. And he formed Fleetwood Mac, and the success that came to Fleetwood Mac was unexpected and unwelcome in a way because he was not suited to that lifestyle. He took massive amounts of drugs as well, and his mind just totally disintegrated basically. I don't know if you've heard that record, 'The Green Manalishi' which he recorded. That is actually the sound of his mind coming apart. It's chilling. That is a man literally descending into madness — haunted by madness, by temptations. He disappeared from the face of Planet Earth for I think 20 years, and now he's just getting his head back together again, but he's definitely not functioning 100%. I went down there to interview him, and the answers that I got did not necessarily correspond to questions that I had asked. And he kept cutting off into these weird flights of fancy where he'd get hung up on a particular phrase being fascinated, and free improvising on this phrase, going off into some weird little place of his own. And obviously he's got brain cells missing, although he was trying desperately to function and to be friendly and helpful but I felt real sort of compassion for him you know. When we got round to talking about drugs, I thought I don't want to

cause this guy pain — he's been through hell. I really felt a warmth for him.

One of the things that I always do... I always treat the people I interview as creative people doing interesting things. That's the basic standpoint I start off from, and I always try to do as much research as I can to try and know what I'm talking about. It's all in there anyway. I listen to it all and take it all in. I've a reasonable knowledge of what's happening even now. I think it's an insult to them if you go along and you haven't done your research — that's part of your job isn't it? To know what you're doing... I did The Stone Roses — I wish I'd kept the

interview tape of that but I gave it away. You get so many tapes you can't keep them all. With Skunk Anansie, I knew more-or-less what they were all about but I didn't know them inside out, so I said I'll do that, and it was set up for a week ahead, so I spent that week getting the records, listening to the records, looking for interviews and getting to know what they did so I could go along and ask intelligent questions. I've never been in a situation when I went in totally blind.

Never just bumped into somebody and taken the opportunity to interview them?

I went down to interview a band called Sheer, an Irish band who were happening at the time, and supporting them was Placebo. I was there to interview Sheer. I watched the bands at the soundcheck, and Placebo were pretty good. I had a microphone and I could see [Brian Molko] from Placebo looking, sort of saying interview me. I could have gone across and done it, but I won't do that because it's not right. So I did the interview I was there to do which was the Sheer interview. Oh, I interviewed Country Joe McDonald from Country Joe and the Fish.

When was that?

That was at the Annual Leeds Folk Festival, but it was the only one there ever was, and it was sponsored by Radio Leeds or something like that. They obviously intended it to be an annual event. It was quite a good festival — there was Georgie Fame on, there was Country Joe and the Fish, there was different people on. I kind of went down to interview him then. I was always into all that psychedelic stuff. Country Joe was a really good guy to talk to because he was kind of intelligent and sharp and witty. We went back to his caravan, and he had these albums out at the time, and I was saying, can I have some review copies. And he said, well you can buy some if

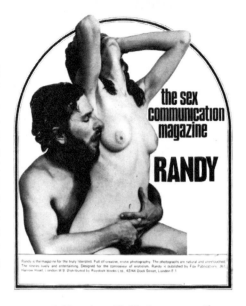

you want. Then he said, I'll give you one if you buy the other one. We were haggling. So I said, if you autograph them for me... So I bought one and he autographed them for me, 'To Andy...' [*We take a break at this point, and come back talking about Elvis.*] I loved Elvis Presley when I was kid, because he was like napalm back in the Fifties. Of course, Led Zeppelin actually met Elvis. Robert Plant shook hands with Elvis in the hotel. They actually did a duet together in the hotel. Elvis asked Robert Plant, what is your favourite Elvis song. I forget which one it was — one of the very early ones — 'Love Me', or something like that — and they actually sung it together. And I actually had that story in the back of my head, that Robert Plant had met Elvis. Robert Plant is a real trainspotter when it comes to early rock'n'roll. He knows all the rock'n'roll records, B-sides, all the obscure stuff — Ral Donner and all these Elvis facsimile people who were knocking about at that time. I was a bit similar to that, so we got talking about all that stuff. I kept the Elvis question right to the very end because I could tell when you interview these people, you're allotted a certain time span, and when the time span is up, there's a PR guy coming in who says your time span is up, next interview please. So I kept this Elvis question right to the very end because the time was running out and it was almost time to go. So I just said, oh I understand you met Elvis. He was straight in there then, Robert Plant was — 30 minute storyboard — sit down and I'll tell you all about it. He was telling me how he met

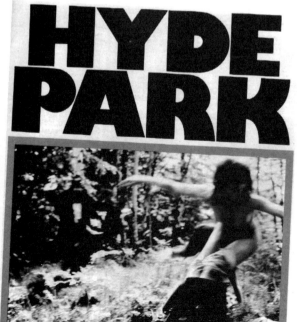

Hello darling. Would you like a rubs me up. It is all over all too quickly with
play around?

him, and then I shook hands with the hand that had shaken hands with Elvis. That's the closest I've been to shaking hands with Elvis. It was funny, going back to Gene Clark thing, you know, him playing at the Working Men's Club in Wakefield. I went into the dressing room afterwards to speak to him, and I'd got a list of questions ready. And he said, 'You know what I'd like — I'd really like some English fish and chips.' So, I thought, I'd walked 10 miles to get his record, I'd worshipped 'Eight Miles High', so this is the one thing I can do for him — I can go out and get some fish and chips. So I went into Wakefield at two o'clock in the morning, looking for a chip shop that was still open, to get some fish and chips. Prowling the precincts and finally I found this shop that was still open, and got these fish and chips, and took them back to Gene Clark, and while I'd been gone, some other guy had come in and started interviewing him. Gene Clark was sitting there eating big handfuls of fish and chips which I'd bought for him, answering questions for this other guy. All the questions I was going to ask, this guy was asking him... Anyway, when this other guy finally got to the end of his questions (he had them printed out — like a computer printout) and when he'd finally finished and packed up and gone, I got my turn. My planned interview had gone out of the win-

dow. I just sat down and we just improvised — did questions sort of kidding around, and that was even better, really because he unwound and got this stuff out of his system. He was really into talking — he just talking about Rick and Bob, and I said, hang on a minute, do you mean Rick Danko and Bob Dylan, and he said yeah. It was amazing — a peak experience that! When I actually got to write the interview up I was saying, Gene Clark is looking fit and healthy and you can tell he's on good form. On stage he did 'Mr Tambourine Man'. Of course, The Byrds only did one verse, and he did the full Dylan version six or seven verses. And I was just saying how fit and healthy he looked. He went back to the States, and a month later he died. Pills and drugs overdose. So I think I was one of the last people to interview him...

How did he go down in this Working Man's Club? I'd seen Lindisfarne before and they were alright — you know, good boozing, sing-a-long type of stuff. Most of the audience were there to see Lindisfarne to be honest. He went down alright with 'Tambourine Man' and the songs that were recognised. To me he was like, up there on the Pantheon. So it was great for me to actually meet him. These writers that go down to London, going to gigs every night and interview-

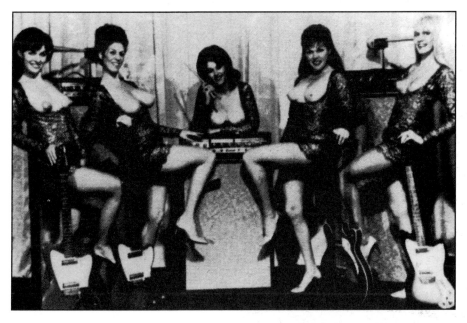

ing these people, they get blasé and get pissed off and end up hating the music, know what I mean? That's never happened to me. I still get off on it. I'm 50, and a couple of years back I went to the V97 festival. Brilliant, I loved every minute. It was raw, there was energy, it was violent — you know. I got that same buzz seeing The Prodigy there that I got seeing The Yardbirds in the Sixties — it was the same buzz.

What were They Yardbirds like live? Who was on guitar at the time? Jeff Beck. In the Sixties I was well into all that. I went to see every band that came through. Saw Hendrix, The Small Faces, The Who dozens of times, The Stones — even The Beatles which is weird. In the local baths — the swimming pool, they used to put boards over and have dances there. Literally. The Yardbirds were there, and you'd be standing and there'd be a drop beneath you — the swimming pool! All my mates used to go to pick up women and that kind of thing, and I was always up for that. If women were an option, I was always into that, but at the same time I was always there to see the band. I was always there fighting to get to the front.

What's your most overriding memory of the Yardbirds gig? They had a Tibetan prayer mat that they put down in the middle of the stage. It had candles at the back because they were always into that slightly esoteric kind of thing.

What was Keith Relf like at that point, because he became quite bad with his booze, didn't he? He was quite together then. He never had a brilliant voice, but that's not necessary to be in a rock band, is it? That's one thing Ian Hunter, the guy from Mott the Hoople said when I interviewed him. He never had a voice — he couldn't sing, but then all of a sudden Bob Dylan came along. Mott the Hoople recorded a Sonny Bono song called 'Laugh At Me', and I always thought that was a joke — that they were taking the piss, because you know Sonny Bono couldn't sing. So I always thought Mott the Hoople were taking the piss. I was talking to Ian Hunter about this and he was saying, 'Oh no, I couldn't sing'. And then Bob Dylan came along, Leonard Cohen came along and Sonny Bono came along, and they couldn't sing, but they were making records and they were selling millions of copies of records, and he thought if they can do it, I can do it. So it was genuine — you don't need a good voice but an effective voice, and Keith Relf had that kind of effective voice for The Yardbirds. It worked really well.

I was into all that Sixties stuff — that was really great but then the early Seventies went

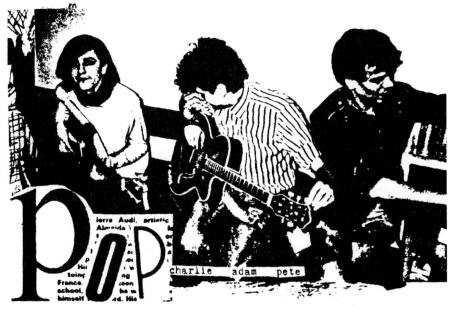

Start your own band!!!

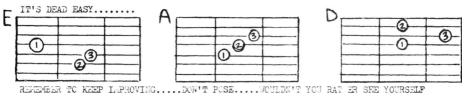

back to the Fifties facsimiles and so on and I lost interest a bit then, although I was working myself into the writing science fiction and getting published. But music wasn't exciting to me until the end of the seventies when you get The Ramones and Talking Heads, and The Sex Pistols The Adverts and X-Ray Spex and all them lot coming along. And the Punk fanzines which tie in with all that. To me it was really exciting because I was trying to get that energy and that visuality. I was using techniques they'd used in the sixties as well mixing it all in. I remember saying to someone that I was trying to reproduce the energy of RIPPED AND TORN and SNIFFING GLUE and all these Punk magazines, but it always came out like me. I interviewed The Fall, and all the punk things, but I didn't feel part of that until a few years later the electronic stuff came out, and I felt totally into that. Their reference points related directly to my own creative processes.

All those alternative underground magazines — they were special times and amazingly good magazines. Where's the market now? I think in a way they were like lifestyle fanzines. I was living in Hull, and I wanted to be part of what was happening, but I felt excluded, I felt isolated because there aren't many hippies in Hull. But I wanted to be part of it. The way that I could be part of it was by buying IT and reading up on all the amazing stuff that was going on.

People were buying IT, OZ and STYNG. They've all fragmented now though, and each lifestyle area has its own fanzine. You know, netheads and WIRED magazine, and each separate form of music has its specialised press. It's still going on, it's still there but perhaps at that time, be-

cause it wasn't quite so diverse there was a kind of bigger potential audience for it. These magazines managed to achieve a reasonable circulation. I don't think anyone was making massive amounts of money out of them. It was like a world wide web of alternative culture.

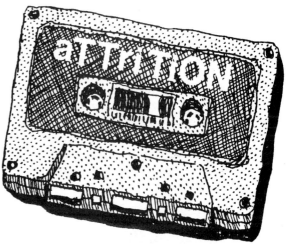

What would you say was your most difficult interview? The one with a band called Danse Society — I think that was probably the worst. They were a band from Barnsley. They were quite good and had some records in the Indie charts... There was this guy, he had the most fantastic hair — all the dreadlocks and beads. I think the entire focus of the band was his hair. I went round to interview them, and they were extremely difficult. I was asking questions about the lyrics — 'Ah well, the lyrics are whatever you make of them. You put your own interpretation on.' It was a get-out. I was trying desperately to get some kind of quotes. They were just totally vague and really bad. I thought that perhaps it was just me, and they hadn't connected with me but later on I saw them on the WHISTLE TEST, being interviewed and it was the same. So it must just be them. People said that Mark E Smith from The Fall was difficult to interview but I found him alright. He had a really sarcastic, witty, down-to-earth sense of humour. I met him at Leeds Polytechnic, and he said, 'Let's go across the pub — you can buy me a drink. I always like the idea of a Yorkshireman buying me a drink'. And he has this thing about putting everybody down. Every interview, he's slagging people off. Anything you mention, he slags it off. So I thought I didn't want that. I didn't want to set things up and him to shoot them down. So at that time he'd done a couple of cover versions, one of which was Gene Vincent's 'Rolling Danny'. So I thought, he must like Gene Vincent, so I asked him about Gene Vincent. I wanted something positive from him. I worked out before what I wanted from him... and I got some really good copy. People say he's awkward but I found he was alright. But then, I always approach people as intelligent people doing creative things.

There's a funny story with this guy I know, who was looking to buy a house. He got a call from the estate agent and went round to view a house which had just gone on

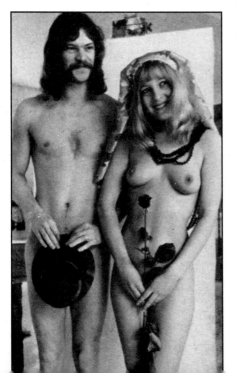

the market in Prestwich. It turned out the house belonged to Mark E Smith, who wasn't happy that the estate agent hadn't given him any warning. My mate thought The Fall might at least make a song out of the visit. Yeah. (Laughs) Everything But The Girl — I interviewed them. He [Ben Watt] was good. He was saying, 'Ask me some more questions', but I was running out of tape — it was only a C90. He was really getting into it. I went round to see them. I wasn't smitten by them, but they were alright. She [Tracey Thorn] is kind of strange-looking isn't she? It's always difficult when you're writing. I like to describe the ambience, their appearance, what they're wearing, their physical mannerisms and that kind of thing. It was hard to describe her in a flattering way, because she's not very attractive. Striking, or distinctive or something... I'd always written pornographic stuff for my own indulgence. I'd always been interested in sexual matters. There was always my serious writing, and then this other pornographic stuff as well at the same time. I never considered crossing the two over, but when I started writing music journalism there were a couple of writers that I thought were really good. There was a guy called Brian Case who used to write for MELODY MAKER — he used to write about jazz. The way he wrote about it, even if you didn't know the musicians involved, he could write in such a way that would inspire you to go out and want to listen to it. He was a beatnik kind of writer and he wrote this spontaneous prose. I thought it was really good that he was using this medium creatively. I wanted to do it in that way. It was the same with erotic stuff... Mike Butterworth wrote for a couple of porn magazines at that time, and he's a guy I've got a lot of respect for. And I also Like Brian Aldiss, the science fiction writer — he wrote some really good stuff. Guy N Smith* and even Kerouac wrote porn. I thought, well they all do it, and they are using it creatively so I can do that as well. So I wrote a story for MAYFAIR called 'Modern as in Mary Quant'† which was the title of a Vice Versa song that had never been released... I thought it was a good title, so I used it for this porno story and they published it in MAYFAIR. And from then on I got writing for KNAVE. I had

Fantastic Offer!

2 New Posters direct from United States – in full colour – yours for only **75p** each!

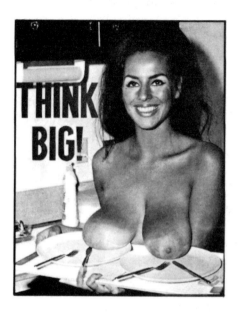

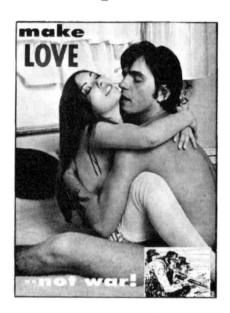

masses of stuff in KNAVE. I still write for FORUM and magazines like that.

What kind of restrictions would the various magazines put on your stuff? People think you can get away with anything, and that there are no rules, but that's not actually true. I think things have changed slightly but there were a number of things that I've censored out. Right from the start, I did set my own agenda of things that I was not going to write about. I've always considered myself to be feminist. From first reading Germaine Greer's THE FEMALE EUNUCH I thought it was really good, and I was with it all the way. So I didn't use the exploitation of women so I set about that from a positive point of view. I've never violated that really. I write from a male point of view of male lust for women who are magical, beautiful creatures. That's the way I tend to write. Whereas male sexuality is sort of grotesque and almost comical. I still think it's true in a way — that's a good point to start off at. So my male characters are grotesque, lusting deviants. Whether that reflects something, I don't know. The women tend to be magical, beautiful creatures, which is the way I see them.

Anal sex. You could never write anal sex. You might be able to get away with it now, but at the time you couldn't. And when I started out you couldn't mention drugs. Sex was alright, but when I mentioned a joint... So oddly enough my version of 'Quest for the Poetry Groupie' is the censored version that was published in KNAVE because it left out all references to drugs. That was slightly tongue in cheek and never actually worked out as I intended it, though there have been moments along the way when it has. One magazine I was writing for had a 'Women Confess' column, which they ran in every issue, and in my naïve way I'd always assumed it was women writing it. But then the editor rang me up asking if I wanted to write some of them.

> *"Oddly enough I was in touch with horror writer Guy N Smith — NIGHT OF THE CRABS, etc — and was surprised to discover him contributing to porn mags, too. This must have been late Seventies."
>
> †MAYFAIR Vol 20 No 2, Feb 1985.

I was a bit taken aback. I'd assumed that maybe a male writer might edit it or sub it down, but that it was basically women speaking. Everything I'd written had my name on it, so if people wanted to take issue to it, it was me they were talking to. It was obviously a male persona, and I was not going to write as a female persona and pretend I was a woman because I didn't think it was right. Plenty of men probably read these features and think, why isn't my wife like this? As a writer, it's fiction and you don't expect it to be totally real, but I do think that some people actually look at these magazines then look at their wife and girlfriend and wonder why they aren't like that. That's when it can be dangerous. I wanted to make it clear that what I was writing was out of my head, and I wasn't going to disguise myself as a woman. There was another thing I was quite surprised about. I wrote a story for them. It wasn't a major work of fiction but the simple story line was that the guy wanted to get into wife-swapping but his wife was initially reluctant but eventually she went along with it and they have sex in a foursome with this black couple. She is so enamoured with this black guy that in the end she moves out with him and leaves her husband. That's where the irony comes in — he's the fall-guy. There was no reason why he had to be black, it was just character really. You make one a Yorkshire character, and you make one West Indian. No reason really other than to give it a bit more depth. I sent this story off to THE JOURNAL OF LOVE and they wrote back and said it was a good story but they couldn't use a story where a black character comes out winning over a white character! I would have had to re-write it and make the white guy alright. I wasn't going to do that. It totally stunned me.

Yeah. I'm surprised they thought like that, particularly given the shoddiness of some of those magazines... Yeah. It must have been intended only to flatter the ego of the white reader. So in the end I decided I wasn't going to change it, and I took it somewhere else. That is racism. I'm not racist. I'm not anti-gay or what-

ever. In FORUM there was a censorship issue concerning gay male sex. Again, things like this married couple, they get a guy to go along with them. He's fascinated by the woman. It started off when I was working at this print shop, and I was really hung up on this woman and I went round their house (she was married). I was really fascinated by this girl but they had this weird kinky sex thing going too. I took that as the jumping off point — that's where reality finished and the story took over. If the guy in the story was to have sex with the wife, he had to have oral sex with the husband first. That was the Catch-22 thing. It was like the Meatloaf song — I will do anything for love, but I won't do that!

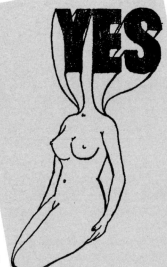

What exactly would you do for love? How far would you go for love? What would you do to make love to this woman? And that was the cut-off point, the fact that he had to give this guy a blow-job. I wrote the story and they said I couldn't do that, and have male homosexuality portrayed in that way. But it was just like an ironic twist to me — where do you draw the line? But they took offence at that. I altered the ending to that to allow it to be published.

I've always been interested in science fiction, but unfortunately that doesn't pay as well as porn or rock n roll. You can sell a good porn story and get £250, which is good money for me. Or for 3,000 words interviewing a rock star — that's good money. But you write science fiction and you get £40 for it. When I write science fiction, I really take a pride in it. I can take 18 months doing a short story, whereas a porn story I might do in two sessions. I sit down and write the basic outline, typing it in, then I will go back and sort out what I've written and write the end. Some of that is totally spontaneous and it comes out really well. I'm not bragging, but it's to my own satisfaction. It has a spontaneity to it and I think if I could write science fiction in that way it would be great. Science fiction is a major investment in time. 🕊

PLAYING DEVIL'S ADVOCATE

Five reasons why The Exorcist isn't Scary Any More

Adrian Horrocks

Britain, 1999. In a packed cinema, a young audience are watching *The Exorcist*. Long banned on video, the film was recently re-released to mark its 25th Anniversary. But as the tale of the 12-year-old Regan MacNeil's possession by a demonic spirit unspools, general indifference pervades the auditorium. Unlike the audiences who saw the film on its original 1973 release, no one leaps at the screen to try and 'get the demon'. No one vomits in the aisles. Instead, there are a few embarrassed giggles, some sighs of exasperation at the film's slow pace. Occasionally, there is a burst of laughter. It's not laughter as a cover for terror. It's laughter that recognises how dated and unscary *The Exorcist* seems to those seeing it for the first time, shorn of its original context.

A few days later, I was able to attend a University seminar on *The Exorcist*. The students loudly decried Friedkin's film as 'boring,' 'dated,' and 'stupid.' Many spoke of their anticipation to see the film, which was dissipated by the slow build-up of the early scenes. One said, 'We thought it was going to be scary, but nothing happened,' while another blandly stated 'It was slow'. One girl pitied the film's original viewers: 'They didn't know any better, so it seemed scary to them.' No one spoke for the film, but it was noticeable that young women were the most vocal in their complaints against it. There was no anger, they simply found it silly. Later, while searching the Internet, I found an *Exorcist* web site, recently created by a British 16-year-old. To him, the film was never meant to be scary, being simply a classic, not horror at all. He said his friends were disappointed by how unscary it was.

What's happened? How has *The Exorcist* gone from making audiences puke, to making them yawn? How is it that a teenager that respects the film, still has to admit that it isn't scary? Of course there have been endless rip-

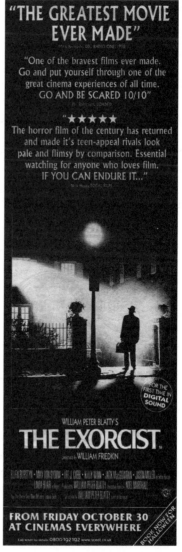

offs, tributes and imitations since it first scared audiences. But beyond that, there are several reasons why *The Exorcist* no longer supplies the scares that it once did.

IT'S DATED

In his book *Censored*, Tom Dewe Mathews claims that *The Wild One* (starring Marlon Brando) was banned by the BBFC in 1953 because they perceived it to be an incitement to juvenile delinquency, and a direct cause of teddy boy violence. The film didn't receive a certificate until 1967, when hippies had replaced teds on the streets of Britain. Today, *The Wild One* seems silly. It's camp, it's funny, but nothing more. Which is why we're allowed to see it. When the censor suddenly allows a once-banned film to be exhibited, this isn't evidence of sudden leniency by our moral guardians. Quite the opposite, it is more an indication that time has passed the film by, and whatever power it once held has been diluted by changes in society.

Thus it is with *The Exorcist*. At the time of its release, America was gripped by social upheaval, making the movie contemporary and gripping. It came at just the right time, capitalising on the fear and distrust with which parents regarded their horrid hippie children. It exploited widespread worries that Mommy and Daddy's little girl might be having sex and smoking reefer instead of staying 'nice' and Catholic. As Stephen King wrote in his non-fiction genre study *Danse Macabre*, "Religious trappings aside, every adult in America understood what the film's powerful subtext was saying; they understood that the demon in Regan MacNeil would have responded enthusiastically to the Fish Cheer at Woodstock." Today, that moment has passed, and those once rebellious children are now parents themselves, leaving *The Exorcist* looking dated.

'GIRL POWER' NOT 'FATHER KNOWS BEST'

The Exorcist was always a perverse film, an attempt to construct a reality in which two men tying a girl to a bed and abusing her was not only permissible, but essential for her survival. In his book *Easy Riders, Raging Bulls*, Peter Biskind reports that John Boorman refused an offer from writer William Peter Blatty to direct *The Exorcist*, as Boorman "thought it was a story about torturing a child." This element is undoubtedly there, and it has always seemed strange to me that any adult man would claim *The Exorcist* as his favourite film of all time.

These days, young women play a more active role in the genre. Films such as James Cameron's *Aliens*, Wes Craven's original *A Nightmare on Elm Street*, and Jonathan Demme's *Silence of the Lambs* all established able female protagonists as part of the genre. Women are now allowed to be full characters in horror films, and the final survivor may well be female: the so-called Final Girl.

Young women today may resent *The Exorcist*'s depiction of them as problematic, evil, and needing to be controlled. If they don't seem to be angered by it, this may be because sexual relations in the post-feminist world have moved on to such an extent that *The Exorcist* has as much relevance as the patriarchal sitcom *Father Knows Best*. Today, young women regard the gender war as being over, with themselves as clear victors. Young women's achievements are far outstripping those of their male contemporaries, leaving 1973's serious attempt to constrain feminism looking like ancient history. No longer even offensive, it is now simply something to laugh at. The ex-BBFC director James Ferman was particularly worried about what effect *The Exorcist*'s appearance on video might have on young women, saying in *Sight and Sound* in July 1998: "We know that when *The Exorcist* came out there were a lot of traumatised teenage girls being helped out of the cinema." This is no longer true. Showing *The Exorcist* to an audience of young women today is not a terror inducing experience. The film is a museum piece, reflecting concerns and fears whose time has gone.

CHANGING GENRE DEFINITIONS

Film genre functions as a short-hand to let viewers know what a film will be like. Each genre carries with it certain audience expectations: a Western will have cowboys, a porn film will have sex, a musical must contain song-and-dance numbers. A film that seems to be of a particular genre, but fails to fulfil the audience's genre expectations, will probably be disliked. But of course, how a genre is defined may change over time, leaving yesterday's classics looking 'wrong' when judged by the new criteria.

Additionally, in Britain, *The Exorcist* has long been spoken of not just as a horror film, but as the most frightening of all horror films. It was banned on video for years, the implication being that it was simply *too scary*. The unavailability of the film added to its stature, and it became almost a genre in itself, something beyond even the limits of the horror genre. This created a keen anticipation amongst those who had not seen the film, and an unrealistic expectation of what it would be like.

The Exorcist has a long build up before anything supernatural occurs. This slow start used to be a staple of the horror genre. However, in the post-MTV world, horror films start quickly — with action, with a scare, with a knowing nod to the audience. *The Exorcist* does none of this.

Modern horror films also mostly feature protagonists who are teenagers. The core film-going audience is young, and they want to see characters of their own age facing problems, fears and concerns that they can relate to. They don't want to see their parents' problems played out on the big screen, and they definitely don't want to see youth portrayed as the problem, the monster, the horrible 'other' that must be stopped. More than most, *The Exorcist* was a horror film targeted at adults. It aligned itself with the parents, the Church, the supporters of Nixon and 'Nam.

Comparison with Wes Craven's recent horror hit *Scream* (1997) reveals other reasons why *The Exorcist* might seem somewhat quaint and old-fashioned to modern eyes. *Scream* hits home immediately with a ferociously strong set-piece in which a teenage girl is menaced at home, and her boyfriend graphically gutted before her eyes. Before the first reel has finished, she's dead too, stabbed and hung from a tree. Only then is the real (female) protagonist introduced. Throughout, the dialogue is sharp and sarcastic, constantly taunting the audience. By contrast, the same amount of time lapse in *The Exorcist* has featured an old man wandering around in the desert. There is virtually no dialogue, and no laughs, scares or jolts. It may be that *The Exorcist*'s quiet, understated filmmaking is better than Craven's full

volume yell. It just doesn't fit in with current genre rules.

SPECIAL EFFECTS

Special effects that initially look stunning, and unbelievably real, can date horribly. The morphing computer effects in *Terminator 2* have been cheapened through their use in other films, and in adverts. The effects in *The Exorcist* were used in an effective, low key manner. Nevertheless, a frequent criticism amongst the students was the shaking bed, which was seen as being some kind of theme-park gimmick, rather than something real. At the time of the film's release, the spinning head effect was seen as being horribly real, unbelievably so. Now this looks quite obviously like the dummy it is. Viewer sophistication increases as special effects become more advanced, with the unfortunate result that previously ground-breaking effects work looks old fashioned.

IMPROVEMENTS

There have been many direct *Exorcist* rip-offs, most notably the progressively more tedious *Omen* cycle. But *The Evil Dead* improved on it, taking the scariest element — the possessed Regan look — pumping up the pace, and replacing the religious atmosphere with some keg-party humour. With *The Evil Dead*, director Sam Raimi essentially made *The Exorcist* redundant, as the same scares were now available in a swifter-paced package, without the need to sit through the more portentous movie. It's also noticeable that *The Evil Dead* is still heavily cut on video, perhaps proof that the film still possesses power that *The Exorcist* itself now lacks.

The BBFC's long refusal to grant *The Exorcist* a certificate for video was cruel to the film. Existing solely as a semi-legendary memory, it was denied its proper place and context in film history. Seen today, it is perhaps not surprising that *The Exorcist*'s devout tone sits ill with new viewers. Now the ban is over, *The Exorcist* should be seen not as the scariest film ever made, but as a skilful piece of work that spoke to the concerns of its time with a power born of excellent direction, acting and effects.

I SAW HUGE SPIDERS

Meddlesome Christians flush your stash down the toilet

Martin Jones

The Sabbath quiet was suddenly shattered by Pete as he struggled down the stairs and called out, 'Dan, I'm having the horrors, you've got to help me.' I sat him down in the lounge and tried to calm him down. 'My hands are growing longer, look,' he said, holding out his hands.

Good Samaritans. Helpful Christians. Sometimes, benevolence doesn't come cheap. And if the hand of friendship extended to you happens to be attached to a Christian, especially a born-again one, then there's a fair chance you'll be led along to the nearest church to proclaim how it wasn't just human assistance, but the love of God, that dragged you out of your own personal hole…

Meet Dan Wooding: journalist, family man, and Christian. With his Birmingham-based group of young Christians ('The Messengers'), Dan is very willing to offer help to those who society has passed by, especially those caught in the Hell Of Drugs. Unfortunately, Dan is operating in the class-A, amphetamine-soaked inferno of the mid 1960s, so a hard task is ahead. Luckily, his fellow pew-lickers could read about the struggle with easily-led Beatnik types in his book, *Junkies Are People Too*, published in 1969 by the Scripture Union. Daddio.

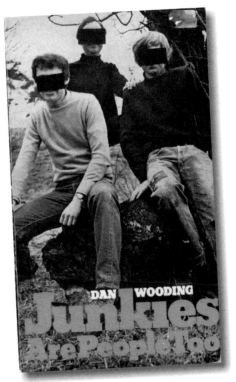

strosities in awful detail. Only those who have known the full horror of it can realise what I went through.'

It's as if the addict were talking through Dan, directly to the reader. Clever, that. In fact, some of the stories are a little *too* fact-filled, occasionally bordering on self-analysis, as is the case with Joe:

'I have an insatiable urge for knowledge concerning death. One of the most interesting forms of death, to my mind, is suicide. I've tried it five times now. Gassing, then hanging. That didn't work either. Then slashing my wrists and a couple of overdoses. I guess all drug-addicts have an urge to destroy themselves which is stronger than the average person.'

Here's Charles, star of chapter four:

His story is going to shock you. I hope it does. His story is going to take you into hell itself. Turn to the next chapter if you are prone to nightmares...

Charles is just one of the sorry individuals in *Junkies* to tell his misfortune verbatim to Dan. Curiously, every time the author hears a bit of background information, it seems to be set down on the paper in exactly the sort of way *he'd* like the horrible message to come across:

'I remember being in an ambulance and being taken to All Saints Hospital in Birmingham — to the Drug Addiction and Alcoholics Unit. I remember crying out for a drink...then my first bouts of delirium tremens. I saw huge spiders...insects blown up to fantastic sizes...crawling everywhere. Mon-

On their own, these tales might just sound depressingly familiar; but filtered through the stained glass of a young Christian viewpoint, you don't know who, or what to believe. Equipped with a slightly judgmental tone and enthusiastic! Exclamation! Marks! Dan Wooding has reported from the fringes of a culture he is at least ten years behind, a coffee-bar and Olympia paperback lifestyle where someone is always introducing someone else to drugs...

'I had a drag, and that's how it all began...'

Dan drifts through this world like a glowing deity; patient, knowledgeable...

'You'll have to do a cold turkey. It's the only way.' After all, I knew; I had read all of the books written by the Rev. David Wilkerson of *Teen Challenge*, New York (an organisation for helping American addicts).

but not afraid to hit home with the sordid truth. Chapter 5 is entitled 'David is dead now':

> Joe said, 'Dave was a lovable, friendly and wonderful guy, and if anyone deserved not to die, it was him.' But with drugs there is no discrimination.

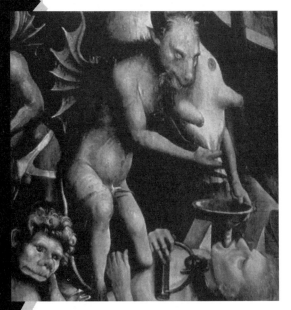

Dan obviously wanted *Junkies* to be read with the same serious concern he gave the Reverend Wilkerson's books, but he got off to a bad start with the front cover photo: three casually-dressed men, their features hidden by those Pools-winners blanks of old, pose around a rock. Judging by this, the book could just have easily been called *Homosexuals Are People Too* (I swear the polo-necked bloke in the background, with his Ian Hislop chin, is Dan Wooding). Unable to understand that society requests nothing more of Christians than to hold the odd bring-and-buy sale, his book is more a cautionary tale to fellow parishioners than a plea for compassion; a chance to show that God is sometimes waiting at the end of 'a cold turkey'. Because we all know how resistant to religion ex-drug addicts are, don't we?

In the beginning, there was a farm. A derelict farm in Worchestershire that Wooding and his wife want to turn into a rehabilitation centre for addicts. This sort of thing takes money, so he enlists the help of a local Christian businessman

> ...who, I had heard, owned a Silver Cloud Rolls Royce. 'He must have a few bob in the bank if he has a Rolls Royce,' I thought.

With this peculiar strain of naïve optimism (who was he a journalist for, *The Beano*?), and never questioning the 'various ways' the funds were mysteriously raised, Dan soon oversees the reconstruction of Hill Farm. Although dubious businessmen were not the only persons he consulted along the way:

> Sunday morning came and it was time for me to give out the church notices. 'If the Lord wants us to have Hill Farm we will have the deposit within seven days.' I don't know why I said it. It just came out. I thought of what I had just said. '£900 within seven days...' I swallowed hard and thought.
> Monday morning came and I dashed to the front door. Letter after letter I ripped open looking for a £900 cheque. Alas, all that came was a £1 note from my Aunt Ethel in Liverpool. 'Thank you, Lord,' I said. Only £899 to go.

Soon enough the place is full of godless beatniks. Leave your bongos at the door, please, and bring forth tales of your own downfall:

> 'We had a good scene going. Most of the time we used to listen to jazz, folk, rhythm and blues records; read books by Camus and Sartre and also have poetry reading. A lot of the time was spent hanging around the town

conning people for money — most people are a very easy con — at night we used to smoke charge.'

Wooding and his wife, Norma, are quickly confronted with horrible reality and all its little tricks:

Joe had a lighter. 'He is sure to try to smuggle drugs in there...' I said to Norma as we looked at it. He had just finished his bath and was now in his bedroom, so I slipped his 'drug-smuggling tool' into my pocket and then locked myself in the steamy bathroom. My fingers shook as I undid the midget screws that held the lighter together.

Some residents, though, are very willing to please:

'You are quite good,' said Bill as I nervously checked him for drugs. 'But you haven't checked my mouth.' 'Your mouth?' I queried. 'Yes, man. It would be easy for me to slip in a contraceptive loaded with my works and drugs, put some string around it and attach it to one of my teeth.'

So said the addict with the widest throat in the Midlands...

And with each chapter, Wooding gets to know his charges and tell their sordid stories to the reader. Not all are beatniks, although they might just as well be in the eyes of the author. There's George, who starts each sentence with "man", is 'a driller' by trade, and is described by Wooding on the first page as 'drilling heroin into his arm'; Pete, who calls psychiatrists 'trick cyclists', and constantly breaks the rules by having a crafty 'smoke'; and not forgetting Joe, a walking mass of autobiography, the living embodiment of beat-

nik on Hill Farm. He's also Example A: Drug Addict, for Dan's readers, just in case they spot one:

I don't know what junkies are supposed to look like, but Joe was all that I had expected. He had long hair, very dark and long sideboards, a mandarin moustache and sallow skin.

All the lads muck in with the farm work, bible studies and occasional sing-songs, each abstaining to various degrees, some occasionally seeing the light, although towards the end of the book you sense that Dan wished he'd stuck to discussing the Bible with his friends over tea and biscuits:

Cars always slowed down when they saw the Hill Farm sign...'Look, there's that drug-addict farm,' you could hear them say.

Sounds like Dan's getting a touch of the horrors himself. He shows great perseverance towards a group of men you wouldn't piss on if they were on fire, but the rewards for the kind of test that The Lord has set him are of a decidedly spiritual nature; a quick visit to the metaphor clinic finds that faith is a big anchor for these drop-outs to cling on to

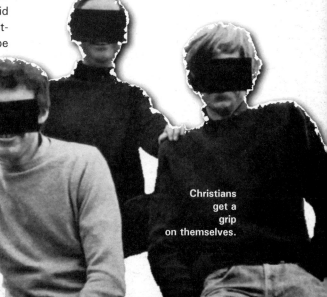

Christians get a grip on themselves.

as they flow past:

'I knew it was God speaking to me. I knew that the only answer was full and absolute surrender, to throw myself on His mercy.'

Thank you, Charles. Even better is Bill, a prototype Iggy Pop (although that's something Dan wouldn't be aware of):

As he climbed into the bath I felt sick as I saw on his body many scars, slash marks, track-marks and scabs. It was awful!

When Bill goes through a particularly bad cold turkey, Wooding calls for Mr. Mantle, the Christian businessman behind Hill Farm, and something of a Brummie Bill Graham:

'Okay, Bill. Uncross your legs and sit up.' He laid his hands on Bill's head and prayed, 'Oh, God, please help Bill at this time.'
Within minutes Bill was walking about. Gone was the pain, gone were the pleas to be taken to All Saints. His physical withdrawal had ended as quickly as it had begun.

But the best is kept for the penultimate chapter, where Dan — through the words of another — finally gets his message across. Acting as best man to Vic, who is marrying fellow Christian Eva, it's moments such as these which prove that the lies, the vomit, the cold turkeys, the strange dialogue have all been worth it...
It had been a long journey for Vic, who has been through the sort of Drugs Hell ('All around me were hallucinatory rats') that Dan Wooding now knows and understands. As the man himself states, Vic can tell you how this miracle took place in his life:

'Just as I was coming round from my

withdrawal, a group of Christians called *The Messengers* came round the ward and started to talk to us about Jesus Christ. I tell you, I thought they were barmy, and should have been in the ward here with me, Saturday night at that! They kept giving me Bibles and tracts and I kept slinging them into my locker...To tell you the truth, I had my eye on one of the Christian girls, and one day I said to her, being a decent sort of chap, "Look here, dear. It's no good you giving me all these Bibles and tracts, I just don't want to read them for various reasons." And she said, "Well, Vic, will you read a book? It's not too religious and it's about some boys in America who have your problem, and how Christ helped them."'

The book, *Twelve Angels from Hell*, sounds like the best Mick Norman novel that New English Library never released; but, unfortunately, it ain't:

'I read that book and for the first time in my life I realized what was wrong with me. Christ was missing.'

Success at last for Dan Wooding! Who no doubt not only had his fingers crossed for Vic, but also the hope that others would read *Junkies Are People Too* and see the light. By the end, Wooding and his family have left Hill Farm, passing it on to other Samaritans, ready to capture more souls in the net, but he has learnt 'that for better or for worse, junkies are people, too.'
So spare a thought for our forefathers, those beatniks, hippies, bikers and rockers who sometimes only had a choice between the tablets and The Tablets; and, when temptation glances over your copy of *Howl* in some coffee-shop or other, always remember the wise words of saintly Peter Cook: 'just say: "mmmm, maybe."'

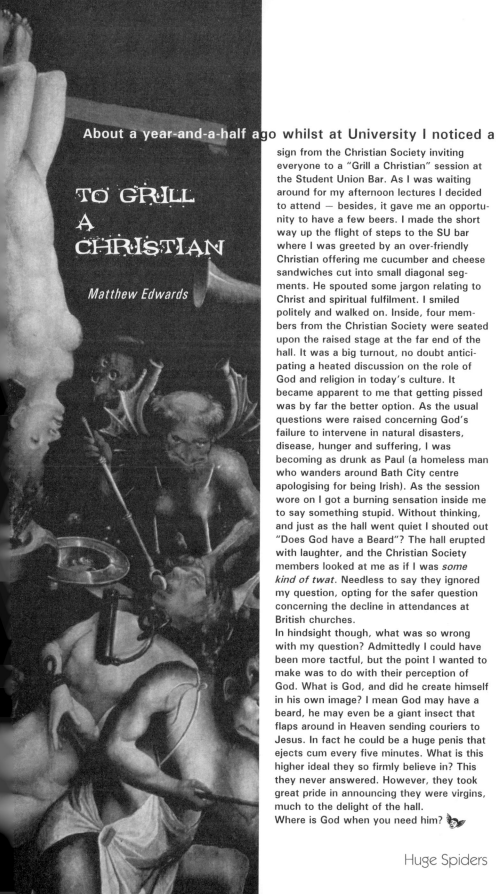

TO GRILL A CHRISTIAN

Matthew Edwards

About a year-and-a-half ago whilst at University I noticed a sign from the Christian Society inviting everyone to a "Grill a Christian" session at the Student Union Bar. As I was waiting around for my afternoon lectures I decided to attend — besides, it gave me an opportunity to have a few beers. I made the short way up the flight of steps to the SU bar where I was greeted by an over-friendly Christian offering me cucumber and cheese sandwiches cut into small diagonal segments. He spouted some jargon relating to Christ and spiritual fulfilment. I smiled politely and walked on. Inside, four members from the Christian Society were seated upon the raised stage at the far end of the hall. It was a big turnout, no doubt anticipating a heated discussion on the role of God and religion in today's culture. It became apparent to me that getting pissed was by far the better option. As the usual questions were raised concerning God's failure to intervene in natural disasters, disease, hunger and suffering, I was becoming as drunk as Paul (a homeless man who wanders around Bath City centre apologising for being Irish). As the session wore on I got a burning sensation inside me to say something stupid. Without thinking, and just as the hall went quiet I shouted out "Does God have a Beard"? The hall erupted with laughter, and the Christian Society members looked at me as if I was *some kind of twat*. Needless to say they ignored my question, opting for the safer question concerning the decline in attendances at British churches.

In hindsight though, what was so wrong with my question? Admittedly I could have been more tactful, but the point I wanted to make was to do with their perception of God. What is God, and did he create himself in his own image? I mean God may have a beard, he may even be a giant insect that flaps around in Heaven sending couriers to Jesus. In fact he could be a huge penis that ejects cum every five minutes. What is this higher ideal they so firmly believe in? This they never answered. However, they took great pride in announcing they were virgins, much to the delight of the hall.

Where is God when you need him?

Meeting
Jan Švankmajer *pt 2*

Darkness Light

Will Youds

Welcome readers*! In the last edition of* HEADPRESS *I told you all of my enthralling encounter with Mr Švankmajer. Well, good news — you can now enjoy this candid and eye-opening interview I have conducted. So, put the kettle on and make a nice cup of tea as my words shape perfect imagery in your mind...*

To fully appreciate the work of Jan Švankmajer, one has to know a little about this illustrious and yet mysterious man. Born in Prague, Czech Republic in 1934, Švankmajer has led a varied and intelligent career as an artist. He began work life as a puppeteer before concentrating more on free form creative work, devoting most of his time to the art of collage, drawing and sculpture. Staring from this precipice he made his first celluloid leap with the debut film *The Last Trick of Mr Schwarzewalde and Mr Edgar.* The Czech Republic was going through major changes that had severe effects on Švankmajer's career too. The country had gone from Nazi occupation to Communism. There was even a period between 1973 and 1980 when the then Communist State banned him from making any films whatsoever. One can sometimes experience this anxiety in the work he produced (in secret) around this period with films adapted from the works of Poe such as *The Castle of Otranto* and *The Fall of The House of Usher.* Since then he has produced a breathtaking portfolio of something around 28 films to date.

Švankmajer is now working on his new film and even has a few scripts on the go.

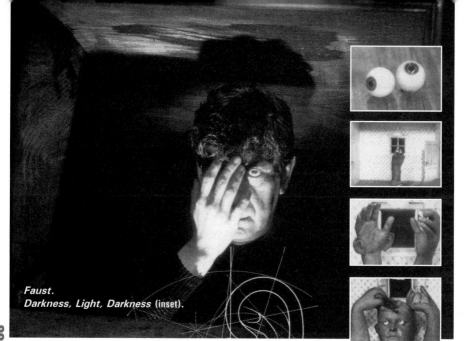

Faust.
Darkness, Light, Darkness (inset).

Last time we spoke you told me you were writing a script for a new film, could you tell me about that?

To be honest I'm not quite sure which of my scripts I was talking about. It was either OTESANEK or SILENI ('Going Mad') — which I have been working on for a few years but haven't had enough time to finish. OTESANEK is currently being filmed and is half-completed. The story of OTESANEK is based on an old Czech fairytale about a couple whom cannot have children. The man goes to the wood, digs out a tree stump and carves a baby boy. The carving turns into a real boy and eats everybody up. My version is set in the present, in reality. It's a black grotesque comedy. I leave it up to the viewers to find out what the character of Otesanek might denote. There is really a lot of possible meanings.

The script SILENI is inspired by two novels by Edgar Allen Poe. It's a psychological horror, in which the line between common sense and madness becomes vague.

You are a member of a surrealist group of artists who live all over the Czech Republic and Slovakia. Is working in a group important for you?

I have been a member of a surrealist group for about 30 years. In the Seventies and Eighties all activities of this group had to be carried out se-

cretly. Working in this group helped me and all the other members to survive the blunting era of 'normalisation'. Thankfully, the change in the political system did not affect our artistic orientation. Surrealists have always disapproved of 'crap' civilisation. In my opinion, Communism (Stalinism) and Capitalism are just different sides of the same coin, robbing people of their freedom.

Our group publishes a magazine called ANALOGON and puts on various thematic exhibitions. An exhibition called 'Svatokradez' ('Sacrilege') is on in Prague at the moment and Surrealists from many other countries, including Great Britain, are displaying their work. The exhibition will be moving to Pilsen this autumn. It is really important for me to be a member of this group

You have adapted many pieces of literature for film, from Poe to Lewis Carroll, are they great influences?

We all have our own teachers. We all have met people who have 'showed us the way'. For me it was my wife Eva and a Czech poet called Vratislav Effenberger. Also some artists who passed away a long time ago and with whom we communicate by means of their works: Edgar Allan Poe and Lewis Carroll and other 'masters' such as Arcimboldo, Bosch, Max Ernst, as well as English authors of black novels and German romantics.

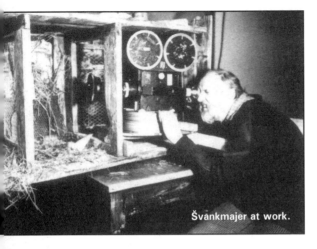

Švankmajer at work.

Do you like to work with a strong narrative?

[No reply.]

OK... What are the advantages and disadvantages of making a feature-length film compared to a short film?

I don't see any big differences. It obviously takes longer to shoot a feature-length film. It requires more persistence and stamina, as well as financial support. I use the same money resources for short and long films, that's why making long films takes me much longer than other directors.

Why did you choose to make ALICE? What did you think you could bring to the story no one else had?

Lewis Carroll and his tale about Alice in Wonderland have always been part of my 'mental morphology'. My first attempt to work with this story is a film called JABBERWOCKY and also — in a way — the film DO SKLEPA ('Into the Cellar'). ALICE is not transferring Carroll's book into a film version; it's a dialogue with him, subject to interpretation. It's an interpretation as a process, not an adaptation. I use this same technique in other films.

You have lived and worked in Prague all your life seeing many changes such as the Nazi occupation and Communism. Your work has been subjected to censorship. How has this affected you?

I was a child when the Nazis came to occupy my country. I was deeply influenced by my mother's feeling of despair which she suffered from. Later, in the Stalinism era, a huge amount of information was hidden from the public and we had to search — illegally — for the truth. I think my generation has much stronger and deeper desire for 'knowing the truth' than most people of the same age in western countries. The Sixties, when Stalinism started losing its power, brought a massive liberating period of creativity, which lasted until the Russian occupation in '68. Between the years 1973 and 1980 my life and my work were strongly affected. I was not allowed to make any films and had to work as an occasional graphic artist in Barrandov televi-

FILMOGRAPHY

The Last Trick of Mr Schwarzewalde and Mr Edgar (1964)
JS Bach: Fantasy in G minor (1965)
Play with Stones (1965)
The Coffin House (1966)
Et Cetera (1966)
Historia Naturae (suite) (1967)
The Garden (1968)
The Flat (1968)
A Picnic with Weissmann (1968)
A Quiet Week in A House (1969)
The Ossuary (1970)
Don Juan (1970)
Jabberwocky (1971)
Leonardo's Diary (1972)
The Castle of Otranto (1973–1979)
The Fall of the House of Usher (1980)
Dimensions of Dialogue (1982)
Down to the Cellar (1982)
The Pendulum, the Pit and Hope (1983)
Alice (Something from Alice) (1987)
Virile Games (1988)
Another Kind of Love (1988)
Meat in Love (1989)
Darkness, Light, Darkness (1989)
Flora (1989)
The Death of Stalinism in Bohemia (1990)
Food (1992)
Faust (The Faust Lesson) (1994)

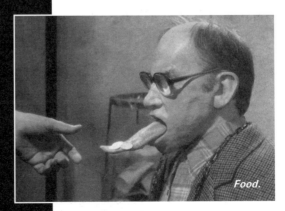

Food.

sion studios. At that time I was involved in all activities in the surrealist group. Thanks to surrealism I learned that there is only one poetry, no matter how we look at it. That's why I didn't feel hurt when I had to stop shooting films. Instead I did graphic designs, made collages and other things, all of which are rather different from audio-visual films. I do not think those seven years were wasted years.

What are your own views on censorship? Does Art have boundaries that should not be crossed?
Censorship is rubbish and the outcome of it usually turns out completely wrong. There shouldn't be such things as taboos in authentic art production.

Your films and art sometimes can come across as dark and grotesque with many elements of horror. Would you say it is an intentional act to bring fear to your audience?
I do not make films with 'intentions', as intentions only show the outer side of author's work. Authentic production — unintentionally — always indicates the inner sides of author's work and their lives. It's the viewer's interpretation that matters, whether they find signs of horror films or absurdity in my own work.

Do you prefer to use puppets or actors?
I always use just the kind of material that I need for expressing particular thoughts and ideas. I work with actors, puppets and other tools of the trade. 🐝

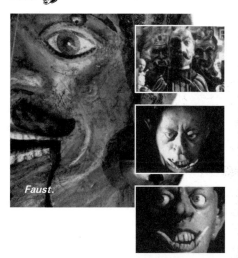

Faust.

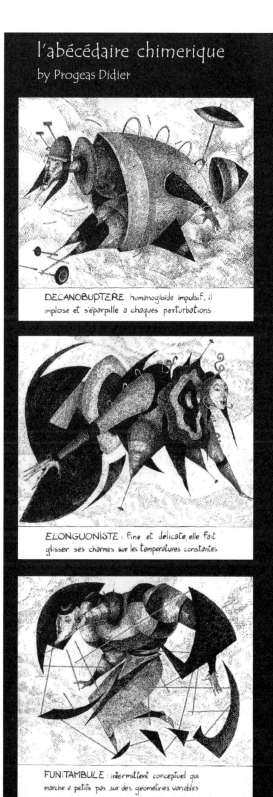

l'abécédaire chimerique
by Progeas Didier

DECANOBUPTERE : humanogloïde impulsif, il implose et s'éparpille à chaques perturbations

ELONGUONISTE : fine et délicate, elle fait glisser ses charmes sur les températures constantes

FUNITAMBULE : intermittent conceptuel qui marche à petits pas sur des géométries variables

to be continued…

oh, dr kinsey!

swinging sex and pseudo science

Mikita Brottman explores the library of the Kinsey Institute for Sex Research

magine a library completely devoted to erotica. Imagine shelf after shelf of dusty piles of porn, from Swedish sex magazines and lingerie catalogues to pulp fiction imprints with titles like HOUND HUNGER, TENDER BOTTOMS and L'AMOUR VIRGINALE. Imagine big piles of cardboard boxes spilling out loose copies of COME!, POP SHOTS and THE FLAVOR OF THE FEMALE, all waiting to be reshelved. Imagine a carton bearing the following label, scrawled in a rather shaky hand: BLACK GARTER, BLACK LACE, BLACK MAGIC, BLACK NYLONS, BLACK SATIN, BLACK SILK STOCKINGS, BLACK STOCKINGS, BLAST OFF! Yes sirs, such a library really does exist — and not just in the wet dreams of Rocco Siffredi, but in a quiet college town here in rural Indiana. This, my friends, is the library of the Kinsey Institute for Sexual Research.

Dr Alfred C Kinsey was the author of the groundbreaking 1948 study SEXUAL BEHAVIOR IN THE HUMAN MALE, better known simply as the Kinsey Report. A sex researcher based at Indiana University, Kinsey was one of the first people to insist that sexual activity should be separated from traditional moral judgements. In the first Kinsey Report, the good doctor conducted face-to-face interviews with thousands of American men who revealed habits that were both shocking and liberating at the same time. Most men admitted that they jerked off; many described having sex before and outside of marriage; lots had gay experiences, and a small number even 'fessed up to doing it with animals.

Kinsey also collected countless sexual histories, including those of pimps, paedophiles, prisoners and prostitutes. The second Kinsey Report (SEXUAL BEHAVIOR IN THE HUMAN FEMALE), published in 1953, kicked off the new sexual freedoms of the Sixties, and helped lead to the emergence of sex education in school, gay rights, sex therapy and no-fault divorce. Kinsey was a *bona fide* hero of the sexual revolution. In fact, no less a man than playboy impresario Hugh Hefner credits Kinsey with opening his eyes to the joys of guilt-free sex. During Kinsey's lifetime, the Institute was seen as a groundbreaking facility at the forefront of sexual research.

After Kinsey's death, the morally conservative climate of the Eighties led the Institute to begin to play down its public profile somewhat. And then, in the Nineties, the shit really hit the fan. Two recent biographies of Kinsey — one by James H. Jones in 1997 and the second by Judith Reisman in 1998 — have painted a picture of the good doctor as being less of a scientific marvel than a lecherous old quack. According to these two biographies, Kinsey was a pervert and a charlatan who made everybody who worked for him — even the janitors — submit to revealing questionnaires about their sex lives. In his research, apparently, he used child molesters, rapists, hookers, sadists and masochists to represent the "average American", and re-classified prostitutes as "married women" when he couldn't find enough married women to fill out his questionnaires. A notorious child-hater, he used paedophiles to document "orgasms" in hundreds of boys and girls as young as five-months, and once even apparently hid the identity of a child-murderer from a police investigation. Nor was the good doctor a model of domestic decorum in his married life. He often dabbled in homosexual one-night stands and practised some increasingly painful sado-masochistic and voyeuristic techniques. Scandalously, both biographers describe regular husband-and-wife swapping antics amongst the staff of the Kinsey Institute, whose recurrent orgies took place in the attic of Kinsey's home in suburban Bloomington, where they were apparently captured on film for posterity.

Whatever his feelings as a scientific researcher, Kinsey certainly knew his BLACK NYLONS from his TENDER BOTTOMS. The Kinsey collection is one of the world's most fascinating and specialised

	per cent
Masturbation	60.2
Intercourse	26.2
Homosexual contacts	7.0
Nocturnal emissions	4.6
Petting	1.3
Animal contacts	.7

depositories of kinky erotica. Unfortunately — though perhaps understandably, given the circumstances — the Kinsey library is a private collection, not open to the public, and a polite but sharp-eyed assistant was assigned to "supervise" me as I worked my way through about twenty rows of dark, disorganised stacks.

The first sets of shelves contain all the "legitimate" medical journals — back-issues of PSYCHIATRIC QUARTERLY, Kinsey's collected papers and correspondence with Kenneth Anger and Gershon Legman, books on infidelity, menstruation, menopause and breast-feeding. Here, amongst the urology manuals and handbooks on VAGINAL INFECTIONS, INFESTATIONS AND DISCHARGE, I came across a slim volume entitled FARTS AND FARTING, which, had

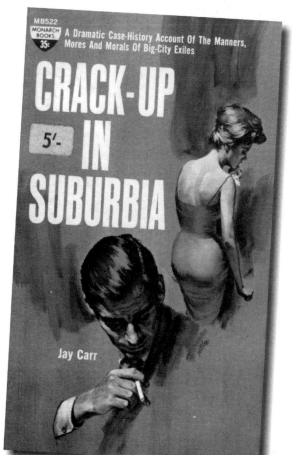

MB522
MONARCH BOOKS
35¢

A Dramatic Case-History Account Of The Manners, Mores And Morals Of Big-City Exiles

CRACK-UP IN SUBURBIA

5/-

Jay Carr

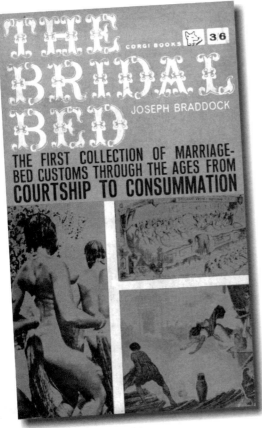

THE BRIDAL BED

CORGI BOOKS 36

JOSEPH BRADDOCK

THE FIRST COLLECTION OF MARRIAGE-BED CUSTOMS THROUGH THE AGES FROM COURTSHIP TO CONSUMMATION

material. This includes complete collections of SWING, GAY BLADE, THE SAN DIEGO GAZETTE and THE SEVERE QUEER REVIEW OF SAN FRANCISCO, as well as oddities like THE GAY COOKBOOK and EFFEMINATE ENGLAND (a tautology if ever I heard one).

And then finally, hidden away right at the back, comes the hard stuff — pulp magazines from the Sixties and Seventies with titles like ANAL SEX ACTS, PETTING GIRLS and THE NIGHT AUDREY'S VIBRATOR SPOKE. Here also were those great piles of cardboard boxes spilling out reams of spanking and bondage magazines just begging to be rooted through (interestingly, the library doesn't have a lot of straight porn — no copies of HUSTLER or PLAYBOY, for example — just stuff that's good and kinky). Then there are the cupboards full of uncatalogued materials "in need of preservation", sex-themed board games (SEXUAL DILEMMAS, RAUNCHY TRIVIA), and even a section devoted to erotica with a Kinsey theme to it (titillating pseudo-scientific pulp novels entitled THE FLIMSY REPORT and OH, DR KINSEY!).

I poked around discreetly in a pile of 16mm film reels, vainly hoping to stumble across footage of Kinsey and his staff indulging in a spot of suburban wife-swapping, but unfortunately none of the reels were labelled. In my enthusiasm, however, I accidentally knocked over a hardback copy of PIERRE AND DANIELLE, which fell on to the film cans with an embarrassingly loud clatter, earning me a stern glance from the librarian. Not wanting to outstay my welcome, I decided that my time as the guest of the good doctor was just about up, even though I'd barely touched the tip of the iceberg. But I'll certainly be back. Whether scientific genius or pornhound extraordinaire, Dr Kinsey has left us an archive of erotica so unusual and eclectic that you need a PhD just to spend an afternoon sniffing around in it.

I been in the aisle of a grocery store, would have gone straight in my basket.

Further back came the *art books*, tomes with titles like DANISH FORMS IN COLOR, YOUR PHYSIQUE, CLASSIC FEMALE LINE AND FORM and, most enticingly, TABU: CROSS-RACE LESBIAN PHOTOGRAPHS FOR THE PHOTOGRAPHIC ART COLLECTOR (and nobody else — do you hear?). This section also contains volumes of etchings and engravings, including the early works of Aubrey Beardsley, collections of photographs by Richard Kern and Robert Mapplethorpe, and comics by Robert Crumb. Close by are the European underwear catalogues like FROU-FROU and LINGERIE LIBERTINES (whose pages, I might add, felt suspiciously sticky), as well as journals full of sex ads and "personals". There's also a section on sex in the cinema (HOLLYWOOD'S SEXUAL UNDERGROUND) and a large collection of gay

Men in RUBBER SUITS

I NSPIRED BY THE SUCCESS OF THE NEW Godzilla series in the early Nineties, the Japanese production company Daiei de cided to wake up their very own giant monster from the Sixties — the atomic turtle Gamera. Yes, that's right. Almost unnoticed by the rest of the world, the Japanese are still making films where sweaty stuntmen squeeze themselves into tight rubber suits that look like monsters (more or less), and jump around on beautifully constructed toy cities. Six new Godzilla movies where made by the Toho company from 1989–95. Godzilla merchandise is constantly invading Japan. Even Roland Emmerich's American lizard-like version of the Big G couldn't harm the Japanese original, as proven by the Christmas 1999 release of *Godzilla 2000 Millennium*.

The first new film for Daiei was *Gamera: Guardian of the Universe* (1995), more or less a remake of one of the most hideous films of the first decade (*Gamera vs. Gyaos*, 1967). The Gyaos are a race of bat-like monster birds, thirsty for blood. Gamera has to fight it out with the birds in a sports arena. A cute psychic schoolgirl by the name of Asagi — who is in mental contact with the monster turtle — is introduced to the series. Monster nerds all over the world were amazed by the freshness that this fast and entertaining film brought to a tired genre. It also managed to be true to the spirit of the Japanese 'kaiju eiga' — giant monster movies.

In 1996 came the second instalment, *Gamera 2: The Advent of Legion*. A very bizarre creature (you are never quite sure which is the front or

Jörg Buttgereit (below right) talks to Japanese Monster-Film director Shusuke Kaneko

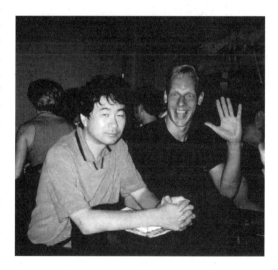

the rear) is nesting in the middle of Tokyo. As with an anthill, we see hundreds of small Legion-soldiers rampage through the city until the mother finally bashes its horns and tentacles with Gamera. It's so hilariously Japanese that your eyes start to hurt. The movie has amazing miniature explosions. Destruction is always a big part of these movies…

Gamera 3: The Revenge of Irys brought us a more serious, character-driven movie in 1999. A beautiful girl called Ayana feels nothing but hate for the giant turtle, ever since her parents and pet cat where killed during the destruction of the Gyaos fight in 1995. Her hate breeds this strange creature called Irys, named after her dead kitty. Like Asagi, Ayana is mentally connected to one of the giant creatures rampaging through the city of Kyoto.

The man behind these insane monster flicks is Shusuke Kaneko. I met up with the gentle, soft-spoken Japanese director at the Fantasia festival in Montreal, Canada in July 1999.

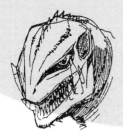

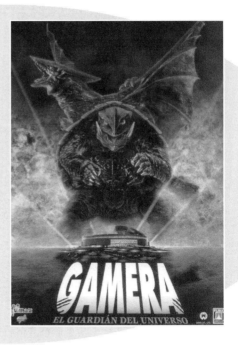

GAMERA
EL GUARDIÁN DEL UNIVERSO

Jörg **You told me yesterday that you had a background in comedies. How was it that they asked you to do a Gamera movie?**

Shusuke Actually when I was a child I used to watch many monster movies, and my interest was from my childhood, but to tell you the truth, in the beginning I didn't think I would be producing monster films because I thought that they were very 'narrow minded'. When Daiei, the company that first proposed the direction of the monster film series, came to me I thought maybe there was some kind of overture or approach I could use to develop this.

They approached you? Yes. At the time, Daiei didn't have a contract director for this kind of project — that's why. Not as a joke but just to test myself I had sent my résumé to Toho studios to propose myself as a Godzilla director. Obviously there was somebody already in charge of the project for Godzilla so I wasn't accepted, but in this small filming community people heard I was interested in making monster films. So Daiei approached me and that's

how the initial contact started. And also they proposed a competition — let's beat Godzilla with Gamera.

That was going to be my next question. Were you really given the order to top the new Godzilla movies with your first Gamera film? Because of course, Godzilla's the big guy. Yes, when I got back and told my wife I had been invited to direct a Gamera series to compete with Godzilla, she said "What? A round turtle is going to compete with Godzilla?" Actually, before I started the series, Gamera was not very well known to the general public, and I myself was not very fond of Gamera because Godzilla was a much more famous monster. But for Daiei, this was their main way to get the competition — the main effort was directed at Gamera. So at the start I intended to make a very appealing Gamera for the public that was quite different from the normal Gamera. Not good looking, but kind of very attractive in an aesthetic sense. Daiei was quite opposed to that. But then of course, the objectives of the company and the objectives of the director are completely different. The things you're aiming towards are not always corresponding.

Baby Irys.

The old Gamera films were mainly done for little children with actors of about five-years-old, but your films are done for a different audience. What kind of audience did you have in mind? I actually felt that a lot of films that were directed for a larger, more adult audience, were a lot more interesting than the films directed at children. So for the first series of Gamera I thought about High School — a teenage audience who would appreciate the film. That is probably the major change that I brought to the Gamera series. They were not only for children, but were produced in a way to appeal to a larger, broader public. I still feel like I have to broaden and amplify my target audience, in terms of age and whatever — really just searching for a larger public. The big masses.

The new Gamera movie, GAMERA 3: REVENGE OF IRYS, has a lot of strong female characters. Might this be the first Japanese monster movie for girls? I planned for it to have a larger female audience, but the opposite happened. There were more boys coming to see the movie, to see the girls! So I'm thinking that maybe I should have chosen nice looking boys in the film because they might have appealed more to a young, female audience.

The film is very character driven. There is a lot of human drama, compared with other monster movies — normally the monsters are the big stars and have most of the screen time. When you wrote the script, did the producers have any objections to the space allocated to the actors and the drama? I didn't have that kind of pressure, because the producer had agreed to have the monsters and the people in the drama. But there was a kind of battle with the producers... They were very opposed to presenting a character called Asagi . That was the main conflict during the making of the film. Because Asagi was the character that was there since the first *Gamera*, the cute girl who has a psychic connection with Gamera. The producers were insisting that if you put her in the series, the public that sees only *Gamera 3* won't understand what her role in the film is, nor Ayana, whose

hatred towards Gamera has created this new feminine monster Irys. They were kind of two sides of the same mirror. Asagi and Ayana are like positive and negative poles of the same personality, so I couldn't really get rid of one of the characters because they depend on each other. In that sense, I wanted to keep both. The producer didn't understand the reasons for the lives of those monsters. The moon and the sun, and the opposite poles that revive the monsters. The producers couldn't understand that kind of dichotomy, so that was the hardest part — to convince the producers.

Adult Irys.

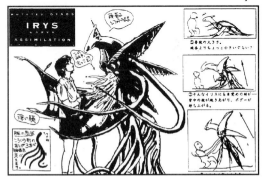

I think the way the scenes with the monsters are presented are quite different than in other monster films I've seen (which tend to focus on the human point-of-view, how they see the monsters evolving, etc). I think the one main element to differentiate things from the old monster series was that the monsters here kind of unite, and have a kind of karma and spiritual connection. In the old productions you don't sense this kind of construction, and that is what is interesting.

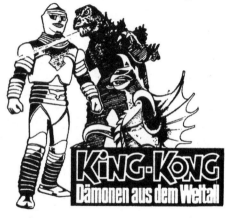

I am interested in how the monsters were shot, because I think there's a lot of difference with the camera angles. Or was this down to the special effects supervisor? I think that the main difference from a technical point of view — the camera angles, the shooting, the way I shot Gamera and so on — is that the old monster films were usually directed by people who belonged to production companies. They had to shoot what the company wanted with no individual creativity, so it was a kind of custom-made monster movie as opposed to what I do now. I'm independent and was hired to work on the Gamera series, and felt like I wanted to do these monster films, which is different from being hired for a project from within the company. You're working for the company but you're hired to do a specific project. That's the main difference for innovation, changing camera angles and so on. It's like the changes in the economic environment. Many years ago you had Akira Kurosawa who had his own budget for big films. But now things are very different. Japan was in economic crisis a few years ago, so the conditions for working are also different... Compared to those times, now you are more free to create your own works and follow your own expectations, but you have less money. That's the contradiction in the film industry.

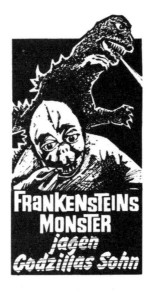

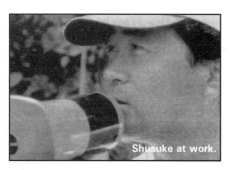

Shusuke at work.

You told me about 'suit-mation' — the guy-in-the-rubber-suit technique — and that it is mainly because of budget limitations that you're using this kind of technique. Do you think that you could do a Japanese monster movie <u>without</u> a guy in a suit? It depends, because I think that it's actually good to have the suit-mation.

Everyone would be disappointed if it looked <u>too real</u>. For me, it's part of the fun to see that this is a sweating stunt man in a rubber costume. It has more 'soul'. **In the Sixties and Seventies the Japanese monster movies were popular all around the world. They played in America and Germany. Today it is different. It seems that these films are mainly done for the Japanese audience and the rest of the world don't know what to do with them. How do you feel about that?** I think that the policy for making those Japanese films known outside Japan hasn't changed, but I do have the impression that the people who work in the international marketing departments of the Japanese companies are kind of incompetent. They don't really follow the strategies to publicise the films. There is something interesting going on in Japanese companies, particularly the international departments. Compare for instance, the car makers in Japan. They are excellent in exporting the products and selling abroad. They even manufacture abroad. Film companies, because of the conflict with television, feel threatened by television, so all they are really trying to do now is preserve the internal structure. The people who are assigned to the international departments are people who are just waiting for their retirement or they are sitting there by the window waiting for something to be done, but they are not the ones who are going to be doing it. It is very unfortunate that international departments don't have more power to publicise the films.

With German movies there are the same problems! That's it — thank you! 🦋

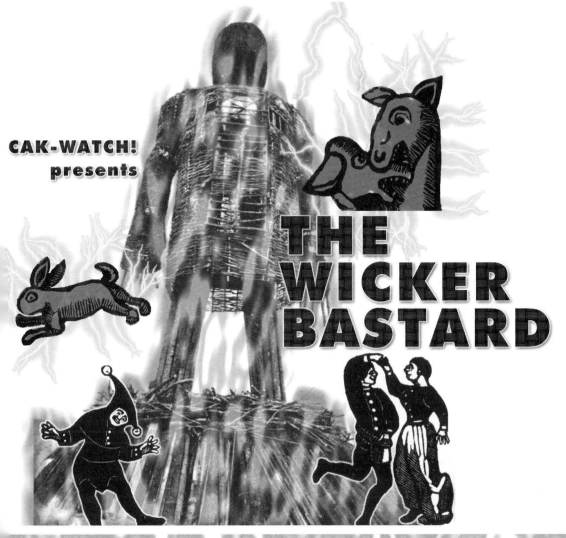

CAK-WATCH! presents

THE WICKER BASTARD

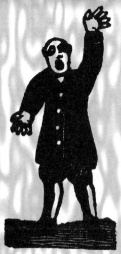

Hello again. Before we begin you can all relax. I'm not going to be slagging off that fine film *The Wicker Man*. On no. I think it's a classic of British cinema, and although it is a little over-rated it justly deserves its cult status. What this Cak-Watch is doing is using *The Wicker Man* as a case in point — the case being... *"FILMS THAT EXIST IN SEVERAL VERSIONS AND YOU GO FUCKING MAD TRYING TO SEE THE LONGEST PRINT."* I hope you're all clear about this now. If you're familiar with the film, read on, as you may find out some exciting information. If you're not, well you might just develop a nervous twitch. A quick whizz through the film...

By Phil Tonge

THE WICKER MAN starred Edward Woodward[1] as "Christian Copper" Sergeant Neil Howie of the West Highlands Constabulary; who flies out to remote Summerisle[2] to follow up a report of a missing girl by the name of Rowan Morrison. The locals deny all knowledge of the girl, even though she's in the school register and her birth is logged in the local Public Records Office.

During his stay, Howie is outraged to discover that the residents are all practising (and somewhat shag-happy) Pagans! (dramatic chord).

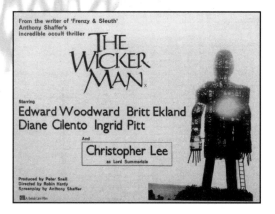

Meeting with the local aristo-parasite Lord Summerisle (Christopher Lee in a born-to-play-it, corking performance), we find that Summerisle's Grandad, a horticulturist and free-thinker had not only turned the island into a successful fruit-producer; but had also encouraged the islanders to reject Christian beliefs and replace them with the "old gods".

Howie, disgusted with all the rumpo/heathen weirdyness surrounding him, renews his search for Rowan.

He finds evidence that last year's crops failed and tomorrow being May 1st — that certain pagan practice demands a human sacrifice to appease the gods of the fields.

After a fine botty-slapping dance from Britt Ekland's Body Double, Howie disguises himself to take part in the May Day Parade, where as he rescues Rowan from what he thinks is *her* sacrifice…

Yeah. Cue big fuck-off wicker man with the bloke from *Callan* inside. Note the effective use of smoke and flame.

A fine multi-layered film, taking a pop at many subjects, blind faith, closed systems of thought and so on. A bit of a treat. So, you want to watch it? Beware!

1973. Here comes a chopper to chop off your head

British Lion (under Managing Director Peter Snell) the film company behind *The Wicker Man*, were taken over during post-production of the film by the Thorn EMI group. Thus when director Robin Hardy presented his cut footage to his new boss Michael Deeley (head of Film Operations EMI) he told Hardy to fuck off and brought in his own gang of snip-happy bastards led by Barry Spikings. During this first round of "trimming" out went most of Ingrid Pitt's performance, yards of Christopher Lee's dialogue scenes (much to Mr Lee's dismay), Sgt Howe's bike- ride and much, much more[3]. So, after this attack by the pinking-shears brigade, Hardy and screenwriter Anthony Schaffer are presented with a 102-minute print intended for a British cinema release. Unluckily for the boys, Deeley had other ideas, and during his efforts to sell the Stateside distribution rights, he approached the legendary Roger Corman and his outfit New World Pictures.

Corman, turning down the film, suggested to Deeley that if he cut 15 minutes from the 102-minute version, he'd have a sure-fire winner on his hands. So, in late '73, a 87-minute version of *The Wicker Man* crawled into British cinemas on a double bill with the second-release-run on *Don't Look Now*.

It died on it's arse.

1974. A Broad Bean in its natural state is not normally turquoise

Failure, like an old-man's wee-wee filled pants, hung heavy on *The Wicker Man* and EMI dropped it (like the wee-smelling pants) on to a firm called Beechwood Properties (a US based tax shelter group). Beechwood bought the film as a tax loss (not giving a Crispy-Woodward whether the damn thing made money or not) and acquired the services of a Luigi Vercotti style mob called National General Pictures to get the thing into a cinema and lose money. However, the curse of

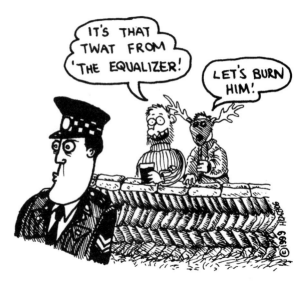

The Wicker Man was in full effect and NGP went tits-up before they could even approach a cinema chain. Into all this mayhem stepped the film distribution arm of Warner Brothers who agreed to "handle" the film.

Evil corporate panty-waists WB, time-serving sods that they were, merely shoved the film on in Atlanta and San Diego, promoting the film as an Amicus/Hammer style horror flick (which it plainly wasn't). Even after *Variety* had given the film a rave review[4], Warners simply shelved it.

After all, Warners were doing a paid bump-job for a tax-shelter company and everyone who mattered was happy, so who gave a shit about some bizarre limey film with lots of folk songs?

1976. Lovely March Hares not silly old Rabbits

By fair means the distribution rights were purchased by Abraxas Film Corporation, a tiny firm operating out of New Orleans. AFC was run by John Alan Simon and the host of a local film-based TV chat-show, Stirling Smith.

Smith had come into contact with Robin Hardy, who was out in the states trying to kick-start his directing career. After a few meetings Hardy informed the boys from Abraxas that a 102-minute print might be up for grabs at EMI.

EMI, in the guise of Mike Deeley began to receive phone calls from the men at AFC, Mr Hardy, Mr Schaffer, Mr Snell (remember him?) even that nice Mr Lee. At first Deeley was evasive, then dismissive and finally silent as he'd stopped answering the calls at all. Nice.

So the "Lads" went looking for the Butcher of Borehamwood, Supervising Editor Barry "Who?-Me?" Spikings. Poor old Barry did not have the front to just blank their calls so he gave it the old moody. First he said that all 360 cans of negative had been "accidentally" burned. When the Wicker Mob checked their sources, and told Barry that the burning story was "Total Bollocks", the little fellow changed his story and now said that the cans had been used as "Motorway Filler". Yeah, right.[5]

The trail had gone cold.

Or so we all thought. Just when you needed them up popped New World Pictures. Turns out before returning the 102-minute print to EMI, the crafty sods had struck off a copy. So, three years after the fact, AFC made a dupe negative from the Corman print and the 102-minute version was back in circulation.

Ah, not quite. The version that AFC released in October 1977 was a 95-minute version they'd knocked together with the help of Robin Hardy's bag of bits. The yanks would have to wait a couple more years before the 102-minute version

THE WICKER MAN
A British Lion release, 1973
director: ROBIN HARDY
producer: PETER SNELL
screenplay: ANTHONY SHAFFER
cinematography: BARRY WAXMAN
music: PAUL GIOVANNI
original editor: ERIC BOYD-PERKINS

N.B. *All timings in this article, unless otherwise stated are at film speed of 24fps.*

turned up in US art cinemas, and then on video in 1991[6]. But as for us Brits, if we wanted to see the 102-minute print, we could go jump bollock nekkid over a fire.

To recap, there are three main versions of *The Wicker Man*:

(A) THE 102 MINUTE VERSION
The story of which you have just read.

(B) THE 95 MINUTE VERSION
The AFC/Hardy print for US cinemas in October 1977.

(C) THE 87 MINUTE VERSION
Also known as the "one-night version". This is the only version available on home video in the UK and was the version shown in its most recent transmission on Channel 4 (1996).

And that's it, is it?

No. This is where the Cak! creeps in.

(D) THE 85 MINUTE & LESS VERSIONS
These are the versions that turn up on American television, and as you'd expect certain midwest types don't dig that sexy, pagan groove thang. I have heard reports that there was a version cut to 72-minutes but that's too horrible to contemplate.

(E) THE 1988 MOVIEDROME VERSION
Now we're fucked. In 1988 the BBC2 cult film slot Moviedrome[7] wanted to show the A version for the first time ever to a British television audience. So the requisite forms were filled in, acquisition departments alerted, budgets were allocated and very shortly everything went pear-shaped. Firstly, no-one had access to, or knew who had access to an A print (the contact at the British Film Institute allegedly said "There is?" when told of it's existence). Secondly, the American contacts, the people who now held the US rights, started leaving everything too close to the deadline for comfort. Eventually with about a week to spare, a spool of NTSC[8] format videotape arrived at the BBC.

On it, the now totally panicked Moviedrome team were presented with a very murky, fuzzy, scratched, damaged, spliced and filthy print of the (B) version which had been dubbed onto NTSC-VT for TX. Realising the dilemma of "How the fuck do we get anything remotely transmittable from this?" the BBC crew leapt for the editing booth and the whiskey.

In the end, the Moviedrome team took the B print and compared it to the (C) print, banging the two together to make the longest possible version fit for transmission. So, where the film was identical the cleaner (C) footage could be dropped in to replace the crappy (B) footage. Alas life with *The Wicker Man* is never easy. In the hurry to get the damn thing ready, certain corners were cut…

So, when Alex Cox introduced he admitted it was not the longest version existent of *The Wicker Man*, but the longest ever seen on British TV, he was quite correct. However, somewhere in the dubbing and re-dubbing the (B) 95-minute version had shrunk to a puzzling 92-minutes. Whoops.

The Moviedrome (E) version was last seen on BBC1 in 1992. The terrestrial UK rights have now gone to Channel Four, who only use the shorter (C) version. Twats.

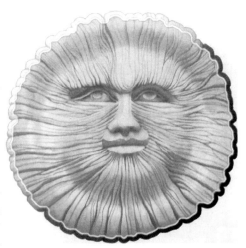

So, what's in the (A) version?
Well, the extra bits come mainly at the beginning…

The film start with Sgt Howie coming up come harbour steps from his nifty seaplane. He engages in "banter" with PC McTaggart (John Hallam who is only in [A] but appears on the closing credits of all prints!). We see more banter by some "Jesus Saves" graffiti. The opening credits have been running through this scene, and as the two coppers walk to their police Mini Cooper (!), Chris

Lee's credit appears. We then have a very *Z-Cars* scene in the Mini and cut straight into the "Lay Preaching" scene in the church. This appears pretty much intact in (B) and (E), and as a flashback in (C).

🕮 We have a shot of a cheeky postman on a bicycle carrying mail to the cop-shop. We see a letter addressed to Sgt Howie that is clearly postmarked "Summerisle Apples". We get a banter scene between the postie and PC McTaggart that fingers Howie as a dull, sexless religious maniac who still hasn't as much as touched his fiancée, Mary Bannock (played by Alison Hughes — you can see her next to Woodward in church). We also see Howie read the letter and look at the photograph of Rowan.

🕮 We have the plane take off as on all other versions but we have differing aerial shots and opening credits. John Hallam's name only appears in these opening credits and the band are credited as Lodestone as opposed to Magnet (B, C & E). [9]

🕮 The ribald Landlord's Daughter song has an extra verse which features the landlord, Alder MacGregor (played by Derek Jarman's mate, the mime Lyndsay Kemp) playing the optics with spoons. There's also a later shot of Kemp leaning by the missing Harvest Festival photo and blowing Fag smoke at the empty space.

🕮 In the graveyard there's a unique shot of Howie next to Rowan's grave.

🕮 Howie bumps into the island's doctor (John Sharp) who tells him that Rowan was burnt to death.

🕮 Before Howie comes in with the dead hare, Lord Summerisle and Miss Rose have an extra verse of their naughty song.

🕮 There is an extra verse to Willow's tasteful and really very moving tits-out-arse-slapping song.

🕮 When Howie is looking at photos in the chemists, there's an extra "thinks" voice over and two flashbacks to his first meeting with Lord Summerisle.

🕮 There's a longer version of Howie researching Paganism in the library — which includes explicit references to the wicker man.

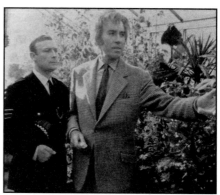

Lord Summerisle discusses his apples with Sgt Howie. A lost scene.
(Inside The Wicker Man)

🕮 Howie's final search of the village is longer and incorporates a bizarre visit to the hairdressers and a fall down a flight of circular stone steps into a room full of scantily clad ladies in the Benny Hill style.

🕮 There's a different shot of Lyndsay Kemp tied up in the bedroom.

🕮 Mr Woodward has more dialogue preaching to the islanders from the confines of the wicker man, to the effect that God is going to do 'em.

So, if I have the (A) version, I've got everything, and need not want for anything more, yeah?

No, not by a long chalk.

This is where you bang your head against a wall and try to pull out your teeth with pliers. Let me explain…

1. *The caption "Sunday 29th April 1973.* This only appears in the (B) and (E) versions.

2. *The picture of the Sun God.* Yeah, after the end credits, there's the Sun God zooming away from the camera into the distance against a black background. It's evocative, it's spooky and it's only on the (B) and (E) versions.

3. *The three villagers watering the graves.* You know, when Sgt Kindling looks over the wall, well that's only in the (B) and (D) versions.

4. *The long-shot of the harbour.* When Howie tries to get back to the mainland there's an establishing shot of the harbour. (B, C & E, but not A.)

5. *Willow brings Howie his cup of tea in the morn-*

ing. Directly after the stone owl fondling, buttock bashing, fancy a quickie dance sequence. Only in (B, C & E).

6. **The master-shot of Howie lay-preaching**. This is a right bastard. The scene in church of Woodward preaching only appears in the (C) print as a flashback just before Britt's "We'll Bang the House Down" dance. Watch it and you'll see a master shot of Sgt Firewood at the pulpit with his back to the camera. Only in (C), the "short" version!

7. **The over-dub**. Just plain irritating this one. When Sgt Howie has his tea in the Green Man pub, and he's complained that all the food is "canned" (odd that, in Britain we usually refer to food in metal containers as "tinned"… (Mmmm), he decides he wants an apple for his duff. When Willow (Britt Ekland) tells him there are no apples, in the (A) print he chokes on his half of bitter and says "No apples, on Summerisle!?" — mainly because in this version the mainland banter has established the island's reputation for fruit. In the (C) versions it is "No apples? On an island famed for its fruit and vegetables?" Seamless, but very clunky.

8. **The caption slide**. On the video version I have of the (C) print just after the end credits is a red on black caption card telling you that *The Wicker Man* was filmed by British Lion on location in Scotland. That's the only place I've seen it.

So there you go. How frustrating it that? You see a film, you enjoy it, but then you find out that what you've seen is a crippled, stunted version. So you go slowly insane as you try to track down any information you can on fuller, more "complete" versions. You end up trying to make you own "Home-construct" of the film[10]. It isn't just *The Wicker Man*. There are people out there still trying to see the longest possible non-disco version of *Metropolis* (1926) (what is it now? 120-minutes down, only another 80 to go?). Or the devout filmophiles who have waded through the 92-, 99- and 114-minute versions of Fritz Lang's *M* (1931).

The Pekinpah maniacs who after finally tracking down the 143-minute print of *The Wild Bunch* (1969) go rooting around film fairs and late-night TV to see the fullest version of *Major Dundee* (1964). 120-, 124- or 134-minutes. Mind you, there might not be many of you asking after the 212-minute print of the 1959 version of *Ben-Hur*…

As a postscript: The 102-minute version of *The Wicker Man* finally turned up at the Leeds Film Festival a couple of years back, introduced by Robin Hardy. Nice.

Notes & Sources

1. A television actor popular in the UK for roles in such series as *Callan*, 1990 and *The Equalizer* (no sniggering at the back, thank you). Now stuck doing *The New Professionals* (you may now snigger).

2. Just to clear things up for the gullible. Summerisle does not exist. For the authors of certain web sites in the states, there is no Lord Summerisle. There are a small group of uninhabited mossy rocks called the Summer Isles just off the coast of the North West Highlands of Scotland. About five miles north of Gruinard Island, where the Army tested the Anthrax bombs. Heh, heh.

3. For more details of footage filmed but never used, check out *The Various Versions of The Wicker Man* web site. Address below.

4. The rather glowing review advised Warners on how to handle the film, promising a rewarding financial run for the film if it was promoted correctly.

5. People are still sticking to this story, although I notice as the years go by, the film has filled in bits of the M4 or the M25, to, in more recent years, filing in a pothole during widening at either Borehamwood Studios or the old EMI Elstree. Shovels in the crisp dawn mist anyone?

6. 1991 US release from Media Home Entertainment/Magnum.

7. When it was good. Introduced by the urbane and informative Alex Cox, as opposed to the trite and nasal Mark Cousins.

8. NTSC is the standard television format used in the US and Canada. It uses a 525 line system that scans at 24fps (frames per second) - the same speed as film projection in the cinema. As opposed to the UK/European system PAL (except the French, who being contrary buggers use the slightly different SECAM system) which uses 625 lines at a scanning speed of 25fps, which means slightly shorted films but superior colour and detail. British TV technicians refer to NTSC as "Never The Same Colour".

9. Apparently there was a band by the same name in existence.

10. Yes, I have made a home-construct and no, I don't know where you can get a 102-minute print. My construct is just over 93-minutes. And it's mine. Ha Ha.

Cult Movies 2, Danny Peary 1983 Bantam/Doubleday/Delta
Cinefantastique, volume 6 £3. Article by David Bartholemew
Film Comment, Nov-Dec 1977. Article by Stuart Byron
The Various Versions of The Wicker Man http://www-phm.umds.ac.uk/ Steve_P/WM/history.htm

inside the wicker man

an interview with allan brown

Sun Paige

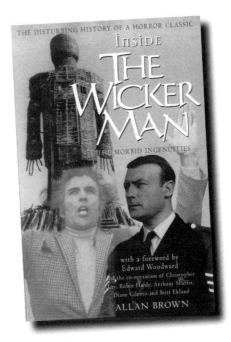

THE RELEASE OF ALLAN BROWN'S NEW book, INSIDE THE WICKER MAN, is proof that interest in "one of British cinema's most notorious films" has never quite burnt out, and instead this 25-year-old film flickers a little brighter with each twist and turn of its convoluted story. Covering the film's conception, creation, release, reaction and resurgence, INSIDE THE WICKER MAN is written with input from many of the main players both in front of and behind the camera. These quotes, frequently contradictory and usually indicating some amount of disgruntlement at the way the film was shot, cut, distributed, written, directed or dubbed, are enlightening, and their collection clearly represents many years of difficult and painstaking research.

There are many surprises too. Who would have believed that Bible Belt Americans would approve of THE WICKER MAN, for a start? Yet the film can inspire extremes of reaction, not least from the cast members. The wonderfully enthusiastic Christopher Lee tirelessly plugged the film despite the fact that huge chunks of his dialogue were cut, and personal payment was not forthcoming. Yet Britt Ekland was clearly not glowing with love for all things WICKER when she remarked to the SUNDAY EXPRESS that the film's Scottish west coast location was "the worst place in creation". As Allan Brown says: "it is easy to be reminded of the film itself, when Summerisle

and Howie watch the local virgins leap through fire. They are looking at the same event. Yet carrying their ideological and cultural prejudices on their backs like bags of rocks, somehow neither of them sees the same thing at all."

There's too much in the book to even hope to summarise, but even the most ardent fans of the film should discover plenty they didn't already know, including rare stills, info on film locations, analysis of the film's Paganism, lost footage and much more. And WICKER MAN fans are apparently most appreciative of such efforts made on their behalf. Jonathan Benton-Hughes who was responsible for the release of the film's soundtrack on Trunk records in 1998 stated: "I just couldn't believe the scale of the response. I've met obsessives, but these WICKER MAN fans were way beyond that. When they started sending me lumps of charred wood, I decided I'd had enough. I'm doing a project based on THE CLANGERS NOW."

INSIDE THE WICKER MAN is informative and fascinating, well researched and obviously the work of a writer with a genuine interest in his subject matter. More importantly Allan Brown does a great job of making sense of the history of this flawed classic.

I had the pleasure of talking with him recently about the unenviable task.

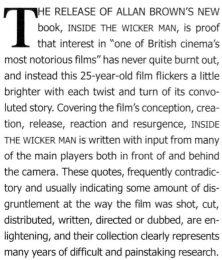

INSIDE THE WICKER MAN
The Morbid Ingenuities
by Allan Brown
Pub: Sidgwick & Jackson, 2000

HEADPRESS It's good to see a book on THE WICKER MAN. **What pushed you towards writing it, and is the story really as convoluted as it seems?**

ALLAN BROWN I originally decided to write the book because Ingrid Pitt claimed in an interview that she had finally located all the missing footage. I figured that if the last piece of the WICKER MAN jigsaw (I was a long-time fan of the film) had been found, it made sense to tell the story of the whole jigsaw. It turned out, of course, that Pitt was mistaken, there was no extra footage, but by that time I had found an interested publisher, made contact with the cast and crew, and was deeply into the project. Yes, the story is extremely convoluted, not to say tortuous. I don't think anybody involved knows all the ins-and-outs. I hope the book is a good stab at unravelling these twists but I'm resigned to some aspects of the story remaining mysterious forever.

Originally marketed as a 'horror' movie, THE WICKER MAN clearly doesn't fit the standard horror mould. How would you define the film?
I like the description in one 1970s American review: "a philosophical soft-core Scottish thriller-musical". I think that about says it! Obviously in several sense the film is a horror film: the film builds towards the revelation of a singularly horrific circumstance; what Dilys Powell called an

Scriptwriter Anthony Shaffer at the site of the second Wicker Man, erected for close-ups.
(Inside the Wicker Man)

ending too barbarous to justify the lighter tone which preceded it. The film was written to be a horror film with literary aspirations. But in the most crucial sense THE WICKER MAN is not a horror film. Horror films tend to dramatise, either explicitly or metaphorically, the transgressive power of sexuality. In horror, submission to the sexual impulse leads to the death of the victim. In THE WICKER MAN, though, Howie's submission to sexual temptation (Willow) provides his one chance of escape.

There is so much discussion about the 'lost' footage, and the negative treatment the film has received at the hands of the industry. Conspiracy, corporate stupidity or incompetence?
A bit of all of those. Despite the conspiracy theories, it seems likely that the film's negative and all its unused footage was accidentally removed from Shepperton and destroyed. So that's stupidity. But I think there was also a degree of callousness in the attitude of its distributors British Lion, who didn't like the film, weren't overly bothered how it was treated. It seems likely that this attitude fed into and created a situation where nobody was particularly concerned what happened to the footage.

The missing footage is said to be in a number of locations — under at least three motorways, or even under Borehamwood Studios or the old Elstree. Are there any other clues you've uncovered as to their whereabouts? More to the point, has anyone ever actually found anything?
No, nobody has found anything and it's deeply unlikely they ever will. It seems the negative and left-over footage went into the M3 as landfill, which was quite a common practice at the time. All we have is the 102-minute version, and that's all we're ever likely to have.

In the introduction to INSIDE THE WICKER MAN you describe how the fans are distinct from say, STAR WARS fans because of their quietly nurtured, contemplative quality. Yet still the young male fans bathe themselves in the morning dew where the

film was shot, and try to dig up various motorways in order to find the cans of missing footage. Is there a definitive fan?

At WICKER MAN events I've had to sit with any number of deranged folk who feel this film has somehow reached into their mind and yanked out the contents. The girl who does the WICKER MAN fanzine has had to stop using her home address because of the kind of mail, calls etc she was receiving. Whenever religion becomes involved in anything, the loopiness of those concerned increases by a factor of five. I've known people who've travelled for five hours on a train just to get to Plockton in the north of Scotland and look at the fishing boat which features in the film. It obviously touches people very deeply and some have the burning urge to touch back.

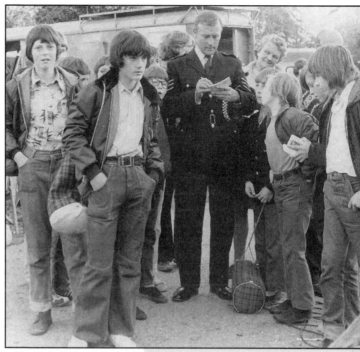
Teenage kicks. Edward Woodward, of CALLAN fame, is surrounded by fans on the set of THE WICKER MAN.
(Inside the Wicker Man)

What's the annual Burning Man festival held in the Nevada desert all about? Is this another case of direct fan response to the film, or is it connected less directly?

The Burning Man festival has no direct connection to the film, although obviously many of those involved will be aware of THE WICKER MAN through various New Age, alt-lifestyle connections.

You draw some parallels between THE EXORCIST and THE WICKER MAN as you claim that both films represent battles between good and evil. Could THE WICKER MAN actually be interpreted almost as the opposite of THE EXORCIST? Where the first film has clear contrasts between good and evil, THE WICKER MAN has fewer easy answers.

Yes, exactly. It is a difficult film, while THE EXORCIST's reputation is sustained by it being this kind of cinematic endurance test, this gory rollercoaster. THE WICKER MAN is so deeply superior to THE EXORCIST that it's almost funny. THE EXORCIST isn't about anything, unless you find the sight of a crucifix plunging into a teenager's vagina a deep, meaningful one.

How do Pagans react to the film?

The Pagans seem to like it; they're pleased to have their beliefs represented, even if it is in a less-than-wholly-flattering way.

I'm not really aware of the David Pinner controversy, i.e. he claims that his 1967 novel RITUAL was the starting point for the film — a point which is strongly contested by Anthony Shaffer. What's the story?

It's all in the book. David Pinner's RITUAL was briefly considered adaptable by Anthony Shaffer, and then ditched. It has similar themes to THE WICKER MAN, something David Pinner never fails to point out, even into the present day.

What about future developments for THE WICKER MAN?

There is talk of various remake/sequel projects. We shall see. 🦋

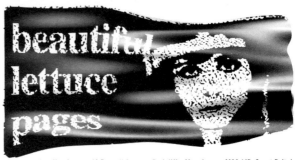

id you ever come across a zine called *Blunt Slug*? I put it out around five years ago — it lasted two issues, mainly because I'd done a 4000+ print run which was a total mistake, with no distribution 'cept a travel card and my legs! Nearly drove me mad seeing it piled up in my flat everyday... Good incentive for shlepping it around week-in, week-out. Getting used to THE HORROR of a pimply faced YTS assistant saying "Eh? No thanks". We've all been there... You should ask for people to write in their zine-shlepping experiences! Much more nerve racking than toilet gigs! We did do our own 7" single which required a big bed to put them under till they sold. We got played on John Peel and a deal in the end so things do work out in different ways. Also I did manage to get rid of all the zines by way of trying different covers... the first was too obscure.

Rick Hollywood,
London

 really enjoyed HEADPRESS 19. The Brando article inspired me to hunt out the *Dr Moreau* film. I picked it up at my local car boot sale last week, and thought it was a hoot. Especially his mutant dwarf thingy — I'd love one of them and that's for sure.

Steve Bickerstaff,
19 Burlington Road,
Ipswich, Suffolk, IP1 2HS
Steve has a limited edition number of his Parsnip Boy pictures for sale. Each set contains 10 drawings on quality card, priced at £10 a set, inclusive of p&p worldwide.

write **Headpress, 40 Rossall Avenue, Radcliffe, Manchester, M26 1JD, Great Britain**
email **david.headpress@zen.co.uk**

M ark Griffiths' Adam Ant article [HEADPRESS 19] summarised in a very thorough manner what I'd thought for years. For me, Adam Ant and the on-set of pubescence went hand-in-hand. What strange imaginings he created! Our only 'music system' was an old radiogram that sat in the hallway. As such, I had to listen to *Dirk Wears White Sox* very quietly because I knew the lyrics would cause some consternation. It remains an odd LP, but to my 11-year-old ears it was genuinely discomforting. I had to psych myself up to handle "<u>a wallful of handicapped / some wearing green hats and all sucking chocky bars</u>". But it was those lines — "<u>she was a wide-mouthed girl / Cleopatra did a hundred roman centurion for after-dinner mints</u>" — that did it for me. After that I knew there was *something else going on...* If Adam Ant had expected to pick up such a young audience, I don't think that S&M/bondage imagery would've wound up in the *Kings of the Wild Frontier* booklet. I bought the *Daily Star* (I think) every day for a week to read what was nominally his lifestory, but seemed only to be concerned with his sex life. I recall one tale of Adam's prowess driving one young lady "up the wall" proving to be decidedly confusing. *What exactly*

could that involve? I wondered. These days, the pop charts ring to the cry of young people having "sex on the beach" and Adam Ant's pro-sex agenda seems kinda quaint and definitely of its time (pre-HIV). Ruined my head though...

Douglas Baptie,
Scotland

 letter in the last HEADPRESS mentioned Wayne County's kitschy 45 'Eddie And Sheena'... a firm fave in this household as we were kinda it in reverse (I was the punk, my girl the ted). The 45 was a touching attempt at taking the piss outta the ted vs punk wars, which were mostly fuelled/caused by our chums in the tabloid press. Over here, punks and teds got along pretty well. I guess the music came first. I know in London it did get kinda nasty at times. That 45 also tied in the attempts by the late, great Johnny Thunders and his Heartbreakers to do a series of gigs with (then) real neat rockin' combo Shakin' Stevens And The Sunsets. Wayne/Jayne's chum (ex bedfellow?) Leee Black Childers managed The Heartbreakers then and got beat up by punks 'cos he had a suave quiff. He also went on to manage Levi Dexter, whose killer combo The Ripchords mutated into the long forgotten but *very* influential band the Rockats, who jammed with Thunders and his buddies on stage. The point of alla this slop however, is that there was a great one-sheet comic done to promote the 'Eddie And Sheena' 45 which was drawn by Antonio Ghura no less! (I think he also did some stuff based on Bowie lyrics.) And less of this heavy metal crap in HEADPRESS pulease... I didn't fight the punk wars for Led Zeppelin and their shaggy ilk to resurface in any shape or form!

Brian Young,
N. Ireland

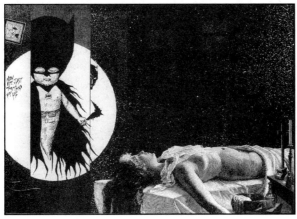

In Search of 'Instant' Ladies
Rubber Dolls

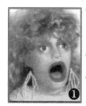

- **Real-feel vibrating vagina with hair**
- **"True to Life" realistic feet**
- **Holds up to 20 stone (127kg) in weight**
  Code 289 £199.95

More reader-responses to the Rubber Doll article in HEADPRESS 18. Submissions have been of a visual nature recently. *Keep your stories, anecdotes and pics coming in!*

Fig 1 This clipping from a sex aid catalogue features the face of <u>Glenda</u>, just part of the Super California line of love dolls. Submitted to HEADPRESS by HE Sawyer, who draws our attention to the weight restrictions.

Fig 2 <u>Bachelor's Life Size "Instant" Inflatable Play-Girl</u>. Taken from an ad in some bygone US real men's magazine (exact details not known). Submitted by Rik Rawling, who asks "What the fuck is going on with that neck?"

Fig 3 Lezbo rubber doll porn! This mind-boggling concept featured as the centre-page spread in the Danish publication, <u>Cats Magazine</u> (genitals obscured by HEADPRESS). One partner is live, the other is a "Living Doll", a pliable ultra-realistic sex toy. The sender of this particular clipping wishes to remain anonymous, but says it's the "freakiest thing I ever saw"...

Yup, a definite contender for the just-when-you-think-you've-seen-it-all stakes.

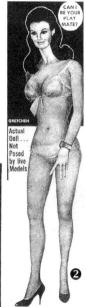

CAN I BE YOUR PLAY MATE?

GRETCHEN

Actual Doll... Not Posed by live Models

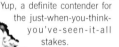

BLONDE OR BRUNETTE

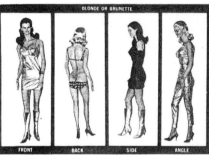

FRONT   BACK   SIDE   ANGLE

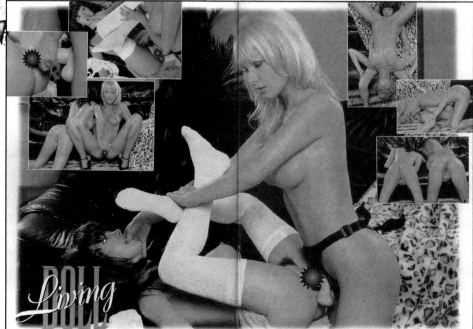

Living DOLL

generation Xploitation

Simon Collins

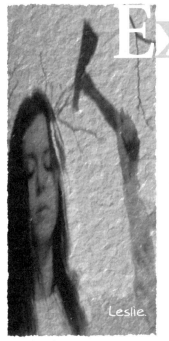

Leslie.

Exploited are the new kids on the block in horror and exploitation film distribution in Britain. Formed in the summer of 1998 by David Gregory, Jake Shaw and Carl Daft, they have since built up a small but punchy range of some 10 titles available on video, specialising in early-to-mid Seventies American product. The distinctive white Exploited boxes are steadily infiltrating such main-stream high street outlets as HMV and Virgin Megastores, as well as being available by mail order. Highlights of the Exploited catalogue include the 1974 cult classic **DERANGED**, based on the deeds of infamous Wisconsin necrophile Ed Gein, Todd Phillips' repellent yet strangely compelling documentary **HATED**, about late scum-rocker GG Allin and his band The Murder Junkies, and the short films **ROADKILL** and **MY SWEET SATAN**, the first works by celebrated American underground filmmaker Jim Van Bebber to be made legally available in the UK.

I met the Exploited crew on Halloween weekend 1999 at the Phoenix arts cinema in Leicester, where they were showcasing a number of their films in an all-day event entitled 'Bent Minds and Bloody Maniacs'. Then in early December I rendezvoused with David and Jake in a dark and gothic corner of the Via Fossa pub in Nottingham, to discuss film distribution, censorship, the BBFC and other stuff…

HEADPRESS Let's kick off with some back-ground details on the three of you, and on how Exploited got started.

DAVID I've been making films since I was quite young, and I've been <u>into</u> films since I was ex-tremely young. The video boom of the Eighties was a very exciting time. I watched a lot of films then, and got into the video industry at 16. I went to America, studied film, came back to England and decided to snatch up the rights to a few films that weren't available.

JAKE I left school at 16 and started work as a runner for an editing company in Manchester, and worked my way up through the production side of the industry. After being made redundant in 1990, I went off to Germany and worked on films there, then came back, bumped into Dave and we started working together on Exploited.

DAVID I knew Carl from school. His was the house that I could go in order to watch video nasties cause my parents wouldn't let me watch them at home. This was the early Eighties, pre-Video Recordings Act, and we watched the obvious ones like ZOMBIE FLESH EATERS and not so obvious ones like NIGHT OF THE BLOODY APES. We were friends just because of this common interest. Carl studied law in London, and now does other work as well as working on Exploited. He doesn't have the same film industry background as Jake and me.

How long has Exploited been running?

DAVID We released the first films in August 1998, which were DERANGED and HATED. Prior to that, we had actually been trying to get licences for films for some time. We did a deal for THE TEXAS CHAIN SAW MASSACRE and for DERANGED at the same time. We wanted to release them together. That would have been a nice little double act, but we were told by the censors that TEXAS CHAIN SAW would never get through. A company called Blue Dolphin has the rights to it now, and it's distributed by Universal, so obviously it has a much larger distribution than it would have got through us, but still it's annoying that as soon as it was submitted by a 'respectable' company, it was allowed.

How do you set about acquiring the rights to a film? Do you pursue specific properties, or do you just see what you can find?

DAVID We have a list of 50-100 possible titles, and then we work out which ones we'd most like to have, and then it's a matter of trying to

trace the producer, or finding out if it's available anywhere in the world currently, so you can track down a rights owner through that.

I'd imagine, given the kind of films you deal with, that this is often not very easy.

PAGE 93: Exploited A-Z. PAGE 101: Interview with Alan Smith, organiser of 'What's Wrong With This Picture?' and Exploited cinema event.

DAVID Absolutely! There are loads of titles that we want to do, things like the mondo film THE KILLING OF AMERICA and I DRINK YOUR BLOOD, which are just impossible to find the rights to. [*Exploited have since found the rights to* KILLING OF AMERICA *and the film has been passed uncut by the* BBFC—*Ed.*] Lots of these films were made by companies that only existed for the production of that one film, and the producers never made anything afterwards.

So you don't just go looking for whatever's up for grabs in your particular fields of interest?

DAVID Well, that happens too. When, for example, we found out that we could get CALIFORNIA AXE MASSACRE, we bought ZOMBIE CHILD with it.

How did the Phoenix event go from your point of view? Did you enjoy the audience discussion, and have you participated in similar events before?

DAVID It actually all starts with DEADBEAT AT DAWN.

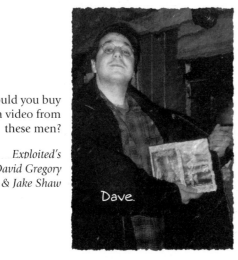

Would you buy a video from these men?

Exploited's David Gregory & Jake Shaw

Dave.

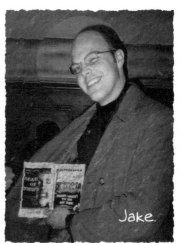

Jake.

Photos this page and page 101 © Simon Collins

JAKE It had gone in to the BBFC, who had recommended a cuts list that was fairly draconian. We cut it and sent it back, and were told we were going to get our certificate, and then Andreas Whittam-Smith turned around and decided, 'This is not the kind of film we want to give certificates to!' so it was banned. Effectively, we were told, 'Yes, you can go ahead,' then we were told, 'No, you can't!'

DAVID We'd spent £1,500 on the film, then there was the censoring, and we'd already advertised the film.

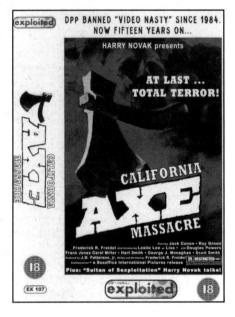

The BBFC charges so much per minute to review a film for certification?

DAVID They certainly do. It's about 11 quid a minute, and you don't get that back if they refuse a certificate. We'd already had MANIAC banned, so we weren't doing very well...

JAKE We had a discussion about how we could recoup some money, and the idea we came up with was doing a cinema tour, which turned out to be really difficult. When people talk about there being an independent cinema sector in this country, it's just not true. There are the arts cinemas, which basically take the same programme of films all over the country, so effectively you're facing the same lockout problem as with Odeon or MGM or something like that. I spent about a month on the phone finding cinemas that would

actually take our films. A lot of the arts cinemas wouldn't show a 'banned' film unless it was within the context of a season of controversial films or bad taste films or whatever. We did a limited tour to a number of very independent cinemas like the Cube in Bristol, the Birmingham Electric Cinema, the ICA and Dublin Irish Film Centre. And the tour did quite well, because people turned out to see the movies. Leicester was a situation where Alan Smith, who runs the Leicester Phoenix, set up the gig, and it was reasonably successful.

DAVID He got complaints from MPs and vicars! He was very happy with the day, though, because it all went fine, and it was all new people coming to the cinema, essentially, not people who generally hang out at the arts centre. The turnout was pretty good. THREE ON A MEATHOOK was the most popular of our films to be shown.

JAKE I think the chat we had with the audience helped, because Alan remarked that American audiences would watch a film like that and laugh and chuckle and scream all the way through it, whereas English audiences will watch the film from a technical and artistic point of view and examine every shot. I think what he said had a major effect when MEATHOOK came on, because people laughed all the way through it!

With a script and camerawork like that, I don't see how it could have failed to get big laughs.

DAVID That's true. But the reason why this came up was because AXE [CALIFORNIA AXE MASSACRE] had just played — which is actually my least favourite of our films — and the version we showed is actually missing the axe murder, which is in the video.

I found it hard to believe that it was ever classified as a video nasty!

DAVID Well, even the axe murder's not <u>that</u> violent! But I <u>like</u> these films. It's important to me to choose films that I like to release. It's generally films that we like, and because we like them, we assume that there's a market out there for them! We also have commercial considerations, obviously. With AXE, it was a more commercial decision, because it had been a video nasty.

You say that the video of CALIFORNIA AXE MASSACRE is actually less cut than the theatrical print?

DAVID Yes, there is more violence in our video version than in the version that you saw at the Phoenix. The reason is that Harry Novak, the world-wide distributor, actually gave us a master without this scene in. Then I was later told that the video nasty version had the axe murder in it. I called Harry Novak, and he called Something Weird Video — because he doesn't know anything about his films, and Something Weird control them in America — and they told him that that scene doesn't exist. So I had to get a German print of it. Luckily there's no dialogue in the scene, so it spliced in quite well. We had to restore the film, essentially, because we couldn't get a full master.

JAKE What I'd like to say about these movies is that I don't think they're bad movies. They're made within the budgets and constraints of the time. I personally think that anybody who's aspiring to make films should watch these films to see that you can get up and make a film, without conforming to this general pattern that you get in England where people think that they've got to make it look sumptuous. Whereas with these films, you know, people just went out and made them, and that energy to go out and make the film is sometimes missing in this country.

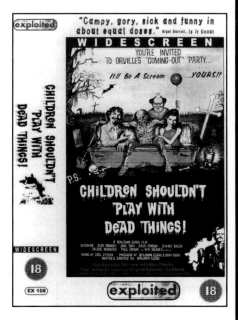

CALIFORNIA AXE MASSACRE

(aka *Axe*, *California Axe Murders*, *Lisa Lisa*)
dir: Frederick R Friedel
USA 1974, 75 mins, Exploited Films, Cert 18

It is a useful rule of thumb that the number of alternative titles a film has is usually in inverse proportion to its worth as a film. Whilst there are notable exceptions to this rule, *Axe* isn't one of them. Its unique selling point is that it's still on some official list of 'video nasties', and Exploited have managed to bring it to the gorehounds of Britain with only minor interference from the BBFC. Unfortunately, like most video nasties, *Axe* is wretchedly bad, and also like most video nasties, it's nowhere near as gory or nasty as you might be expecting.

The plot of *Axe* is simple: three criminals on the run hole up in an isolated farmhouse with a withdrawn young girl (Leslie Lee) and her paralysed, catatonic grandfather. One by one, the cons start to take liberties with Lisa, but she's a no-nonsense chicken-decapitating kinda gal who knows how to handle a straight razor and a hatchet ('axe' is frankly a bit of a stretch!), and she takes two of them to pieces before the last one gets gunned down by the cops.

I only really liked three things about *Axe* — its sickly, brooding atmosphere, the stark white American Gothic production design, and the truly demented electronic score, which I'd swear was recorded on a Stylophone! *Axe* is a bit of a laugh, but seekers after serious sickness will be disappointed. It's the runt of the Exploited litter, for sure, and I can't see why you'd lay down your spondoolicks backing this pony (if you'll allow me the solecism of a litter of ponies!) when you could get a film that was actually <u>good</u> for the same money.

The video release of *Axe* also boasts an interview with Harry Novak, the self-styled 'Sultan of Sexploitation', responsible for foisting hundreds of sleazefests — such as *The Touchables* and *Midnight Plowboy* — on an unsuspecting world... in addition to *Axe*.

CHILDREN SHOULDN'T PLAY WITH DEAD THINGS!

dir: Bob Clark
USA 1972, 85 mins, Exploited Films, Cert 18

YOU'RE INVITED TO ORVILLE'S 'COMING-OUT' PARTY... IT'LL BE A SCREAM... *YOURS!*

This is the third film in the Exploited range to have some sort of connection with Alan Ormsby and Bob Clark (the others being *Dead of Night* and *Deranged*), and the first film they made together. They co-wrote the screenplay, Clark directed and Ormsby did the make-up and took the lead role. He plays an egotistical young theatre director (imaginatively named Alan!) who leads a reluctant troupe of actors to a spooky cemetery island to engage in necromancy and devil worship, using a grimoire Alan has somehow acquired. The first corpse they dig up turns out to be an actor 'planted' by Alan to hoax his long-suffering employees. But then Alan decides to prolong the fun by exhuming a real corpse, dubbing him 'Orville', and marrying the body in a bizarre travesty of a wedding ceremony. However, Alan's conjurations have been more successful than he knows, and (aw, you <u>guessed</u> already!) the dead rise to avenge themselves against the impious Alan and his hapless hangers-on.

Made for only $50 000 whilst Ormsby and Clark were still drama students, and featuring a cast composed largely of their friends and acquaintances, *Children...* is a fairly spirited low-budget romp, though Alan Ormsby clearly demonstrates that he was wise to pursue a career behind the camera after this first outing. The standout performance of the film comes from Ormsby's wife Anya, who plays the superstitious, psychically vulnerable member of the group with a pop-eyed intensity worthy of Peter Lorre. *Children...* benefits from some hilariously (deliberate!) camp dialogue and acting, Seventies fashions which exhibit the same 'living dead' characteristics as the zombies, and pretty good resurrection sequences near the end. Unfortunately, the first two-thirds of the film are slow, slow, slow, so you may find your interest waning before it manages to get in gear. And even at its best, the film is but a paltry imitation of Romero's *Night Of The Living Dead*, which was doing great business in Florida drive-ins around about the time that Ormsby and Clark were wondering what sort of film to make. *Children Shouldn't Play With Dead Things* is no classic, but an amusing curiosity with a groovy title!

The tape includes as a bonus the first part of an interview with Alan Ormsby (concluded on the *Dead of Night* tape). You also get a free 'authentic replica' of the original promo gimmick insurance certificate, which guarantees you a free burial if you are attacked by a cannibal ghoul whilst watching the film. So that's a relief!

DEAD OF NIGHT

(aka *Deathdream*, *The Night Walk*, *Whispers*, *The Veteran*, *The Night Andy Came Home*)
dir: Bob Clark
USA 1972, 90 mins, Exploited Films, Cert 18

I DIED FOR YOU... NOW WHY SHOULDN'T YOU RETURN THE FAVOUR?

Ormsby and Clark return! Alan Ormsby wrote the story for this one, which is, as he freely admits, a loose take on MR James' classic ghost story 'The Monkey's Paw'.

Andy is a Vietnam combat veteran who unexpectedly reappears at his family's home in an unspecified American small town on the very night that they've been informed he's been killed in action. They're naturally overjoyed to have him back, but soon start to notice that Andy's, well... different somehow. But this time it's not post-traumatic stress disorder. No, what ails Andy is a severe case of death. And being one of the walking dead, as any fool knows, requires one to prey on the living. First it's the truck driver who gives Andy a lift into town, next it's the family dog, and after that the body count really escalates. Andy's parents simply don't know what to do — his authoritarian father finds himself at odds with his indulgent mother, whose attitude seems to be, 'He may have bits dropping off him, and he may need to drink the blood of our GP, but damn it, he's still my son!' Interestingly, the increasingly uneasy, fractious conversations between Andy and his father seem to reconfigure zombiedom as a kind of teenage alienation (*Rebel Without A Pulse*, anyone?).

Dead Of Night has a satisfying amount of gore in it, and the stages of Andy's physical disintegration are nicely outlined by Tom Savini's makeup work (this was Savini's first film). And when Andy goes out on a double-date, he dons wraparound shades and black gloves to conceal his dete-

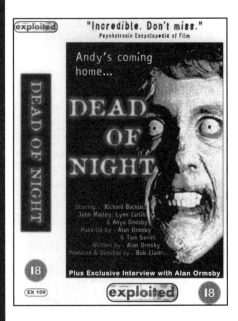

"Incredible. Don't miss."
Psychotronic Encyclopedia of Film

Andy's coming home...

DEAD OF NIGHT

Starring: Richard Backus,
John Marley, Lynn Carlin
& Anya Ormsby
Make-Up by: Alan Ormsby
& Tom Savini
Written by: Alan Ormsby
Produced & Directed by: Bob Clark

Plus Exclusive Interview with Alan Ormsby

EX 109

exploited 18

DAVID Purely and simply as entertainment for the people who like that kind of film, rather than trying to do something important or making a social comment...

THE BLAIR WITCH PROJECT and THE EVIL DEAD would be good examples of what you're talking about.

JAKE Absolutely. When I was at film school, the big film was RESERVOIR DOGS, and all the director students were saying, 'Oh yeah, we could do that! One or two locations, lots of dialogue...' I was back at a film school a couple of months ago, and all the students were saying, 'Wow, look at that! BLAIR WITCH PROJECT, it only cost $35 000!' It's great that it inspires people, but I think that what we need to do in this country is try and make _original_ movies, instead of looking at American product. Inevitably it ends up being some kind of watered-down English version. Distribution is a big gap in the British film industry. It's where a lot of things go wrong. I was told that 50 per cent of films made in the past two years in this country have never been distributed, and have therefore never been seen. Maybe because they're shite, admittedly!

Is getting a film passed by the BBFC a major hassle?

DAVID Absolutely, yeah. It's got slightly better

since [James] Ferman left, but not much. People are all excited that they're relaxing standards, and that's completely not true. What has improved is the amount of time that it takes. It took us 12 months to get a rejection letter on MANIAC, which is a long fucking time to be waiting. And of course you have to fork out for the rights up front, then you have this two or three month period while you're waiting to get the certificate — particularly if you've got to get cuts — before you can actually put it out, then you've got another period of time to get your advertising in, and that kind of stuff. We were trying to butt all that up together, and we lost out in the

case of DEADBEAT AT DAWN, because we'd already put the adverts out by the time we found out that they weren't going to let us release it. So now we have to do it end-to-end — once we've got the certificate, we can start planning the advertising, print the sleeves, whatever.

But it's still very difficult to get to speak to the BBFC if, for example, they demand that you have to cut something, and you want to argue the point that it's a valid scene in the context of the film. Like the head-stomping scene at the end of MY SWEET SATAN, which was cut in the video. As far as I'm concerned, that's very important to the actual power of that final scene.

ROADKILL was passed completely uncut, which

rioration, exuding a good deal of mod cool in the process (compared to all the Seventies effusiveness around him). Their evening out culminates in Andy causing mayhem at a drive-in. Eventually, Andy's mother, in an unbelievably Freudian gesture, drives her rapidly-decaying son to the local cemetery, where she looks on fondly as he literally digs his own grave. His return to the comfort and security of the womb could hardly be more literally depicted.

It is possible to discern in all this an allegory of American involvement in Vietnam — Andy bringing the violence of the firefight back to shatter the complacency of small-town America, and so on — though I think Dead Of Night has a rather slender pair of shoulders on which to bear all this ideological baggage. Suffice it to say that it is consistently entertaining, and a worthy addition to the Exploited range.

DEADBEAT AT DAWN
dir: Jim VanBebber
USA 1987, 80 mins, Exploited Films, Cert 18

HE QUIT THE GANGS. THEY KILLED HIS GIRL. HE BECAME... *DEADBEAT AT DAWN*.

This is the film that VanBebber and his mates made using their tuition fees rather than finishing film school, and it's an impressive directorial debut. *Deadbeat* is a gory revenge drama featuring urban street gangs, set, like *My Sweet Satan* (see below) in Dayton, Ohio. VanBebber plays Goose, a member of the Ravens (how can a goose be a raven?!), who wants to quit whilst he's ahead and retire on the proceeds of his speed dealing. But he finds it's not easy to leave his past behind. Disgruntled Ravens beat his girlfriend Christy to death, and Goose is forced into hiding at his crazy junkie/wino father's crib. The Ravens then hook up with rival gang the Spiders to pull off an armoured car robbery, and Goose gets involved. He's soon pursuing his own agenda of violent retribution for Christy's death, however.

It's a simple enough plot, the characters are mostly flimsy caricatures (a big dumb brute called Bonecrusher? C'mon!), and the script is badly clichéd. Where *Deadbeat* really picks up points, though, is in the excellent fight sequences, which are dynamically filmed and chokka with nasty violence of the tooth-spitting, face-slitting, punch-daggering, finger-shooting-off, larynx-ripping-out kind. Baseball bats and golf clubs are used for non-sporting purposes, and, most problematically for the censors, UK-banned 'ninja' weaponry, shurikens and nunchuks, appear quite a lot.

Also worth a mention is the edgy, atmospheric music by A-OK and Ned Folkerth. Mike King's cinematography has a grainy, bleak, underlit look, well-suited to the film's downbeat mood, and is interspersed with lyrical passages of nature photography and psychedelic kaliedoscope effects. Just to add to the film's violence and drugs, Goose's girlfriend is messing with the occult and using Ouija boards, and there is just a tad of nudity here and there. There is also a great dream sequence, where Goose sees the mutilated corpse of Christy in a cemetery.

As he does with Ricky Kasslin in *My Sweet Satan*, VanBebber throws himself into the role of Goose with gusto, riding a motorbike around, flashing his butt briefly, and (seemingly) doing his own stunts.

Deadbeat At Dawn is an entertaining film, and would make a good double bill with *Vigilante* (see below). Sadly, however, you're unlikely to be able to see for yourself, as the BBFC decided that it was just too violent to be seen in

Britain — even with two minutes of nunchuks and stuff removed — and refused it a certificate. Oh well, see if you can find a bootleg!

DERANGED
The Confessions of a Necrophile
dir: Alan Ormsby & Jeff Gillen
Canada 1974, 84 mins, Exploited Films, Cert 18

PRETTY SALLY MAE DIED A VERY UNNATURAL DEATH! ...BUT THE WORST HASN'T HAPPENED TO HER YET!

Ed Gein, the necrophile, graverobber, cannibal and murderer apprehended in Wisconsin in 1957, has been, and continues to be, an *eminence grise* in modern horror cinema. As well as inspiring *Psycho* (1960), *The Texas Chain Saw Massacre* (1974) and *The Silence Of The Lambs* (1991), countless forgettable exploitation flicks have pawed over various aspects of the Gein legend. *Deranged* is one of them...

After a modestly successful stint on the Midwestern drive-in circuit in the mid Seventies, *Deranged* has remained virtually unseen for over 20 years. In fact the negative was believed to be lost at one point. As detailed in the main article, Exploited originally intended to secure the UK video rights to both *Deranged* and *Texas Chain Saw*, but the latter deal fell through. Nonetheless, *Deranged* became Exploited's first release (and their best-selling one to date), and the company deserves massive kudos for making the film available after such a long hiatus.

Roberts Blossom (that's how it's spelt), if a quick trawl through my film guides is any indication, has had a fairly undistinguished Hollywood film career as a character actor, appearing in such disposable fare as *Candy Mountain* and *Citizen's Band*, as well as garnering minor roles in rather more memorable projects (evidently he played the 'Aged Master' in Scorsese's *The Last Temptation Of Christ*, though I can't say I remember it). In *Deranged*, though, he gives the performance of his life as Ezra Cobb, the Ed Gein character, managing to come across as simultaneously camp and convincing, his face an assemblage of tics and grimaces conveying the psychosis raging beneath the unassuming surface of 'ol' weird Ez', handyman, babysitter and all-round good neighbour. Blossom's performance can easily bear comparison with that of Anthony Perkins in *Psycho*, and it makes you wonder how much more celebrated an actor Blossom would now be, had he got roles that allowed him to shine out.

When *Psycho* was first released, it caused a sensation on account of its graphic (for the time) sex and violence, and its themes of deviant sexuality and murder. Little did many of its viewers realise that Robert Bloch, the novelist who wrote the book on which *Psycho* was based, had in fact toned down the unsavoury truth about Ed Gein considerably! *Deranged* makes no such effort to spare the viewer — the Wisconsin necrophile is presented here in all his human-skin-vest-wearing, shrunken-head-making, brain-eating, barking-at-the-moon glory, and the gross-out gore effects (courtesy of a young Tom Savini) can be appreciated to the full in Exploited's fully restored version, which reinstates all of the footage excised for its original theatrical release — in particular a scene where Ezra scalps the head of a freshly-disinterred female corpse, opens the brain pan, scoops out the contents, peels off the face and places it over his own. Tasty! The production design is generally

was weird, because if <u>any</u> of our films were going to be banned, I thought it would've been that one; there's no context to the violence, there's no anything, it's just a showreel with loads and loads of violence in it!

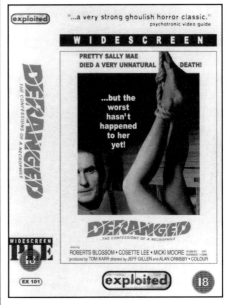

DERANGED — the contentious sleeve.

How consistent are the BBFC's decisions?
DAVID Very inconsistent!

JAKE They make arbitrary decisions, absolutely arbitrary. I've heard that when Spielberg was putting SAVING PRIVATE RYAN through, he went off for a weekend of tea and cakes with James Ferman. Is that a valid way of classifying or censoring movies?... The BBFC are lenient on some films, not just mainstream or big films. The annoying thing is that they insist that they can't charge small companies any less, because it's the same process that all the films are going through. Which is fair enough, but when LOLITA got passed it was announced in a press release, and the BBFC were talking about how they got child psychologists and police and experts in to watch the film and assess whether it was acceptable. Well, you can bet your bottom dollar they didn't do that for MANIAC! It was like, 'Fuck it, it's just some little film, ban it.'

You think they have an institutional prejudice against exploitation material?
DAVID They do have a disturbing tendency to

assess artistic merit in a film. Essentially, it's a bunch of middle-class, middle-aged males who decide what's artistic and what's not, and that's not fair. What do they know about it?

JAKE It's bound to happen with an organisation like that, where there is no recourse. If we want to appeal against the BBFC, then we have to pay their legal costs!

DAVID We couldn't take DEADBEAT and MANIAC to appeal, because we just couldn't afford it. It was probably a bit naïve of us in those early days to pick up MANIAC in the first place. But I did call up the BBFC and ask if it had ever been submitted before, and they said no it hadn't. So I thought OK, there's a chance, it's got to be less cut than the Intervision version that was released over here. But then I was told by Ferman, 'You know, you really should do your homework before submitting a film, because it has been submitted before, and it was rejected,' and I said, 'Well, I did call the registration office, and they told me it had never been submitted before.'

But with DEADBEAT, there was no way we could know. That is not a film that I would have thought would be banned. Cut, yes, because it's got a lot of nunchukas in it, but banned?!

So which of your current releases have had cuts imposed?

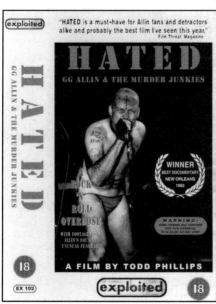

of a high calibre, and the scenes of Cobb's farmhouse full of human relics and bodies arranged as if for an undead tea party are claustrophobic, Gothic and genuinely creepy. Whilst *Deranged* is pretty strong meat, there is also a rich vein of coal-black humour running through it, particularly evident in the scenes where Ezra meets with a lonely and frustrated widow, who contrives a séance in an attempt to convince Ez that her dead husband wants him to take over on the old 'conjugal duties':

WIDOW: ...HE MISSES THE CARNAL ASPECTS OF MARRIAGE.
EZRA: CARNIVAL?

With this film now generally available, it may finally acquire the cult status it so richly deserves. Two final points: the video is available in a choice of sleeves, the limited edition mail-order one being rather more 'hard-edged' than the one for release to retail outlets, so snap one up if you can! As a bonus the video includes a short documentary on the making of *Deranged*, featuring interviews with co-director Jeff Gillen, producer Tom Karr, and FX man Tom Savini. Exploited, aiming to give the public what they want, also do *Deranged* posters and T-shirts... though surely a range of *Deranged* carving knives and cooking pots would be more apposite?

HATED
dir: Todd Phillips
USA 1993, 60 mins, Exploited Films, Cert 18
Todd Phillips' award-winning documentary about the infamous GG Allin and his band The Murder Junkies is just about as in-yer-face as they come. Allin, for the uninitiated, was a crazed NYC biker-scuzz-punk whose stage performances plumbed depths of self-destructive abjection and raw aggression which left Iggy Pop looking like Michael Bolton. Sadly, unlike Iggy, Allin's artistic vision was quite unsullied by talent. Still, Allin must be given his due as one of the most extreme performers ever vomited forth from the bowels of Rock'n'Roll. As he shuffled off this mortal coil in 1993 — overdosing on alcohol and heroin and thus reneging on his repeated promises to commit suicide on stage, possibly taking a few of his fans with him — *Hated* offers as close a look as you're likely to get (let alone want!) at the GG Allin phenomenon.

Allin's onstage persona combined the gross-out sensationalism of a carnival geek with the relish for audience confrontation of a WCW wrestler. As he says at one point in *Hated*:

MY MIND IS A MACHINE GUN, MY BODY THE BULLETS, AND THE AUDIENCE IS THE TARGET.

Nor is there much indication that he was any different offstage. In the interview sections, Allin comes across as a man with a lot to say, but no real brain behind the mouth. He's more articulate than you might expect from a man with 'LIFE SUCKS SCUM PUCK' tattooed in big wobbly letters on his shoulder and no teeth (he knocked six of them out with the mic one night), but Nietzsche he ain't. Despite the unconvincing attempts of his cronies to depict his act as some kind of terrible indictment of society, he looks more like a man with some heavy personal issues to grapple with. Rather than seeing a shrink, though, Allin acts out — and how! He shits on stage, rubs it on his face and throws the rest at the punters. He sticks a banana up his ass. He runs around naked, revealing one of the smallest dicks I've ever seen on a grown man. He punches out anyone who makes eye contact. Allin's antics, both on- and offstage, brought him to the frequent attention of the authorities. Murder Junkies' tours had to be fitted in between stretches in the pokey, and frequently involved violating parole.

Unsurprisingly, Allin's friends and fans are a pretty hardy breed — after all, not everybody would be happy to risk life and limb, purely for the pleasure and privilege of hearing some piss-poor two-chord punk rock behind a barrage of verbal abuse from a naked lunatic. His brother Merle Allin, bassist for the Murder Junkies, sports a shaved head, Hitler moustache and huge mutton-chop sideburns, and appears only marginally less unbalanced than good ol' GG himself (I'm sure their mother loves them)! Dino the drummer, another compulsive nudist, has a criminal record for weeny-wagging in front of little girls, and in a stoned drawl describes GG as 'God, Jesus and Satan all rolled into one'. (Now, where have I heard that before?) Chicken John, a disaffected ex-guitarist, offers what seems like a pretty cogent critique of the Murder Junkies, then spoils it all by smacking himself repeatedly in the head to prove that he's as hard as GG.

As chronicled in Jack Sargeant's book *Deathtripping*, Todd Phillips took *Hated* on a coast-to-coast tour of the States with much carny-like hustle and promotional brouhaha, resulting in a series of screenings scarcely less outrageous than GG's live appearances. Allin had already handed the young filmmaker a publicity windfall by dropping dead just three days before the film's New York premiere. Trash potentate John Waters dubbed Phillips 'the next Kroger Babb' for his exploitational flair (Babb was a veteran of the grindhouse circuit of the Forties and Fifties).

The whole scene is beyond parody, really. If you want to see just how low-down, dirty and downright degrading rock music can get, look no further than *Hated*. It's an unedifying spectacle to be sure, but the film is a lot more entertaining than most band documentaries, or even (saints preserve us!) 'live videos'. *Hated* also boasts a soundtrack full of timeless classics like 'Suck My Ass It Smells', 'Fuck Authority', 'Gypsy Motherfuckers', 'Cunt Sucking Cannibal' and 'Bite It You Scum'. The end credits roll over scenes from Allin's funeral, an open-casket affair where he looks even worse than he did alive. Still, it was probably the first time he'd ever stayed sober at a party.

LEMORA, THE LADY DRACULA

(aka *Legendary Curse of Lemora*, *Lady Dracula*)
dir: Richard Blackburn
USA 1973, 80 mins, Exploited Films, Cert 18

RUN, LITTLE GIRL... INNOCENCE IS IN PERIL TONIGHT!

Lemora is something of a lost vampire classic, and the availability of this remastered uncut version, a quarter of a century after its original release, will be welcomed by many [*The editor of Headpress among them—Ed*].

Lila Lee (played by Cheryl Smith, who went on to enjoy a degree of B-queen notoriety as Rainbeau Smith in such films as Jonathan Demme's *Caged Heat*) is the flaxen-haired and sickeningly pious 'Singin' Angel' soloist of a Southern Baptist church. Lila has become a ward of the church (following the disappearance of her ne'er-do-well gangster father), living in the rectory with a slimy preacher (played by director Blackburn). After receiving a mysteri-

DAVID Recently, we've been doing all right. As I said, the ROADKILL thing got through uncut. CHILDREN SHOULDN'T PLAY WITH DEAD THINGS, DEAD OF NIGHT and THREE ON A MEATHOOK are completely uncut. AXE has a token cut of about three seconds. We had to tinker about so it was a 'different' film than the one that was banned as a video nasty! According to the BBFC, they legally have to change a film that's been prosecuted in order to not get prosecuted themselves. But the recent films have been doing OK. I guess we might be getting a bit more tame in the kinds of films we're picking up.

I didn't think ROADKILL or MY SWEET SATAN were particularly tame!
DAVID Well no, that's true.

A lot of your tapes feature bonus material of this sort. Is this easy to arrange? I believe you did the interview with Jim VanBebber yourself.
DAVID No, actually, I gave the questions to Mike King who shot DEADBEAT, because just before I got to LA VanBebber left town. It turned out all right, though, because they shot it on Betacam SP, and it's a more professional-looking interview than the ones I did with Harry Novak and Alan Ormsby. I tracked down Alan Ormsby through William Lustig, who directed MANIAC and VIGILANTE. I called him, and Alan was very keen to participate.

Things like THE MAKING OF DERANGED and THE CONFESSIONS OF LEMORA (which is on the release of LEMORA) — they're productions that were already shot. I just edited THE MAKING OF DERANGED.

So you plan to continue putting bonus material on future releases?
DAVID I think it's important. As a film fan myself, I'm always a bit sceptical about picking up movies in Britain, because there's always that fear that they'll be cut. And mostly it's just paranoia. But if there's an extra thing on the tape, it seems like that makes it more worthwhile. We put trailers and bits and pieces on the tapes that film fans, who are obviously most of our clientele, are going to enjoy.

Is there an overall philosophy governing what you release? Is it just material that you happen to like yourselves? I'm thinking of Nigel Wingrove at Redemption Video.

DAVID I'm going to be a bit humble here! I think Redemption put a lot more effort into making a house style for the kind of films they were releasing than we have done. What they did with their packaging, for example, which, whether you like it or not, was very original. I'm not that keen on a lot of Redemption films, those Euro-horror type films. I know a lot of people are, and that's fine, but we're more into hearkening back to the early days of video where they had the original poster on the front.

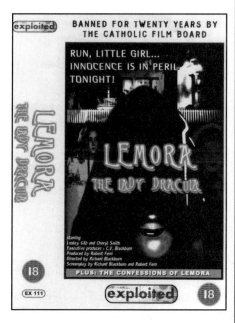

The maddening thing about Redemption packaging is that whilst it always looks smart, it gives you absolutely no indication whatsoever about the quality of the film itself! Some of the films on their list are horror classics by anyone's reckoning, and some of them are just garbage!

DAVID It's very clever how they've created an image for themselves that's far removed from the films, and they captured a whole market-place out there which they had to themselves for a while. Screen Edge is a label that's dedicated to films that you definitely would not see

ous message from her father, Lila runs away to find him, taking a bus to some spooky woods. The bus gets attacked by howling ghoul-creatures, but Lila escapes, running through the woods to an isolated farmhouse, where — surprise! — she is taken captive by the crazy inbred acolytes of Lemora, a vampiric witch-queen (played by Leslie Gilb with a firm-jawed forbiddingness, looking like nothing so much as Matt Dillon in drag!). Lemora, for no very clear reason, has kidnapped Lila's father, and now seems to want to seduce Lila herself into her web of evil, tenderly bathing her, plying her with drugged wine and luring her to join in with the abandoned dancing of her weird menagerie of demonic children.

Soon, the very pictures on the walls of the creepy old Gothic farmhouse are urging Lila to get out while she still can! As Richard Blackburn interestingly observes in *The Confessions Of Lemora*, the 20-minute backup feature which rounds out this tape, *Lemora* is a film which blurs the boundaries between arthouse and exploitation. Basing his narrative on the fevered imaginings of HP Lovecraft and Arthur Machen, Blackburn evokes a gloomy romanticism interspersed with brief moments of gore and ickiness, not unlike the films of Jean Rollin transposed to a shit-kickin' hillbilly milieu. The Rollin comparison also holds good for the distinct lesbian undertone to the pursuit of Lila by Lemora, although there is no explicit sex or nudity. And like Rollin's films, *Lemora* is long on atmosphere and short on sense. Lemora's motivations are never made clear, Lila's father is an irrelevancy, and the director seems unable to decide whether he's making a zombie film or a vampire film. The Sadean innocent-in-peril theme follows a child-like 'and then... and then...' narrative trajectory, degenerating into a mad chase which climaxes in a frenzy of jump-cut images of zombie destruction.

All this apart, *Lemora* is pretty good fun, although it's let down by its wretchedly bad soundtrack, which sounds as if it was recorded on a Dictaphone in a dustbin. Couldn't something have been done about this during the remastering process?

Leonard Maltin's Movie Guide calls *Lemora* 'perfectly awful,' rating it as a 'BOMB', but genre fans will like it fine. Evidently, the film languished on the banned list of the Catholic Film Board (who wield a disproportionate amount of influence in America) for 20 years, but it's difficult to see why as there's no seriously disturbing or graphic content. It's an atmosphere thing!

ROADKILL / MY SWEET SATAN
dir: Jim VanBebber

USA 1993, 35 mins (see below), Exploited Films, Cert 18 (in spades!)

Roadkill, subtitled *The Last Days Of John Martin*, was originally conceived as a full-length feature film, but VanBebber failed to secure the necessary financial backing. The 15-minute short that exists was made as a trailer to show to prospective backers, but is in fact a memorable little slice of ultraviolence in its own right. The first part of the film documents the unsavoury lifestyle of a demented loner living in incredible squalor — human and animal body parts litter the house, vying for space with empty beer bottles and swarms of rats. When John Martin goes out for a drive and stops on a desolate country backroad to offer help to a young couple with car trouble, the discerning viewer somehow senses that he's unlikely to take them to the nearest AA phonebox, and indeed he doesn't. The hapless victims are swiftly knocked into submission and taken back to the farmhouse. Here, the woman recovers consciousness to find herself naked in a chicken wire cage on top of the stove in the killer's cannibal kitchen. She watches, screaming in terror, as Mr Loonytunes dismembers her boyfriend in front of her, occasionally breaking off to torment her. Finally, he lights the gas rings under her, leaving her to cook alive. And that is more or less that. No explanations, no motivations, no back story, no redemption. We are never even told the victims' names. *Roadkill* is a short, toxic one-way ride to Hell, and is certainly one of the most repulsive films I've ever seen. The compression of the narrative only adds to *Roadkill*'s shocking immediacy and intensity. I was lucky enough to see this one on the big screen, and my girlfriend (normally no milquetoast) cried out, 'Fucking Hell!' as John Martin fired up the gas rings. And she was right. I can't imagine what possessed the BBFC to pass this film uncut — not that I'm complaining! Grab yourself a copy of this tape before they change their mind.

My Sweet Satan is a 20-minute short based on a real-life murder case. In June 1984, teenage Heavy Metal dropout and wannabe Satanist Ricky Kasso messily stabbed an acquaintance, Gary Lauwers, to death in front of two witnesses, whilst they were all on acid. The murderer sadistically taunted Lauwers and forced him to declare his love of Satan before killing him. Kasso was caught in short order, and hanged himself in his prison cell before standing trial, having written on himself 'Satan lives' and 'I'm coming home master.'

This tawdry tale of suburban anomie and stoner violence has inspired a book called *Say You Love Satan* and at least two other films (*Where Evil Dwells* [1985] and *River's Edge* [1986]). VanBebber took the decision to update the story to 1992, to take into account the considerable 'hardening' of Heavy Metal culture since the mid-Eighties. This means that Kasslin (as Kasso is called in the film, played with scary conviction by VanBebber himself) and his buddies sport a lot of tribal tattoos, piercings etc, and listen to a lot of gnarly Death Metal sounds. Actually, the sole glaring anachronism in the film is in the choice of Kasslin's T-shirts — I really can't see a teenager in 1992 trying that hard to be threatening and then wearing AC/DC and Iron Maiden shirts! Other than this time shift, and the moving of the action from Long Island to Dayton, Ohio (presumably for budgetary reasons), VanBebber remains pretty faithful to his source material. And whilst *My Sweet Satan* isn't quite as appalling as *Roadkill*, there is still plenty here to rot the moral fabric of society: Satanic ritual, animal sacrifice, drug abuse, what looks like an authentic nipple piercing that made me squirm (and I have multiple body piercings myself!), and, of course, some very graphic and bloody violence. The climactic headstomping of Gary was too much for the BBFC however, and suffered minor trimming, but what's left is certainly nasty enough. The subject matter is perfectly suited to VanBebber's brand of voguish nihilism, and he approaches the Heavy Metal stoner subculture with an empathy that a more mainstream director would be most unlikely to possess.

Although both *Roadkill* and *My Sweet Satan* are brilliant, their combined running time is only 35 minutes. Don't worry that you are being short-changed on this tape, however, for this is Bonus City, with fully 40 minutes of additional material after the two shorts. There is a lengthy interview with the Bebster himself, plus a behind-the-scenes look at the filming of his long-awaited Charles

any other way! I don't know whether that's a good thing or what, but what Screen Edge have done is very original. I think they're having a bit of a hiatus at the moment, which is a shame. Because a lot of their films are independents and very much unknown, it's difficult to tap the retail market. The video market's changed. You can't just release something on rental, hoping it's going to get into all the rental stores. Retail has taken over. The Video Recordings Act had a lot to do with that as well — it changed the face of the industry. A lot of independent shops went out of business because a lot of their stock was uncertificated. The rental industry, in some ways, has never really recovered from that.

What's in the pipeline?

DAVID We're in talks for a number of films. The problem at the moment is that video is on its way out, so to get five years of video rights, you don't really want to be paying too much. We tried to get a couple of Italian zombie pictures, but the money we were talking about was way below what they were expecting. Although we <u>are</u> going to move into DVD, at the moment the process of mastering to DVD is a bit expensive. It's not like burning a CD. But inevitably, if we're going to carry on, we've got to move in that direction.

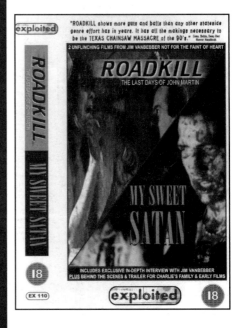

alan smith
season to taste

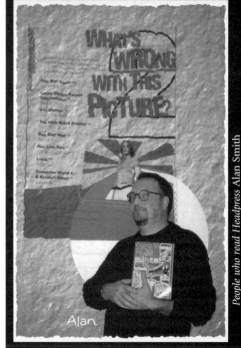

People who read Headpress Alan Smith

Alan.

Alan Smith is Head of Cinema and Media at Leicester's Phoenix Arts Centre. In October 1999 he staged a two-part season of films entitled 'What's Wrong With This Picture?', dedicated to films that were challenging in terms of either content or form. It featured such notorious works as THE TEXAS CHAIN SAW MASSACRE, STRAW DOGS and AI NO CORRIDA (IN THE REALM OF THE SENSES), as well as the one-day Exploited event and the rarely-seen HAXAN. I talked to him about the difficulties of mounting the season and the opposition he faced.

HEADPRESS How did the season originate?
ALAN I had it in mind from more or less the first day I arrived here. It fulfilled several functions. It enabled me to gauge the Leicester audience, to find out how far I could push things, and whether there would be an audience for this kind of material. And also, there is cinema which is unseen, denied, neglected, which I'm always keen to push back into the mainstream, even if it's the independent mainstream. I have an affection for these kind of films.

Is there a conflict in putting films like that on here, because whilst you can argue that they're minority cinema, some of the material will offend many people? Yes, we're committed to screening minority interest films, and we show black and Asian movies, but I think it's also correct to screen movies that have a minority interest out of taste. There are people

Manson epic *Charlie's Family*, together with a trailer for the film itself. The inclusion of these items is a major incentive to buy this tape, particularly given the fact that these are the only glimpses of *Charlie's Family* you're likely to see in the foreseeable future, due to VanBebber's ongoing completion and distribution struggles — to say nothing of the inevitable censorship wrangles that will ensue if and when this film ever makes it to the marketplace. Last but not least, there is an enchanting selection of very early Super-8 material by VanBebber, short on coherence and long on imagination and brio, with a lot of stop motion animation. Think Godzilla and Ray Harryhausen movies made by a 14-year-old with no money, and you'll have a fair idea what these are like.

THREE ON A MEATHOOK!
dir: William Girdler
USA 1973, 80 mins, Exploited Films, Cert 18

A PADLOCKED SHED, HOOKS OF COLD STEEL
-- A MANIAC ON THE LOOSE

VideoHound's Complete Guide to Cult Flicks and Trash Pics complains about the 'unwarranted amount of attention' lavished on this 'dull cheapie' as a result of its Ed Gein connection — well, here I am adding to it.
Billy is a good-looking but rather slow kid living down on the farm with his hard-drinking dad. When Billy offers to help three girls whose car has broken down and brings them back home to stay the night, Pop blows a gasket, reminding Billy that he, 'can't be around women… you know what happens.' Sure enough, all the damsels in distress come to a variety of sticky ends that night. Pop assures Billy that he must have done it, although Billy can't remember having done anything. Billy next meets a groovy chick waiting in a bar downtown (cue an intolerable amount of footage of some lame Seventies soul-funk band playing in the bar), and invites her and her friend out to the farm for dinner. And so it goes…
Billy really does take an unbelievably long time to work out that it's his dad doing all the killings rather than himself, and that's not all — *Three On A Meathook!* boasts a

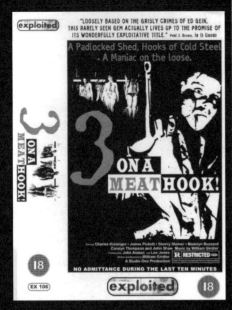

"LOOSELY BASED ON THE GRISLY CRIMES OF ED GEIN, THIS RARELY SEEN GEM ACTUALLY LIVES UP TO THE PROMISE OF ITS WONDERFULLY EXPLOITATIVE TITLE." Pete J. Brown, In It Uncut

A Padlocked Shed, Hooks of Cold Steel - A Maniac on the loose.

3 ON A MEATHOOK!

'surprise' twist ending that will have you groaning in torment rather than gasping at the ingenuity of it all. Not that watching this film is devoid of all pleasure. There's some truly berserk camerawork. For example, during conversations, the camera veers off to spend long minutes examining light bulbs and curtains for no obvious reason, while there are many leisurely pans across the trees surrounding the farm revealing precisely nothing! Add to that deathlessly camp dialogue, like the following:

HE REMINDS ME OF SOMEONE... SOMEONE I KNEW A CENTURY AGO... A MONTH LATER WE WERE MARRIED. AH, THAT WAS A WONDERFUL SUMMER. EACH HOUR WAS A DAY IN HEAVEN. THEN THEY SENT HIM AN INVITATION TO DIE IN ONE OF THEIR WARS. THEN THEY SENT ME A TELEGRAM THAT HE HAD. BUT THEY WERE ONLY HALF-RIGHT. I DIED TOO. TAKE ALL THE HAPPINESS YOU CAN. AT BEST, LIFE'S A SHORT RIDE, AND IT ISN'T ALWAYS A ROUND TRIP!

The gore content is disappointingly low, and the climactic scene in the shed which is the inspiration for *Meathook!*'s charming title is over far too quickly. It's complete bollocks, really, but don't let that put you off too much. Get some beers in, invite some mates round, and you might even enjoy it.

VIGILANTE
dir: William Lustig
USA 1983, 90 mins, Exploited Films, Cert 18

YOU WANT YOUR CITY BACK?
YOU GOTTA TAKE IT!

Lustig is probably best known for *Maniac* (denied a video release in the UK by the BBFC — see main article) and the *Maniac Cop* trilogy. *Vigilante* is an ultra-gritty morality tale of urban mayhem and bloody retribution set on the mean streets of New York. Evidently much-loved by Quentin Tarantino, the film relates the story of a peaceable family man and steelworker (Forster) driven to take the law into

out there who like sleazy sex films, gruesome horror movies, absurd space movies. They have as much right to have their inclinations seen to as ethnic groups or certain classes or whatever. The films themselves ought to be given the airing. Films don't exist if they're just sitting in a tin can in Perivale... which is this vast warehouse in North London where all of cinema heritage lives. The sad thing is that there are lots of very interesting films at Perivale, but the rights to them have lapsed years ago and nobody's going to pick them up.

How did you hook up with Exploited? Did they approach you? Yes. We had a meeting up in Nottingham, and we had an A-list and a B-list. The A-list contained some material that was uncertificated, and the B-list was all certificated. We went for the latter because I was testing the audience. If I'd shown these films and nobody had turned up, that would be it. I wouldn't need to go out of my way to show these films, because there simply isn't an audience for them. I said to Rachel Thomas, our director, who was getting a little worried at this point, 'When you need to worry is if these films get audiences, because that means we're going to do more of this!' In fact, the figures were incredibly impressive. We did something like a 65 per cent average, and our normal average is about half of that. Even the BFI was very surprised, because a lot of these films are thought to have been played out. The other side of that, of course, is the 'anti' letters that we got. I saw some the other day that had been sent to advertisers in the brochure, and also to the council and other venues. To the credit of the council, they responded very positively on our side, saying, 'Some people like this stuff, some don't. If you don't like it, don't come in.' We got about a dozen letters of protest, and they were rigged too. They would all have the same phrases, and were clearly from the same five people or so. Somebody said that God had my soul in his hands, and let's hope that Satan didn't take it away! The objection was that these films are vile and hideous because they rejoice in violence and they show the dark side of humanity.

The only walkout I'm aware of was with HAXAN,

the witchcraft film, and we had three people walk out halfway through. A couple of days later I got a letter, saying that they felt the film had been misrepresented, they weren't frightened enough by it and they wanted their money back! I wrote to them saying, 'Well, it does clearly state that the film was made in 1921, and it's b&w, it's silent, what did you expect?'

So Exploited approached you and they fitted in nicely with the season you were planning? Yes. They were happy to provide five features for us to screen, and we gave them the opportunity to sell videos and merchandise downstairs. It was a very amicable affair.

The other thing that fitted in well with your season was the high-profile un-bannings of films by the BBFC last year, notably THE TEXAS CHAIN SAW MASSACRE and THE EXORCIST, which you didn't show... Because we'd shown it a couple of months earlier. It didn't do terribly well here. I think the cinema release was a marketing platform so that they could push out more video units. But you're right, THE TEXAS CHAIN SAW MASSACRE was the catalyst. It's been around for a long time, notoriously banned, unavailable, and suddenly here it is, in a more or less completely uncut version. The BBFC used that as a linchpin to fit all the other bits and pieces around... STRAW DOGS is massively banned. You never see it on TV, there isn't a video of it, the only place you can see it is at the cinema, and I'm still at a loss to know why that is. Yes, it's a difficult film, but there are other films which are equally difficult, yet which are in full availability. It got the highest turnout of any film in the season. It got practically a full house.

Was there any local press coverage? There was, and it was all very positive, thank God! One of the things that worried us was the possibility that we would open the paper and find a 'Kiddie Porn on the Rates' kind of thing. It never happened. I'd actually gone as far as preparing a response, which I left at the box office in case some journo came in asking loaded questions.

When we talked before, you mentioned

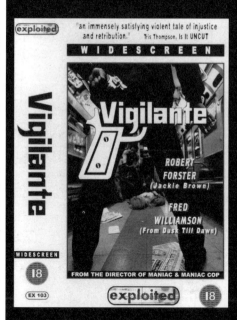

his own hands after his wife is raped and battered and their child is murdered by an improbably ethnically mixed street gang (shades of *The Warriors* and *The Wanderers*). One of his co-workers (Williamson) has started to organise a rather proactive Neighbourhood Watch scheme, and Forster hooks up with them to wash the scum off the streets. So far, so humdrum, but *Vigilante*'s chief virtue is the lurid directness with which its theme is addressed — Lustig has a camera eye that simply doesn't know when to quit. Thus, when a minor baddie gets tossed off a rooftop, we not only see him go over, we track his fall, his impact, and <u>then</u> the camera lingers for several more nasty seconds on his bloody remains. Dial G for gratuitous! *Vigilante* doesn't miss a trick in justifying the bloody vengeance wreaked on its villains. The viewer is offered the very simple, almost primal, emotional pleasure of watching bad people who do <u>really</u> bad things (kiddie murder, assaulting women and defenceless old men, dealing smack to children, tormenting the handicapped!) come to <u>really</u> sticky ends. There is no room for equivocation or moral niceties here — they are all guilty, they all must die. And when at the end Forster car-bombs the limp-wristed liberal judge who let the gang leader walk in a misguided plea bargain, you find yourself just cheering him on.

Vigilante has other incidental delights to gladden the heart of cheese connoisseurs everywhere — its curiously dated look and feel, for instance, plenty of *Starsky & Hutch*-style car chases, kung fu fighting, and streetwise, jive talkin' black dudes. Not forgetting the big laugh you'll get when Fred Williamson is beating information out of a drug-dealing pimp

Q: WHO ARE YOU SELLING FOR, MAN?
A: I, I, I'M SELLING FOR MISTER T!

So <u>that's</u> how he paid for all those gold chains, then! Leonard Maltin's film guide gives *Vigilante* a 'BOMB' rating, and describes it as 'truly distasteful', but here at *Headpress* we are made of sterner stuff, and this film is recommended. Consistently entertaining.

ZOMBIE CHILD

(aka *The Child*, *Hide and Go Kill!*)

dir: Robert Voskanian

USA 1977, 90 mins, Exploited Films, Cert 18

Another film from the stable of Harry Novak, *Zombie Child* is a curious hybrid of the evil-little-girl film and the walking-dead film, coming on like a cross between *The Exorcist* and *Night Of The Living Dead*.

Alicianne Delmar (Laurel Barnett) takes a job as a nanny for Rosalie Nordon (Rosalie Cole), an innocent-looking little blonde girl living in an isolated farmhouse with her father and older brother. We watch her arrive at the house, having ignored a slew of warning signs, such as car trouble, getting lost in the woods, and meeting the old neighbour, who informs her that 'Rosalie regards these woods as her own private property...' Indeed! Rosalie spends an unhealthy amount of time playing by herself in the old cemetery. It soon transpires that she has powers to raise the dead (feeding them on sweet fluffy kittens!), using them to wreak vengeance on those she holds responsible for the death of her mother. Before long, Alicianne has found a disembowelled lynx (?) in the woods, the mists close in, and the walking dead come out to play. A fair amount of bloody mutilation ensues, and Alicianne and Rosalie's brother Len attempt to flee the mayhem...

Zombie Child has plenty of atmosphere, and doesn't stint on the ketchup during the violence. The film <u>does</u> lag, however, during the lengthy and stodgy dialogue scenes. The acting is mostly indifferent-to-bad, though Rosalie Cole turns in a surprisingly assured performance.

The tape also features the conclusion of the Harry Novak interview begun on *California Axe Massacre*. Novak waxes nostalgic about his roster of horny hillbilly movies (which, incredibly, were in production up to the mid-Eighties), and opines of *Zombie Child* that

YOU GET YOUR MONEY'S WORTH FROM THE PICTURE... EVERYTHING'S TOP QUALITY.

Well... that may be a mite overstated, but the film <u>is</u> good gory fun of a modest and uncomplicated kind.

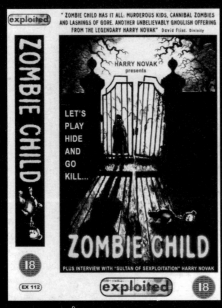

" ZOMBIE CHILD HAS IT ALL: MURDEROUS KIDS, CANNIBAL ZOMBIES AND LASHINGS OF GORE. ANOTHER UNBELIEVABLY GHOULISH OFFERING FROM THE LEGENDARY HARRY NOVAK" David Flint. *Divinity*

HARRY NOVAK
presents

ZOMBIE CHILD

LET'S
PLAY
HIDE
AND
GO
KILL...

PLUS INTERVIEW WITH "SULTAN OF SEXPLOITATION" HARRY NOVAK

EX 112

the idea of getting club status for the Phoenix to show uncertificated films. Is this a possibility? It's the way Soho clubs used to operate, isn't it? And the NFT and the Watershed in Bristol and the Lux in Hoxton and lots of cinemas! Yes, it's ongoing. Our licence from Leicester City Council indicates that we can run a club, but we must still show certificated films, and this is a kind of contradiction. I've asked other venues that have club status, and the whole thing is fairly ambiguous. The Lux, for example... 80, 90 per cent of everything it screens is uncertificated. What they do is simply send a list of everything they're going to screen to Hackney Council once a month, and that's it! As far as I know, everywhere there's a club, the circumstances seem to be entirely unique, and it's a question of negotiation.

I wanted to ask about AI NO CORRIDA, because the version you showed was very different from my dodgy bootleg copy – not only was yours better quality, but there were extra scenes in it, a different set of subtitles, and even more sex! It was the National Film Archive copy. It comes from the BFI, and they always have the best copy!

Can you briefly assess for me the current state of UK film censorship? Do you find that there's less stringent regulation of film than of video, which is what the BBFC claims? Yes. Catherine Breillat's ROMANCE typifies one aspect of the change in thinking, but I find it absolutely poisonous and inexcusable to allow this film through uncut on the grounds that it's French. This notion that this is a film <u>about</u> sex, not a sex film, is lost on me. It indicates a thought pattern that if you intellectualise something, you're allowed to get away with all sorts of things. The BBFC seem to be going that way, and I find it extremely spurious. In terms of sex, they're becoming more relaxed, but they're not at all relaxed about violence, children etc. In other countries, you just <u>get</u> a general warning that a film is unsuitable for certain ages. Here, the BBFC do that, but then they cut things up as well! It's infuriating, but it's the British mindset. 🦋

Jade Marcella is, quite possibly, Porn's Perfect Slut

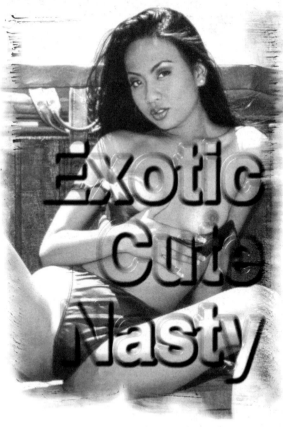

From Indonesia With Lust

Exotic Cute Nasty

Anthony Petkovich

"IT JUST KEEPS GETTING WORSE AND WORSE with her," cockmeister Max Hardcore recently told me about the lovely Jade Marcella. "I mean, there doesn't seem to be a rock bottom with what Jade'll do. Her sluttiness is like a bottomless pit."

Yet initially looking at the cute, darling little Marcella, you'd never think that this seemingly angelic, Jakarta-born 19-year-old could be so nasty, so heavily into double penetrations (DPs), anal, bukkakes, and gangbangs. The proof, however, is in the pudding. And such "sex-positive" evidence — pointing straight towards Jade's superlative sluttiness — can be found in *Gangbang*

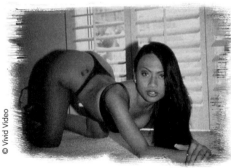

Angels 6 (Elegant Angel), *Luciano's Lucky Ladies* (Extreme Associates), *Color Blind*, *The Watcher 3* (Vivid), *Maxed Out 13*, *Hollywood Hardcore* (Max Hardcore Productions) *Gutter Mouths 12*, *YA 12*, and *American Bukkake 4* (JM Productions).

I interviewed Jade shortly after she relocated from sunny San Diego to the infamous San Fernando Valley (a migration made strictly for the sake of horny little Jade being that much closer to the world of porn). As Marcella spoke to me, her seductive Indonesian accent was still quite detectable, even though (go figure) she's been living in the States for 16 years. And while she's starred in a plethora of thoroughly hardcore movies, her attitude is anything but jaded. Simply put, Jade is one sweetheart of a slut.

HEADPRESS What kind of a kid were you growing up?
JADE A lot of people say that I was spoiled because I'm the only child. But not really.

Are you spoiled now? Of course not! (*Laughs*)

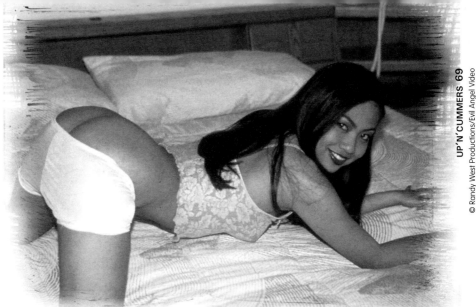

Have you visited Indonesia since you left so many years ago? I actually visited there two years back. I went with my mother to Jakarta and Bali, and I discovered that I'd really love to live in Indonesia; the people are so nice there. Besides, my grandfather, grandmother, and cousins all live there. I stayed in Jakarta for about a month and really liked it because the people are just very polite. And I didn't get sick from the food, either, which is very similar to Thai cuisine… spicy, with lots of coconut.

Seeing as you're so young, did you immediately set your sights on porn after graduating from high school? Actually, I went to college… for one semester. (*Laughs*) I was studying psychology, and I was dancing at this one club in San Diego called Pure Platinum. That's where I met this one producer who got me started in the business. So, yeah, I guess you can say that I went right to dancing after high school. But I really always wanted to be a dancer while I was in high school. I also wanted to get into porn for a while. In San Diego, though, there's not that many people who are in the porn business, so I didn't have the right connections.

After I made the right connections, I did my first video in '98. I was still living in San Diego and so would shuttle back and forth between there and LA, which made it kind of hard to get booked because a lot of producers would see the 619 area code and think, "Oh boy, she's far… we can't get her." That's the one reason why I moved out to LA.

And your first film was…? *I Love Asians7*, it was for a Hawaiian company. I was hyped up! It was a good experience. I didn't do anal in it, though. I didn't even do anal 'til probably two months into the business. As much as I like anal, I like DPs better.

Had you done many DP's in your personal life before getting into porn? Yes, yes. Like when I was in high school. I was 17-and-a-half. It was just me and a couple of friends. We were kind of hanging out after school at my girlfriend's house, and we were with two guys from high school. And we were partying, drinking, talking, and watching a little porno. At one point we saw a DP scene and we kind of got turned on by that. So I'm like, "Ah-ha! There you go. That's the key." But we didn't do many more DP's after that one.

Are you a DP girl? (*Laughs*) Yeah, I would say that. I think that's a good thing. Check out *Freshman Fantasy* from All Good Video. That was one of my better DPs.

Do you often have true orgasms in your scenes or are you simply faking it? Yes! I usually come about twice in my scenes. That's the point where I want to stop shooting, but the producers, of course, want to keep rolling.

Where did you come up with the wayward girl, Indonesian-accented "Hey, Meestar" routine which we see in a lot of your videos? The "Hey, Meestar" thing… (*laughs*)… well, some of it was my idea, some of it was Max Hardcore's idea. The pigtails were his idea. I hate to tell you this but it really turns me on playing those little girl roles. I like older guys like Max Hardcore. That's a little fantasy of mine. (Laughs) The first time I worked for him, it was kind of a difficult thing to do… swallowing his cock like that… you know, the way he'd just jam it down the girls' throats. He's rough and stuff, but I kinda like that. I just like different things. So it was a good thing working for him. Actually, I worked for him for like so many times — probably like nine or ten times — that now I know what to expect and what not to expect, you know? The first time I think it was for *Maxed Out 13* or something like that.

Nine times? Where are these videos of you and Max? I've seen a few, but I don't think I've seen nine of them. Um… we have the pissing videos for Europe. I have four of 'em but I don't remember what they're called. Do you want me to look for them?

Sure, a little later. But let's talk more about these pissing videos? Did you enjoy making them? Pissing?

Yeah, pissing? Are you talking about me peeing by myself or Max peeing on me?

Well, let's talk about both. Peeing… I don't know, that was Max's idea.

But do you like it? I have fun doing it. I don't know why. Do you think it's probably weird?

Not at all. So do you like people watching you pee? Ohhhhhh yeah. (*Laughs*)

In some Asian countries — like Indonesia — it's not uncommon for some natives to squat right there in the street and pee. Would you ever pee in public? When I was small I did. (*Laughs*) But not now, though.

So where does your interest in porn come from? I like sex.

How far does that go back? You mean the first time I had sex? (*thinking*)… The first time that I had sex… I would say… was when I was 16, with a boyfriend who was older than me, six years older. You can count how old that is, right?

I think I can handle it. Let's see… duhhh… he was 22, right? So was it at his place, in his car…? Noooooo, it wasn't in his car. It was at his place in San Diego. I had known him for a while. We went out for four months. It was a good experience. It wasn't, you know, messy or anything.

And what is it typically about a guy which turns you on? I like older guys, they're more

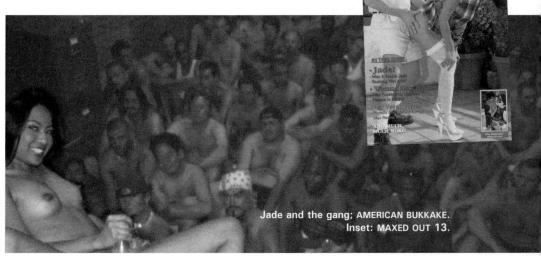

Jade and the gang; AMERICAN BUKKAKE.
Inset: MAXED OUT 13.

mature. They have more of a sense of humour, can talk about more things. It's irritating when certain guys — usually young ones — just talk about themselves, you know? I like to have a full conversation, not just a one-sided one.

Any particular sexual position that you like or dislike? Let's see now…

Very important question. It is?

No. (*Laughs*) Um… I like being on top! I come more easily and you can basically control the whole rhythm of the thing.

Do you have a particular goal with porn? I'd like to do this for the next couple of years, and I'd like to direct some day. Mostly males are directing now. Asia Carrera directed me one time and that was a pretty good experience. It didn't seem like there was much difference between her directing me and a guy.

What did you think of your 75-guy bukkake scene for director Jim Powers? Well, they didn't cut at all when they were shooting that scene because they didn't want me to wipe my mouth; they just kept rolling the video tape right until the seventy-fifth guy came on my face. Afterwards, I had a hard time trying to open my eyes. They told me, "Don't open your eyes too quickly," because, see, the cum burns. And while the guys were coming on my face, one after another, there was a point where I

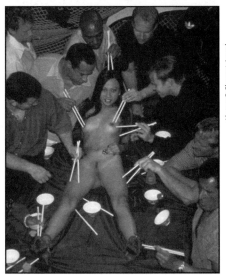

Above © Elegant Angel
Below © Anthony Petkovich

Chopsticks at the ready…
GANGBANG ANGELS 6

was thinking, "Please let this be the last guy" because there were so *many* of them. It was CRAZY! Some guys came about three times each and many times I had to, you know, patiently wait while they jerked off. I mean, the longest time I spent waiting for a couple of guys to pop on my face was two minutes. But altogether the scene took about an hour-and-a-half to shoot.

Did you feel any humiliation during or after the event? I mean, that's really the whole point behind this genre in Japan? No. I walked away thinking, "Hey, that was something different", a new experience. But to tell you the truth, I would never do it again. It was just too much.

So, Jade, what's your fan club address? It's 371412 Reseda Blvd., Reseda, CA 91337.

Last question: A lot of us pornographer's use the term 'slut' in our writing, and it's usually used in a complimentary fashion. What's your take on that particular term? Slut. That's a dirty word! But if you're in a movie, you can call me "slut" all you want. Sometimes I get turned on by guys calling me that. I like it when Max calls me a "fuck hole" and a "fuck toy." I especially like to talk when I fuck. Some people are more quiet. It all depends on the person you're with. If they like to talk, we can talk. If they want to be quiet, let's just be quiet. 🦋

People who read HEADPRESS

Korean-born porn star Lee Anne on the set of Hollywood Video's UNDERGROUND SEX EDUCATION 101. A very tasty, outgoing new piece of ass on the block, Lee Anne has high hopes of eventually doing some pretty nasty stuff in LA. "I want do gang bang with 50 men," the Asian vixen said in seductively broken English. "That really turn me on." Well, here's a first plug for you, Lee Anne, and we wish you the best of luck with those 50 slices of well-hung bulgogi. More from Lee Anne next time!

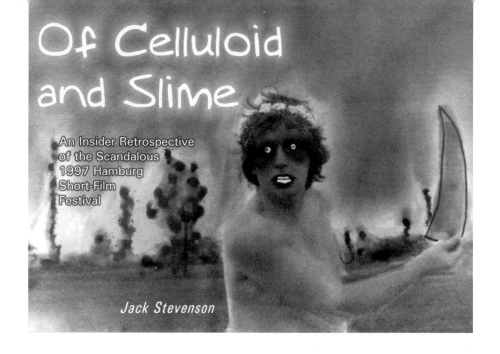

Of Celluloid and Slime

An Insider Retrospective of the Scandalous 1997 Hamburg Short-Film Festival

Jack Stevenson

I arrived at the train station

in Hamburg after a seven hour trip from Denmark, and disembarked onto the crowded platform. I was soon met by two girls from the festival, Judith Lewis and Nicole Newmann. Although I was extremely tired, they convinced me to head out with them to the airport where a celebrity welcome was being prepared for Vito Rocco, who was to serve with me on the No-Budget jury. Months before on the phone they had told me they were "trying" to get Vito to come over from London. I had feigned weak and transparent enthusiasm — I had no idea who the fuck he was. From his bio in the catalogue they handed me on the train, I read that he was an oceanographer in Acapulco who got sucked into the motion-picture industry and ended up filming underwater fight sequences, until his small Mexican studio went bust and he ended up on the streets...

At the airport, we soon spotted a crowd of festival people that included a nurse with wheelchair, a tall party girl in scaly green cocktail dress, and a phalanx of shaven-headed security stooges in head-mics and black suits.

Congregating at the arrival gate, word soon passed that the plane from London had landed. After a stream of businessmen and tourists lasting 20 minutes, the shrivelled spectre of Vito Rocco emerged, nestled anaemically in a wheelchair being pushed by an airline porter. Garbed in white silk suit, prominent neck brace, sunglasses and pointy shoes, Rocco was the essence of effete, exhausted decadence, around whom festival minions and confused onlookers darted.

Filmmakers/jurors Ben Hopkins and Andrew Kötting drifted over to me unnoticed in Rocco's wake. We killed time. Neither seemed to know exactly who or what Rocco was. Andrew had vague recollections of meeting him a few years ago but couldn't match this prone vision with what he remembered. "I think he's better known in Germany than England," ventured Hopkins as we cooled our heels and waited for someone to tell us what was going on.

Two vintage Mercedes with fender flags aflutter awaited us outside. Eventually the bullshit subsided and Rocco was bundled into the lead car with a

Above *Hummeln Im Kopf*
All photos in this article are taken from the collection of Jack Stevenson.

driver and two "handlers". Ben, Andrew and myself were stuffed into the tiny backseat of the second vehicle with Nicole up front.

On the drive into Hamburg the two cars became stuck side-by-side in traffic, giving the verbose and beefy Kötting a chance to lean out the window, over Hopkins, and harass Rocco with a jovial stream of bellicose cockney vulgarities and arcane hand gestures that were all vaguely related to the act of masturbation. The rest of us reacted with embarrassed smiles. Rocco's imperviously pleasant expression of celebrity certitude glistened bullet-proof and inhuman through the reflecting window glass.

The festival entourage, swelled by two or three vans, spilled out at the Hotel Wedina on Gurlittstrasse (where I could have been sound asleep hours ago), with the increasingly fragile Rocco holding up traffic for a block as he was carefully helped by three festival goons out of the car and into the building. Me, Ben and Andrew unfolded ourselves out of the backseat and tried to walk again.

After resting, I dined on a donner kebab and strolled the six or seven blocks over to the Markthalle, a kind of black-walled punk concert venue with a big main room, bar, dance floor and irregular ancillary spaces. This was the festival headquarters, and here tonight the jury was to meet the press.

By the time I got there, Rocco was already holding court with a TV crew. I got a beer and took a seat near the door. Soon after, the TV crew departed with shit-eating grins all round. Either they got too much or they got too confused...

After the opening ceremonies, a selection of films were shown. I went back to the hotel after that as a party in the bar area raged into the wee hours. Hamburg and Oberhausen were Germany's main short film festivals. From all reports Oberhausen was a deadly dry academic affair. Hamburg, in contrast, was run by anarchists.

The next day, both the No-Budget and the International juries met at 7PM in the Markthalle to receive instructions. Joining Vito, Andrew and myself on the No-Budget jury — and raising the glamour quotient considerably — were Annebelle Gangneux (who programmed the Super-8 festival in Tours, France) and Margaret Von Schiller (who co-programmed the Panorama section of the Berlin festival). We were each given an envelope containing 500 DM expense cash, and the meeting came to a quick close for the lack of any intelligent questions.

I didn't see Rocco, but the plainly dressed, sunburned guy who hung quietly at the edges of our group came over after the meeting and stuck out his hand. "Remember me? Rik Bolton?" Indeed, four years ago I had stayed a weekend with Rik and his girlfriend, Liz, in Enschede, Holland where they had arranged a couple of film shows for me. So *this* was the fake-flake celebrity, Vito Rocco! I'd not recognised him in his guise as the fame-hog Rocco, since I'd only managed to catch the glint off his sunglasses which had appeared welded to his head.

That evening in the Markthalle we watched the first of two blocks of no-budget short films, each block weighing in at almost two hours running time. Six blocks in total were stretched out over the next three nights. It was an onslaught of Super-8, video, 16MM and 35MM, with the films running a wide range from the divinely inspired through the utterly incomprehensible to the simply appalling. ("Utterly incomprehensible" being my favourite category.) It was hard work at times, especially the long bouts in the Markthalle with those uncomfortable folding chairs. We came to share the kind of exhausted, battle-scarred camaraderie normally only experienced by soldiers in major wars. I took copious notes and by the end counted 73 films, even though the festival catalogue and all other documentation listed only 69. The International jury was meanwhile watching short films of considerably higher budgets that were almost exclusively on 35MM.

I was happy to be a castaway in a low-budget wilderness, where one feels like a true explorer and not just a marketing middleman. In the nitrogen gases of the no-budget compost heap was the stuff of life — warped, extreme and highly imperfect visions produced by obsessives and delusionals who either don't care or don't know how to polish and structure their stories for the proverbial wider audience. A few years back the No-Budget jury decided that nothing they saw was good enough to win the prize, and gave the money back to the festival. I hereby publicly damn those faceless predecessors of mine for the arrogant fools they are!

After the screenings, came another late night party with a DJ and much dancing.

The next afternoon two vans ferried all the festival guests from the hotel down to the harbour for a buffet in a long glass-ceilinged canal boat. Walking into the boat we found ourselves ambushed by a luxurious corporate spread that had been underwritten by a cigarette company and a TV station. Two big tables lay heaped with fancy platters of cascading cold meats and gastronomical creations sculpted in mayonnaise. There were cheeses girded with garlands of grapes, various rich pates and creamed desserts next to dished assortments of Herring in 10 different sauces and tinctures. At the other end of the cabin a cook in dress-whites stood ready to carve

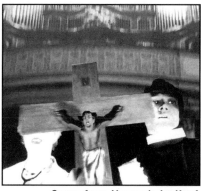

Scene from *Hummeln Im Kopf*, voted first place.

up a sizzling hunk of high-priced meat.

Our party of 50 was seated as waiters attired in black suits and bowties hustled about with bottles of wine. Free packets of cigarettes and lighters lay on the linen-clothed tables.

I still felt somewhat overwhelmed by the long train trip, the excessive drinking of the night before and the donner kebab I'd eaten earlier, unaware of the impending dimensions of this buffet which now exerted a Jupiter-like gravity. But I was helpless in its grip and submitted to its sensory omnipotence. In other words I dove in.

We shoved off. The boat was soon consumed in tobacco smoke as it began its tour of the industrial heart of Hamburg's giant port.

The richness of the food, drink and tobacco smoke was pushing me to the brink of nausea.

Once docked, we disembarked and scattered in smaller groups. Nicole guided Annabelle and myself back to the main train station. Nicole tried to talk us out of buying tickets, counselling us that we could all just run away if transit cops showed up — probably not the kind of advice handlers give to guests at glamour fests like Berlin or Cannes.

That night the No-Budget jurors gathered to watch another four hours of short films. The venue this time was the beautiful art-deco Metropolis theatre on Dammtorstrasse. All the experimental/Avant Garde selections were slotted into this block, and although Andrew and myself rather enjoyed the obscure psychic/electronic journeys, relentless special effects and imponderably abstract lightshows (not forgetting the comfortable seats), the stuff did not sit at all well with Margaret, who had spent the afternoon drinking champagne with the Norwegian contingent as they travelled from bar to bar.

Following the session at the Metropolis, we all went back to the Markthalle where "Die Trash Nite" festivities were about to begin.

Saturday was a period of languid recovery. I had taken to hanging out at the train station, trying to read the English language newspapers without buying them.

At 6PM we met back at the Markthalle for the final two blocks of No-Budget screenings. As we approached the end, we were hit with two or three particularly atrocious video productions, one of which I refer to in my scribbled notes as

The No-Budget jury of the 1997 Hamburg Short-Film Festival. The closing awards ceremony. L–R **Margaret, Jack, Rik (alias Vito Rocco), Andrew and Annebelle.**

Utterly incomprehensible!... video... apparently in Turkish with Iranian voice-over... a shaky travelogue of every unpronounceable Turkish town... endless! Just when you think it ends, long pause and another blast of Turkish horn music strikes up... camera aimed out of car, blurry roadsides, endless last closing shot of sky out dirty windshield... Jesus Christ!

Only the misery of my fellow jurors — at one point Andrew was holding his head in his hands — made me feel better.

Soon after that we ended up in the lonely back room of a cheap Italian restaurant, recommended by Nicole. Here we ate, drank, smoked, pondered over the film entries and kept the polite waiters up far too late. We had our verdicts.

We took cabs back to the Markthalle — by now it was about 2:30 in the morning. We were just in time for the second running of the Super-8 projector race. All the seating had been cleared out of the main hall and 10 projectors had been outfitted with roller-skate style wheels. When the starting bell sounded the projectors began to trundle forward, feeding along lengths of Super-8 film secured at both ends of the race course. It was a sweaty, boozy, gambling affair with all the atmosphere of an illegal cock fight. Some projectors advanced steadily in straight lines while others started going sideways and tipped over.

The party went on until daylight, helped along by bottles of Vodka which Nicole had talked the bartender into selling her at an unbelievably low price.

We gave Nicole the names of the four films we'd chosen. One of them was a three-minute, Super-8 silent entitled *Mullet*. It was a simple yet playful and surefooted parable of a spurned village idiot who wears a fish on his head. Produced by Australian Rick Randall and the Back to Back theatre group, it displayed a vital, collaborative group spirit and managed to turn its humble production specs to its advantage. Also it came at the end of the Experimental/Avant Garde block and dazzled us with images of actual human beings.

I had been the chief advocate of this film and in return for their acquiescence to a fourth place special mention (dressed up as the Bronze prize), my fellow jurors insisted I wear a fish on *my* head. For her part, Nicole volunteered to go down to the harbour that morning and buy a fish at the seafood market.

And I thought she was just making conversation in a forest of empty vodka bottles...

Around 7AM, with the sobering light of day upon us, Annabelle, Rik, Margaret, Andrew and myself walked back to the hotel, stopping to drink for another couple of hours at the outdoor table of an all-night bar. Finally, getting back to the hotel, we found breakfast was out.

For the closing awards ceremony that evening at 8PM, the Markethalle was packed. An overstuffed couch and stand-up home organ console were installed on the stage.

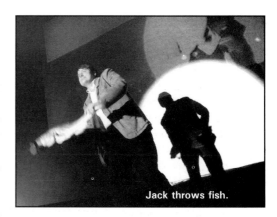

Jack throws fish.

The International jury started off with Ben delivering the news from the bar. First prize went to *Flatworld*, a funny, polished and innovative — if perhaps overlong — cartoon by the Englishman, Daniel Greaves. Second prize was given to the Brazilian production *O Bolo*, by José Roberto Torero, which chronicled a series of everyday moments between an elderly couple with a dry and witty touch. Both films were then screened.

After a short intermission, there came the awards for the best "three minute quickie", with the primitive yet retardedly seductive *Rebell Für Einen Tag* by Harald Koch being the standout.

The No-Budget awards followed and we piled onto the couch. Vito was re-splendent in powder blue leisure suit, matching head-bandage, neck brace and fold-up cane. Nicole had brought out the large cod she had bought and sat it on an upturned metal pan in front of the couch with a rose in its mouth.

Margret emceed our presentation, and, after a series of obligatory thank-you's, she announced *Mullet* as our Bronze prize winner. She then publicly nodded to me with profound intent: it was my turn to do something. I had to haul my ass off the couch and pull something funny out of the hat in front of a crowd that was still pretty reserved. For lack of a better

idea we'd decided that I'd present the fish back to Nicole, since (1) we all loved her so much in her green vinyl mini-skirt, and (2) she was the one who had bought the goddamn fucking thing in the first place! But surely this had no "grand gesture quality" about it, I thought, standing there ready to fizzle out in front of a full house.

The original idea was that I would wear the fish on my head like the fellow did in the film — which we weren't showing. I did actually put it on my head and capered about briefly to scattered and lukewarm audience reaction that clearly indicated we had reached rock-bottom. I then announced we were presenting the fish back to Nicole, which, if nothing else, was a way out. Nicole started to make her way to the stage as I cradled the slimy monster in my hands. Seized by the moment, I declared that if she didn't come and claim it, I'd have to lob it into the audience. The crowd instantly came to life... Nicole stopped in her tracks and melted into the confusion. Rocking the fish back and forth in three theatrical heaves, I then let it fly as the audience erupted. Blinded by the stage lights, I couldn't see where it landed.

With the buzz still resonating through the hall, Annabelle's uncertain English struggled for dominance and she announced that the Silver prize was going to *Sunset Strip*, by Kayla Parker of Plymouth, England. This three-and-a-half minute piece had impressed everybody at the Metropolis screenings. Comprising 4,000 images, created frame by frame using materials such as bleach, nail varnish, magnolia petals and net stocking, it recorded the impressions of 365 sunsets on a broad and overwhelming 35MM canvas.

Andrew announced that Gold was going to *Quel Giorno*, a moving and emotional 35MM treatment of contagious despair on an Italian street corner. Director Francesco Patierno wasn't present, so the certificate was given instead to the Festival's Italian projectionist.

After *Quel Giorno*, a fellow came up on stage carrying the fish in a blue plastic bag, put it on the floor next to me and told me I owed somebody an apology. I grabbed the

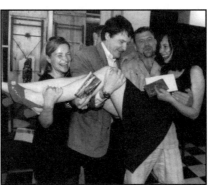

L–R **Margaret, Jack, Andrew and Nicole (Rik obscured in background).**

mic: "I want to say that I *do* apologise to the person that got hit with the fish, but I don't think there was a soul in the place that didn't mind seeing someone *else* get hit — the public demanded it and I am a man of the people!"

There was a confused murmur from the crowd as I'd blurted out my English too quickly for the mostly German audience to digest. But at least now I realised why I had done it. Yeah, it was a Political Act!

It was becoming clear that what I'd really thrown into the audience was a giant Red Herring (in keeping with the spirit of many of the films they'd thrown at *us*)... something highly theoretical and metaphorical... except to the girl who got hit by it.

Margaret announced our first place prize which went to *Hummeln Im Kopf (Bumble Bees In My Head)*, a surreal and visually intoxicating young-girl-in-her-bedroom fantasy. Employing a lush array of visual processes, from hand-painted frames to step printing and animation, the seven minute, 16MM work won both the jury *and* the audience prize — a festival first. *Hummeln Im Kopf* was screened and filmmaker Dorothea Donneberg, from Kassel, came on stage to accept the award.

All the festival staff and guests filled the stage to sway and sing along with Vito Rocco's infectious and sloppy celluloid kiss goodbye, *Ciao, Ciao*, as the movie played on the screen behind us.

The show closed with Kiki and Herb's *Total Eclipse Of The Heart* as people started filing out to the bar. I dragged the fish back to the dressing room where a small crowd gathered in the exhausted glow of rosy anticlimax and farewells. We hoisted Nicole in our arms to careen unsteadily around the room as flash bulbs and beer bottle caps popped.

Later on, Nicole told me the girl who got hit with the fish wanted it back in order to fry it up. I handed it over instantly.

My grand political gesture pretty much split the audience: some thought it went too far, while others came up to me that night in the bar and offered their solemn support and heartfelt encouragement. "I just want to tell you, you did right by throwing the fish," declared one fellow in deadly earnest as he shook my hand.

Some people make great films and some people throw a fish into the audience. I know which side of the fence I was on *that* night (...since I've never had any desire to make a movie). 🦋

PAUL SCOTT

ARTIST AT LARGE!

Drew Lawson

NSURGENT ARTS, Paul Scott's graphics company, is something of an underground anomaly. Producing wild shirts and screen prints of his unique work, Paul takes the DIY ethic to heart. And while he could easily adapt and cash in on mainstream America, Scott seems content to stay low-key, and share his work with those who really understand it. Paul is not only a gifted artist, he is a very cool person, and a good friend. Recently we sat down and talked about his art, big business, and selling out.

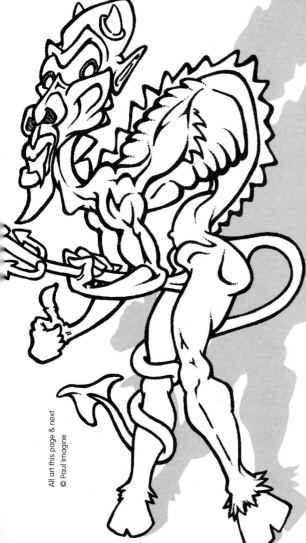

All art this page & next
© Paul Imagine

Describe your typical day.
That's a retarded question. Well, I wake up, draw, screw around, and go back to bed.

What got you started drawing like this, I know you don't take drugs!
I used to take drugs. Just being bored in school, not wanting to pay attention in class. So I just drew all the time… my version of art school.

Who were some influences on your drawing style?
Oh lord. Er… I love Derek Hess. Um, I like Bacon, he's the man! Robert Williams, R. Crumb. All the goodies, you know.

I like your views on doing commercial art, tell me about that again.
Fuck commercial art! Commercial art sucks! I don't want to sell my ass to anyone. If people like my stuff, they can buy it, if not to hell with them.

Being that you draw by hand, how do you feel about traditional illustration being replaced by computers?

115

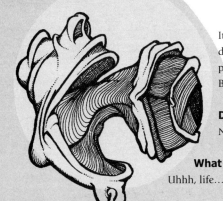

It's cool, if you know how to use a computer to draw. I suck at it. I prefer hand-drawn art over computer stuff because it's got more feel, more style. But I give props to people who are good at it.

Do you consider yourself a rebel?

No, pretty much an *outcast*. Not necessarily a rebel

What inspires your work?

Uhhh, life… stupidity (*laughs*). I don't know…

If you ever put out a line of shirts and got rich, what would you do with all the money?

Retire, relax, uh, pay strippers to take off their clothes.

What would you like to tell readers in England about Americans?

Uhhh, shit. I don't know anybody from England. Everyone's people, it doesn't matter where you're from. Unless you're like a cop or something, or a politician. In England or wherever, people are pretty much the same. Unless you're a jock. I guess they fit in there with cops…

Without God, how can the Devil exist?

I don't know. I don't believe in either. But if I had to pick one I'd go with the Devil. Otherwise you'd have to listen to fuckin' televangalists for all eternity. I'd rather shovel *hot poop* in hell.

What does art mean to you? How does it affect your life?

Art? Art is power! It's communication. That's how the world changes — through art and music, and all that crap. Without art, people would still be scared of everything. Nudity, for example. Art is the voice of the people. Anyone can do it. You don't have to be rich or anything.

Why do think people want to wear name brand logos and advertise for companies that aren't doing shit for them?

Well, everyone knows the brand names, and they want to 'look cool' and look like everyone else! To fit in.

Product identification?

Yeah, pretty much. But I'd like to do the same thing with my shirts. Now if a bunch of fools would wear my crap (*laughs*) then it would be *all* good.

So you got any free shirts for me?

Fuck, no! You don't get nothing free in this world, especially from me! 🦋

Note from Paul Scott: "I'm writing to let you know that by the time HEADPRESS 20 comes out my name will not be Paul Scott; it will be changed to Paul Imagine. You see I got married [July 10th 1999], and me and my beautiful wife Eve decided that it would suck that she would have to change her name and take my last name. So we are both changing it to Imagine."

Paul Scott/Imagine can be reached at: insurgentarts@hotmail.com

The QUEST for the POETRY GROUPIE

The Conceptual Writer, And How To Be One

Andy Darlington

POETRY? NO TA. YOU'RE STEAM-rolled punch-drunk by an aversion therapy of exam-based education, right? Lobotomised without anaesthetic by a system so rigidly syllabus-bound no chink of literate light can penetrate? Finally cut loose bleary-eyed and well stomped-on at 16, totally conditioned against picking up a book or reading a poem <u>ever</u>, right? But then there's grizzle-bearded Allen Ginsberg sat crosslegged on this TV stage motor-mouthing about jacking off in Cuban modern bathrooms, about visions of **ultimate cunts and come eluding the last gyzym of consciousness,** surrounded by moony-eyed chicklets with pre-coital adoration suffusing their rapt and attentive faces. There's Charles Bukowski's unshaven NOTES OF A DIRTY OLD MAN on an endless drunk spewing Technicolor vomit into his battered typewriter and free-versing it into a sexually incandescent cultdom clear across every campus west of Moscow. There's Kerouac on the eternal highway verge, thumb stuck out, sharing Neal Cassady's wife in <u>ménage à trois</u> and never without some vagrant hipster nymphet by his side all blowy nightblack hair and itchy crotch. While in London there's Pete Brown time-warping **across the Thames glaring/at its**

neonbanks glaring/to another party getting in by drink/and finding friends and jazz and beds and... 'Commemoration' from Penguin's

For better or verse, poetry is sexy. Poets, even now as I write and you read, are getting <u>laid</u>. Even gay old Walt Whitman gets pursued by a voracious proto-groupie determined to become impregnated by him. Poetry can be the whiff of the perverse, the hint of decadence capable of dislodging even the most massive comprehensive-induced mental block. Try this one: Michael Kelly is writing in GLOBAL TAPESTRY magazine: **she kneels on all fours.../nipples grossly engorged being stuffed/ from behind by a man whose long cock/hairy balls hairy loins stick out from under his shirt /...kneeling to shove (her) tongue stuck out between/bright lips with eyes almost closed she licks /the spurt from the other man's cock.../his bright-headed many-veined free-standing/organ spilling its come to her pink blonde-haired face.**

Art? Poetry? Sure — and sexy as hell.

Poets get <u>laid</u>. Words seduce like expensive aphrodisiac, only cheaper. Skipping reels of

Children of Albion.

From 'George Grosz — Erotic Pictures'.

rhyme liberate the female libido — and then some. Sure, Rock Tsars mega-touring midway through the mid-West States hook in more backstage nubiles, but Rock requires upfront investment in amplifier stacks, stratocasters, wedge-heeled glitter boots, plus musical ability sufficient to pick out a three-chord riff. Poetry needs a biro and a few lines of cheapo surrealism thefted from cryptic crossword clues autowrecked into each other and served up as symbolism. Tony Hancock (through the medium of Galton/Simpson) hips the jive and accurately shoots down the sharp end of schlock-modernism in his East Cheam Poem soirée (**straw in the wind/straw in the wind/straw in the wind/fly, fly, fly**) on the Emperor's New Zoot-Suit unprincipled principle that if you can't dig it you got no vision. It's a flash one-upmanship that comes cheap and pulls as much pussy as a flash new Porsche (well... nearly!). Hell, even THE OBSERVER writes with

The Observer, December 29, 1985.

confidence about **the cosy phallocentric world of contemporary British poetry**. Here, the quest for the Poetry Groupie remains valid.

Perhaps you caught the excellent movie REUBEN REUBEN? Tom Conti as Gowan McGland, a poet of the cosmic jester/holy fool school. An impecunious sexual anarchist on an inspired pussy-hunting verse-reading trip across an American campusland of female adulation. "Will you dedicate a poem to me?", they plea apres la gig (huge eyes glistening, huge breasts trembling), "maybe it'll give me a kind of... immortality". That's the Poetry Groupie. That's what I had in mind when I started versifying. When I began gallumphing up and down this blighted Isle word-slinging. It was something like the yearning idealism in that girl's eyes, allied to the seismic tremble of those breasts that first set me on the quest for that elusive breed: the Poetry Groupie. Girls to whom the penis reaches on through the physical into the metaphysical. Girls who sublimate themselves to your muse. They're Bohemian. They're Beat. They're post or neo-Hippie. Sometimes they're even leather-Punk vamps or Gothic weirdo. They wear long mystic-black pre-Raphaelite hair that shadows their faces into numinous plays of intimate secrets and sensual promise. Their lips part in a private hypertumescent curl, moist with thoughts and anticipations nice girls aren't supposed to have. Their decadent-chic garrets are always half-lit, always aromatic of subtle drugs and duplicator ink, hung with Art Nouveau or Aubrey Beardsley prints. They're designer-sex machines who wear no underclothes 'cos they want nothing to impede their freedom, they like to be nude because truth is naked. They have pubic hair in coils and curlicues like nests of spiral galaxies. Sometimes they don't shave their armpits because they believe in what's natural; they like to fuck — that, too, is natural. They'll suck your cock till their jaw aches in the hope of inspiring a couplet. And after the coupling, lying together while the sex-sweat cools on your mutually bare and sated skins, you discuss Rimbaud, Apollinaire, or Andre Breton...

How do you acquire these fabulously erotic creatures? Are they supplied with your first

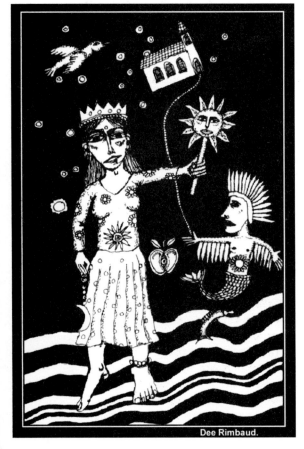

Dee Rimbaud.

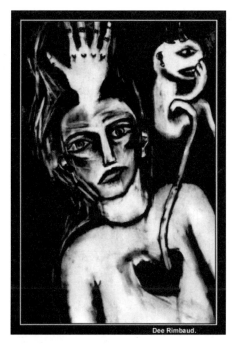

Dee Rimbaud.

magazine acceptance slip? I hit on the archetypal Poetry Groupie fantasy by accident; 17, maybe 18, living in Hull. Seeking enlightened opinion on early poems (a stew of Dylan — Bob, not Thomas — garnished with crude acid-Dada) I venture to the trendy loft apartment of one Maximilian Cantos who brags a local Lit. bigshot reputation. Down a long melancholy avenue of Regency houses subdivided into low-rent flats squatted by students or whores, then around the back treading leaf-silt and dog-turds, past a dustbin betraying the odd syringe or two in amongst the hash or rotting Chinese Take-Aways (No 40 & 69 with fried rice). To this simple Working Class would-be Bard it's a real Desolation Row scenario, a real stomach-churning hint of romantic sleaze, a tantalising glimpse of otherness beckoning as clear as semaphore. And a head through a window way above me concedes "yes", I'm free to ascend if I must — and I must, I must. The hallway and creaking stairs stink of musty decay and last month's stewed cabbage. A twilight room, yet he wears shades to admit me into his presence, an inner sanctum where he's stood in velvet smoking jacket and cravat, a book clasped stylishly open at the page bearing his name. And he starts into a long free-association lecture on the elitist art opin-

ions he assumes I feel myself suitably privileged to hear. Every now and then he'll illuminate some arcane point with an elaborate flourish of his cig-holder, sending spirals of dissolving smoke into the surrounding gloom. But I no longer care; I've seen <u>her</u>! She's sat at a polished-wood table preparing some kinda green salad — but her eyes never leave <u>him</u>. She's hung on his every poseur's gesture, his every pseud's syllable with an expression at once docile and adoring. Her hands — glistening with salad oil — move like they're performing some intimate service on his body. A long loose Laura Ashley skirt with a cheesecloth peasants blouse that's dimpled by nipples that are the perfect punctuation to the kind of haiku I could live in for the rest of my days. And as she tosses that salad in oil, working it around the wooden bowl, those nipples describe patterns of small perfect circles jiggling up, down, and around, against that blouse. I'm sweating like a garden sprinkler under my Double 2, even my sweat's sweating, surely she must smell my undeodorised funk? But just as I'm watching her, scarce daring to breathe, convinced I'd endure light-years of Cantos' pontificating just to watch the rise and fall of those delectable nipples beneath that thin thin material — she's transfixed on him. She never speaks. He never introduces her, or even alludes to her presence, as far as she's concerned I don't even exist. But for that half-hour she graces my life so intensely it switched my head around, reprogramming my future so my options narrowed down to just one thing; the quest for someone like that <u>for me</u>! For months after I lie awake obsessed with the things she'd do to me, the things we'd do together. Pulling myself off like it's a chicken neck with a new theme for a wet dream... sometimes the penis is mightier than the pen is!

Then, picture search forward to a shiny new redbrick Arts Centre besieged on all sides by urban-clearance dereliction — amber street lights coming up on acres of surrounding maps made up of absent buildings razed to ghost floorplans. And inside — a bored Poetry Workshop, 18 would-be scribblers with ballpoints and ring-binder files of carefully typed poesy involved in games of taking each other seriously, mutual crit. and Samaritan-style mutual support. I've had more than several Dutch courages already and reality is fraying at the corners. A guy with shoulder-length circa-'69 frazzle-cut hair and paisley shirt, legs folded over the Formica-top table, says "anyone mind if I smoke?" "Dance naked for all I care," a woman next to me in a tone of contrived libertinage, fussily if precisely dressed in a tight skirt with chess symbols on it. Middling in age and class. My mind wanders drunkenly as he ignites a strange ragged and bulbous cigarette, and starts reciting. Then she's reading and I catch the drift of his smoke until by the time I'm reading it no longer seems quite as important. I'm watching the walls fade in and out of focus and the nervous twitch-pulsations of a faulty striplight spraying spasms of spacey luminance. But when I'm done she leans over, fixes me with an intensity sufficient even to penetrate the surreal unreality that's now afflicting me, "you must think very deeply. I'd love to hear more". Only the way she's saying it operates on more levels than I'm capable of functioning on — saying, in code, "I fucking lurve you, man, you cut clear through the crap to the goddam asshole bone of truth!"

Then things are disintegrating and people start for the bar or the street, or the street via the bar. I'm telling the hippie with the strange ciggie what she'd said at me. He leers. "Yeah — Cass. She's like that with all first-timers. An orgasm addict suffering from penile dementia." He slips me a stick of bubble-gum and homes in close with an air of scandalous indiscretion. "What she really wants is to be written into someone's memoirs — and she hopes, by being laid by each and every aspiring poet, that statistically she's bound to make it with one or two who'll be famous, eventually."

We're in the car-park, Cass and me, zoning in on what I see as two Fiestas, or is it three? I choose the middle one and slur in beside her. She thumbs the radio up but starts into some dialogue about Byronic Romantic intensity, sturm and drang. I have difficulty

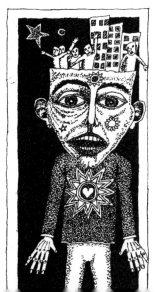

keeping track. The Arts Centre empties and lights decay into darkness until we're alone in a car marooned in acres of nothing. She turns on me, snoogling up close, first she's kissing me, then her tongue's snaking down my throat (failing to discover the bubble-gum artfully trapped behind my teeth) with a suction sufficient to send shivers down my spine clear along the length of my penis to spark in a series of high-voltage pulses across the glans. As she draws back I find her blouse is open — and so is my fly, her chair horizontals and she's drawing me down onto her by the cock. She's murmuring, grunting. Some of is do it with dinky retractable biros, but she's shoving me head down between her splayed legs reeling into a well of stocking tops and bare bare skin. Ovid might've penned an ode to this, but then he wasn't troubled by the problem of what to do with bubblegum during cunnilingus. I resolve the dilemma by adhering it to the gear lever as I'm sucked by sexual gravitation inexorably beneath a bridge of thighs into the yawning knickerless black hole. A cunt pink and moist, hungrily flexing in a nest of coarse black tentacles, a deliquescence of warm dissolving softness closing in on my tongue, tiny rippling muscles gripping. Memories blur beyond this point, coming at me in a storm of moist flesh-coloured penetrations, her pudenda rasping like steel wool on my chin. She's mewing with metaphysical pleasure, her released breasts falling like Gowan McGland's "condemned men through the trapdoor of the scaffold". Now the muse has me in her well-manicured grasp and she's lapping up spermatic pearls of culture direct from priapus; now I'm sinking as pussy-deep into her as the handbrake tangled in my Y-fronts will allow, in so tight I got her nipple-prints indented into my chest, and I'm shooting drops of sticky white love where it most counts. Mate and checkmate...

Back on the tarmac watching her tail-lights recede, it's hardly the initiation into poetry groupiedom I'd anticipated, I never even got to retrieve my bubblegum from her gear-shift, but it's a start. No Beat metaphysical wordfire from leather lady scribblers with spiky pens on the cutting edge of style. No pubic hair dyed green and trimmed heart-shaped. But I've made the lower rung on the way up to where the literati meets the glitterati.

Me, who can't tell an iambic pentameter from a clerihew, I begin slotting into journals with names like GLOBAL TAPESTRY, MELODIC SCRIBBLE, PUNK-SURREALIST CAFÉ, PERSPEX HEMORAGE, and KRAX, doing reading 'gigs' up and down the length and breadth of old Albion. It's an entire subterranean multiverse of rat-arsed mail-order magazines; faded mimeo A4's to instantprint Xerox A5 zinettes side-stapled so viciously they open up your thumb as you slide them outta the envelope. And upmarket tasteful type-set offset glossy digest-size Arts Council-funded coffee-table tomes publishing poems in the vanguard of the avant garde, new vibes for new scribes, new lit-art for the new Literati. Each zine designed as a prestige propaganda pack promoting its editor. A Literary Movement, sez Steve Sneyd (quoting someone else), consists of two writers in the same town who hate each other. Both of them run magazines. Outside contributing poets freeload into such a closed system as the padding necessary to surround the editors' own writing. Contributors generally read only their own poems to marvel at their own profundity; yet, against the odds, good writers do emerge. Dave Ward painting out the drabness of recession-blitzed Liverpool overspills. Dave Cunliffe, prosecuted in the Sixties for obscenity and grabbing DAILY MIRROR shock-horror space in the Eighties by performing naked from a mixed-sex Jacuzzi. The aforesaid Sneyd rewriting West Yorkshire into mutated SF symbolism...

There's David Tipton writing (in TRIANGLES) **sunbathing on the lawn/half-asleep I have this vision/(my imagination working overtime/of her giving him a blow job/his prick is enormous, swollen/...how can such a small girl/take such a goddam BIG one?** In the USA there's Lynn Van Eimeren FUCKING IN THE KEY OF E, and Ron Androla's DON'T READ THIS POEM (**her sweet**

mouth/boy'd she suck nice/all over me like/a puppy on speed/squiggled a couple fingers/opening her lips/ she panted hot on my/wet cock -- stick 'em in/she demanded/I was being gentle/I wasn't thinking fist-fucking/C'mon you bastard/yr whole hand/she insisted...

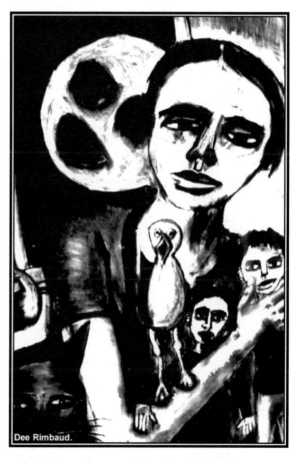

Dee Rimbaud.

And the readings... thumb-tripping the M1 to a Birmingham pub slotted on between an R&B band and a Feminist mime duo in dungarees and Thatcher masks. Datsuning down to a concrete Spielberg mothership of an Arts Lab in Sheffield with a poet dressed like Batman reading over vari-speed backing tapes. In the Cheltenham Poem Fest with conveyor-belt poets, rappers and ranters scattered through shredded vowels and nouns accelerating on the tongue, beards quivering with stolen Dylan Thomas impressions. Hunting a venue in rain-smudged Manchester at 10:57 PM dogged by inquisitive prowl-cars and drunks pissing in shop doorways. Then there's gigs in Punk cells where you go on with a fistful of lager and a mouthful of rhymes, never using an innuendo where four-letter precision will do. And a reading in a psychedelic head-shop over a disco where the bass-lines throb up physically through the floor so you have to lip-sync your lines to their rhythms, delivering poems you hope will violate language with the raw essence of razor-wit and Dada shock cluttered with the snakes and jewels of bile and arsenic. Poems alive with lies and lives that defy explanation hung on the brink of hallucination, madness and utter chaos taking their cue from

Dee Rimbaud.

1847.

Bakunin — **we can be happy only when the whole globe is in flames**...

And after one such event we drift, stumblebumming home. Mark, his close-shaven skull goose-pimple bald, talking faster-miles-an-hour about future events he's promoting. Mandy, his lady — passive, in owl-eye specs — smiling apologetically. A vindaloo take-away taken away to their 'place' which is poised mid-point between decay and a conversion programme to bring it into the 20th Century, the front room crawling

with cats and Airfix spacecraft, strewn with DIY beanbag furniture that's partially deflated like soft sculpture suffering from Brewer's Droop. She sits demurely, still smiling inanely while he unearths a plastic tub of home-made wine that cuts the palette like lasers. He hasn't paid me for the gig yet and I'm none too sure how to broach the subject, but soon we're suitably reeling and incoherent, mutually embued with that special love for each other and the planet that only drunks can share. Upstairs, driven by the wine's corrosive effect on the kidneys, there's dark low beams looming lethally at shoulder-height, there's trays of suspicious-looking plants pricked out in rows of polystyrene cups, and eventually a bathroom of sorts. I raise the seat-cover and unzip, attention cut loose and drifting numbly, and there, draped over the bath-edge is black suspender belt, black stockings, black basque with peek-a-boo cut-away nipples, their cumulative effect so stunning I've pissed all over the carpet before I discover my weapon's delivery misalignment. Downstairs the conversation gets increasingly loopy and suddenly I can't take my eyes off Mandy. Meek, eyes of denim-blue with long flutter-up lashes pleading innocence, no erotic body language, can it be there's less here than meets the fired imagination? He's into this convoluted anecdote about a lecture theatre, a speaker name-dropping William Burroughs, another guy pelting the podium with potted shrubs because he claims a closer relationship with the NAKED LUNCH writer: "I once shared a cab with him." But I'm watching Mandy, trying for the double-whammy blue eyes compassion-shot, but don't quite provoke a reaction. He's into Subliminal Generation, Reality Adjustment, Xerox Art, Neo-plagiarism, strongly peppered with contrived beatist expletives like 'Boperation' and 'Blatarootie'. I wonder how to bring the subject round to hard cash, reaching absently for an Airfix phallus, a Saturn booster or Gemini multi-stager, lifting it carefully by the Lunar Landing module at its tip, it gets into orbit about... so high, then it achieves perfect first-stage separation, the abruptly discarded lower segments splashing down clear across the floor.

And, as if it's a signal, the whole thing goes into overdrive, like an import video. There's no bed, but we're all together embracing beneath a huge crosspatch patchwork quilt on mounds of deflated beanbags. She's wriggling outta her dress pretty-pink naked beneath, and better than I could've hoped or imagined, we're squashed together and she's kissing us both, shivering with anticipation, my cock nearly raping my navel in its tumescent eagerness, her hands crawling erogenous patterns in the hair of my lower gut — and stealing lower. Her tongue's lapping and impaling my ear, and we're lost in a writhing mesh of hair, body-juices, entwined limbs, long sharp-nail fingers and deep yielding pools of bare skin. Who's tongue-tipping my glans, a delicate pout away from the full gob-job, I daren't think, but now I'm seeing shapely naked legs with a bald head jutting out between them. And now we're pumping away at both ends of Mandy's voluptuous little anatomy. I'm watching Mark's sprung-to-the-perpendicular length disappearing between her demure lips, then sliding back out in vigorous lusty thrusts, the loose foreskin bulging as it rides up with the forward drive, tightening red-veined slick on the withdrawal stroke, her sweet little tongue lap-lapping all the while hotly on the jerking underside. While the soft slurpy suction of her salaciously lubricating fuzzbox is drawing me in. I wonder if — without her specs — she can tell which cock is which, but by the way she's moaning, she doesn't seem to care. And a moment later I'm past caring too. I swear I can count each one of the 120 million sperms I'm spewing into her.

In the morning, with some ceremony, she drapes a tacky gold chain round my neck, her bare breasts shivering up against my chest as she tiptoes to reach. There's a ring-pull threaded onto the chain. Obviously part of a regular ritual. It seems churlish to mention I still ain't been paid, and in retrospect, sure, it works out an expensive stab at troillism — but the ring-pull reveals a whole new world of erotic symbolism. I still watch out for poets who wear them. I'm wearing mine now. But the financial element, the fact the Mandy belongs to Mark and is there in lieu of payment, knocks the incident outta the mainframe of this thesis; which is 'Poetry Groupiedom and the Quest thereof'. I mean, how do you acquire these fabulously erotic creatures?

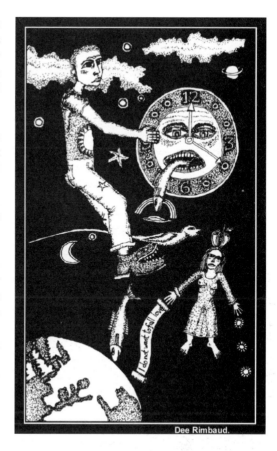

Dee Rimbaud.

Where the hell are they? Within a limited word-age I can't detail every thrust by thrust sexual run-in, prick-tease and quickie-quick near miss; there was that girl at the crazy magazine-launch party, a Debbie Harry, a Bardot, and a Patsy Kensit all in the same tight sweater, the stuff of sweet (and sticky) dreams. And there was the hitch-hiker who shyly confesses that she, too, is a writer of sorts, and can I give her some, er, pointers...? afterwards...?

But despite such pleasant diversions un-healthy patterns emerge over a period of years. The results of this dedicated research into what triggers the stimulation zone south of the navel, I'm only now prepared to pass on. Now I'm al-most out of the game and into writing for Men's magazines — where the real pussy is to be found!

I now know Poetry Groupiedom to be a sub-division of BIRGing: Basking In Reflected Glory.

I think it was Henry Kissinger who called power the greatest of all aphrodisiacs (I could be wrong, and in case of litigation I'm prepared to retract). But ain't poets among the most powerless dregs of this most non-literate of cultureless cultures? Poets don't make money either — which is the other major institutionalised sociosexual turn-on. Poets don't even grab much media celebrity, which is the third accepted way of hypnotising nubiles outta their knickers. So what's the secret? What indefinable quality is it that Gowan McGland and Maximilian Cantos share? Quality of literary output's a non-starter. Expert syntax in no way equals sexpertise — indeed, it's hardly necessary to write at all! What's important is image! Cantos has carefully contrived the visual affectations of what's popularly considered 'poetique'. McGland is a meticulous assemblage of deliberate Bardic cliché and tired stereotype extracted from all manner of recognisable cultural archetypes. They both present images that people (and for that read 'groupies') can readily identify as Poets with a capital 'P' for penis. They play a part, overstating ludicrously, but necessarily — because it's the gilt by association, the reflected glory of that image that's the groupie bait. Groupies — like Cass — want to be written into someone's memoirs, like in REUBEN REUBEN they want the kind of immortality a poem dedication might bring them. Hence advertising is important, the correct poses should be posed, and you must become 'the conceptual writer'. They want poet — you give 'em Poet. There are, obviously, a number of different off-the-peg literary 'types' on offer — from the angry young working class rebel image, through to the dour priggish young fogey. Even the arty camp poet has some currency value — but the sharper the definition the more restricted its audience, so a blurry mix'n'match of broad hints is a better shot.

A certain defiant down-at-heelness is usually expected. Facial stubble can help — in Literary demonology it denotes an inner-directed rejection of material values and conventional standards. A drink problem denotes vulnerability — always a plus, shorthanding disguised emotional need and a bacchanalian visionary drive. Sometimes a tousle-headed Celticness is worth cultivating, a Jewish intellectual quality is as good, but more difficult to sustain. But in every potentially pre-coital conversation it's important to drop the CORRECT NAMES to properly impress. East European Dissident poets are a good bet, equally applicable to both Left or Right-wing biases; invented foreign-sounding names are even better, saving the possibility of being out-argued on their merits, it also intimates that you're better versed in verse than your soon-to-be bedmate. Such lines should be delivered with an air of jaded world-weary cynicism, a post that has the added bonus of actually gaining conviction with advancing age; while in any given argument it's worth remembering that a knowing negative position, delivered in witty put-downs, is more easily defensible than any positive opinion you may be later called upon to justify. These dialogues can be slurred, and should be scatological; references to bodily functions show (A) street credibility, (B) an earthy awareness of the real biological truths of everyday existence, and (C) that your conversational motives are physical and not merely academic.

Finally the writing itself, which is not necessarily the problem it may at first appear. Indeed, all this assiduously contrived imaging could be destroyed by a misplaced couplet. So it's worth either investing in the East Cheam school of schlock-modernism (the Emperor's New Zoot Suit, remember?) or, even better — once the initial image has been established and placed within an acceptably Literary setting — you merely describe the poem (or even better, the poem cycle) you're working on! That way you can't be called to account for this duff line or that phoney metre. It also allows the gullible Poetry Groupie the hope that — by temporarily filling the emotional/sexual need by sucking your dick or getting you well-laid — she can be muse to the work's eventual completion and perhaps grab a dedication on the published manuscript.

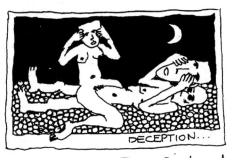

DECEPTION...

Dee Rimbaud

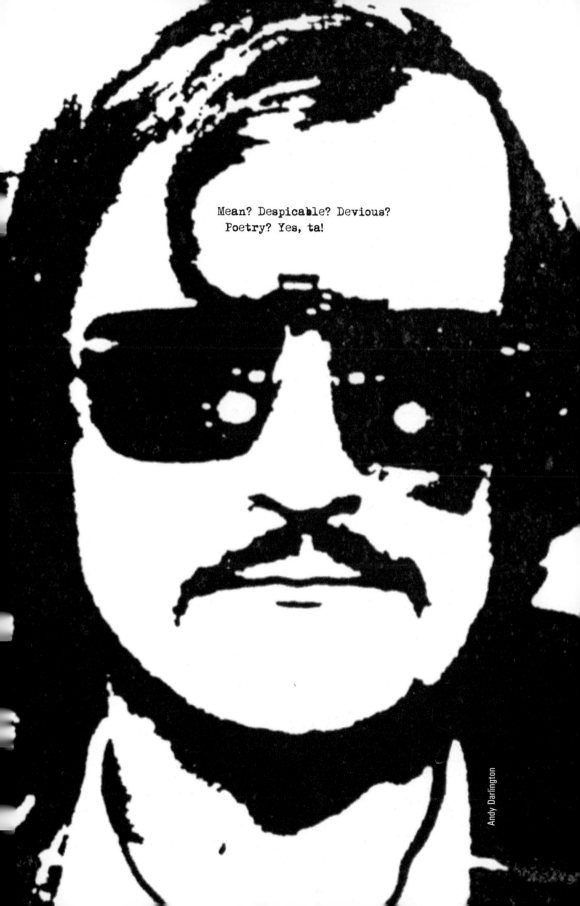

Mean? Despicable? Devious?
Poetry? Yes, ta!

Andy Darlington

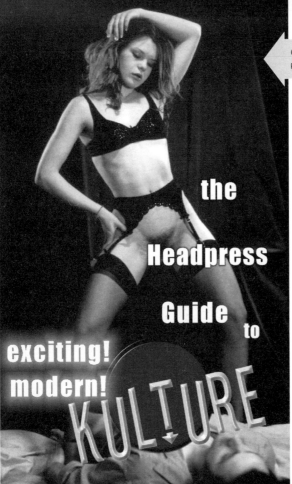

the Headpress Guide to exciting! modern! KULTURE

GIULIA. Review on page 153.
Photo © Roy Stuart

Howard's idea of fiery is that 'girl power' kind of pose where an open mouthed snarl or kung-fu style fist is supposed to signify some kind of liberation. It winds up being about as emotionally involving as a Spice Girl photo shoot, with Tammy Balinewski and Julie Strain seemingly competing to see who can look more like a topless Emma Peel who's just eaten a giant chilli pepper. Howard also provides the single most boring photo of Nina Hartley's elysian backside I've ever seen. Talk about achieving the impossible! I'm not as convinced as Justice that tattoos across the biceps or body-piercing automatically convey any sort of authenticity, whether fiery or feminist. Sporty Spice can get three new face studs and two new tattoos (as she did, apparently, for her new album) but that doesn't turn her into either a singer or a feminist, just a consumer of ink and metal grabbing at the pocket-money of impressionable pre-teens. It doesn't help that Howard can't write (sample: 'both books, signed copies all, grace my coffeetable'), but she and the magazine are caught in the same dilemma, trying to create a self-justifying rationale for work that flies (if not anything else) in the face of the philosophies they claim to espouse. Stripper Jessica Haskin's sophomoric 'attack' on suburban life, which lists 'thou shalt not get a tattoo' as one of the Ten Commandments of Suburbia tells you less about the suburbs than mainstream movies like *The Ice Storm* or *American Beauty*, and winds up feeling more conformist than the culture it attacks. Even better (or worse), Athena Douris details her attempt to produce a feminist porn mag that would humiliate men. She's now writing a monthly lesbian sex column for *FHM*. Reading *FHM* is indeed pretty humiliating, but it takes a special kind of disassociation to write a sex column for them with a feminist straight face! In the same way that these theoretical feminists wind up producing the same sort of sex stuff as the most unliberated men, *Gauntlet* itself appears to have been 'marked' for the sex industry, and it's starting to bear the same relationship to sexual reality that wrestling magazines do to their sport. Mimi Miyagi's 'I'm a Cyber Feminist' is a simple two-page plug for her various money-making enter-

REEL WILD CINEMA, No 5
32pp Aus $3
HIP POCKET SLEAZE, No 2
26pp Aus $2; John Harrison, 2 Glenbrae Court, Berwick, Victoria, Australia 3806
Two Australian fanzines from the cut-and-paste school. The first costs more and looks like shit, shoot the cover artist! Anyone old enough to remember the boom in horror fanzines during the late Eighties will think they have fallen through a time warp. *Reel Wild Cinema* is basically a review zine, detailing anything from Fulci to Hong Kong Cinema, classic B's to video slashers. Strangely, it reads like a UK-based zine, with articles on David Lynch at the Edinburgh Film Festival and many references to UK video censorship. It's all too familiar. Publisher John Harrison should concentrate more on his other zine *Hip Pocket Sleaze*, a much more mature looking publication dipping its dirty fingers into the world of trashy pulp fiction novels and art work. This has at least some constructed direction to

it and looks good, an antipodean *Sheer Filth* if you will. Dedicated to reviewing printed material, *Hip Pocket Sleaze* concentrates on the likes of Eric Stanton, Herschel Gordon Lewis (his film novelisations) and artist Dave Burke. At only $2.00, I shouldn't moan! **David Greenall**
[*John Harrison also has a mail order service comprising film memorabilia, comics and books.*]

GAUNTLET 18
$6.96 from 309 Powell Rd Springfield PA 19064 USA
The theme of this issue is 'The Feminine Mystique' and it seems to mark a continuing change of attitude for *Gauntlet*, which for a while stuck sharp teeth into censorship issues, but recently (see review of *Gauntlet*'s 'Porn in the USA' issue in HEADPRESS 18) has been more like a toothless puppy gnawing at the boner of the sex industry. The centrepiece of this issue is Justice Howard's photo-essay on 'fiery feminists'. As a photographer,

prises. In the end that's what it's all about. Money talks and bullshit walks. Susan Bremner, who writes to 'educate and promote a non-stereotypical view of women in the stripping industry' dances once a week to support herself while she strategizes and implements her 'new entrepreneurial endeavours'. Stripping may have liberated her from her own sexual hang-ups, but her livelihood still depends on exploiting the hang-ups of its audience. Will Bremner educate herself right out of a job? Will *Gauntlet* 'educate' the johns out of giving her dollar bills? On the positive side there is an update on the *Hitman* and *Natural Born Killer* cases, keeping in vague touch with the censorship issues, and Nina Hartley offers a hopeful sounding column that pleads for understanding and tolerance. Tolerance is one thing, but creating something worth the reader's interest is another. Even with Nina on board. **Michael Carlson**

BIZARRISM, No 7

40pp $5; Chris Mikul, PO Box K546, Haymarket, NSW 1240, Australia
Email: cathob@wr.com.au

The latest issue of Chris Mikul's chronicle of kooks and charlatans makes a fascinating read, with articles on the anatomy of conspiracy theory, the great rip-off of the sea-monkeys, Donald Cammell and *Performance* and the first in a series on 'My Favourite Dictators' (No 1: Ceausescu). Equally entertaining are the book reviews and illustrations, also by Mikul (check out his crazed comic-strip adaptation of AG Major's 1915 poem 'The Idiot Boy'). Dann Lennard has an illuminating piece on the Von Erich pro-wrestling family dynasty ('an obsessive father who guided five sons into wrestling only to see four of them die through drugs and/or suicide'), and there's an interesting article by James Cockington on pervy Australian sculptor Lyall Randolph. But the bulk of the work is Mikul's, which happily gives the magazine a nice coherence and unity of tone and style. Mikul has a connoisseur's eye for the uncanny coincidences and freakish details of these bizarre, neglected and not-so-charmed lives, which makes this bi-monthly publication a genuinely compelling read. **Mikita Brottman**

BIZARRISM, No 7

Details above

Bizarrism has been going since the early 1990s, but my first taste of it

was through Critical Vision's recent book of the same name [*order details on page 160!—Ed*]. If one of the purposes of good writing is to prompt the reader to dig deeper into the subject matter, then that 'best of' book succeeded. Subjects in the first new issue since then include Donald Cammell, Screaming Lord Sutch, Nicolae Ceausescu, the Von Erich wrestling family, prolific mystery author Harry Stephen Keeler, and the Tichborne Claimant, an impostorous 19th century heir who has also been the subject of a recent British film. With a few notable exceptions, Chris Mikul writes and illustrates everything in this A4 magazine, and — despite the occasional error (Edward Fox in *Performance*?) — it's a great read. *Bizarrism* may bring forth cries of 'not more Fortean stuff!' from some quarters, but, unless you're prepared to rise to the same obsessive level that Mikul obviously occupies, it's not really a valid criticism. Buy it now. **Martin Jones**

BLACKHARVEST, No 2

40pp £2.50; payable: A. Young; PO Box 292, Huddersfield, W Yorkshire, HD1 4YF

A DTP'd zine of 'Cybergothindustrialfusion', i.e. covering much the same ground as the American mag *Industrialnation* does (what have these people got against spaces between words?). This issue contains interviews with Darlingos ('Webmistress of Digital Darkness,' apparently) and bands Spahn Ranch, Faithful Dawn and Narcissus Pool. There are features on hanging (as in death penalty, not spending time with your mates!), a scene report from InFest 99, and a pretty tacky piece on murder sites in and around Huddersfield. Quite well-produced of its type, with plenty of photos — one for wannabe Trenchcoat Mafia members, potential readers of Tony White's *Satan! Satan! Satan!* (see below), and people who read in the dark using infrared glasses. Haven't you heard? Bela Lugosi's dead, but the pesky bats just won't leave the friggin' belltower! **Simon Collins**

DESIRE DIRECT

138pp, £4 or 6 issues for £10; Moondance Media Ltd, 192 Clapham High St, London SW4 7UD

While you could probably beat your meat to it, this isn't really a porn mag as such. The readers' letters seem a little fabricated, true, but cover such topics as a girl getting her boyfriend

to go with another man. That just doesn't happen in porn mags [*see the interview with Andy Darlington on page 44 for proof—Ed*]. There's also an article on the pleasures of chubby-chasing (complete with beached-whale photos), which you don't get in porn mags — not many porn mags anyway. No, *Desire Direct* is for singles and couples with an interest in sex and the erotic, hence articles on cyberporn, readers' porny poems (including, somewhat incongruously, 'Working Girl' the melancholy tale of a junkie prostitute who tops herself), David Flint on Michael Ninn, Tuppy Owens on honeypot-holing (that's fisting to you), a shit heap of contacts and a shit heap of ads. One of the ads is for Fiona Cooper's videos — she's got a better class of model these days. Some of the writing is a little prosaic, but I like this magazine; it has joyful, non-exploitative attitude towards its subject matter. **Anton Black**

HEAD, No 9
Survival

118 pp £4.95; contact: BM Uplift, London, WC1N 3XX; www.headmag.com

Our estimable near-namesake continues to go from strength to strength, benefiting in this latest issue from a new format, reducing it from A4 to an odd squarish size, which in no sense diminishes it. The theme of survival is tackled in the broadest possible sense, and the contents of *Head* 9 range from dodgy 'for-information-only' pieces on knives and guerrilla warfare techniques to serious stuff on water fluoridation, bio-diversity and ecology. Ex-TOPY dude John Eden contributes his musings on the very meaning of 'survival', eco-warrior Merrick offers 'Tribal Brain, Global Village', and other pieces tackle geodesic domes, workers' and housing co-ops, LETS (Local Exchange Trading Schemes), ibogaine therapy for addiction and alcoholism, Internet encryption, CS gas, rave culture and the maverick American book company Loompanics. Lest this all seems too, too worthy and dull, Mogg Morgan's translation of 'Tantrik Blow-Job' is entertaining, and Gyrus interviews the magnificently out-to-lunch Man-woman, last heard of (by me, anyway) in RE/Search's *Modern Primitives*, and now founder of the Friends of the Swastika network (though I must say, walking around with 200-odd swastikas tattooed on you doesn't seem like much of a survival tactic to me!). Less successful, to my mind, are the fictional pieces 'I Don't Live today (Maybe)' by X-Chris and 'No Number Zen' by AKCT (sci-fi Kung Fu skinhead Zen monks? Spare me!). Well may you hide behind pseudonyms! But overall, *Head* is an excellent read, nicely produced, good value, and an altogether recommended purchase. Issue 9 comes wrapped in a smart urban camouflage cover, making it one of the coolest magazines to pose with in trendy cafés (along with HEADPRESS, natch). **Simon Collins**

NETWORK NEWS
No 13: Secret Power of Music
No 14: Total Eclipse
24pp & 28pp, £1.50 each; 4 issue sub £5; contact: N Ayers, Earthly Delights, PO Box 2, Lostwithiel, Cornwall, PL22 0YY
Having, by a strange coincidence, actually visited Lostwithiel, I can testify to the appropriateness of something this weird and marginal coming from somewhere as remote! *Network News* is a quarterly newsletter produced by the ambient/industrial band Nocturnal Emissions. These two issues, though, contain little in the way of 'news', being instead given over to an ongoing fictional narrative set in the crusty eco-squat scene of London and elsewhere, involving cults, sacred architecture, free festivals, stone circles, witches' flying ointment, sex magick, performance art (that old urban legend about the self-amputating performance artist John Fare gets a fresh airing), civil disorder and Throbbing Gristle. It's illustrated with bizarre photographs and interspersed with shameless product placement for Nocturnal Emissions recordings and merchandise.

This is very much a personal project — how much you like it will depend on how attuned to the author's preoccupations you are. At least there is a discernible level of irony present — it's always reassuring when someone writing about this kind of heady stuff doesn't appear to take it all completely seriously. **Simon Collins**

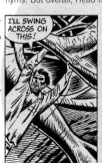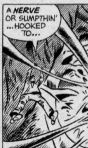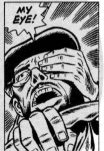

© Skyward Publishing Corp

A not-too-fantastic voyage, after all! Panels from 'The Inner Man', *Nightmare* #3. GHASTLY TERROR!

HOG, No 4
40pp £2.50; Turbodog Comix. Rik Rawling, 94 Emet Grove, Emersons Green, Bristol, BS16 7EG
Email: richard.rawling@virgin.net
At long last, here's some new *Hog*. Still as obsessed with sex and violence as they are with winding up Forbidden Planet habitues and PC nuts, issue four nonetheless contains some surprising diversions: Stephen Hawkins goes megalomaniac in John Welding's 'Philosophical Iron'; Derek Gray offers the strangely calming 'Spitzy Reinhart'; and Cat Andrew's 'A Life In The Day Of Picasso' uses a mere two pages to sum up the old beach-bum. Merchant and Ivory, take note. But some things don't need to change. Jim Boswell is still stuck deep in a pit full of porn queens from which I feel he never wants to escape, and Rik Rawling... well, Rik offers two new 'Rats Bastard' strips here, but who gives a toss about that saggy old mutant when there's delightful eye-candy like Suzi Suzuki and Wanda Wolfen to drool over (although no Jasmine Jackson this time round). Raven-haired, gun-packing, big-booted, firm-bodied; they're exactly the kind of dangerous babes you'd expect to find in your local gothic nite-spot, but never do. My favourite? Wanda. Mmmmm. One minor gripe: Rik's occasional habit of copying poses direct from his (no doubt extensive) collection of jazz

The latest page-turner from the author of *Pigs: The Homeopathic Approach to the Treatment and Prevention of Diseases* and *Goats: Homeopathic Remedies*. It's hard to see what use most HEADPRESS readers would have for this compact paperback manual of homeopathic remedies for animals, unless it's to browse through the various descriptions of 'old dogs' stools'. Like most medical encyclopedias, however, this book makes a pleasantly graphic read, made only slightly less enjoyable, perhaps, by the fact that the ailments described are suffered by animals, rather than other people. Interesting symptoms to look out for in your four-legged friends include 'catarrhal and purulent discharge occuring from the womb', 'greenish slimy diarrhoea expelled in explosive motions', 'mucous vomiting' and 'profuse black stools'. Call me a cynic, but if I were a goat in this condition I'd expect a bit more from my vet than some alfalfa root and a bowl of camomile tea. **Mikita Brottman**

More things to do with snipewort and star of bethlehem, this time to treat emotional maladies in human beings. Edward Bach, apparently, was a physician who gave up his 'big London mags. But it's only minor. How could you not love a comic that sticks a photo of Fred West's bedroom door on its back cover? Or slips in references to The Cramps, The Stooges and *Withnail & I*? The increasing diversity of *Hog* is gonna make it a force to be reckoned with. Like the song says, they got good taste. **Martin Jones**

GHASTLY TERROR!
The Horrible Story of the Horror Comics
Stephen Sennitt

224pp £13.95; Critical Vision, 1999
Order details on page 160

The world of the illustrated comic can be a troubling one. And often for all the wrong reasons, conjuring images of an overly moral universe, of caped super-heroes and flashy villains, set loose in some juvenile morality play. But back in the Seventies, some of us were infected by darker, more ambivalent material. To our peers, gorged on the above banality, such reading seemed deviant, even dangerous. We were viewed as 'Midwich Cuckoos'; sullen fanatics, seeking out these large b&w horror magazines from the States. Early exposure to this unusual brand of highly literate, visionary horror, has led to life-long changes of attitude, habit, even outlook.

Such was the power of those early Warren titles, *Creepy* and *Eerie*. And, most remarkable of all — the phenomena that were Skywald's *Nightmare*, *Psycho* and *Scream*, the inspired work of editor 'Archaic Al' Hewetson and his 'Horror-Mood' team of artists and writers.

Ghastly Terror! navigates a long-awaited journey down the dark, rotting highways and by-ways of the horror comic field. It is so refreshing to find a volume rich with the unbridled, but critical enthusiasms of a true aficionado. There is a wealth of detail and handsome illustrations here to delight the connoisseur, but this opus is not so dense as to exclude the first time adventurer. Indeed, like the very best of the comic titles themselves, the author acts as your host, welcoming and beckoning with a warm, tattered grip that will cut you to the bone. Stephen Sennitt has done us all a great service. He strikes out boldly from the well documented history of

practice' in 1936 to devote himself to preparing remedies 'amongst the wild flowers of the countryside'. This book lists various maladies identified by the good doctor, and gives the names of the plants that apparently function as remedies for them. So those suffering from 'very great hopelessness' should brew up a tincture from the hairy stalk of a gorse root, and 'those who have a feeling of uncleanliness' should ignore the soap and reach for the crab apple. And 'those who have fears of the mind giving way' should simply pluck a branch of cherry plum, boil it into a solution, dilute it with brandy and stick it in the bathroom cabinet for the next time they find themselves teetering on the brink of insanity. **Mikita Brottman**

PASTEUR EXPOSED
Germs, Genes, Vaccines, The False Foundations of Modern Medicine
Ethel Douglas Hume

Bookreal, Australias, 1989
First published 1923

This history of germ theory seeks to prove that Louis Pasteur was a plagiarist and 'monumental charlatan' who actually stole his ideas from a fellow scientist and 'ignored genius' named Pierre Jacques Antonio Bèchamp. More significantly, according to the author, Pasteur actually got it all wrong. By taking Bèchamp's discovery that homeopathy, acupuncture and holistic therapies can cure disease, and distorting it into the concept of vaccination, Pasteur has apparently caused the loss of millions of lives. This book claims that virtu-

known to humanity has been linked to vaccine damage, and there's an 'unaccountable' connection between the AIDS epidemic in Central Africa and the massive vaccination campaigns that occurred there. As a non-scientist, it's hard for me to comment on the evidence for this. And, whilst its always nice to see idols being smashed, I think Hume would have a more convincing argument had she drawn Bèchamp as less the humble savant, and Pasteur less the egomaniacal monster. **Mikita Brottman**

THE COCKROACH PAPERS
A Compendium of History and Lore
Richard Schweid

232pp £10.99; Four Walls Eight Windows, 1999; ISBN 1 56858 137 8

This is an absolute gem of a book. Even if — like me — you've got no particular affection for cockroaches this is a book that you have to read. Richard Schweid takes us an a grand tour of the cockroach world, and along the way we learn about the life and times of the cockroach, about pest exterminators, forensic pathologists dealing with cockroach infestation in dead bodies, the effects of globalisation in Mexico, the bead trade in sub-Saharan Morocco, entomologists and other scientists, cockroaches and asthma in working class children and a whole lot more. Interspersed with straight reportage (and the piece on Ciudad Juarez is especially good), are anecdotes and extracts from cockroach appearances in literature.

Having worked in the catering trade, and having lived in a Mediterranean

unless you're up close to a cockroach you just can't imagine how alien the thing is. I remember working in the kitchens of a big Victorian hospital in South London, where there was all out war between the staff and the roaches. The stock-pot in the centre of the kitchens was on day and night, home to left-over veg and always bubbling away with a nice thick vegetable stock. When the lights came on late at night the roaches used to scurry for cover. (The extra protein probably never did anyone any harm, honest.) That pales into insignificance compared to some of the infestations listed in this book. Some of the stories are enough to make all but the most ardent animal-liberationist reach for the strongest insecticide to hand. But the fact that roaches were here before us — in fact they were here about 150 million years before the dinosaurs — suggests that we're the infestation, not them. Still, most of the thousands of cockroach species seem to do fine without any contact with us at all.

Skilfully written, the writing is matched by the excellent design of the book. While the b&w photographs of roaches aren't especially stunning, the flip book showing two roaches mating is a nice touch that's cleverly done. Having read this I'm more than eager to read more of Schweid's work.

In the eyes of some people the fact that I raved about this book marked me down as a weirdo much more than confessing to a love of industrial white noise, fetishism or extreme politics. Hell, if you need an excuse to buy this book then get it for the 'yuck!' factor alone. **Pan Pantziarka** the William Gaines EC titles, into a nefarious labyrinth of precode horror from the Fifties, rarely documented until now. We enter a printed universe gone mad, a delirium of sewer-living monsters, of ultra-violent, grotesque sadism, each horror admirably rushing to top the last in terms of bloody excess.

If Skywald represent the horror comics field in its highest form — as convincingly argued by the author — it becomes no less a pleasure to peer into the Sixties sepulchre of the obscure Eerie Publications, whose weird titles achieved some new 'bottom-of-the-bloody-barrel' nadir. Their vivid cover art alone seems a triumph of vicious, absurd lunacy.

In all, this is an invaluable work which serves to resurrect the masters of the genre for fresh appraisal — those great writers and artists, by whose example we are given proof that contemporary imaginations are slack, tired and formulaic. Hell, this book could even herald some bloody, dark renaissance! Let's hope so! **Mark Farrelly**

RAPID EYE MOVEMENT
Simon Dwyer

255pp £17.95; Creation Books, 2000
ISBN 1871592690

I can still remember the first time I came across the first volume of *Rapid Eye Movement*, it felt incredible, like I'd just stumbled across something so wonderful that it couldn't be true. I grabbed the copy there and then, convinced that it was important. This was where I wanted to be, I realised. It wasn't just that the content covered areas I was already interested in (Throbbing Gristle/PTV/ToPY, industrial music, conspiracy theories etc), it was also that it was well-written, extremely intelligent and obviously a labour of love.

Years later I can remember the launch party for the third and last volume of *Rapid Eye Movement*. It was held in some dingy art space near Clerkenwell. Mr Andy Weatherall was doing his stuff, Gilbert and George were there in a corner with a couple of pretty boy minders, Stewart Home was due to spout his stuff... And where was Simon Dwyer? I was looking forward to meeting him at last. I asked one of the Creation Books crew and was told that he was in hospital. With what? My answer came a little while later when Peter Colebrook took the stage to deliver a message from Simon, in hospital with AIDS. I was

stunned. It seemed so unfair that he should be ill on a night like that.

I was never fortunate enough to meet Simon Dwyer. Jealously, selfishly, I had hoped that he would recover to continue with *Rapid Eye*. Where was volume four? I wanted so much to contribute, to add something back to a project that had given me so much. It was never to be, as Simon fell victim to the disease.

Creation Books have taken the best from those three volumes of *REM* and created a tribute edition, dedicated to Simon and his widow, Fiona. Reading back over some of those first articles I can still feel a sense of excitement, even though my interests have moved on. There is still much to be admired about it as a work. Simon's critical intelligence is clearly evident, and his passionate interest in art, creativity and the state of the world shines through. If you've never read *REM* then this must count as vital reading — primary material for anybody interested in 'industrial' culture, modern art and the state of the world. **Pan Pantziarka**

RAPID EYE MOVEMENT
Details above

REM-founder Simon Dwyer died in 1997, leaving behind a large body of writings on the political and fringe-cultural scenes. This collection, the last in the series that began in 1989, is a distillation of his final musings. Dwyer tackles well-proscribed 'outsiders' in essays and interviews that are always readable and articulate, and often bone-dry funny. Genesis P-Orridge, Burroughs, Jarman, Gilbert and George, and Warhol, are among his human artistic subjects and he makes a good stab at saying something original about all of them (not easy). The piece on Psychic TV and Genesis P-Orridge is a good primer for the uninitiated despite the callowness of Dwyer's opinion that the man has shunned fame and riches to retain his punk credibility. I should cocoa. Originality doesn't always equal mountains of sales. Dwyer hardly had a bad word to say about artists on the fringes of mass recognition, conveying respect that can spill over into obsequiousness, and, again, the pieces on P-Orridge and Gilbert and George sometimes wallow. Other pieces on human rights erosion in the UK and the extract from 'The Plague Yard', his long essay on US culture, go far to rectify his indulgences, paradoxically by in-

dulging even further. Dwyer was best when not honing-in solely on his icons. The essay on the hallucinatory properties of the Dreamachine has finally convinced me to make one and give it a go — so simple, can it really work?!

The book finishes on a disenchanted note with Dwyer regretting the lack of originality in the early Nineties cultural scene. More regrettable was that he didn't appear to be looking in the right places. He was too busy hobnobbing with Tim Leary to be busting the VR labs of Silicon Valley or Manchester's club scene. Frontier-making art and culture is always happening. To pronounce that it doesn't exist presupposes a kind of omnipresence. More ominously it's an oblique admission of jadedness; never a good thing. Leaving this aside, his final almost apocalyptic overview of the state of things in early Nineties America, nourished by awareness of his HIV-positive state, is lyrical and transcendentary. 'Cherish your questions, not your answers,' he writes at the very end.

Dwyer's subjects are all a bit respectable now, all a bit 'done' in a Channel 4/*South Bank Show* kind of way. The embrace of The Beast is wide and benevolent. Body piercers appear on afternoon chatshows. Church of the SubGenius books are available on Waterstones' shelves. If there is such a thing as fringe-mainstream, this volume is the perfect guide to its sacred cows. It may even be a proscribed text one day. **Eugene Carfax**

BODY PROBE
Mutating Physical Boundaries
David Wood (Ed.)

192pp £19.95; Creation/Velvet books, 1999; ISBN 1-84068-004-0

This fascinating volume of essays and images offers a real primer of cutting-edge information about today's cyber-fetish scene; and in this context seems light-years ahead of its obvious model, RE/Search 12: *Modern Primitives* (now amazingly over 10 years old!) and more in keeping with Mark Dery's *Escape Velocity*. In fact there's only one tired-old tat article (Alex Binnie again...) amongst a disturbing morass of mutational manifestos; the most thought-provoking of which comes from the pen of Dr Rachel Armstrong, cyborg anatomist and 'Post-Futurologist' (the last phrase is mine!). She offers the provocative weirdisms, 'Sex in Space' and 'Alien Abduction and

Fetishism'; some of the most disturbing ruminations on the outer limits of sex symbology you're likely to encounter in a long time. *Body Probe* is exciting, lively and extremely well designed — it also contains 50 colour plates, making it good value too! **Stephen Sennitt**

PILLS-A-GO-GO
A Fiendish Investigation into Pill Marketing, Art, History and Consumption
Jim Hogshire
£11.99/$16.95; Feral House

Everything you ever wanted to know about pills, from those ever useful mother's little helpers to the drug of the long distance lorry driver, slam dancer and cramming student: speed. This volume collects together such useful trivia as pill songs and book covers from the Sixties/Seventies to pill pulps and medical 'fact' books. Alongside such fascinating ephemera are numerous pieces rich in hard facts... for example, chapters on pills with multiple uses, a history of pill development, an essay on law and pills, so-called rape drugs, and a guide to pre-Viagra sex pills, amongst others. Easy to read, and comprehensively illustrated with graphics ranging from chemical molecules through to comic book style images, this book is a must-have for anybody who has ever popped anything. If you keep cookery books in the kitchen, then this is the first volume you really need to keep in the medicine cupboard. A definitive reference book. **Jack Sargeant**

PILLS-A-GO-GO
Details above

Pills-a-go-go is neither a guide to getting high nor a dreary, academic pharmacopoeia, but rather a history of pills written for unrepentant drug takers of all kinds. The concept for the book first emerged in a 22 issue zine devoted to 'Which pills worked, which pills didn't, and how they could be hacked so as not to ruin one's internal organs'. The best of this information, along with further high-dosage active ingredients, is collected here in *Pills-a-go-go*.

There is plenty of stuff on the ingestion of recreational drugs, and also genuine, registered pharmaceutical product — albeit not for the usages approved, i.e. extracting codeine from painkillers. Readers seeking new highs should find the book useful, though possibly a little too diverse,

delving as it does into many other areas, like pharmaceutical-style drug marketing. Nestling amongst the heavier articles on alternative uses for over-the-counter medicines and lists of controlled ingredients within prescribed drugs, are song lyrics about pills, lists of pill-popping celebrities, and overly cute marketing gimmicks. More radical are the sections on prescription forging, and on how to get your pharmacist to give you exactly the drugs you want.

Pills-a-go-go is well researched, detailed, stylishly laid-out and informative, with a large bibliography and a section on online reading. However, the lack of an index means the book seems stuck as a collection of writings and pictures, rather than the definitive reference work it could have been. Worse though, are the many errors which render entire sentences unreadable or illogical — consider 'Getting pills that have aspirin instead much better' from pg. 223, or 'She takes her attitude a step further when she exalts the pill to holy status she feels the drug is being profaned' from pg. 10. **Sarah Turner**

WHITMAN'S WILD CHILDREN
Portraits of 12 Poets
Neeli Cherkowski
$18/£12; South Royalton,
Vermont: Steerforth Press

Walt Whitman is a good place to begin any examination of the Beat poets. Ginsberg acknowledges his debt explicitly in his wonderful 'A Supermarket in California'. More than the sense of Whitman as gay icon, the liberating flow of his American free verse influenced Ginsberg, as well as the sense that Whitman was a man of the streets — constantly out among the public, writing about ordinary people, to the extent of visiting Civil War battlefields where he would comfort the wounded. Cherkowski's idea of a 'man of the streets', may be more an image of a proto-hippie Walt cruising the docks for willing sailors, but love beads were never a part of Whitman's image, not even when his hair was long.

Actually, Whitman is a role model for Cherkowski himself, because this book might better be subtitled 'Song of Myself'. Neeli in Wonderland, as it were, and sometimes this preoccupation with self is downright hilarious. Ginsberg's first words on meeting Cherkowski were 'You're fat'. Neeli riposted 'You're old'. He then reports,

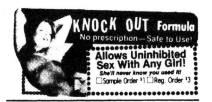

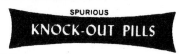

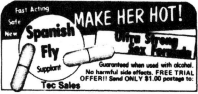

Before Viagra... Ads for questionable sexual stimulants. PILLS-A-GO-GO.

deadpan, 'Things were never smooth between us after that.' Johnson shat on Boswell from greater heights than that without creating undue bumps in the relationship road! The high point of Neeli's life appears to be when his own poetry is praised by some youngsters who mistake him for Ginsberg in his beads and buttons, or else when he beats the great man at Trivial Pursuit, which turns out to be one of Ginsberg's favourite pastimes. That's appropriate, because this really is a Beatnik Trivial Pursuit game between covers. We know the Beats have become an industry, and there is a lot of mileage in constantly recreating a neighbourhood tour of San Francisco in the late Fifties, or the Village in the Sixties. Hell, Michael McClure (one of the 12 poets discussed here), who was adept at riding the waves toward the next celebrity or grant, once wrote a book called *Scratching the Beat Surface*. That would seem deep by Neeli's standards. Critically, Neeli lets it all flow over him. He makes no bones in refusing to make critical distinctions about Harold Norse. He is overcome by the *faux* sentimentality of Jack Micheline — he just gives up and lets it wash over him. When he's asked to review John Wieners' *Selected Poems*, he's overcome with emotion, yet actually his take on this unjustly neglected poet is probably the best in the book. And it's nice to see attention paid again to people like Philip Lamantia.

Otherwise, there is better stuff out there on the major subjects: Ginsberg, Ferlinghetti and Bukowski. Neeli says Buk 'didn't buy the Eisenhower Fifties, didn't buy the Kennedy Sixties' but misses the point: that was when he did his best writing, and when he did buy into the Reagan Eighties, he lurched into self-parody. Of course, self-parody is a staple of the Beats, and Gregory Corso's ever-inventive riffs are the other highlight here. Corso tells him: 'I'm the elder now. A daddy. You who do so love the Gregory got the goodie gumdrops from me.' Then Neeli, calling him a pied piper, marches off with Corso through the streets of North Beach, reminding me of nothing so much as a happy hamster. The other link to Whitman, which Neeli ignores, is that Walt was a major league mama's boy, sleeping at the foot of her bed long into adulthood. This is a theme that runs through the Beat poets, most notably Kerouac. And so with Neeli. When he takes 250mg of bad acid in 1978 what does he do? He calls mom, and she advises him to find Lawrence Ferlinghetti, who's sitting in a café reading the *New York Times*. Far out. Maybe Neeli's mom could have drawn us a better map, that would've got us to Ferlinghetti sometime before disco became king. **Michael Carlson**

CRASH
Iain Sinclair
£6.99; BFI Publishing; ISBN 085170719X
As Iain Sinclair makes clear in this slim but interesting little book, *Crash* exists not as a single work by Ballard, but as a sequence of projects that have mutated and evolved over time. *Crash* exists as a set of works by Ballard, as an exhibition piece, as a documentary, as a film by David Cronenberg and now as a series of essays by Sinclair. This abundance of works, over-lapping in terms of media, time and intent are ably uncovered by Sinclair. With an almost surgical precision he delves into *Crash* to reveal the different agendas at work in its various incarnations. Sinclair's critical intelligence posits Cronen-

berg's film as a work that obscures Ballard's subversive fictions. He makes it clear that the film is a re-writing of Ballard. And, just as persuasively, he shows us that the film is a necessary step for Cronenberg, according him the critical respect that his earlier films did not garner. *Crash* was an inevitable and logical progression from *Naked Lunch*.

With this as a central thesis Sinclair also examines JG Ballard and James Ballard — the blurring of fact and fiction, author and fictional creation, is a central theme of Ballard's work. *Empire of the Sun* and *The Kindness of Women* are written as a means to an end, according to Sinclair. Ballard writes Ballard in order to recast himself — to control the picture of the man and the myth.

Anyone who seeks to understand Ballard needs to read this book. It is the most incisive and interesting commentary on him to date. And, one has to ask, what of the hidden themes that underlie Sinclair's *Crash*? Just as Ballard and Cronenberg seek to change or control public perceptions, so too does Sinclair. This book is as much a part of the uncovering of London — in particular the relationship between the urban and the suburban — as it is about Cronenberg's not very interesting film.

I look forward to seeing where Sinclair takes us next. **Pan Pantziarka**

YOUR VIGOR FOR LIFE APPALLS ME
Robert Crumb Letters 1958-1977
£9.99/$14.95; 250pp; Fantagraphics Books, 1998; ISBN 1-56097-310-2
All the letters in this collection were written by Robert Crumb to his close friends, Marty Phalls and Mike Britt, both of whom shared Crumb's passions for life and art. Crumb talks of his family ('...Max lives alone in San Francisco. Lives on welfare and is a weirdo-hermit who eats sparingly and never does anything for pleasure'), music ('... the more I hear of early blues records, the more I like them'), everyday life ('I'm now making a feeble attempt to get a job') and art ('Haven't made any friends in school... There isn't anybody interested in cartoons...'). Unlike many autobiographical works where events and opinions are conveniently mis-remembered or omitted, Crumb's letters are largely un-edited, and it is gratifying to discover that Robert in

1977 is still very much the same person he was in 1958. *Your Vigor for Life Appalls Me* is an attractive and compelling book (which unusually for this kind of work, contains an index) and — unlike the usually perceived image — reveals a surprisingly self-assured Mr Crumb. **Sun Paige**

CONFUSION INCORPORATED
A Collection of Lies, Hoaxes & Hidden Truths
Stewart Home
224pp £7.95; Codex, 1999
ISBN 1-899598-11-1
The cover and blurb of *Confusion Incorporated* centres around Stewart Home's piece in *The Big Issue* that suggested ex-KLFer Jimmy Cauty kept a comfortable arsenal of weapons at his Devon home. It's the most clear-cut hoax in the book. As I know cock-all about modern art, philosophy, or whiskey, articles related to these subjects mean nothing to me. But, for provincial bumpkins (such as myself), there's some great stuff amongst the interviews, travelogues and lecture notes collected here: 'How To Be An Art Tart' seems to be aimed specifically at *Guardian* readers; the 'Royal Watch' columns paint our favourite inbreds as drug-dealing occultists; and 'Dennis Cooper Does Drugs' (from HEADPRESS 17), in which Home attempts to guide the tripping cult novelist around Jack the Ripper murder sites, manages to be both depressing and hilarious. Of the interviews, the best are with ex-Art Attacks members Steve Spear and Edwin Pouncey ('we went all over the place to promote that *Streets* album, mostly Yorkshire'), and Laurence James — aka Mick Norman — author of the classic NEL 'Hell's Angels' quartet from the early 1970s. James makes you nostalgic for the days when it was possible to knock out a novel in a couple of weeks in order to pay the rent. The working methods of 'hacks' such as himself (165 books in 20 years!) and Peter Cave put today's 600-page-plus bloated 'serious' novelists to shame. The excellent interview is the highlight of a book where some articles (hoaxes?) went so far over my head that they carried passports. However, if I ever happen to find myself at an art premiere, literary event, or, godforbid, dinner party, then Stewart Home — a self-confessed worshipper at the shrine of his own image — is exactly the kind of gatecrasher I'd want around. **Martin Jones**

SEX AND ROCKETS
The Occult World of
Jack Parsons

John Carter

£15.99 $24.99; h/bk; Feral House, 1999
ISBN 0922915-56-3

'John Carter' is the Edgar Rice Burroughs-inspired pseudonym of American occult researcher, Paul Rydeen, who has a background in the more lightweight or popular end of this subject-matter via appearances in a multitude of small-press UFO/Fortean magazines and booklets. However, *Sex And Rockets* is lightyears away from the home-made atmosphere of such publications (just as one would expect from a publisher like Feral House) sporting a colour dust jacket wrapped over a nicely produced hardback, with sewn-in binding and quality paper. Pity, then, that the content of the book is still so amateurish and 'light' in tone, offering few real insights into a character as complex as Parsons. 'Carter' just seems happy to write-off this pioneering rocket scientist, poet, and Thelemic magician as a naïve, moody failure with a mother-fixation, and he leaves all the more complex occult ramifications to 'hardcore' researchers such as Kenneth Grant and Michael Staley. This is a shame, because the author had a golden opportunity here to extend our understanding of Parsons who's still a relatively obscure figure in 'underground culture'. Instead, 'Carter' offers a rather bland, colourless account of Parsons' dual career; touching all the bases, but only in the most desultory and totally lacking in any insightful arrangement of the obviously voluminous and painstaking research notes he must have assembled. **Stephen Sennitt**

BROTHERHOODS OF FEAR

Paul Elliott

255pp £18.99; h/bk, Blandford

Brotherhoods of Fear is a book that promises much more than it delivers. In looking at such diverse groups as the KKK and the Red Army Faction, one would hope that Elliott would apply some kind of theoretical or psychological framework to link the different groups together. Instead we get the sketchiest kind of definition imaginable, which boils down to the fact that these groups are (a) violent and (b) they don't give a toss what the rest of the world thinks of them. If that sounds like a Readers Digest view of the world then you'd not be far off the

mark. There's a bias here, of course. Given the author's hazy definition of what constitutes 'a brotherhood of fear' (and hey, don't a lot of these groups have women in them?), it's no surprise that he doesn't include such vicious and violent brotherhoods as the SAS and the Metropolitan Police. But of course, they're alright because they're on the 'right' side of the law. What this leads to is a survey of a number of different, unconnected groups and it attempts to offer some degree of insight into their histories and motivations. And it's a pretty mixed bag, starting with the Inquisi-

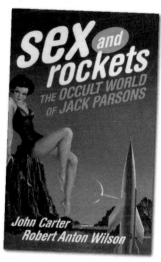

tion and the medieval witch-burnings and ending with Aum Shinrikyo's poison attack on the Tokyo subway. Along the way we meet 19th Century Anarchists, the Mafia, British neo-Nazis, Baader-Meinhof, the Klan and more. In each case we get a smattering of history, some facile analysis and then we're off onto the next group.

There's little depth here, and no understanding of the ideologies which underpin these disparate groups. For example the section on Anarchists focuses on Anarchists as lone assassins and ruthless bombers. There's no mention of Anarchism as a mass movement or as a coherent ideology, and no mention of the Russian Revolution or the Spanish Civil War. The author doesn't even mention the phrase 'propaganda by deed', which even the most cursory research on 19th Century Anarchism would have turned up.

The treatment of Anarchists is indicative of the whole book, which is superficial, poorly researched and likely

to appeal to people who find long words problematic. If you're interested in any of the groups included in *Brotherhoods of Fear* then take my advice and seek out something better.
Pan Pantziarka

LUCIFER RISING
Sin, Devil Worship and
Rock'n'Roll

Gavin Baddeley

256pp £12.99; Plexus, 1999
ISBN 0-85965-280-7

This is something of a departure for Plexus, a company which usually publishes books on relatively mainstream stars of popular culture. More surprisingly, it's an entirely sympathetic treatment, and an enormously entertaining read. Looking much like an old issue of HEADPRESS, with a backprinted motif of a woodcut demon recurring throughout and a b&w illustration on virtually every page, the book is broken into three sections: the history of Satanism, Satanism in 20th Century culture, and the Satanic millennium. The book's not really exhaustive enough to work as a general overview — hardly any films are mentioned, and there's not much of an account of Satan as a literary figure past Baudelaire. This is fair enough as each of these areas is worth a book in its own right. Where the author really has done his work, however, is with Satanic music, in a far broader sense than *Lords of Chaos*, although the two do intersect at times. I don't know much about the current state of 'black metal', but this seems to be a pretty solid account of Satanic imagery and beliefs in bands from the Stones and Black Sabbath through to Cradle of Filth, through backmasking scandals, Satanic ritual abuse hysteria and electronic industrial bands. As you might expect, some bands see it as a gimmick, a marketing tool, while others are more grimly serious about their relationship to the Hornèd One. One thing all the bands have in common is the same cheesy gothic look. Surely if you've done a deal with the devil you can look better than that? But Baddeley doesn't raise the issue with his interviewees, probably realising that types like Count Grishnackh ('If I, for example, murdered a person, I could steal his aura and add it to mine, so I would get a more powerful aura') and Danzig ('If the situation happened right here where I had to cut your throat, I would do it') wouldn't take too kindly to comments about their sartorial elegance.

There's also an informative and entertaining history of Satanic organisations, from the Hellfire Club to the Order of the Nine Angles. LaVeyan Satanism is gone into in some detail, with lengthy interviews with LaVey himself and other pretenders to the throne. The interviews with contemporary groups (Baddeley covers some which are not explicitly Satanic) reveal a disturbing if well-documented trend in modern occultism — the celebration not only of the imagery of the Third Reich but also of its ideology. In a way this seems to be both a reaction against the cosiness of established organisations such as the Church of Satan or Michael Aquino's Temple of Set — they're just not evil enough — and a deliberate attempt to bait the liberal media. A number of the interviewees give evasive answers when asked about ritual sacrifice. LaVey's take on all this? To advise his followers to become 'Jewish Nazis'. To his credit, Baddeley doesn't skirt round the issues involved here. He doesn't attempt to censor the voices of anyone involved, and nor does he justify or condemn. This kind of objective approach to such an emotive topic is rare and extremely welcome. While I would have welcomed more on the contemporary occult scene and less on black metal bands — a few of the interviewees in the latter category are virtually indistinguishable — I can't fault Baddeley's research or his approach. Highly recommended.
James Marriott

COME PLAY WITH ME
The Life and Films of
Mary Millington
244pp £14.99; FAB Press, 1999
ISBN 0-9529260-7-5

Mary Millington was a sexual and lifestyle icon for her generation, but this porn-star, model, kleptomaniac and libertarian killed herself after being arrested for a little shoplifting. Unlike the 'turncoat' Linda Lovelace who changed her ways and protested innocence after porn had made her famous, Mary had no such regrets or hang-ups. According to contemporary reports she genuinely felt that full-on porn should be legalised so, unlike many porn-star suicides, sexual guilt did not defeat her — harassment by the authorities did. In addition to her shoplifting problem, she also owed a fortune to the tax-man. Easily one third of Come Play with Me comprises

Mary's filmography; walk-on parts, starring roles, and contemporary reviews. The most interesting bits are about Mary the person, her friends, family, animals and attitudes. She was happily bisexual and overtly promiscuous (though she was outraged when friend Diana Dors requested Mary have sex with her son to check if he was gay). Even if you're not a fan of Mary, this book is a colourful and well-written peek into the world of Seventies British porn, discussing many of the unsung 'heroes' — like composer David Whitaker, and poster artist Tom Chantrell — as well as those whose faces graced the big screen (Bernie Winters among them).
Sun Paige

THE ALFRED HITCHCOCK STORY
Ken Mogg
192pp £29.99; h/bk; Titan Books, 1999
ISBN 1-84023-091-6

The majority of *The Alfred Hitchcock Story* is devoted to chronological film-by-film coverage, offering a synopsis of each, critique and plenty of rare stills and posters. A companion piece to Titan's earlier *The Hammer Story*, this hardback carries forward the same lovely production values, splitting Hitchcock's career into convenient, easily digestible segments (from 'The Early Years 1899-1933' through to the 'Languishing 1965-1980'). Along with the film coverage there's info on the director's cameo appearances (what Hitchcock book would be complete without them?), radio work, unrealised projects and the novels he (even posthumously) lent his name to. I preferred *The Hammer Story* but that in no way is intended to belittle this fine volume. **Sun Paige**

THE ENCYCLOPEDIA OF WESTERN GUNFIGHTERS
Bill O'Neal
386pp £12.50; Pimlico

Bill O'Neal is a quick draw when it comes to shooting down reputations. His encyclopedia describes Wyatt Earp as a 'Farmer, section hand, buffalo hunter, horse thief, saloonkeeper, gambler, bunco artist, sportsman, law officer, and prospector.' Roughly in that order, though not necessarily consecutively. O'Neal is one of those who considers the Gunfight at the OK Corral a case of premeditated murder by the Earps and Doc Holliday; he implies Earp's two other killings, revenging the assassination of his

brother Morgan, were murder as well. O'Neal doesn't suggest Earp was responsible for the mysterious death of Johnny Ringo, found under a tree with his boots off, shot through the head, but it's clear that debunking the mythology of western novels and movies is O'Neal's business, and business is booming. Thus America's West becomes a farce of drunken con-men, petty thieves, and greedy ne'er-do-wells, skulking about dirty little towns occasionally shooting someone in the back if they got drunk enough or if the perceived insult was bad enough. You start to think the amazing thing is any civilization at all emerged from what appears to be absolute chaos. Then you realise what has emerged is a country filled with cities like Atlanta. Indeed, the big difference is that the towns aren't quite so dirty, the demarcation lines for the bad sides of town are drawn even more sharply today, and of course, the weaponry is more sophisticated.

It's lucky for gunfighters that western firearms were nowhere near as accurate or reliable as portrayed in the movies. Even a direct hit from a pistol ball was not necessarily fatal. One of the best lines in this book refers to Billy Breakenridge: 'In 1881 he shot Curly Bill Brocius in the mouth, thereby persuading Curly Bill to hang up his guns.' Indeed, the quicksilver skills of gunmen turn out, inevitably, to be somewhat exaggerated. When John Armstrong arrested John Wesley Hardin, Armstrong was already walking with a cane because he'd shot himself in an accident. Despite having Armstrong's gun levelled at him, Hardin drew his own and might have killed the lawman, had his pistol's hammer not become caught in his braces.

Many of the west's leading figures, from Billy the Kid on down, actually hailed from the East. I discovered two gunmen from my home state of Connecticut, a long way from the West. One, Mysterious Dave Mather was rumoured to be a descendant of Cotton Mather, the fiery fundamentalist preacher. There was nothing very mysterious about Dave, but gunfighters did get good nicknames. Texas Jack Vermillion was called Texas Jack because he came from Virginia. In Britain, he'd have been called 'Vermsy'. Texas John Slaughter would be 'Slaughters.'

Henry Plummer deserved a colourful nickname, but never got one. He was a baker elected City Marshal, and in the final year of his term, a man named John Vedder caught Plummer in bed with Mrs Vedder. When he ordered Plummer to leave, the Marshal shot him dead. He was sentenced to 10 years in prison, but was pardoned after a year. A year later he killed a man in a whorehouse fight. The next year he killed a man who made fun of his Yankee accent. Eventually Plummer was shot in the arm while laying in wait with a shotgun to ambush a sheriff. The sheriff quit the West, while Plummer taught himself to shoot left-handed.

This is an invaluable book to anyone interested in the origins of modern American killers. You can argue a direct line, say, from Jesse James coming out of Quantrill's guerrillas in the Civil War, to the Bonnie & Clydes of the 1930s, and from there the line is easy to follow through the mythology which grows up around killers. Perhaps through O'Neal's eyes it all seems funny after a century has passed, but even the art of our greatest westerns, the films of John Ford, or Budd Boetticher, or Sergio Leone, or Sam Peckinpah, pales in the face of the black comedy of the West as it really was. **Michael Carlson**

HIGH ART
A History of the
Psychedelic Poster
Ted Owen & Denise Dickson
176pp $30.00; Sanctuary Publishing, 1999
ISBN 1-86074-256-4

FUCKED UP & PHOTOCOPIED
Instant Art of the
Punk Rock Movement
Bryan Ray Turcotte &
Christopher T. Miller
240pp $35.00; Gingko Press, 1999
ISBN 1-58423-000-2

These two books should reside next to each other on one's book shelf. Invaluable collections of paper ephemera, from the psychedelic posters of the Sixties, through the flyers of the late Seventies and early Eighties punk/hardcore scene of certain cities, and the musical denizens thereof. Essential for anyone interested in the paper trail left by the youth culture of the late 20th century.

High Art will warm the heart of the most wizened afficianado of psychedelic posters and art. The posters reproduced (all in color and many full page) range from the Art Nouveau influences of Jan Troop, Beardsley, Klimt etc to their Sixties' counterparts

who took things even further towards Surrealism and Symbolism. The text is well written and informative and even covers such topics as the artwork on sheets of blotter acid. It is mind blowing and it is a trip!

Starting with the earliest work of the nuculei of San Fran artists (Wes Wilson, Alton Kelly, Stanley Mouse, Rick Griffin and Victor Moscoso — all of whom have biographical sections), an historic overview of origins is given. Individual artists and poster companies are profiled throughout. Lesser known artists and their work are also represented. The book is basically in three parts, the first concerning the US, the second the UK (which covers OZ magazine, the UFO Club and Big O Poster company, also with individual artists profiled) and the third, a chapter on the 'New Wave' of poster/flyer artists such as Frank Kozik, Alan Forbes and the 'Coop', amongst others. The Appendix is about collecting the posters themselves — if one has enough time and money. If not, this book is the next best thing and well worth the price.

Fucked Up & Photocopied is a 180 degree turn in the direction of the punk/hardcore scene and the multitude of 'instant art' flyers it spawned, some deliberately crude yet others coming close to their Sixties forerunners in innovation and talent. Fleeting, ephemeral, timeless, surreal street trash that covered the telephone poles, walls and gutters across the US. This book is page after page of full color flyer reproductions, the chapters breaking them down by cities and sections of the country. Some of the flyers would not be of much interest by themselves, but they have been arranged and juxtaposed, many to a page with added background graphics and text to make a most aesthetic whole. Featured are artists like the always enigmatic and interesting Raymond Pettibon(e) of Black Flag flyer fame; in addition someone who went by the name of 'Pushead', and some early Kozik are here, along with the unknown and anonymous. Some of the bands heavily represented by these flyers are Dead Kennedys, Black Flag, Weirdos, X, Misfits, Fear, and Circle Jerks. A lot of the images are bizarre and extreme, as per the music they advertise.

The youth cultures that these two books encapsulate seem at once very different and closely linked. The psychedelic posters taking time,

thought and care to create and print, were made to be looked at over and over again, at length. The flyers of the punk/hardcore scene were, in many cases, literally 'instant art', quickly done and cheaply printed (or Xeroxed). More often than not they were black ink on colored paper, made to be handed out, tacked up and thrown in the street. But where High Art and Fucked Up & Photocopied come together is in the combination of the newly aquired freedom of youth in the later half of the 20th Century, and the advent of the technology to express it. **Tom Brinkmann**

AMOK FIFTH DISPATCH
Sourcebook of the Extremes
of Information
Stuart Swezey (Ed.)
561 £14.99/$19.95; Amok, 1999
ISBN 1-878923-12-9

Snowdomes — those tacky souvenir panoramas in Perspex bubbles which, at the flick of the wrist, become pretty snowy winterscapes. Except they weren't always that tacky and their history is often intriguing. Dating back to the 1800s, some snowdomes are intricate pieces of art, while some others (made in Hong Kong) were banned in the 1960s for having untreated, polluted water inside.

Snowdomes by Nancy McMichael is just one of the many fascinating books featured in Amok Fifth Dispatch. A random flick through this tome's pages reveals other esoteric delights, like The Prisons (a book of 'grandly brooding etchings depicting imaginary prisons executed between 1743 and 1745 by the frustrated Italian architect Giovanni Battista Piranesi'), Amputees and Devotees ('scholarly study of female victims of lost limbs and the men who eroticize them'), and Countering the Conspiracy to Destroy Black Boys (which 'describes how African-American boys are systematically programmed for failure').

Continuing where Amok's own Fourth Dispatch of some years ago left off — but ditching the pulp look for superior paper stock and a more pleasing layout — Fifth Dispatch still doesn't offer much by way of a critique of any of its entries. Many titles are represented with an extract from the book's own publicity blurb, and in some particularly vague instances no text at all appears other than title, author and publisher details. Although Amok no longer claim to be the mail order source for this material, Fifth Dispatch remains to all intents a sales catalogue, albeit one that has mutated out of all natural proportions. But I'm not really complaining, I haven't actually used it to source anything but have spent many a happy hour leafing though its pages, delighting in the sheer diversity and wealth of material covered... which is illustrated with plenty of contentious images. And if you turn the book upside down it snows. Only kidding.

FRAGMENTS OF FEAR
An Illustrated History of British Horror Films
Andy Boot
288pp £14.95; Creation, 2000
ISBN 1-84068-055-5

A welcome reissue of *Fragments of Fear*, in which author Boot chronicles British horror cinema with plenty of anecdotal asides. One of the major drawbacks of the original edition has been addressed with this reprint, and filmmaker Norman J Warren — hitherto completely absent from Boot's original overview — gets an appendix devoted to him and his work. This is what differentiates the book from its previous incarnation.

Joe Scott Wilson

THE ESSENTIAL MONSTER MOVIE GUIDE
A Century of Creature Features on Film, TV and Video
Stephen Jones
448pp £16.99; Titan 1999
ISBN 1-85286-935-6

There have been many encyclopedias devoted to horror film. This one's a little more genre specific (monsters only) but still manages to turn in a wide selection of foreign language obscurities, some British obscurities (lacking in most US-centric guides), recent TV series (like *Poltergeist The Legacy* and *Eerie Indiana*) and plenty of fresh movie minutiae. Hardcore porn cash-ins, sitcoms and old cartoon shows also feature. For instance, who's ever heard of the Japanese/US co-production *The King Kong Show*? This mid-Sixties animated series for children contained characters designed by Jack Davis, and 'features the once-mighty 60-foot ape as a 'loveable' hero who teams up with Professor Bond, his son Bobby and daughter Susan to battle evil scientist Dr Who'. While episodes from *The Young Ones* ('Nasty'), *F Troop* ('V is for Vampire') and *The Muppet Show*

(starring Vincent Price) might seem a little leftfield for a monster movie guide, their inclusion does liven up the proceedings. Together with it having rather more credit info than most books of this ilk (seemingly in favour of actual 'comment' at times), *The Essential Monster Movie Guide* is deserving of a place on the cineaste bookshelf.

A TASTE OF BLOOD
The Films of HG Lewis
Christopher Wayne Curry
252pp £16.95; Creation, 2000
ISBN 1-871592-91-7

God bless Creation. Presumably richer than Midas due to a certain Mancunian rock band, they use their wealth wisely. This marvelous little outfit publishes interesting and erudite titles on overlooked cinematic talents, talents that Faber are unlikely to touch without the use of asbestos gloves.

Talents like HG Lewis. Visceral auteur Lewis has been ripe for literary reappraisal for some time now. Despite and because of the nauseating trend towards retrokitsch culture, he has been both rediscovered and ridiculed afresh. What your average flares-wearing irony-enslaved twat doesn't realise though is that Lewis made great films. *2000 Maniacs*, *Wizard Of Gore*, *The Gore Gore Girls* will all stand the test of time long after *Independence Day* and other shite made with a million times the money Lewis had have been discarded to the cinematic dustbin.

So it was with some eagerness that I started this tome. And with much disgust that I put it down. I had been hoping for an intelligent analysis of Lewis' movies, with a little cultural context thrown in *a la* Jack Stevenson (or at least Jack Sargeant). And what did I get? A fucking *fanzine*.

> I COULD HAVE DIED. I NEVER THOUGHT I WOULD ACTUALLY SPEAK WITH HIM... SEVERAL MILLION ENDORPHINS WERE SUDDENLY RELEASED IN MY BRAIN. I WAS EUPHORIC.

Author Curry is too hopelessly infatuated with his subject to be able to produce a probing, objective book. Plus, he's a crap writer. In all fairness, he does admit as much at the start of the book (which is quite endearing), and his research is impressive [*Not so impressive when one realises much of it is drawn from The Amazing Herschell Gordon Lewis by Dan-*

iel Krogh & John McCarty, the out-of-print status of which was the inspiration *for Curry's own Lewis project!— Ed*]. *A Taste of Blood* stands as a solid factual reference tome. If you found it as a b&w photocopied tipsheet and paid a few quid for it you'd be happy. But it's certainly not a book worth paying a disgraceful *seventeen quid* for. I've changed my mind about Creation — bollocks to them for such shameful money grubbing. If they want to charge this much they could have at least got someone in to write some actual *criticism* on top of Curry's collated facts (and filled in many blank spaces while they were at it). But no. The author is so puppy doggish in his adoration of everybody that ever walked past a HGL set (check out the fawning interviews) that the book amounts to little more than *Hello!* with intestines.

There are some amazing ad mats, and the reader is left with sense of the here-today-gone-tomorrow/wing-and-a-prayer excitement of such filmmaking, but it's not nearly *enough*. What a frustrating book. A book I really wanted to like. There is no reason HGL shouldn't merit the sort of first-rate job recently done by Stephen Thrower on Fulci (*Beyond Terror*). When that Lewis book comes out I daresay it'll be courtesy of FAB, not Creation, and will probably cost less than this arse-kissing festival.

Anton Black

PORNOCOPIA
Porn, Sex, Technology and Desire
Laurence O'Toole
416pp £9.99; Serpent's Tail, 1999
ISBN 1-85242-720-5

'Porning' is how Laurence O'Toole defines the growing trend of sexualising the look and content of many mainstream magazines — a trend which has increased dramatically these recent years. While this itself may not be a bad thing, the editorial hypocrisy concerning pornography evidenced in many of these same titles is. People may be more open with regard to matters of sex, but there remains a stigma attached to pornography and its use. Look across any newsagent rack and you'll be hard pushed to spot a magazine — regardless of its content — that doesn't feature a bikini-clad babe on the cover displaying her ample charms. Hardly in a position to deny that sex sells (or that they're selling it), look *too* hard however and you're liable to fall into the sad, raincoat category, so regularly vilified in those same pages. Where does the boundary of sexual 'coolness' and social acceptability finish, and where does the 'sad wanker' start? Is the boundary governed by the revenue sex generates for these publications?

An article in one mainstream publication proposed to be an investigation of video porn, conducted by a male and female journalist, who together endured a marathon hardcore video-viewing session. The result was obvious cock-a-snoop stuff and the marathon viewing session understandably was not very arousing for the intrepid viewers. In the one instance when the journalists admit to the stirrings of arousal, they immediately pull themselves into check and laugh it off.

And that, in a nutshell, is the dilemma that is pornography: something that we don't want to be seen looking at or enjoying.

This updated edition of *Pornocopia* contains a new chapter, covering porn's many developments since the book was first published in 1998. With a refreshing British vantage point that also takes in the phenomena of softcore sex mags and the necessity of buying hardcore under the counter, *Pornocopia* comes highly recommended. [*Laurence O'Toole was interviewed in* HEADPRESS 19.]

ALL I NEED TO KNOW ABOUT FILMMAKING I LEARNED FROM THE TOXIC AVENGER
The Shocking True Story of Troma Studios
Lloyd Kaufman & James Gunn
336pp $14; Berkley Boulevard, 1998
ISBN 0-425-16357-1

Troma are the independent film company responsible for dumping such charmless no-budgeters as *Bride of the Killer Nerd* and *Surf Nazis Must Die!* onto the world. Often, the most exciting thing about a Troma movie is its title. They deal almost exclusively in tasteless movies full of juvenile sight gags, shoddy effects, and a cost-cutting veneer that makes the lowliest Monogram picture sparkle in comparison. But the company hit paydirt with *The Toxic Avenger*, a movie which played up to the 'cheapness' as if it was some kind of artistic statement. It followed the story of a hideously deformed mop-carrying superhero with a no-nonsense ultra-violent attitude

towards lawbreakers. Should you be thinking Christopher Reeve and *Superman* right now, well, don't. The Toxic Avenger isn't out to save the world from any single-minded, power crazed megalomaniac — his crooks are smack heads, happy to drive repeatedly over a child for kicks, rape blind girls and shoot guide dogs. As wholesome as that might sound, *The Toxic Avenger* managed to spawn not one, but two sequels, and Toxie himself became a Marvel comicbook hero and a syndicated cartoon character for kids, with his own TV show (for which the name was changed from Toxic Avenger to Toxic *Crusader*, should any little viewers go insane and become demented vigilantes).

One of the co-founders of Troma is Lloyd Kaufman, a roving publicity package with a self-styled 'wacky' personality. One glimpse at *All I Need to Know About Filmmaking*, Kaufman's book on the story of Troma, and you'll want to throw it quickly down again, on account of his big stupid face leering right back from the cover — as it does again several times throughout the book. Bracing yourself against the 'zany' mug shots and silly asides, you might care to delve a little further and decide that the story Kaufman has to tell isn't uninteresting. Indeed, parts of it are very interesting and sometimes quite funny. Read how Kaufman's first big break into film work came via porn movies, notably *A Dirty Western* (thankfully, not in front of the camera), and an early student film of his co-starred Lynn Lowry, the ingenue who was to become a minor cult figure through her appearances in *Shivers*, *The Crazies* and *I Drink Your Blood*.

In a section discussing the making of the film *Troma's War*, Kaufman admits to being genuinely surprised that people were offended at the concept of 'The AIDS Brigade', one of the fighting teams he had scripted, and around

whom a 'rape joke' had been constructed.

Troma's War is Kaufman's favourite Troma movie. *Big Gus, What's the Fuss?*, on the other hand, is one that Kaufman would rather forget. Following a conversation with a guy called Ami, who guarantees that his idea for a film will return an original investment ten-times over, Kaufman travelled to Israel to shoot *Big Gus, What's the Fuss?* This supposed 'family film' which, Kaufman recalls, concerned 'a pudgy Israeli running from place to place in Tel Aviv', was filmed in both English and Hebrew, and starred people of no acting capability who in real-life refused to communicate with one another. Ami effectively hired himself as co-director but promptly disappeared when the film was over, leaving no trace of the big money backers he promised would be funding the movie. Kaufman and Troma partner Michael Herz were left broke with a film no one wanted. Their only option? To try and rent the Hebrew language print to synagogues around America. Only one synagogue actually took the film, but after screening it refused to pay the $100 rental fee, accusing Kaufman and Herz of being a 'disgrace to Jews'.

Beneath the kooky façade, Kaufman

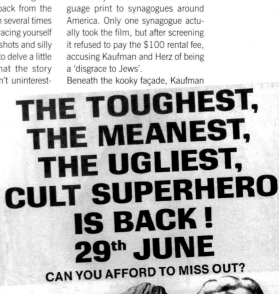

comes over as though he could be a likeable and conscientious kind of guy. He makes some interesting points as to why mainstream movies like *Forrest Gump* and *Pretty Woman* have a far greater corrupting influence on audiences than *Blood Sucking Freaks* (despite the latter being the one film in the Troma library that Kaufman is queasy about distributing), and he states in writing that a McDonald's restaurant which opened next door to the Troma office brought with it rats.

STRUWWELPETER
Fearful Stories & Vile Pictures
To Instruct Good Little Folks
Heinrich Hoffmann
Illustrated by Sarita Vendetta
178pp $24; Feral House, 1999
ISBN 0-922915-52-0

In the autumn of 1844, a respectable bourgeois doctor in Frankfurt named Heinrich Hoffmann went shopping for a picture book to give to his three-year-old son Carl for Christmas, but he was disappointed by what was on offer — all the children's books available seemed too sentimental, preachy and didactic. So he sat down to write and illustrate his own, and the result, *Struwwelpeter*, was published to great acclaim in 1845. Although out of fashion now, it has been one of the world's most perennially popular children's books, and a constant source of fascination to psychiatrists.

For what makes *Struwwelpeter* remarkable is the high level of sadistic violence displayed in both pictures and text. As the psychoanalyst Wilhelm Stekel dolefully observed in his classic monograph *Sadism and Masochism* (and he had *Struwwelpeter* specifically in mind): 'It seems to give adults satisfaction to tell children cruel and gruesome stories.' In a typical poem (the stories are all written in doggerel), a child commits some offence, frequently trivial, for which a hideous and completely disproportionate retribution is exacted. Thus, Romping Polly plays a little more boisterously than a good girl ought, after being warned against it by her aunt. She promptly breaks her leg, and is crippled for life. Augustus refuses to eat soup, and starves to death in an improbable five days. Pauline plays with matches, watched by her horrified pussy-cats, Minz and Maunz — predictably, she catches light and is incinerated. In a delicious last image, the cats are seen quenching her ashes with a flood of tears. Cruel Paul is a seriously disturbed child. He tortures and mutilates any animal he can lay his hands on. Yet his punishment is no worse than that of the lesser transgressors. Most memorably and terrifyingly, perhaps, young Conrad is warned against sucking his thumb. Of course, he continues sucking, and in comes a 'long, red-legged scissor-man'…

CRUCIFY ME AGAIN
Mark Manning
(aka Zodiac Mindwarp)
224pp £8.95; ISBN-1 899598-14-6; Codex Books, PO Box 148, Hove, BN3 3DQ
www.codexbooks.co.uk
codex@codexbooks.co.uk

I've been waiting for this book for over 13 years now, ever since I heard Zod's 1987 hit single 'Prime Mover' and realised for the first time that I wasn't alone in this howlingly mad world. It came with an accompanying video full of space god rock Stormtroopers, teenage slutvixens and exploding nun heads that was *so close* to my dreams that it was frightening. The lyrics, the Sven Hassel imagery, and the knowingly adolescent celebration of the female sex's base appeal was a White Dwarf dense compression of every potent visual stimulant from my childhood, *Warlord* comics, Paul Raymond magazines and Motorhead album covers. It truly fucking blew my mind and came at a time when heavy metal (my only church) was daubed in mascara and spandex and needed a serious injection of the grease and hogsweat that *true* metal would always be lubricated by. Over the years I followed the band's breakneck decline into obscurity, trudging along to decrepit toilet venues like Rio's in Bradford to witness the very definition of desperation played out on stage. Zod, Cobalt Stargazer and the ever-changing line-up of under-mutants would pummel through the 'hits' and unleash the occasional blitzkrieg of new material from albums destined to be released only in Germany. They always looked up for it — perhaps driven less by enthusiasm than a brainstem compulsion to get the job done. Like soldiers in 'Nam they knew they were fucked but had only the combat to justify their existence. Little did I suspect that behind the façade of showmanship there was a fusion reactor of neuroses and electric snakes writhing in a pit of Freudian slurry. *Crucify Me Again* is a submersible dropped into that pit. Nothing like an autobiography, this is a collection of anecdotes from Manning's life: his childhood in Leeds, his adventures in the Rock Wastelands and his Troubles with Women. I suppose the closest literary comparison would be Bukowski — the same world-weariness, the same sexual obsessions, the same alcoholic self-indulgence and the ever-enduring image of a damaged man hunched over a keyboard.

Behind a wildly inappropriate but amusing cover image of scowling Chinese Army DeathBitches are 190 pages of lies, madness and the often hard and unpalatable truth, loaded into chapters as short and no-nonsense as a Stanley Knife blade. With titles like 'Sympathy For The Paedophile', 'Fucked By Rock', and 'Menstruating Nazi Fucker' the lazy and uninterested reviewer might think they could hawk up a quick slating of the book without actually reading it but they would be wrong, wrong, wrong. The label is not the contents, the map is not the territory and these ironic stabs at tabloid succinctity are designed to draw you in and then hammer home their point with ball-peen accuracy.

Manning is more than comfortable with his chosen lexicon — an exuberant gutterspeak collision of Milton, Burroughs and Leeds boot boys — and revels in veering from one extreme to another across the pages. He eases the reader with unsentimental tales of his youth: growing up in the shadow of Elland Road football ground and Armley Jail, schoolyard scraps, tap room initiations and mindless destruction — all numb responses to the grey monotony of life on a council estate in Seventies England. As grim as these tales may be to some, to my eye they brought a dewy tear as I fondly remembered the 'old' Leeds before the yuppies descended on it like locust and turned it into one huge café bar and hair salon. These experiences gave a solid foundation for the curious young Manning to build upon. At 16 he went to Bradford Art College where his mind was raked open by extravagant homosexual lecturers who weaned him onto books by Reich and Burroughs. It was a short step from there to LSD psychosis and then he was ready for a bruising by the Great Beast Itself: ROCK!

The chapters covering his experiences

SNIP! SNAP! SNIP! THE
SCISSORS GO; AND CONRAD
CRIES OUT -- OH! OH! OH!
SNIP! SNAP! SNIP! THEY GO SO
FAST; THAT BOTH HIS THUMBS
ARE OFF AT LAST.

Are you beginning to see why followers of Freud groove on *Struwwelpeter*
so much? There is no hint of the sickly
Christian piety so prevalent in most
19ᵗʰ Century children's literature —
the peremptory way in which hubris
is punished is more akin to Greek tragedy than anything else. I was
unsurprised to learn that Hoffmann
went on to found a lunatic asylum —
whether he himself was aware of it or
not, the stories in *Struwwelpeter*
seethe with neurotic fantasy. The ti-
tle-poem itself, 'Struwwelpeter' or
'Shock-Headed Peter', is rather different. There is no narrative of crime and
punishment here, only an extraordinary iconic image of a boy in a medi-
aeval-style tunic with wildly tangled

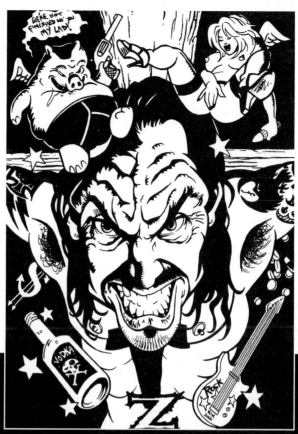

Zodiac Mindwarp
Art © Rik Rawling

in the music industry are perhaps the
least interesting. He mentions a few
interesting characters such as Joe (the
giant black Nazi who wore a 'White
Power' T-shirt) and Clive (lead singer
of Dr & The Medics who had a magical ability with turds), but seems to
have ditched a lot of that baggage in
the scummy wake of endless tedious
tours around Europe. There's no mention of any pleasure gained from being a rock star, just a palpable sense
of relief that it's all over and best put
down to experience. He does point out
that it's pretty rare for the actual cul-
prits involved to write their own story
— these days it's left to the hagiog-
raphers at *Mojo* and the roadies who
remember which testicle Keef liked to
shoot heroin into. The tone becomes
less detached when he discusses the
women he's collided with over the
years: the three mothers of his three
children and the dozens, hundreds,
of others — some of whom were nothing more than 'Road Gash', some who
were teetering on the edge of sanity
and some who, for one reason or another, managed to leave their crampons in his heart. He attributes his
attitude to most of his 'conquests' (that
some would knee-jerkingly react to
with howls of 'misogynist') as the inevitable result of a life spent on the
road in a rock band where the rules
of consensus reality are skewed by un-
checked indulgence, testosteronic
overload and a gradual slide into an
unreedemable state of psychological

squalor. Here's an example of how
bad it got:

I COULDN'T BE ARSED WANKING
MYSELF, BUT I HAD THIS HARD-
ON THAT JUST REFUSED TO GO
AWAY. I GOT UP AND DRAGGED
THIS LITTLE BLONDE INTO MY
GRUESOME LITTER. I COULDN'T
BE ARSED FUCKING HER BUT I
THOUGHT SHE'D BE ALRIGHT TO
JUST TOSS ME OFF SO I COULD
GET SOME SLEEP. BLONDIE
STARTED SLURPING AROUND...
I BLOBBED OFF ONTO HER
TONSILS AND WENT TO SLEEP.

It seems cold but who's to say we
wouldn't end up the same way in
those same fucked circumstances? It's
the beast in all of us, which is ultimately Manning's main point and his
favourite subject, and it's the lifelong
wrestle with this Tasmanian Devil that
has left him emotionally napalmed
and shuttered away from the outside
world in his Clerkenwell hovel. With
his days of howling at the moon on
stage now consigned to the past, he's
left to communicate his ideas via the
medium that was always his best —
as originally evinced in his lyrics. His
casual mastery of language is not

designed to win Booker prizes — it's
the peacock display of a man who
dragged his intellect out of the gutter
of diminished expectations and into
the league of articulate deviants like
DeSade and Burroughs. It delivers a
punch of communication that intellectual (as opposed to intelligent) pif-
fle merchants like Martin Amis would
have to offer up a lifetime full of virgin
sacrifices to Yahweh to match. Amidst
the hilarious and breathtaking sexual
metaphors ('cock snot', 'nad jam',
'fuck hammer') are genuinely profound declarations on the human condition, my favourite being

...LANGUAGE, CUSTOM, RELIGION
AND CULTURE ARE THE THIN
PAPER THAT COVERS THE
CRACKS IN THE WALLS OF A
HAUNTED UNIVERSE.

That pretty much sums it up for me.
In case you haven't figured it out, this
is an important book. Mark Manning
has nailed a portion of his soul to the
masts for all to see. He's walked paths
that many couldn't imagine, let alone
dare to follow, and is reporting back
on the ruined state of the destination
he's found. He did it so you don't have
to. Now go read his book. **Rik Rawling**

hair and enormous talon-like finger-nails, looking like a poster boy for extreme yoga.

Hoffmann's own illustrations for *Struwwelpeter* are naïvely charming in their folksy Teutonic 19th Century way, but are admittedly rather crude. Feral House's beautifully-designed deluxe reissue, however, boasts not only a facsimile of a 1915 American translation, complete with the original illustrations, but also modern illustrator Sarita Vendetta's b&w takes on some 15 of the poems, and a full-colour plate of her fetishistic vision of the Scissor-Man (capering about in rubber with his thighs stuck full of pins and needles, a jar full of severed thumbs on the floor behind him, and a naked child in a cage behind that). 'WARNING! THIS CHILDREN'S BOOK IS NOT FOR CHILDREN!' screams the back cover of the book, and whilst many modern parents would doubt the pedagogical wisdom of giving any child a copy of *Struwwelpeter* to mull over, Vendetta's pictures are the main reason for this admonition. In a painstakingly pointillist pen-and-ink style, she lays bare the outrageous psychopathology of the poems, with their undercurrents of abjection, castration and trauma, in a series of vivid tableaux of child abuse. Like Paula Rego and Angela Carter, Vendetta is evidently fascinated by the repressed content of much children's literature, and like Trevor Brown (of Whitehouse cover art infamy), she excels at rendering images of children in pain. These pictures will give a lot of *adults*, let alone children, nightmares!

Also lurking beneath the tastefully spot-laminated cover of Feral House's *Struwwelpeter* are an informative introduction by Jack Zipes, professor of German and expert on children's literature, a foreword from Adam Parfrey, and a facsimile of an historical curiosity called 'Struwwelhitler', a British propaganda parody from World War II depicting prominent Nazis as naughty children. This book reaffirms my opinion of Feral House as being one of the most exciting and innovative publishers currently active, and is highly recommended. **Simon Collins**

ICON
Frank Frazetta
No price listed; Taschen, 1999; Note: This is a reprint of the 1998 Underwood book which is already a collectors' item. Like most Taschen books, it is available in remainder shops. The original price was £12.99 but it appears to have dropped since then. At £12.99, it was a bargain.

PULP ART
Robert Lesser
No price listed; Gramercy Books, 1997
If we accept that fantasy fans are life's seven stone weaklings, used to having sand kicked in their faces while they sit on the beach engrossed by Robert Heinlein or William Gibson, then Frank Frazetta's art is designed to conjure up the very Charles Atlas figures that, as the old ads in the comics said, 'made a man out of Mac'. In Frazetta's imagination, the world is filled with men whose muscles were Hoganic centuries before anyone discovered steroids. His women are beyond pneumatic: tautly muscled themselves, with feline faces that alternate innocence with seduction, and breasts that would get them talk shows on Channel 5 the first time they were bared.

Frazetta was already a legend in the world of comics when his covers for Lancer Books' reprinting of the Conan stories shot him into prominence in the slightly more mainstream world of SF. A generation of fantasy fans created by Tolkien in the mid-Sixties went looking for something else to read, and Frazetta's Conan was what drew their eyes. Frazetta had a way of anchoring his larger than life figures in a very real sort of action — movement that we can recognise, that must owe something to a sportsman's past. What *Icon* demonstrates so well, however, is the wide range of Frazetta's talent, and the way he was almost always working, often anonymously, at the higher-paying ends of the market: as an 'assistant' to Al Capp on 'L'il Abner', or with Will Elder on *Playboy*'s 'Little Annie Fanny' for example. The relatively small number of actual comic books he drew, for EC and others, have, by their very rarity, helped contribute to his legend, as has the occasional high-profile mainstream advertising and magazine work. The influence of talented graphic artists like Roy Krenkel, Al Williamson, and Wally Wood is apparent. But one of the beauties of *Icon* is the reprinting of some of his SF covers from *Weird Science Fantasy* and *Famous Funnies*. The reproduction of these covers is wonderful, usually a full page with a smaller, related piece of art decorating the brief explanation. The sometimes impressionistic colouring in the background helps set the mood for Frazetta's best work, contrasting with the obvious energy in the foreground: when he calms the action in the foreground, as in 'The Moon's Rapture', which closes out the book, the effect is stunning.

Some more of the background to Frazetta's work can be gleaned from another impressive volume, Robert Lesser's *Pulp Art*. This is a collection of cover art from the pulp magazines which flourished in the 1930s and Forties, and is also reproduced to a high standard. They are quick to trace the influence of the Howard Pyle school of book illustrating, particularly NC Wyeth, which is also quoted as a major influence on the young Frazetta. Looking at J Allen St John's Tarzan book illustations and his jungle pulp covers gives you a good idea of Frazetta's roots. In fact, Frazetta's first paperback cover, for *Tarzan and the Lost Empire*, looks like a more direct

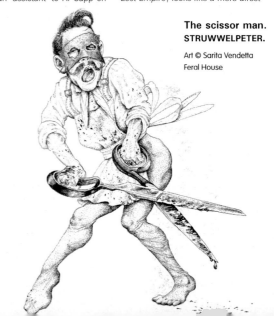

**The scissor man.
STRUWWELPETER.**

Art © Sarita Vendetta
Feral House

version of St John.

But in a more general sense, what impresses the most about this art is its sheer inventiveness. There are different conventions to each writing genre, and general conventions too (like the use of diagonals to attract attention on newsstands), but within those formulae artists like George Rozen (*Shadow Magazine*), Edd Cartier (*Unknown Worlds/Fantasy Fiction*), Rafael DeSoto and many more can create an often surreal tension.

Lesser's own text for *Pulp Art* is augmented by numerous brief essays, including an effective, if brief, overview by Roger Reed of Illustration House in New York, an artist's perspective from Jim Steranko, and a short interview with J Allen St John from 1950.

In virtually uniform format, these two books will stand happily side-by-side on the shelves of anyone interested in popular art. Indispensible. **Michael Carlson**

DIGITAL LEATHERETTE
Steve Beard
282pp £8.95; Codex, 1999
ISBN 1-899598-12-X

Praised by William Gibson as 'an exuberant, neurologically-specific neo-Blakean riff-collage', this piece of 'ambient hyperfiction' fuses fictive text samples from internet websites, court transcripts from a complex espionage case, briefing documents, screenplay excerpts and some faux-Elizabethan drama. A writer for the 'style press', Beard uses his journalistic experience to add some authentic details to the dense, abstract, metaphor-laden prose of this tightly-knit conceptual 'anti-novel'. Significant themes include MI6, Morrissey, drugs, raves, the millennium and something about Battersea Power Station; psychogeography is a futuristic London as reflected through the eyes of William Blake, Iain Sinclair and JG Ballard. Fragmented, convoluted and ultimately highly irritating, this is strictly a book for boys. **Mikita Brottman**

CHARLIEUNCLENORFOLKTANGO
Tony White,
158pp £7.95; Codex 1999
ISBN 1-899598-13-8

'Lissen yew cunts', begins our tale — with one single phrase printed in the middle of each page — 'Coz yore proble wundrin wot we woz do-inn there in the ferss place & ow we cum ter be juss dryvin aroun din the fuckin dark myles & myles from fuckin enny ware...' As the opening of *CharlieUncleNorfolkTango* makes clear, this is hardly your traditional roman policier. Three officers — Lockie, Blakie and The Sarge — are driving around at night in a police van. After they've been abducted by aliens from 'a soddin spay ship or summink', we find out that one of the trio isn't exactly human. But which one...? Not quite the 'lode a bollux' it might sound, *CharlieUncle...* basically presents us with a stream of consciousness from the perspective of the narrator, Lockie, whose musings cover subjects as diverse as mad killers prowling the streets, 'blokes and birds', the anatomy of *Charlie's Angels*, and the lights of the city streets. Lockie's thoughts are interspersed with various atrocities and acts of corruption which make the police seem as trapped in their alienation as the criminals they're out to get — or even the 'free-fingerd fuckers' who abduct them. Starsky and Hutch it surely ain't. *CharlieUncle...* works if you read it as a long poem. The problem with reading it as a novel, however, is that there isn't really much of a plot. In the case of the best writers to use this kind of experimental, phonetic prose — Anthony Burgess, for example, or Hubert Selby Jr — the idiosyncrasies of the style quickly fade into the background as matters of character and plot become more and more absorbing. Here, though, there seems to be little more than the style itself, which never becomes unobtrusive, and the narrative voice is foregrounded to such an extent that in the end the whole thing sounds a bit like a pathological Frank Butcher. Still, if you can handle it, you'll find a lot here that's brutal, poignant, penetrating, even funny. And if you like stories of 'fuckin coppers' being abducted by aliens, you're going to eat this up. ain chew mate? **Mikita Brottman**

CUNT
Stewart Home
192pp £7.50; Do-Not Press, 1999
ISBN 1-899344-45-4

Hey kids, dig those crazy London novelists! Could you really give a dog's 'nad about them, or anything they write? Dead parents, emotionally-retarded men, lonely alcoholic women, gay librarians, blocked writers. Boo-fucking-hoo. *Cunt* is a novel about a London novelist. Sort of. Thankfully, author Home dogs the heels of Sinclair and Moorcock more than Amis and Self, and so this book is a long way away from queeny literary tiffs...

THE GIRL SAT DOWN ON THE TOILET BOWL AND I LICKED HER CLIT WHILE SHE TOOK A SHIT. SHE STOOD UP AGAIN AND SAID I COULD FUCK HER UP THE ARSE. WE DIDN'T NEED A LUBRICANT, HER LUNCH HADN'T AGREED WITH HER AND SHE'D JUST HAD A VERY LOOSE CRAP.

Meet David Kelso. A cunt is what he is, cunt is what he's after, and *Cunt* is his journal; it charts the final stages of his attempt to re-fuck the first thousand women he ever had. As protagonists go, Kelso is somewhere between *Complicity*'s Cameron Colley and *American Psycho*'s Patrick Bateman, but without the morals of the former or the social etiquette of the latter. Travelling through the bleak landscapes of East Anglia, Finland and Scotland, Kelso translates his mission onto hard disk, give or take a few distractions: as he also happens to be a money-burning, whiskey-devouring, teen-shagging superman. We discover this in chapter one — in which our hero fellates a she-male — and there's no let up thereafter. *Cunt* is so over the top it reads like nothing more than a novelist's megalomaniacal wet dream: Miller, Bukowski and Crews all jacked off into the gene pool and out popped David Kelso — one hand holding a bottle of fine malt, the other up a 15-year-old's skirt. Home has injected every clichéd vice into one character and let him plough his own course, as well as adding some genuine pranks — such as Kelso inventing a Dead Young Poet and secreting his 'work' on the shelves of charity shops, then sitting back and watching a cult of nothing emerge. OTT, yes, but give me Home's book over 'I don't think you really realise what it's like to be a 35-year-old single man' record shop shelf-fillers any day. Buy it for the female English literature student in your life. **Martin Jones**

MURDER BY NUMBERS
Anna Gekoski
310pp £17.99; h/bk; Andre Deutsch
ISBN 0233991387

If there's one thing the world needs more than another serial killer it's another serial killer book. Right? Someone ought to chart the rise of serial killings against the number of words the subject generates. What's

FANTASY WORLDS

Deidi von Schaewen & John Maizels
340pp £24.99; h/bk; Taschen, 1999
ISBN 3-8228-7190-7

BUILDING A NEW MILLENNIUM

Philip Jodidio
576pp £19.99; Taschen, 1999
ISBN 3-8228-6390-4

Large, beautiful and crammed with glossy photographs, *Fantasy Worlds* pays tribute to the creators of fantasy architecture and their alternative and eccentric worlds. But don't let the word 'architecture' put you off. Anyone with even the remotest interest in art, interior or garden design, sculpture, madness, inspiration and obsession will find the book fascinating. Though *Fantasy Worlds* includes certain classics of off-the-wall architecture — such as the Sedlec Ossuary in the Czech Republic or the Tarot garden in Tuscany — this book is at its best when delving into personal and domestic madness. People decorating every free surface in their house with broken pots, for instance; entire house façades covered in retrieved junk; the Watford Shell Garden with its stuffed toys encased in concrete and shells… These are quite rightly as prominent

within *Fantasy Worlds* as professionally created large-scale works of religious grandeur.

From Europe through the East to America, each fantasy is different, and each is inspired. "The Garden of Eden" is set in the garden of a log cabin home and consists of large sculptures in concrete tree shapes, representing the creator's political and religious beliefs. Stranger still is the fact that their creator, Samuel Perry Dinsmoor (1843–1932), not only married a 21-year-old at the age of 89, but also lies buried in a glass-topped coffin in the garden's very own mausoleum.

As wonderfully colourful as the *Fantasy Worlds* creations are the glimpses of the creative, scavenging, recycling and obsessive single-minded visionaries who brought them to life.

Another Taschen architecture book, *Building a New Millennium* is sure to have Prince Charles quaking in his boots at the "daring innovation in space, light and form" which will seemingly shape the buildings of the future. Many new structures are photographed, notably the 'Pharmacy' Restaurant designed by Damien Hirst and Mike Rundell in which the pharmacy theme is explored in the pill-

shaped chairs, the cold, sterile atmosphere and the pharmaceutical product in glass cabinets lining the walls. Also included is the Eden Project in St Austell, Cornwall — a huge "showcase for global biodiversity". *Building a New Millennium* represents a cleaner, more organised and more modern view of built structures than does *Fantasy Worlds* and therefore will likely have less general appeal.

Sarah Turner

DIGITAL DIARIES

Natacha Merritt
256pp £16.99; h/bk; Taschen, 2000
ISBN 3-8228-6398-X

I first heard of Merritt in an erotica special issue of *Juxtapoz* magazine. The artist and work were fascinating: a teenage girl photographing her fuck-partners on digital camera and downloading them onto the internet. This book presents a collection of those photos — from Merritt's early works on low-grade digital cameras to recent work on hi-tech digital cameras (most sections are named after the camera on which the work was shot). Again and again Merritt and fuck-pals expose all for the pixel gaze of the camera. But something strange is happening. The further the 'reader' gets into *Digital Diaries*, the more he or she will realise that, for all the fucking and sucking (and there is a lot of sucking), Natasha is above all interested in taking photos. On occasion she appears to be looking into the distance during seemingly random acts of copulation, until the viewer realises she is actually looking at the liquid crystal display on her camera. Also fascinating is the fragmentation of the male body. Men are all hard cocks and tight testicles. There are few male faces in the book (I think there are only two, in fact), contrasting with the claim made by some feminists that heterosexual pornography depicts women as fragmented. Intellectual ideas and technology aside, *Digital Diaries* contains the same pleasures as reader's wives magazines, i.e. watching 'amateurs' depict and participate in their own pornography (of course, the tanned hard bodies of Merritt and the California girls may be more attractive than some of the contributors to reader's wives, but each to their own). The pleasures in this volume not only make it a coffeetable classic but also a good masturbatory aid. Hey, it functions on all levels!

Jack Sargeant

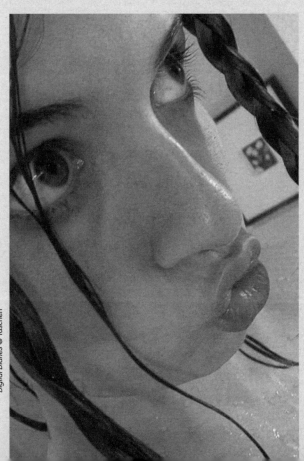

Digital Diaries © Taschen

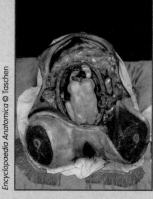
Encyclopaedia Anatomica © Taschen

ENCYCLOPAEDIA ANATOMICA
A Complete Collection of Anatomical Waxes

704pp £16.99; Taschen, 1999
ISBN 3-8228-7613-5

From medieval times onward the art of the waxworker has been a poor relative to practitioners in the 'elevated' sculptural media of stone and bronze, and never afforded the respect that the considerable craft deserved. But, as Georges Didi-Huberman observes in one of the several introductions to this collection of full-colour photographs, wax is the material of all resemblances, and its virtues are so remarkable that it was often attributed with magical properties. *Encyclopaedia Anatomica* makes this immediately apparent with around 1,500 studies of the human body from the Museo La Specola in Florence, the cream of 16th and 17th Century wax-artists working when medicine was starting to take a serious interest in the mechanisms of the body.

Everything from the brain to the metatarsals, the viscera to the voicebox, is depicted, often with such astonishing accuracy and clarity (or as far as I can tell, not having a pass to the Royal College of Surgeons) that you might think you are looking at real dissections. The full-figure studies of flayed men reclining — as if in some tortural ecstasy — on silk cushions, or the advanced representation of a young woman with her removable skin and organs, are especially hypnotic. (I still can't look at some of the pictures without wincing. The final section on reproduction is a particular challenge.) It is one of the central mysteries why when we look at the insides of our own bodies we confront horror and beauty in such close proximity.

Taschen are to be recognised for bringing such an important collection to a wider audience. If a criticism can be levelled it's the lack of size for such detailed images. There's a fair amount of white border on each page and,

even taking into account the chunky A5 size of the book, the images could have been 10, maybe even 20 percent larger. On the whole, though, this is a definite must if you have any interest at all in anatomy or curious museums and collections. **Eugene Carfax**

JAMES BIDGOOD

175pp £24.99; h/bk; Taschen, 1999
ISBN 3-8228-7427-2

Anyone remember 'The most infamous and erotic Gay film of all time' shot by 'Anonymous' and featuring the first ejaculation shot to be given an 18 certificate? No? Can't say I'm surprised. The film in question is *Pink Narcissus*, and the 'Anonymous' none other than Mr James Bidgood.

Bidgood spent six-and-a-half-years (1964–1970) filming this homage to the young male body, only to have his footage taken away from him before he'd finished shooting and — in his own words — 'ruined' in the final editing. The film was finally released in 1971. (A remastered version was released for video in 1994.) Bidgood was furious and disappointed with the end result and refused to allow his name to be connected to the film in any way, hence the 'Anonymous' credit. Then in 1985 after the death of his partner, Bidgood fell into a deep depression and destroyed all his prints and sketches from *Pink Narcissus*. Luckily he kept the still shots and many of these are included in this volume, along with sessions from his physique photographer days. The detail in his photography is quite astonishing, and obviously a big influence on the likes of Pierre et Gilles. Without the help of digital technology, each set, each costume, each camp scenario is designed to the finest detail and caught on camera in the comfort of his own apartment.

This book takes us through Bidgood's career, notably his work for *The Young Physique*, *Muscleboy*, *Demi-Gods* and other magazines; his 'off-Broadway' shows and drag performances at the infamous Club 82; his first meeting with the seriously cute Bobby Kendall in 1962 who 'Had the look of a deer caught in headlights', and right through the making of *Pink Narcissus*. Unfortunately, due to his depression, very little new work has been realised. But he is presently working on a biographical film, *FAG: The Pretty Good Life of Jimmy Bundle*, the release of which I await with baited breath. **Rick Caveney**

the correlation? Not that I'm going to do a Colin Wilson and blame serial killing on pornography, or even on the pornography of true crime writing. It's just that with the death of religion we're no longer scared of Satan, hell or eternal damnation. The supernatural, currently undergoing a bit of a revival, doesn't frighten most of us. Instead we like to scare ourselves with something of the here-and-now, and yet possessed of that quality of evil that separates it from the 'normal'. Is it any wonder that Robert Rossler, ex-FBI and the man who coined the phrase 'serial killer', entitles his books *I Have Lived In The Monster* and *Whoever Fights Monsters*. Demonisation is the name of the game; in this secular and confused age we'll invent devils to frighten ourselves, and, just as importantly, to confirm to us the parameters of our 'normality'. Which brings us in a round about way to Anna Gekoski's *Murder By Numbers*. This is a detailed look at the life and crimes of British serial sex killers. All of the usual demons are included here: Christie, Ian Brady, Myra Hindley, Dennis Nilson, Fred and Rose West. However this isn't just a case of going over the same old ground. There are chapters here on Robert Black and Colin Ireland, for example. The latter is interesting as there is practically nothing in print about this man who preyed on men from the gay SM community.

The book looks closely at the childhoods of these deadly, twisted individuals. And even on the nth reading, the crimes these people committed are frightening. If you're a sick fuck, of course, you'll even find these sickening crimes arousing. However, Gekoski takes her task seriously. What made these people commit crimes awful enough to cast them forever as demons? And in asking that simple question she steps away from the standard line. She does much more than make us shudder and check the locks on the door at night.

But looking at these people as people, by probing their young lives she gives us a picture of young souls that are seriously damaged, of personalities that are recognisably vulnerable and which elicit sympathy as much as their adult crimes evoke revulsion. If you want to understand rather than sample a frisson of fear and disgust, then this book is highly recommended. **Pan Pantziarka**

TEMPLE OF BLASPHEMY
The Black & White artwork of Trevor Brown

Approx. £30 if you can find an importer to touch it; Mondo Bizzarro Press, Piazza S.Martino 3/D, 40126 Bologna, Italy

For those who don't know: Trevor Brown is an Englishman living in Japan, a self-propelled exile brought on by the total lack of a home market for his 'transgressive' (to say the least) artwork and his inclination for Japanese females. A long-time contributor of artwork to the Susan Lawly label (home of Whitehouse), he specialises in airbrushed paintings of dolls and young girls where he toys with a personal aesthetic that could be construed as 'paedophilic'. He denies any overt intent in that direction, but lovingly rendered paintings of bruised and cut doll-girls with lizards scooting off up their snatches and obviously pre-teen punkettes squatting to piss would seem to offer little by way of a 'defence'. However, Trevor Brown is an intelligent man who has long since tired of the 'child porn art' debate that surrounds his work. Many of his fans and customers are female, drawn to the same often surreal expressions of sexuality and iconography that neither they nor the artist themselves can fully explain.

Along with the paintings which make up the majority of his output and income, he also produces b&w artwork using Radiograph pens. This is the medium with which he first chose to express his ideas in the Eighties, in booklets such as *Graphic Autopsy*, *Necro Porno* and, inevitably, *Graphic Autopsy 2*. *Temple of Blasphemy* collects all his output from that period to the present in one volume, enhanced by enviably slick production values. The early work now looks quite amateurish and seems deliberately intent on shock value: cut-up images, laid out like comic-strip panels, juxtapose Himmler with babies on respirators, young girls bound and gagged with splayed vaginas sporting gaping cyclopean eyes. Myra Hindley. Son of Sam. Intravenous drips. Car wrecks. You can spot the influences and from today's perspective it all looks a bit like the empty magazine of a gun, the 'shock bullets' having long since been spent by lesser triggermen. But, this is where the man was learning, developing his technique and exploring aesthetic sensibilities. The drawing style is sparse: one thickness of line throughout and flat blacks for shading. Occasional use of zip-a-tone and splashes of blood red add little to the overall effect, which is as grim as an ambulance parked on Saddleworth Moor.

Brown's move to Japan had an obvious impact on his work — suddenly it's Oriental girls sporting the bruises and the bandages. Inspired by the extreme pornography of the Far East, his images become full of Kinbaku rope bondage scenes and depictions of truly unpleasant degradation: shit, piss and menstrual blood sluicing across the pages.

Here his drawing style is more fluid but still obviously reliant upon detailed photo-reference to capture the looks of jaded pain and the 'glib smiles' that Brown claims to find so appealing. Sparse medical dungeons are the backdrop for the perversions — white tiles, chairs and a cloying astringent stench to mask the bodily discharges. Whether this is the man's sexual inclination or his response to the libidinal underbelly of an almost alien society is a moot point; the fact remains that these images, more than the later works featuring close-ups of cocks pissing into women's mouths and bandaged Japanese girls slurping custard-like ropes of semen, are the ones that fix their crampons in your mind. The best image of the entire collection is Brown's famous 'Black Eye Madonna', a fine drawing of the popular female songstress from her early puppy fat 'Into The Groove' years sporting a bleeding shiner — which, in itself, renders Peter Sotos' fatuous introduction utterly redundant.

As all the images are obviously culled from photos, the question that begs is: Why bother? The images already exist in one form and even reduced to a b&w assimilation are still essentially the same image. Perhaps the purpose lies in the fact that Brown has taken the time and effort required to render the original source image in its new form? Perhaps if the viewer spends as long looking at the finished image as Trevor Brown did creating it then the essential truth of its appeal and intent will become apparent? Perhaps. Ultimately, this is a unique (in every sense) collection detailing one man's ongoing obsessions, which is valid in itself, but it's difficult to say just how many other people it would appeal to. And best of luck to anyone trying to sneak a copy past our boys at HM Customs. They will be all over this like flies on shit. **Rik Rawling**

HELLBLAZER
Damnation's Flame

Garth Ennis & Steve Dillon, et al
£10.99; Titan; ISBN 1-84023-096-7

The John Constantine character first appeared in *Swamp Thing* back in the mid Eighties. In his uniform of rumpled suit and trenchcoat with a Lambert & Butler permanently hanging out of his gob he was the bastard offspring of Michael Caine, John Lydon and every single 'supernatural investigator' that has ever lurked in the shadows. Alan Moore, the writer at the time, never really used the character properly and it wasn't until he got his own monthly title — *Hellblazer* — in 1988 that writer Jamie Delano tried to put some flesh on the bones.

The first 10 issues or so absolutely *rocked* with Delano and artist John Ridgway going arse over tit with horror clichés, dragging them into contemporary Britain and loosing them in the underground car parks and council tower blocks, establishing a new gothic landscape for Constantine to explore. Over the years he's been subject to much abuse — going up against mutant soccer hooligans, yuppie demons, thug cops and even lung cancer, overcoming them all with the same 'shit eating grin' (as it is always *tiresomely* described. Who the fuck would grin while eating shit?) and fag in hand.

Garth Ennis clearly relishes the chance to use the Constantine character as a vessel for his own opinions. Making full use of the first-person narrative and world weary cynicism that he's persistently fumbled with on *Preacher* he puts Constantine in New York City for no other reason than to allow himself the indulgence of wading in to 'Big Bad America'.

It's difficult to know where to start with this material. Constantine goes into a bar and gets his drink spiked with some voodoo bollocks. He immediately starts having some 'freaky' visions — fleshless hands, flayed demon cats — and soon finds himself 'witchwalking'. His conscious self is beaten by cops, pissed on by cretinously caricatured street trash and even comes close to a violent buggering (a recurrent Ennis theme is violent anal penetration. Over to you, Freud) while in his 'dream state' he meets a 'Gangsta' philosopher, gets his throat slit by Central Park cannibals and eventually gets to meet and walk through Monument Valley with JFK — who comes complete with gaping head wound. Are you seeing the heavy symbolism here? One page even has a Two-Gun Uncle Sam stood in a dark alleyway with a chained bear bleeding to death and a junkie Britannia slumped in the gutter! And that's about as subtle as it gets. This whole venture is nothing but a hilariously adolescent 'condemnation' of America and all it allegedly stands for, seen through the eyes of a man who wears his influences on his sleeve but has no idea how to internalize them and use them effectively. Whatever 'point' he's trying to make is lost amidst the woeful shock tactics and blind slashing at the stinking hides of long-dead sacred cows. And judging by the amount of 'Frigging' going on it seems that publisher Vertigo have backpedalled slightly on the 'Realistic Language' licence they gave their writers a few years ago — perhaps as a 'moral' response to the Columbine High School massacre where, no doubt, comics in which you can read the words 'Fuck' and 'Cocksucker' were a significant contribution to the mindset of the two young killers? Stirred in with all the 'Bloody Arseholes' and 'Christ's Sake's' it makes for some of the most implau-

sible dialogue ever written. The target audience of 16-year-olds may think this is hard-hitting stuff but I'm afraid it's still the same old comics medium, trapped in perpetual childhood but this time wearing it's older brother's clothes and trying to talk tough. And, frankly, it looks a right twat.

Respect, as ever, must go to the artists who spend far longer than is necessary on scripts of this quality. Having to indulge Ennis' obsessions with 'real' blokes swigging 'real' pints, pub-philosophising, Blarney wisdom and anal rape should carry danger money for the as-yet-unknown psychic damage being inflicted upon the artists.

If this is the best response to superheroics that comics can come up with then I'd rather stick with the X-Men which at least knows it is bollocks and doesn't think it's Ernest Hemingway. No more of this please. Really. **Rik Rawling**

SPAWN
Blood Feud
Alan Moore, et al
£8.99; Titan; ISBN 1-84023-117-3

Alan Moore. Alan. Moore. Back in the Eighties he was the only writer that saved *2000AD* from turning into the pile of shit that it would inevitably

become. With his Future Shocks, the over-rated Halo Jones and the unsurpassed Dr & Quinch he displayed sensibilities beyond the clichés that the other writers had come to rely upon. He soon came to the attention of DC Comics where he revolutionised the then-pointless *Swamp Thing* and went on to produce the seminal *Watchmen* series. He was the main reason many of my generation had come back to comics after abandoning them in favour of football, Grifters, punk rock and crap sex with local slags. He had the Midas Touch back them and as comics were given a brief recognition as 'The New Rock'n'Roll'. He came to believe the medium was ripe for some 'serious' material. By 'serious' he meant rants about covert US Government operations and projected 10-issue series about shopping centres in Northampton! He had, frankly, disappeared up his own arse and the bubble soon burst with crap 'graphic novels' soon piling up in the remainder bins at WH Smiths, and writers of what's best described as 'nebulous' abilities like Neil Gaiman steaming in to steal his thunder. Moore became a recluse in Northampton, exploring 'magick', writing novels that no-one read and only showing his face with the occasional comics work like the acclaimed *From Hell* series.

He seemed to be pretty much 'done' with comics, even claiming at one time that he felt he was contributing to the 'death of superheroes'. I'd have liked to have thanked him for it if he'd actually pulled it off. But no, the fuckers are still going strong and now look at what Moore himself is up to — churning out a whole new universe of pituitary retards and power fantasies for the boys who still get beat up at school for liking *Star Trek*. I guess the man's got a mortgage to pay and, besides, it's the Nineties (or it was until recently) — maybe it's 'ironic' to do superhero comics?

Not that there's anything remotely 'ironic' about *Spawn* — the brainchild of Tod McFarlane who made his name at Marvel before 'controversially' leaving to start Image comics, where he created the phenomenon that is Spawn. One movie, an animated series and fuck knows how many comics later the phenomenon spreads like Ebola across the comics shelves of the Western World, which just goes to prove that you can fool some of the people all of the time. Kleptomaniacally plundering every myth and ar-

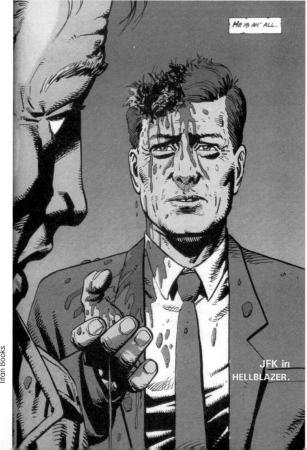

HE IS AN' ALL.

JFK in HELLBLAZER.

chetype known to man, the result is basically Quasimodo on steroids in a Batman outfit — with chains. Except the costume is a living entity in itself and exists in symbiosis with its host who's a dead guy with green eyes and stitches down the front of his head. Confused? I fucking was. There's already been 12 collected books of Spawn so there's clearly a lot of background and history that I'm unaware of, but let's not allow such trivialities so spoil things. It only becomes apparent that this is an Alan Moore script at page five when 'The great iron throats sing out into the dark. They tell of ruin yet to come' gives the game away. Similar pifflings crop up throughout, but mostly it's Moore going through the motions of giving the projected audience exactly what they want and no more. The story is as predictable as shits after a curry: Monster hunter cop in town. Horrible murders. Spawn is fingered for it. It can't be true, he's the hero! Turns out the cop is a super vampire called John Sans Couer (you work it out). Spawn seems doomed. All is not lost. Big fight. Villain gets away for future showdowns/marketing opportunities. Holy fucking shit! Every creaky old plot device is used as Moore milks whatever sour dregs are left from this saggy old tit of a story which is really just an episode of NYPD Blue with CGI and worse jokes. I can't imagine the 'kids' of today — who groove on Buffy and Xena — not seeing straight through it. This is a McDonald's cheeseburger of a comic right down to the gherkin artjob that has obviously taken a long time to produce — every link of chain and shred of cape is there trailing across the pages but unlike the hyperdense detail of Geof Darrow, it adds nothing to the feel or the look of the work. It's just clutter for the sake of it. The entire visual playout, with headspinning point-of-view shots, panel overspills, double page spreads and obligatory shite PC colouring is like a bog-standard rock video loaded with many of the same images and delivering much the same numbing effect to the frontal lobes. The drawing is in the overly-exaggerated cartoon style for which Image are infamous — jut jaws and walrus chins, button noses and sports car bonnet foreheads, steroid-flooded biceps and Cro-Magnon knuckles. It's a heavy metal album cover brought to life. It's a Gene Simmons wet dream without the bitches in bikinis (which may have saved it actually). It's another nail in the coffin of an artform that never really got out of the incubator. It's another triumph for stupidity over intelligence. It's just a comic. Cheers Alan. **Rik Rawling**

BILE
Mark Brand
£6.99; Citron Press; ISBN 0754400603
It's 15 minutes into the future, when Helmut Kohl runs the Euro super-state that invades poor old Blighty. Of

RAIDERS OF THE LOW FOREHEAD
Stanley Manly
159pp £6.99; ATTACK! 1999
ISBN 1-84068-031-8
www.creationbooks.com
New fiction from ATTACK!, an imprint of Creation Books. Fiction for the modern generation. Fiction that knows the best way to assault the old order and tell everyone you mean business is to go wild with the exclamation marks and capital letters, because IT FUCKING WORKS!!!
In Raiders Of The Low Forehead, seven stone duster-boy Vince has been promised blow-jobs for life from Sharon if he does-over the knuckleheaded psychos of the title, who framed her dad and brother and got them stuck in pokey. Mix this plot up with food, sex, violence (sorry, FOOD! SEX! VIOLENCE!), turd curries, slaughtered coppers and sheep shagging; add alliteration and rhyming sentences, and you have something that is occasionally very funny and occasionally headache inducing. I think that might have been the publisher's intention. If Viz was run by a dictatorship of skinheads employing music biz hacks to knock out pocket-size novels, then this would be the result.
But who is Stanley Manly? Chapter 39 of Raiders Of The Low Forehead steals a couple of lines wholesale from TV's Brass Eye, specifically the 'Cake is a made-up drug' episode. Perhaps Chris Morris himself is moonlighting as a renegade teen author?
Martin Jones

SATAN! SATAN! SATAN!
Tony White
TITS-OUT TEENAGE TERROR TOTTY
Steven Wells
132pp & 260pp, £6.99 ea; ATTACK! 1999
ATTACK! With a distinctive graphic style and lots of manifesto-like propaganda at the back of the books, and even a club to join (just like the Beano), this new imprint from Creation is evidently concerned with fostering a strong brand identity and reader loyalty, though I must admit being buttonholed with 'Oi! Reader!' and addressed in horrible sub-Loaded wideboy street talk

IN YOUR FACE, DOWN YOUR TROUSERS AND UP YOUR ARSE LIKE A SHIT-EATING RABBIT ON SPEED...

does not make me feel inclined to join in the fun. As all this is accompanied by a lot of vituperation directed at the literary 'establishment' ('the self-perpetuating ponce-mafia oligarchy of effete bourgeois wankers who run the "literary scene"...'), it suddenly becomes clear that ATTACK! is the hellish mutant offspring of Stewart Home's attempts to update Seventies New English Library 'yoof' fiction for the Nineties. Be afraid, be very afraid... But what of the books themselves?
Satan! Satan! Satan! is by Tony White, author of Road Rage (reviewed in HEADPRESS 18) and Charlieunclenorfolktango (see page 141). The plot concerns a group of Goth girls in Leeds and their visit to the 'Festival of the Night' in Whitby to see a load of bands dressed in black. Bilko, a pathetic small-time speed dealer who has the hots for Debs, one of the Goth chicks, has his entire body tattooed with designs by occult visionary artist Austin Osman Spare in a misguided attempt to impress her. When this fails, he hares off round the country, indulging in a little ritual murder to attain his desires. Meanwhile, Vlad Vargstrom, asthmatic lead singer of mad Swedish Death Metal band The Dogs of Thor, is making elaborate plans for a memorable entrance to the festival at Whitby, and Jeremiah Jones, a demented evangelical Christian cult leader, is rallying his followers to picket the event. Little do they know that he has become possessed by the spirit of Jim Jones, and is planning to restage Jonestown in Whitby... I didn't like this book much at all. The plot was silly, the characters unengaging, and the whole thing culminates in an unholy mess at Whitby, which is doubtless meant to seem

course the spooks in our intelligence services engage in all kinds of black ops, especially in the Anti-Hygiene Underground (the Krauts being world class hygienists of course). Somehow everybody talks in a nasal estuary whine, which is transcribed phonetically for our reading pleasure — it took me ages to figure out who the 'Ow Biw' are. And I won't even mention the massed ranks of rubber-suited gimps. Does it sound a mess? It is. An absolute mess of shifting tenses, points of view and writing styles It shifts in and out at random, switching character and tense mid-paragraph and then back again. But, despite its myriad faults, there's a real page-turning quality about it. For the first hundred pages I wanted to jack it in, but after a while I was hooked, like 'a kant' and had to keep going. And it's funny too, in a warped sort of way. The book is so obviously after cult status that it won't get it.

Pan Pantziarka

THE PORTABLE HENRY ROLLINS

Henry Rollins

324pp £12.99; Phoenix House, 1997

Just what is it about Henry Rollins, the thinking man's Travis Bickle? On the face of it, his deficiencies are more obvious than his talents. He can't sing, he can't dance, he can't write poetry (his prose is more debatable, but more on that later), and those of you unfortunate enough to have seen the dreadful *Johnny Mnemonic* will affirm that he absolutely can't act. Hc looks like a demented Action Man, he has some cheesy tattoos (and some great ones), and he admits to enjoying the music of Dave Lee Roth and Thin Lizzy. His first band, Black Flag, despite enjoying massive cult status now, were frankly mediocre, no better or worse than a hundred other hardcore bands; and whilst the Rollins Band have their moments, too often they sound like Black Sabbath with an even worse singer than Ozzy Osbourne. I know

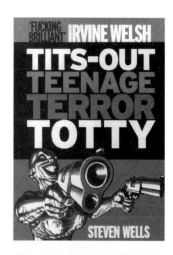

apocalyptic, but just reads like a mess. Even apocalypses need choreographing, if they are to read plausibly. The style is off-putting, too:

THE MAGIC WORDS 'ACCESS ALL AREAS' WERE PRINTED ACROSS THE FRONT... THEY WERE DEAD COOL, AND DEB WAS GOBSMACKED.

Words like 'ace', 'sound', 'wicked' and 'brilliant' litter the narrative, not as part of reported speech, but as the authentic authorial voice. It's very hard to do this kind of writing in slang and get away with it. Mark Twain could do it. Iceberg Slim could do it. Irvine Welsh can do it. Tony White can't do it. I can see that it's meant to give a street feel to the text, but all it does is make the language dull and impoverished. Even more misjudged is the near-exact repetition of entire sentences and paragraphs throughout the text. Why? The device just seems bizarre and irritating. I also found the extensive quoting from Jim Jones' suicide speech a bit distasteful — taking a real-life tragedy like Jonestown and recycling it into pulp entertainment this flimsy and inconsequential seems like pure exploitation, and not exploitation of the enjoyable sort. If you're a dim teenage Goth from oop North who doesn't like reading, you might enjoy this novel. Otherwise, avoid. *Tits-Out Teenage Terror Totty* is a

rather more substantial piece of work, though I still didn't really like it. Steven Wells is perhaps better known as Seething Wells, the rant poet who achieved some notoriety in the early Eighties (alongside Attila the stockbroker and John Cooper Clarke), and he has also worked on the *NME* and the excellent comedy show *The Day Today [Another Chris Morris connection!—Ed]*. He is also the general series editor for ATTACK!, and thus has to shoulder some of the blame for *Satan! Satan! Satan!*.

It's pretty impossible to attempt to summarise the plot of *TOTTT*, or even to quote an extract, as all the sentences in it are about three pages long. Basically it's set in a dystopian near-future UK featuring evil Tory vampires, a girl-power terrorist group led by Justine Justice, Margaret Thatcher sex-golems, weekly resurrections and ritualistic re-killings of Princess Diana, a rock band called Helen Keller's Iron Lung and assorted other highly-coloured but still recognisable exaggerations of the country we live in. The text is almost impenetrably dense, the narrative careers along at a blink-and-you'll-miss-it pace, and there are frequent strange sound effects in large type. The whole thing comes across as a nightmarish circle-jerk involving William Burroughs, Terry Pratchett, Tom Sharpe and Douglas Adams. (This is not a compliment!) I found it

indigestible and annoying after a while — it's just so bloody noisy and hectic. Reading this book is like having a speed-freak yelling in your ear non-stop for hours. Or maybe I'm just getting old. According to the front cover, Irvine Welsh says this is 'Fucking brilliant', but then the front cover of *Satan! Satan! Satan!* has Jesus Christ imploring us to 'Ban this evil book'... ATTACK! books were the subject of an incomprehensibly reverential piece in the *Guardian* Saturday Review section last November ('We're Brutal But Brilliant'), the author of which protested that 'only the most mean-spirited could deny the sheer energy and animation of the... books'. However, Creation are going to have to do better than this before they convince me that the future of British fiction lies in big block letters and exclamation marks. I just get the feeling that these authors would all rather be getting tanked up and pinching traffic cones than writing fiction, and since the yobs they're pitching their product at think that reading anything more than the sports pages and a Haynes manual is for girls, it's difficult to see who's going to buy these books. **Simon Collins**

Three more titles under the ATTACK! imprint have just been released: Tommy Udo's *Vatican Bloodbath*, Jesus H. Christ's *Whips and Furs*, and Mark Manning's *Get Your Cock Out*.

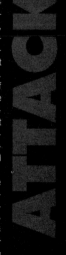

all these things, even if Rollins doesn't, and yet I have to confess to being a Rollins fan. And I'm not alone — his gigs and spoken-word performances now get respectful reviews in the quality press (well, *The Independent* and *The Guardian*, at least), and there is a growing opinion that Henry Rollins is, in some mysterious and indefinable way, cool.

This is largely a personality cult rather than an acclaim for his creative output. Rollins somehow manages to seem much more than the sum of his parts. Not that he's idle: in addition to extensive touring and recording, both solo and with his band, he's produced a dozen or so books, appeared in several films, and he runs the 2.13.61 publishing house, originally a self-publishing venture but now handling the work of many other authors as well. *The Portable Henry Rollins* is a sampler culled from his first eleven books ('Portable' is a bit of a stretch — this is a pretty weighty tome — but I'm sure it's easier to carry around than Rollins himself). The quality of the writing is wildly variable. Rollins is at his best writing travelogues, tour diaries, reminiscences (*Black Coffee Blues*, *Now Watch Him Die*, *Get In The Van*, *Do I Come Here Often?*), but he's embarrassingly bad writing 'poetry' about his various abortive relationships with women. This is some of the worst rock poetry penned since Jim Morrison and Jimi Hendrix gave it a rest (not that I wish to denigrate their respective excellent musical outputs). He lacks the subtlety, the sense of balance, and the empathy to get away with being 'sensitive', and I suspect these are personal failings as well as literary ones. Make no mistake, Rollins sustained some heavy duty damage from his evidently horrible upbringing, but instead of seeing a therapist and trying to rejoin the human race, he has founded his career on roaring like a wounded beast about how lonely he is. Check it out:

CLOSE YOUR EYES
THINK OF THE FILTH
THINK OF THE ALIENATION
BECOME THE ISOLATION
EMBODY THE ALONE
USE IT AS A WEAPON
ALIENATE OTHERS...

Henry, Henry, take it easy! Lighten up, dude! No man is an island, y'know. But of course Henry doesn't know. It's also easy to read the rage Rollins feels against his mother in his fear of women, just as his exaggerated hatred of the police is a transparent reaction to his bullying, militaristic father. Coupled with the hyper-masculine posturing, the obsessive bodybuilding, the boot-camp haircut, and the view of life as an endless combat zone, a picture emerges of Rollins as a frightened little boy who wasn't taught how to love. I hate to think of the level of repression that has gone into the construction of Rollins' tough-guy façade. But this can make compelling reading. At its best, his writing is searingly honest, brutal, visceral and artless (which is why the poems don't work).

This collection is a good (and good value) introduction to all that's good and bad in Rollins' written output, and for the completist it also contains some work unavailable elsewhere, including transcripts of a spoken-word performance from LA in 1992. Just as with Lenny Bruce, a lot of Rollins' humour lies in the physical and vocal delivery, and the spoken word shows are often both funny and affecting, demonstrating a self-deprecating irony which is nearly non-existent in the strident, self-righteous written work. I still don't really know why I like Henry Rollins and buy his books and CDs. There's just something about the guy. Those of you who feel similarly indulgent, or are merely curious, could do worse than to buy this book. **Simon Collins**

LIQUID CITY
Marc Atkins & Iain Sinclair
223pp £14.95; Reaktion Books
Marc Atkins' photos have appeared alongside Iain Sinclair's saturated prose previously, but the content has always been weighted in favour of the writer. Here the balance is redressed — Atkins is given centre stage for his vaguely menacing vision of London; a successive series of photographic essays characterised by unlikely juxtapositions and a pervading sense of gloominess. The Sinclair pieces here, themselves more snapshots than essays, serve principally to further mark out the boundaries of his obsessions, explored in far more detail in his novel *Downriver* or *Lights out for the Territory*, a collection of accounts of London walks; the same figures and themes seem to apply whether Sinclair's writing about JG Ballard or Jeffrey Archer. But the fact that Sinclair's only got a couple of tricks up his sleeve doesn't really matter — they're such impressive tricks, and his knowledge of the territory so thorough, that he's still one of the most inspiring writers around. Recommended. **James Marriott**

NAMELESS AEONS
Peter Smith
1999; Contact: Logos Press, 170 Doncaster Road, Mexborough, S. Yorks; www.phhine.ndirect.co.uk/mailorder/logos.htm

IÄ! IÄ! CTHULHU FHTAGN!

In this, the latest pamphlet I've seen from Logos Press, an attempt is made to explicate the works of 'weirdists' HP Lovecraft, Clark Ashton Smith, Arthur Machen and Bulwer Lytton in terms of practically applicable occult content. The essays are short — none is much over 10 pages long — and of those concerning Lovecraft and Smith much of the content is taken up with autobiographical details. As a general overview of occult interpretations of the writers' works, it's interesting and concise, but anyone wanting actual spells and practical applications will have to look elsewhere. There's an introduction by Kenneth Grant, who's clearly been a major influence on Smith – possibly too much of an influence, as the Typhonian tradition isn't the only way to interpret Lovecraft.

The quality of the essays is a little variable. The only downside to those on Lovecraft and Smith is that they're too short, but some of the later pieces overstay their welcome. Smith operates from the basic premise that the creatures referred to in the stories of the weirdists actually exist — no ifs or buts. I can appreciate the use of Cthulhu-related worship in a personal occult system – as is pointed out in the literature of the Esoteric Order of Dagon. While their members 'do not believe in the absolute existence of the deities which are portrayed in the Cthulhu Mythos, they find the iconography of Lovecraft's work to be a useful paradigm for gaining access to deeper, non-rational areas of the subconscious.' But here Smith really does seem to believe in their existence, which has had the unfortunate effect of shortcircuiting all of his scepticism, so that he throws all kinds of apparently unrelated weirdness into his essays in the service of some demented grand unified theory. One of the essays here, 'The Negative Ones', contains one of the wildest pieces of dream analysis I've ever seen. The following sentence should give you an idea of the breathless and awestruck tone:

AND WAS THE UNKNOWN POWER BEHIND THIS MANIFESTATION NOTHING LESS THAN THE FORESHADOWING OF THE AEONIC SUCCESSION OF HORUS HIMSELF -- IN HIS INCARNATION AS HOOR-PAAR-KRAAT, THE BLACK GOD OF SILENCE, THE POST-NUCLEAR AVATAR OF A COMING ERA OF GLOBAL DEVASTATION AND THE RESULTANT EVOLUTIONARY MUTATION OF THE ENTIRE HUMAN RACE?

That said, this makes an excellent introduction to occult readings of the weirdists, and if some of the other pieces seem a bit nutty, what do you expect from a small press occult publisher? (Incidentally, the Logos Press website is superb.) **James Marriott**

FETISH
Masterpieces of
Erotic Fantasy Photography
Tony Mitchell (Ed.)
223pp £25; Carlton Books, h/bk
ISBN 1 85868 6741

This is basically an updated and glossier version of Jurgen Boedt's *Secret Fetish Photo Anthology*, edited by Tony Mitchell of *Skin Two* fame. Like the original, it aims to showcase work by the best photographers in the fetish scene. However, unlike the original, the production values match those of *Skin Two* magazine — good quality paper, good use of colour, excellent design and generally stylishly done. The introduction by Mitchell attempts to set the scene a bit, but to be honest it's the pictures which are going to sell the book. As one would expect, all of the well-known fetish photographers are here, from Bob Carlos Clark through Trevor Watson to Doris Kloster. Lesser known names include Nic Marchant and Sandra Jensen, both of whom may be known to regular readers of Nexus paperbacks. Many of the images may well be familiar to regular readers of the pervy press too, though there are enough new names involved to keep things interesting. For me, the pictures by Housk Randall-Godard, Jo Hammer, Herbert Hesselman, Giles Berquet and the batch of Chris Bell classics stood out from all the rest.

If there's a criticism of the collection it's one that is generic to all coffee-table photo anthologies — the images are divorced from their context. Collected here in one place these 200-odd pictures soon lose their power to shock or arouse. The pictures risk becoming sexless, divorced as they are from the fantasies which inspire them. Part of the problem is that publishers shy away from the implications. Tony Mitchell probably convinced Carlton Books that this was merely just another fashion book, albeit a slightly risqué one. What no mainstream publisher has dared to do yet is to marry a set of fetish photographs with a set of erotic fantasies or short stories. Come on — somebody, somewhere must be willing to put together the stories of Maria Del Rey, Penny Birch, Jean Aveline *et al* with a set of illustrative photographs? **Pan Pantziarka**

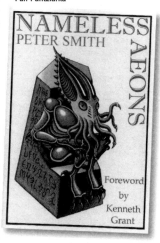

CRIME WAVE
James Ellroy
288pp £15.99; h/bk; Century

It's a problem that Joseph Heller's struggled with since *Catch 22* — how do you top something that's monumental, seminal and so fucking brilliant it redefines an entire genre? Let's face it, the likes of you and I are never going to have to grapple with this one, but it's one that James Ellroy seems to be having trouble with right now. Having produced the nightmarish, twisted vision that is the 'LA Quartet', he's now faced with the task of writing something to match it. And, like Joseph Heller before him, he's having trouble hitting his game. After the detour that was *American Tabloid*, *My Dark Places* was a return to the scene of the crime in many senses. The LA

of the Fifties that he evoked as memory echoed the fictional alternative reality that he had crafted to perfection in books like the *Black Dahlia*. In moving from fiction to memoir he managed to produce a compelling insight into the long journey from kid-whose-mum-was-murdered to maladjusted schoolboy Nazi to druggie panty sniffer to Mr James Ellroy-crime-writer-par-excellence. However, good as *My Dark Places* is, it still left me with the feeling that he's stuck, looking back at what he's done and struggling to find somewhere to move to next. On the evidence of *Crime Wave* it appears that he's not moved anywhere yet, and that he still shows no sign of knowing where to go. *Crime Wave* is a collection of reportage and fiction culled from the American edition of *GQ* magazine with a couple of new short stories thrown in for good measure. The non-fiction mostly reprises material from *My Dark Places*, which is no surprise because that book grew out of a feature from *GQ* in the first place. Aside from his mother's case, he looks at another unsolved homicide in the same area and with a similar MO. He looks at the OJ Simpson case; he spends time with cops; he meets people with whom he went to school. It's all mildly interesting stuff but that's it, perfect magazine fodder but somehow lacking when collected together in book form. The short stories are, if anything, even more disappointing than the reportage. All the Ellroy trademarks are here: alliteration; short, sharp sentences; plot changes aplenty. Unfortunately it reads like a caricature of Ellroy. The alliteration is taken to excess, so that a couple of pages into the story 'Hush Hush' you want to scream. And there's a plot change every sentence, as though he feels compelled to produce fiction that's ever more complex. I like James Ellroy and consider the LA Quartet to be amongst the best works of American literature this century. He illuminates a nether world of cops and corruption, racism and homophobia, paranoia and violence that has been air-brushed out of history. If his relationship to the 'big bad white men' who have the power is at times ambiguous, it's no matter because he pulls no punches. I just hope that he can get it together to write better books than this one. If you want a recommendation then check out the *Black Dahlia*, *The Big Nowhere*, *LA confidential* and *White Jazz*. **Pan Pantziarka**

TIGER TIGER

Aishling Morgan

255pp £5.99+£1 p&p; Nexus, 1999; ISBN 0-352-33455-X; payable Nexus Books; Cash Sales, Nexus Books, Thames Wharf Studios, Rainville Road, London, W6 9HT

Perhaps if I could learn greater appreciation for *Tiger Tiger*'s half-human, half-animal, sexually over-charged characters then I could appreciate the sensuality of this 'study in gothic eroticism' (*'Pull my tail', she hissed*). But, as if the strangeness of the creatures weren't enough, like an outsider at a fantasy convention, I just had to laugh at the animal character's names: Tian-Sha, Pomina, Rufina and Hoat (*'She comes to me whenever she is in season'*), amongst others. Many others. Don't get me wrong. I'm prepared to admit that *Tiger Tiger* may very well be a 'complex plot of erotic intrigue… played out against a background of arcane ritual' as the back cover spouts, but it didn't do it for me. There is certainly a sense of storyline and some reasonable characterisation in *Tiger Tiger*, but personally I couldn't make it past the bestial sex and peculiarly shaped genitals. Maybe it's my failing that I prefer my erotic heroes to be genetically just a tad more than half-human. **Sun Paige**

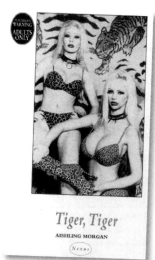

Tiger, Tiger

AISHLING MORGAN

NEXUS

THE DUNGEONMASTER'S APPRENTICE

Mark Ramsden

216pp £7.99; Serpent's Tail, 1999
ISBN 1-85242-623-3

Don't let the garish cover or stereotypical title put you off, *The Dungeonmaster's Apprentice* isn't just another granite-faced exercise in S&M litera-ture. Fleeing New York in the wake of some vaguely outlined murders, Matt and diminutive dominatrix Sasha plan to blend into the London fetish scene, only to have the mysterious Apprentice of the title start leaving them presents involving bits of dead cat. Things go from bad to worse as one of Sasha's clients has an unfortunate asphyxiation accident, and they subsequently get wrapped up in the mechanics of neo-Nazi occultism that also involves a high-kicking Hong Kong tattooist, a Cruella de Vil-style hag, and a longhaired old ponce with Crowleyite aspirations…

There's not a lot of sex, plenty of casual drug ingestion, and splatters of violence, but what makes this novel stand out is the supreme debunking of the lifestyle it describes, with Matt as its cynical narrator. Here, everyone is trying to out-transgress everyone else, and nobody wants to break their 'been-there-done-that' stance for fear of looking uncool. True to the consumerist nature of the late-20th century, if these freaks feel they want something, they demand to have it. This scene is pretentious, expensive, cliquey and so far up its own arse it's probably considered another sexual peccadillo. And, as written by ex-*Fetish Times* editor Mark Ramsden, it's also very, very, very funny.

What I find amusing about people who carp on about sexual activities that are considered 'alternative' is how they either (a) try to portray themselves as just your average working bod, or (b) think that an open relationship, a few bolts through the genitals and a maze of Celtic tattoos sufficiently distances them from the world's wage slaves and *Sun* readers. *The Dungeonmaster's Apprentice* shows that the rules and regulations of such lifestyles are not a million miles away from the *Art of the Barbecue* or *Proper Caravanning Techniques*; there are the usual lines you don't step over, and political correctness rears its freshly scrubbed head at the oddest of times. Some of the scenarios Matt and Sasha strike a pose through are disturbingly akin to Real Ale festivals.

This is an excellent novel, and deserves a much wider readership than it might initially attract; I can imagine *The Dungeonmaster's Apprentice* being ritualistically burned in cabalistic murder ceremonies in some of London's more humourless fetish clubs. I hope Ramsden doesn't feel he has to confine himself to this particular rubber-room of delights in future books. **Martin Jones**

"I'D RATHER YOU LIED"
Selected poems 1980-1998

Billy Childish

219pp £9.95; Codex, 1999
ISBN 1-899598-10-3

**From the wood-carved naked image
Her womb is washed and stained
From flowing tears of Billy Childish
Published on page two.**

**How quickly two decades have raced away
And how quickly our little Billy has grown
The result: the angry young man
Shot paradoxically accross the uni-verse
Determined verse to undermine
Overthrow his inner demon
To rehabilitate the soul and create fever
Throughout his existentialist university.**

**We salute you one hundred and thirty eight
Page compendium.
A guide light through our night
A template to daylight that promises
Bliss.**

**This I give to you, an inspirational high
A proposal of beauty and truth.
Or would you rather I'd lied.**

Will Youds

THE SPLINTERED DAY

V.K. Mina,

214pp £8.99; Serpent's Tail, 1999

Touted as 'a novel about love, multiplicity and the cross-currents of desire', *The Splintered Day* is actually a fragmented series of tales of cross-race and cross-gender relationships in New York City. Indian women cling hopelessly to West Indian men, black lesbians fall in love with straight women, heavy Asian girls date abusive drug-dealers with dreads; 'buppies' and 'b-boys' dance to reggae with lonely bisexual girls in Greenwich Village night clubs. Not quite the 'modern Emma Bovary' it's cracked up to be, *The Splintered Day* nevertheless tells honest, candid truths about the frustrations and complexities of modern human relationships. The main drawback to the book as a whole is that Mina seems to be drawn so regularly to certain themes and characters — surly boyfriends, Indian food, bad sex, tormented lesbians, unwanted pregnancies, sullen Asian girls trapped in miserable relationships with illiterate Rastafarians — that you end up getting the impression that it's a slice of

Art © Mark Farrelly

the author's sad personal life that's being endlessly revisited. A thoughtfully captured series of bad scenes that leaves you craving something entirely different. **Mikita Brottman**

SECRET ART
The Work of Mark Farrelly

8mins £5.00; Rictus Video; cheques payable to M. Farrelly, c/o The Julian Myers Gallery, 196 High Road, Wood Green, London, N22 8HH; commissions undertaken, original works & framed prints available

This is a video gallery exhibition of five works by Mark Farrelly. Though a mere eight minutes long, the viewer is treated to an in-depth examination of paintings and sculptures against a queasy soundtrack of vaguely sinister music, credited to 'Basil Kirchin and the Clockwork Wizards'. Cue Dr Phibes, Farrelly's central obsession in his pursuit of 'perfect' disfigurement. In the painting, *Dark Town Strutter's Ball*, this mildly arcane reference to Robert Fuest's horror movie is juxtaposed with the real-life horrific visage of Falklands hero, Simon Weston. This theme turns up again in *The Facio-Maxilia Nightmare* in which Weston's disfigured visage vies with images from *Dr Sardonicus* (whose rictus grin echoes Dr Phibes), *Eyes Without a Face* and Franco's *Faceless*. *Cantinflas is Dead* examines the rictus grin in the form of Mexico's Day of the Dead where the Aztecan goddess of the underworld lurks behind the flimsy façade of Catholicism. Farrelly's wax sculptures, the *Pickled Punks* are a reference to the deformed or disfigured medical specimens (real or fabricated) of carnival culture. Another sculpture takes the central figures of *Dark Town Strutter's Ball* — those of Phibes and his lover, Vulnanvia — and exposes their visages as three-dimensional topographics for the camera to explore. With gallery space at an optimum, as dictated by the provincially minded orthodoxy of the 'official' art-world, the way forward for artists like Mark Farrelly would seem to be with video exhibitions like this one. Highly recommended, the nicely illustrated box comes with three postcard prints of Farrelly's paintings. **Stephen Sennitt**

SUCKER
dir: Hans Rodionoff, USA

cast: Yan Birch, Monica Baber, PK Phillips 91mins; Digital Entertainment; Cert. 18

Rock band blood-suckers who prey on big breasted groupies. Lots of blood

and lots of naked flesh dripping in comic book primary colours. With Michael Herz and Lloyd Kaufman taking executive producer credits, *Sucker* has Troma stamped all over it! Like most of the Troma catalogue, this has absolutely no idea how to be shocking or funny. It tries but falls flat on its face at every hurdle. With a kung-fu kicking vampire hunting babe out to infect a vampire with HIV, *Sucker* is about as predictable as a bowel movement and arrives on our video shelves a decade too late to be controversial. The latter half switches tone in an attempt to convey sympathy for the vampire as he develops skin cancer and sticks to a regime of combination therapy. It's the type of film Joe Bob Briggs would probably give a thumbs-up to. Anyone with half a brain shouldn't waste their spit renting it. **David Greenall**

SHRIEK
dir: Victoria Sloan, USA

cast: Tanya Dempsy, Jamie Gannon, Parry Allen; 75mins; High Flyers, Cert.15

Desperately trying to cash in on the *Scream/Faculty* boom in teen-horror, *Shriek* is yet another tale of buffed up, tanned Californian college kids vs homicidal monster. But this one has its roots dipping in real quality, taking much of its structure from Jacques Tourneur, ie the brilliant *Night Of The Demon* (1957). You know the score, whoever finds a symbolic scrawl on a piece of paper on their person is next for the chop. The monster in this instance however is nothing more than a two-headed piece of rubber that walks through walls and shrieks with excitement as it kills. Its victims are all photogenic and like to emphasise their hetrosexuality without appearing politically incorrect. They are a bland bunch, except for Robert who lives in the basement and dabbles in the occult. At 75 minutes *Shriek* is painfully long and with a '15' certificate is pretty much void of any decent gore. It simply plods along on autopilot in the usual 'and then there were none' mode. With such credentials it will no doubt turn up on Channel 5 very soon. **David Greenall**

PARTS
The Clonus Horror
dir: Robert S. Fiveson, USA 1979

cast: Timothy Donnelly, Keenan Wynn, Peter Graves; 85mins; Digital Ent.; Cert. 18

Made the year after *Coma* proved a box-office success, *Parts* is based

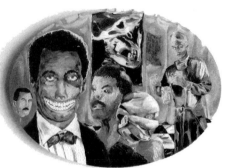

The Facio-Maxilia Nightmare. Oil on wood, 1999. From SECRET ART.

around the idea of cloning people in case they need organ transplants in later life — Clonus being a top secret, government funded medical institute where the clones are raised without knowledge of their real purpose in life. Constantly monitered by men in white, the clones are promised a release in America when their time is right, the reality being deep freeze suspended animation. But trouble is brewing and in typical 'nature finds a way' style, the inquisitive nature of two clones-in-love results in escape and confrontation.

The conclusion is a depressing affair: Clonus escapee Robert eventually returns to his lover only to find her a lobotomised mong. All trace of his existence in the outside world has been wiped-out by Men In Black.

I remember renting this one out pre-VRA and finding it quite enjoyable. Ten years on it doesn't really look too good — the quality is a little washed out and the content contrived. It feels almost Cronenberg at times, but just fails to hit the mark. **David Greenall**

SWEET ANGEL MINE
dir: Curtis Radclyffe, Britain/Canada

cast: Oliver Milburn, Margaret Langrick, Anna Massey, 85mins; High Fliers; Cert.18

Reviewers who write for slick, newstand magazines have developed a tedious propensity in recent years for putting across what *they think* is the most amount of 'information' in the least amount of words: the technique in question could be called the *meets* technique. You know the one I mean — where the reviewer says something like 'John Harrison's new book is Alan Bennett *meets* Reservoir Dogs' (or some such meaningless shite). In the case of *Sweet Angel Mine*, a low-budget and rather dull Canadian horror film with admittedly pretty locations, the slick *Loaded* offers the gem, 'like Psycho meets Twin

Peaks'; an epithet that does little justice to the classic status of Hitchcock's finest film, or the fearsome brilliance of *Fire Walk With Me*. Supposedly, they recombined to even greater effect in *Sweet Angel Mine*! Nothing could be further from the truth. *Sweet Angel Mine* is, not surprisingly, in contrast to its supposed models, wooden, clichéd, uneventful and almost totally lacking in suspense. The characters, though reasonably well played, are uniformly uninteresting and in some cases downright annoying, especially in the case of affected 'Londoner' backpacker Oliver Milburn, complete with his Downes Syndrome hairstyle. But this is hardly the fault of *Sweet Angel Mine* and more the gross stupidity of those reviewers of the 'soundbite' generation for making such poorly considered comparisons in the first place, sacrificing the necessity of judging a work on its own merit for a quick and ill-considered slogan that actually does more harm than good in the long run.

Still, bugger it! Truth be told, I've always wanted to move into the big time as a slick newsstand magazine reviewer. Forget 'Psycho *meets* Twin Peaks', Four Stars. Try 'Texas Chainsaw Massacre *meets* Little Women', one-and-a-half. **Stephen Sennitt**

UFO
Episode 1: Exposed
Episode 2: Survival
Digital Entertainment
The first I heard of Gerry Anderson's *UFO* was a couple of Headpresses ago. I was barely sperm when the programme was shown and have never before seen it. So for me at least the program must stand on its own two feet without the safety net of nostalgia. Just as now-primitive design and SFX do not render an irredeemable pile of crap good (as in 'so bad it's good') neither should they detract from ideas executed with originality and atmosphere, not to the discerning viewer at least.

These tapes have obviously been released to cash in on the never-ending wave of retro-trendy kitsch nonsense, but divorce them from that obnoxious context and they are not without merit. On their own terms there is a philosophy at work. Take the politics of the situation: when our SHADO (Supreme Headquarters Alien Defence Organisation) heroes find a UFO, they blast the living shit out of it. Simple as that. There's no touchy-feely bollocks; the show was made when the Cold War was still going strong, and it shows. The men of SHADO are defenders of their world, killers of aliens and stoic in the face of danger, men on a mission who can't allow their humanity to interfere with the work at band... the product of a bygone age before the whole Western world went into therapy. When their womenfolk can't deal with the long hours and secrecy, their relationships end: there are greater tasks to be done. Still, the SHADO base has certain consolations in the form of the female staff, resplendent in purple bobs, Cleopatra makeup and great silver outfits. Sadly these glam femmes don't do too much in these episodes — save for a good bit where a Chinese girl gets a bloke in a headlock — but they make for fine decor. The aliens dress like someone you'd expect to see at Torture Garden, all red leather and chains. The rocket ships have one big missile protruding from the nose that fires rudely into the distance. And the title sequence shows the astronauts jumping feet first into smooth circular tunnels... what would Dr Freud have made of it all? **Anton Black**

SEX AND ZEN III
dir: Chang Man, HK
88mins; MIA; Cert. 18
Supremely silly 'Red Footbinding Diary'-style softcore goings-on. I haven't seen the first two in this series, so don't know how this compares. It's easy enough on the eye, if surprisingly brutal at times, and clearly has a good grasp of what its target audience wants — production values are high, acres of naked female flesh are on display and the women get a pretty rough ride throughout. For all the popularity of Hong Kong Cat III movies in the UK and US, I'm often surprised by how traditional they are. The plot and characters of this one are straight out of a Seventies Golden Harvest movie, and there's a timewarp feel to the whole thing — which isn't, in this case, a recommendation. Compared to some whacked-out Nikkatsu film, it doesn't really have much to offer. But I'm sure it won't disappoint the punters. Come on, you know who you are. **James Marriott**

SUSAN'S PLAN
dir: John Landis, USA
cast: Natassja Kinski, Billy Zane, Dan Ackroyd; 85mins; High Fliers; Cert. 18
Susan (Nastassja Kinski) wants her ex-husband dead so that she and the new man in her life (Billy Zane) can get their hands on a substantial life insurance payout. Two down-at-heel petty crooks are called in to do the murderous deed and — guess what? — it all goes horribly wrong.
I'm hard-pushed to figure what makes this 'outrageous non-stop action comedy' — as noted on the videobox — a 'comedy' exactly. The only concession to humour seems to be the tired, familiar comedy face of Dan Ackroyd (who's completely miscast here as a love-lorn biker-heavy). From this poor vantage point the film goes rapidly downhill, as several peripheral characters are drawn together for an achingly contrived series of farcical encounters.
However, I thought I had this lame movie pegged as some kind of elaborate joke on the viewer when it unexpectedly shifted gear halfway through with a series of brutally blood-thirsty set-pieces. But I was wrong — it's just a bad movie with the paw prints of a failed post-production salvage job all over it. Completely fucked.

THE LAST BUS HOME
dir: Johnny Gogan, Ireland
cast: Annie Ryan, Brian F. O'Byrne, Anthony Brophy; 96mins; Showcase; Cert. 15
The Last Bus Home concerns the trials and tribulations of The Dead Patriots, a burgeoning Punk band in late-Seventies Dublin who just might have what it takes to make the big time (big like the Outcasts, that is). Pursued by the requisite rival faction (a couple of skinheads) and courted by a record company (who seem *really* easy to please), the band enjoy a brief spell as local heroes before reality comes crashing in.
Following some rather laboured attempts at sparkling wit, the film hits its stride when the group finally develops its own identity and conflicts within begin to emerge. With a record deal looming in London, the band is torn between commitment, emotional baggage, making money, and integrity. This is nothing you won't have seen before, but it remains compelling nonetheless (though we'll not ponder too long or hard on the dumb ending, suffice it to say that lounge music as 'catharsis' is a very bad idea...)
Showcase have a small catalogue of independent British films like this one, encroaching on territory once exclusive to Screen Edge. It'll be interesting to see how they fare in the charts.

GIULIA /
THE GLIMPSE VIDEO
dir: Roy Stuart

For details send self addressed *unstamped* envelope to: Roy Stuart, 19 rue Richer, 75009 Paris, France

Readers may be familiar with Roy Stuart's photographic work through the books published by Taschen (*Roy Stuart* vol I and II — see previous editions of HEADPRESS). These two videos incorporate several of the key themes and ideas prevalent in Stuart's photographic vignettes, and utilise many of the photographer's extremely pretty models.

Giulia is a short film supervised by Tinto Brass for a series intended for cable TV. The story revolves around the eponymous Giulia, a young Parisian performing arts student who secretly works in a live sex show, and whose sister and mother are devout Catholics. When she discovers the real reason why her dance teacher has excluded her from a tour of Italy (he'd rather take his lover Eric), Giulia follows anyway and seeks sexual retribution: first on her teacher, and then seemingly on Catholicism itself. It is this final scene — which shows the naked Giulia openly taking a piss near the Vatican — that stirred up some understandable controversy for the film. The Italian senator Michele Buonastesta announced that *Giulia* should be forbidden because of its 'public insult against religion'.

It's all very pleasant in a Tinto Brass kind of way, but in spite of its rich atmosphere and show-stopping finale, *Giulia* rather pales next to Stuart's *Glimpse Video*. This particular two hour-plus montage is a strange beast indeed, offering a straightforward intimate fantasy scenario one minute, and the next pulling back to reveal the charade of it all: actors and actresses in front of a camera crew, receiving directions. In direct contrast, other sequences show models masturbating to a very evident genuine climax, interspersed with what appears to be playful home-movie footage and clandestine *Candid Camera*-like escapades (a group of beautiful bikini models doing their aerobics in what appears to be an old people's holiday home, for example).

All of this is set to cut-up pieces of music, which give the feel of something out of the New York underground. *Glimpse* opens with a young-looking ballerina being seduced by an older girl. The emphasis is on hands

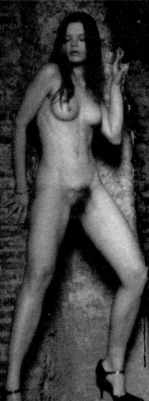

slipping into lycra pants. Next, a girl in the street flashes her soiled underwear to the camera, just as an old woman happens by and raises a ruckus over an irregularly parked car. A woman gets caught short and has to take a piss in an alley — 'wet scenes' are a predilection of Stuart's. We move indoors for some fetish wear and penetrative sex. There is no cum-shot, the film crew is clearly in shot, and the sequence incorporates some very unporno-like edits. A sleeping girl is oblivious to the foot and panty sniffer who has sneaked into her bedroom. A girl is sold in a white slave auction. In one of the few scripted lines of dialogue, a dominatrix says to her trick "You can masturbate now… That's not very good". A sex scene in a tattoo parlour shows a tattoo emblazoned on a guy's arm that reads 'I Love Big Tits'…

Those people seeking hardcore sex would be better advised to go elsewhere. There is some hardcore material on offer here, but not much. The real focus of *Glimpse* lies elsewhere… If your thing is bonny looking, pale skinned teens (and they certainly don't come any bonnier than the long haired hip love-goddess at the film's end),

and you fancy some imaginative and stylish 'Reality eroticism', then you really need look no further than this.

MICHAEL WELDON'S
MONDO PSYCHOTRONIC!!

NTSC; $20+$3p&p (cash, cheque, m.o. or credit card) to Psychotronic, 7549 Rt. 97, Narrowsburg, NY 12764

Email: psychotronic@ezoccess.net

Michael Weldon is the editor/publisher of *Psychotronic Video*, one of the more interesting and — having recently celebrated its 30th issue — longest running independent trash cinema magazines. He is also the author of the voluminous and critically acclaimed *Psychotronic* film guides. This two-hour video is a visual guide to the 'psychotronic credo', courtesy of movie, TV and home-video clips. It's also a slice of shameless self-publicity for Weldon and by the end looks like an off-kilter episode of *This Is Your Life*. But there is so much going on, and at such a fast rate, that it's impossible to get bored by any of it. The tape opens with a promo trailer for an ITC series that never was called *The Psychotronic Zone*, which effectively would have lifted Weldon's ideas ad hoc. Thanks to his lawyers, Weldon successfully scuppered ITC's plans. (Back in HEADPRESS 14, I pondered how Weldon could copyright 'Psychotronic' when the word already existed in the title of a cheap 1980 movie. Well, watching this video and the proposed rip-off antics of ITC, I can appreciate *why* he did so — if not how.) Clips that follow include some rare TV archive stuff (like a vaudeville performer of the Thirties by the name of The Banana Man — a man dressed as a woman dressed as a man), musical excerpts (such as a demented Timothy Carey fronting a Rock'n'Roll band, in a positively electrifying moment from *The World's Greatest Sinner*), and rare film clips (including the opening credits for the hippie musical *Love Commune*). The latter half of the tape comprises mainly of Weldon's TV appearances, and while this is all very painless and entertaining, I'd like to have seen more obscure clips in the vein of Al Adamson, who is seen here briefly on a talk show.

Mondo Psychotronic!! comes with a lengthy accompaniment penned by Weldon, which ties the often seemingly random pieces of film into a biographical whole.

NAKED KILLER
The Director's Cut

dir: Clarence Fok Yiu Leung, 1992

103mins; Hong Kong Classics; Cert. 18

It isn't difficult to see why so much of a buzz surrounded *Naked Killer* on its release, and continues to do so with this special re-release some seven years later. It's got all the right ingredients: beautiful women, lesbian sex, and some stunning Cat III action. A spate of brutal killings leaves the police puzzled, with only a young cop by the name of Tinam believing it might be the work of elite, man-hating female assassins. Tinam gets much too close to the truth when his girlfriend Kitty, trying to avenge the death of her father, is forced to shed her identity and join the elite band of killers. The assassins' seemingly impenetrable façade crumbles however when Princess — a former trainee and 'wealthy lesbian' — returns to the fold just as Kitty is tempted away from it, back to a life with Tinam. All three women meet for a fight to the death, leaving Tinam relegated to the wings on account of his physical aversion to firearms (subtle, eh?).

As to what constitutes the 'sensational previously unseen footage' in this director's cut, I'm at a loss to say. But I'd hazard a guess it has something to do with the multifarious scenes of sexual violence and trauma to the genitals, the preferred method of injury facing the women's 'shiteating' male victims. Then again it might be the block of kissy-kissy exposition which almost draws the latter part of the movie to a dead halt.

JACKIE CHAN
My Stunts

dir: Jackie Chan, 1998

94mins; Hong Kong Classics; Cert. 12

This is something of a 'Master Class' for armchair martial arts movie enthusiasts. While it may guide some young hopefuls towards a career in chock-socky filmmaking, its main audience will undoubtedly be the fans of Jackie himself, anticipating once more white-knuckle adventures with their hero's most dangerous stunts. There is no doubt that Jackie has put his life on the line many times, with even seemingly straight-forward stunts — like running down a *steep* incline in the first *Police Story* movie — taking on a chilling slant when the very real dangers are made apparent. But those in search of bloody mishaps would be well advised to look else-where (like the old episode of Jonathan Ross' *Incredibly Strange Film Show*). For the most part, *My Stunts* leaves out the bruisings and life-threatening close-shaves — the 'freak show' element — for a very entertaining crash-course on Hong Kong action cinema, along with some tricks of the trade from its leading exponent.

It's for good reason that Jackie utilises his own crack team of stunt men whenever possible (they take falls onto actual glass because it looks more dynamic than the fake alternative). In a rooftop fight sequence involving an 'outside' stuntman for the film *Who Am I?*, for example, Chan gets increasingly exasperated as the blows reigned upon him are delivered incorrectly and serve to push him backwards towards the building's edge.

The eight-man team also have a 'Stunt Lab' where they work out inventive new stunts, putting the human body through more twists and turns than seemingly possible. But Chan takes an obstinate pride in having to do things this way, even if it means a thousand takes to get a shot looking just right — as demonstrated by his kicking a vase repeatedly into the face of an opponent!

PLAGUE

dir: Ed Hunt, 1978

cast: Daniel Pilon, Kate Reid, Celine Lomez; Digital Entertainment, Cert. 18

With all the current furore surrounding genetic modification, it isn't difficult to see how this stinker from 1978 might have come up as a plausible title for re-release.

When a scientist flaunts laboratory safety regulations in order to further her experiments in DNA, an unquantifiable side effect produces a lethal bacteria that causes death within hours. The scientist herself is the first to succumb — with so much emphasis placed on a leg calliper that one suspects it to have some great bearing on the antidote that must be discovered before the movie ends. (It doesn't.) The lab is placed under immediate quarantine, but an employee makes a break for it and inadvertently helps to transmit the deadly virus to the outside world.

Not that the viewer gets to witness much of this first hand — death tolls are related via the grim looking officials who bark orders from behind their desk, or look quizzically into TV monitors as a lone scientist works around the clock to come up with an antidote. (If that doesn't give you some idea of the scale of the budget, the cardboard sign outside the laboratory that wobbles in the wind might.) Extremely dull affair, heightened momentarily by the fact the carrier seeks solace from the police in a theatre whose marquee promises *Sexual Freedom in Germany*, *Chain Gang Women*, *Italian Connection* and *Superchick* no less.

Now that'd be something to see.

AFFLICTION

dir: Mark Hejner, 1996

59,95NLG; 2602 Media Madness; Contact: Chainsaw Video, Voorstraat 44, 3512 AP Utrecht, The Netherlands

www.chainsaw.demon.nl

Email: arno@chainsaw.demon.nl

Some of you older readers might recall that *Affliction* featured way back in HEADPRESS 14. Well, courtesy of Chainsaw Video, here is an opportunity for European viewers to tune in and turn off to this risible compilation of underground artists and geeks at work. Performers like Mike Diana and GG Allin will be familiar to most anyone with a passing interest in things transgressive, but few will have had the opportunity to see either in quite the bare-assed light in which they're presented here. Diana — banned-from-drawing by law — takes out his frustrations on a Good News Bible and crucifix. Ingesting a vomit-inducing potion, he sits and waits ashen-faced for the drug to take effect. 'I think I feel a bit of churning in my stomach,' he tells the viewer anxiously, 'does that make you happy?' While we wait for the puke to come, *Affliction* takes time out with segments from the other performers… Turbo Tom uses himself as a human dartboard, sticks a spike through his cheek and places his hand into an animal trap, while the ski-masked Full Force Frank, the producer of a zine that salutes mass murder and women's feet, threatens to kill people because it's what he's 'gotta do'. His philosophy? 'My mind isn't small, it's big. Guns are big too.' Back to Diana: 'I'm just waiting fer it to come up.' Annie Sprinkle performs her tit ballet. Concert footage of the late GG Allin taking a shit on stage and eating it ('What you all went to see,' admonishes director Hejnar), is followed by Allin encouraging a girl backstage to squirt ass-ketchup onto his French Fries before devouring them. And if you think that must be the taste-less highlight of the tape, you'd be

THE PHANTASM BOX SET
Phantasm, Phantasm II, Phantasm III
dir: Don Coscarelli, USA, 1979, 1988 & 1995
£24.99; Digital Entertainment; Cert. 18

Phantasm is something of a horror classic. Its surreal story involves the dead being brought back to life as hooded dwarf slaves, a threatening Tall Man who stomps around the place in slow motion, trepanning silver spheres that fly through the air, an ice cream van that plays its music through the night, a netherworld that can be reached through a pitchfork, and a funny looking kid as a hero. (Oh, and the music sounds like the best bits of Fabio Frizzi's *City of the Living Dead*.) The success of *Phantasm* led director Don Coscarelli to make three sequels, utilising the same cast members on an adventure that gets crazier with each instalment. Watching each film back-to-back (as I did recently) is a weird experience, almost like reacquainting yourself with old friends. By part IV, Angus Scrimm as The Tall Man is looking decidedly doddery. All the episodes have a distinctive atmosphere, with part II being particularly gruesome and bleak (as well as my own personal favourite). Here, our heroes Michael (played in this instalment by James Le Gros) and Reggie (Reggie Bannister) pursue the Tall Man as he pillages the graveyards of small towns, the whole thing coming over like *Evil Dead II* if it had been made as a road movie. Digital Entertainment have recently released the first three *Phantasm* films as a video box set. To commemorate, I spoke with director Don Coscarelli.

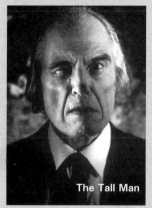

The Tall Man

HEADPRESS Where did the inspiration for PHANTASM and the silver balls come from?
DON Doing a film in the sci fi/horror genre was inevitable for me. As a child, all I wanted to watch were horror films, all I wanted to read was science fiction. During an early screening of my second film, *Kenny and Co.*, there was a sequence involving a man in a monster costume who jumped out, and the audience screamed in surprise. I thought to myself, 'this is an interesting response!' So I decided that in my next film I would go for screams, the more the better. As to the spheres, they came to me in a dream. Honestly! I was in my teens and what I can remember had mainly to do with my fleeing down endlessly long marble corridors, pursued by a chrome sphere intent on penetrating my skull with a wicked needle. As far as I can remember, the spheres never caught up with me. They still haven't.

PHANTASM II follows on exactly where the first film left off. Did you always have a 'bigger picture' in mind when you made the first film? The original *Phantasm* was intended to be a stand-alone film. However, after seeing how *Phantasm II* worked (starting the sequel the moment after the original ended) and the power of the fan response, the pattern of the story line evolved easily. I now understand that The Tall Man is even more enterprising than I could ever have imagined, as I have come to believe he wants nothing less than world domination and the annihilation of our species.

Was Angus Scrimm the ideal you had in mind when you envisioned The Tall Man? Angus was my first and only choice for the part. I had worked with him on my first film, *Jim—The World's Greatest*.

Michael Baldwin — who plays the kid in PHANTASM — isn't in the second film, but returned in the third and fourth. What was the reason? When Universal Pictures decided to finance *Phantasm II* they placed certain conditions and one was that a young, working actor play Mike. As Michael Baldwin had been out of the movie business for several years, the executives insisted on someone else. I was forced to make a choice and cast James LeGros, who did an excellent job. However, when funding became available for *Phantasm III* there were no restrictions on cast and I approached Baldwin about returning to the role.

How did the actors feel returning to their roles after so much time? Reggie seems to be having a ball in part III! Reggie certainly revels in his character and loves shooting! All the actors and I have become close friends over the years. We truly enjoy working with one another.

Each film has a different feel. Was this a conscious effort — to create different tones with each instalment? Yes and no. Part III was definitely an attempt to expand the *Phantasm* world, to include some more characters and add some intentional humour. Part IV was intended as a return to the serious nature of the original. However, I have received many comments that *Phantasm II* is the most serious and grim of the series, and it is not a tone I originally set out to create.

The series on the whole is pretty surreal. How easy is it for you to sell your ideas and films, having this quality? It's very difficult. In fact, all my films have been made independently and then sold for distribution afterwards. I never even dreamed to try and sell the original *Phantasm* to a distributor prior to production. There was no way they would 'get it'.

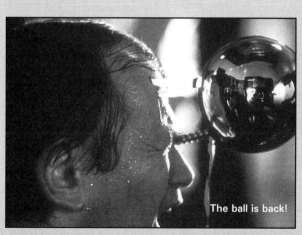

The ball is back!

PHANTASM

mistaken. I'd say that dubious, leg-crossing honour goes to the practice of blood-showering: a pin jabbed into the head of an erect penis on the vinegar stroke, sends a stream of blood and cum (more blood than cum) into the face of young man. Wisely knowing when it's beat, *Affliction* closes on this lovely tableaux. But yes, Diana does eventually manage to puke. He also gets to read one of his outlawed comic strips.

CINEMA OF TRANSGRESSION
Various, US, 1986-1992
147mins; BFI; Cert. 18

As part of their 'History of the Avant-Garde' series, the BFI have dedicated a volume to classics of the Transgressive Underground. For anyone not familiar, these are films that began to emanate out of New York's Lower East Side in the mid Eighties, made by and starring no-good punk kids. Courtesy of the guiding hand of Jack Sargeant, the BFI have done a grand job in collating a fair and varied Transgressive cross-section, amongst them: Nick Zedd's *Police State* (a must-see for anyone remotely interested in how good, funny and powerful no-budget filmmaking can be), Richard Kern's *The Evil Cameraman* (a radical fetish piece that saw the director being kicked out of one venue following its screening), and Tommy Turner & David Wojnarowicz' *Where Evil Dwells* (a loose adaptation of the Ricky Kasso story, the Satan Teen killer). There are some other works that may not be so familiar, such as Tessa Hughes-Freeland's *Baby Doll* (a documentary about two go-go dancers) and M. Henry Jones' short animated adverts. The latter permeate the tape, and while appearing a little too colourful and accomplished in comparison to the other material showcased (which tends to be scratched, grainy and b&w), they do help to create an overall 'party tape' impression. Buy.

ANUS PRESLEY
Music To Listen To When You're Dead
CD; Jazzassin Records/HWE; £10/$12; Jan R. Bruun, Munkebekken 257, N-1061 Oslo, Norway

Hmm. Good cartoons, boys. And great song titles. 'The Glorious Shining Path to Bosnia'. 'Dead Niggers'. 'Nietzsche is a Mommy's Boy'. Whatever you say. The music's not too bad, though, cheap flash-fried noise in a kindergarten Merzbow style, but there's not much to distinguish Anus Presley from other entry-level electronic noise 'artists'. Their amusing name, perhaps? Considering how much of this kind of thing's out there now, I can't imagine anyone actually buying Anus Presley apart from friends of the band. As they themselves admit, the music was recorded at 'a time when nobody had any money or talent'. I'm impressed by their honesty, but they really should get a new copywriter. **James Marriott**

TORTURE GARDEN
Bizarre and Eccentric Music Compilation
CD; Torture Garden Records
www.torturegarden.com

There was I expecting an all-out assault of industrial techno, but instead this is really a compilation of bizarre and eccentric music, and apart from one track it's also extremely listenable. It kicks-off with 'The Tiger Lillies', a kind of decadent cabaret style track. Next up are Von Magnet with an excellent mixture of electronics and Arabic vocals — it's one of the best things on the CD. Unfortunately that's followed by a crud of a track by performance art group Minty. The less said the better. Coil do much better, but then you'd expect them to. I was expecting the worst from Boyd Rice (who performs a duet with Tiffany Anders), neo-Nazi Satanist and misanthrope par excellence. Instead we get a sweetly sung duet straight out the early Sixties. No doubt the lyrics are shocking, the ironic conjunction of sweet melodic sound and downright nasty words being too good to miss, but to be honest I wasn't listening. Death In June, also Nazi-obsessed, are up next in a laughable paean to power. It's just so scary. Mee and Test Dept are much better, the latter's contribution being superb. There's more cabaret with Naked Ruby; a nicely sleazy track from DA Jones for the Dragon Ladies to strut their stuff to; Flesh Fetish sound like Miranda Sex Garden, and Blackfoot and the Voola do nothing for me with their Hammer Horror rock. If only there'd been a bit more of the likes of Coil, Test Dept and less of the likes of Minty and Death In June, this would have been an even better collection. Buy it anyway, it's worth it. **Pan Pantziarka**

VARIOUS
100% Genuine
£6.99; CD; Distributed in UK by Vital

Steve tells us in a gormless Yorkshire accent how he would like to put his Purple Bulb between your lipsticked lips. He imagines the ladies out there getting moist at the thought of it and reckons his nine inches would touch the back of their throats no problem. Tony is from Plymouth and likes wearing stockings, suspenders and *especially* French Knickers. He wants those with a similar interest to speak with him… Sandra is 39, happily married and would like a sexual experience with another woman. Her husband is aware of this… Lee is desperate for you…

This CD is a collection of 40 messages left by individuals placing voicemail 'Personal' ads. Thanks to the judicious selection process the majority of them are bizarre and truly hilarious. Straights, gays, lesbians and bisexuals all feature, and reveal themselves to be staggeringly ordinary people who can find no other outlet for their sexual needs than via this process.

During the first listen I laughed my cock off but by the third or fourth time I was contemplative as to what these messages taken as a whole say about society and human sexuality. Maybe nothing much? One thing that is apparent is that *everyone* is a fetishist. I always knew I was but compared to some of the folks on here I'm fairly predictable. There are leather fans, boot lickers and submissives as you'd expect but there are also sock and shiny DM's fetishists too. There's 'Felicity' an allegedly 'effeminate' transsexual with a voice so deep and overtly male that you have to wonder how he missed his calling doing Action Movie trailer voice-overs. Instead he likes to be a housemaid, forced to submit to 'old-fashioned domestic drudgery'. Then there's Robert who wants a lady who dresses like a tart, acts like a tart and loves long, slow 69's. And then there's the retired schoolteacher who especially likes to hear from clergymen and ministers who want to receive a severe — and I do mean *severe* — beating. Not forgetting Del who's a monk in a semi-silent religious order looking for a woman of 18-25 years old to teach him the art of sexual performance.

These are people looking for something to get them off. Which, I suppose, could be said for all of us. Despite the unintentional hilarity of some of the approaches, I was left with a warped kind of respect for these people: you can either face up to who you are and express it while you can, or you can or bottle it up and stew in your own angst and frustration until you die. So, more power to Ruth, who's 48-28-38 (fucking hell!) and wants 48-38-40 in a male. And Dave who lives on a small island off the coast of Scotland and is looking for phone sex with submissive women in leather. And Stuart who wants guys up to 45 in white socks. And Colin, the submissive bisexual with a machine gun stutter!

It's all too easy to laugh at other people's secret desires, but if this CD doesn't make you sit and think about your own fetishes and fantasies and the lengths you'll sometimes go to fulfil them, then maybe *you're* the one that's not 'normal'. **Rik Rawling**

PJ PROBY
The Waste Land

CD; Savoy, 44 Wilmslow Road, Withington, Manchester, M20 3BW

Is it strange that Savoy has released this CD of rock's lost wild man reading TS Eliot's modernist landmark? Is this pranksterism on their part or a more serious venture? Well, it's Savoy we're talking about — so who the heck knows? Stick the disc in and it becomes obvious... who better than Savoy to treat Eliot's vision of human spiritual devolution to an update? However, whereas Eliot would seem to perceive some (slim) potential for redemption in his work, Savoy sees the world as irretreiveably lost. This is hardly odd, given the locus of much of their output being WW2 — Eliot could have no notion of the theatrical unhumanness WW2 would eventually bring about. David Britton has made a living from eviscerating it, bathing in its every screaming shattered shard. Eliot bewildered us with a groundbreaking slew of mythical references, Britton batters us with a postmodern Burroughsian barrage of

intertextual insanity. *The Waste Land* is a disciplined studied work (especially after Ezra Pound edited it), no stream of noodling consciousness; likewise, *Lord Horror* et al are packed with carefully considered extremity. There is thought and intelligence behind them, not just silly teenage shock-your-mum aimlessness. After all, rock stars invoking the Dark Lord look pretty hopeless when stacked up against Kristallnacht, the Pogroms and Auschwitz. It takes WORK to artistically depict the blackened soul of humanity — mooning at an MP doesn't really cut it in quite the same way. Proby's rasping vocal presence moves the poem from a bewildered UK Prufrock sensibility into Yankee trash dementia. Perhaps America has at this time the most to learn from Eliot? New Roman Empire and all that? PJ is quite controlled here, which is to say: objectively, not much. His drawl doesn't always add to matters — though it's always great to listen to — but Eliot's use of repetition does spring to life by being recited. The intonation is not always random. It goes wild for the hysterical endnote of 'A Game of Chess' but quietens the Hell down for the funeral obit of 'The Fire Sermon'. What next? A 20 CD box set of *Ulysses*, read by Roky Erickson I daresay. **Anton Black**

[*Also available on CD is the Savoy Talking Book,* LORD HORROR, *featuring hardcore excerpts from David Britton's controversial novel, read by Proby.*]

TERMINAL SOLUTION

cassette; Contact: David Chapman, 20 The Dell, Stevenage, herts, SG1 1PH

Terminal Solution? Note the not-so-risque allusion to the Final Solution? Are we meant to be shocked or something? Names like Terminal Solution are more likely to induce terminal boredom than anything else. But that

whinge aside, this tape is certainly worth a listen. The music's reminiscent of Front Line Assembly with a dash of Front 242 and even, at times, of Consolidated. That should give an idea of what to expect: semi-militaristic beats, sequencers, muscular rhythms, white noise and snarled lyrics which are way down low in the mix. It works well enough. It's hard to make out the lyrics, but the usual 'Industrial' concerns with spree killing, mind control and so on are evident in the four track titles: 'Thrill', 'Opium for the Masses', 'Efficiency Born' and 'The Day After'. There's around 20 minutes of music on the tape, and if you like industrial electronics then you'll go for this. **Pan Pantziarka**

EXPOSE YOUR EYES
Z=z²+C

CD; Paul Harrison, 18 Canal Road, Sowerby Bridge, HX6 2AY; mail order list available

This is fancy! I'm feeling all warm and gooey on the interior because this CD is numbered 15/31 and I got one! Truly a limited edition, and frankly I can see why. I think these are some of the most Goddamn annoying tones ever committed to disc. I don't know what the point is... If it's supposed to be annoying, well then it's a rousing success; if not, it's a pitiful waste of 650 megabytes.

This is all junior-got-a-laptop-with-virtual-analog-synths nonsense, except in the case of track eight where junior got a phase shifter too. This baby clocks in at 74:19 and you'll be filling your ears full of molten lead long before that to make it go away. As much as I don't like this, I have to admit that the whole idea that someone made this at their house is incredibly appealing in a medieval basketweaving kind of way. The cover is printed on glossy inkjet photo paper with an obscure mathematical video thing on it. Puzzling... Fascinating... I wonder what the current NHL standings are?

Carl Sagan samples and vague references to the actor Rip Torn are beyond me. This whole thing is beyond me... I have a headache. I think this could make someone very angry. As this is an extremely limited issue, and utterly transgressive, I'd be willing to let it go for, say, £75. Any takers?
Mark Deutrom

NUNCHAKU
Best Of, 1993-1998
CD; Howling Bull, PO Box 40129, San Francisco CA 94140, USA
www.howlingbull.com

These guys are really hauling ass... 15 songs in 35 minutes. They are in a real hurry and positively sound like they are racing each other to the end of the song. This is 100mph Japanese crossover hardcore metal, heavily influenced by the California East Bay metal scene of the mid-1980s.

As far as this stuff goes, these guys know how to do it. Wall o'chocolate puddin' guitars, tub thumper drums, completely indecipherable lyrics (they're Japanese) and a solo bass riff every once in a while just to let you know there is a bassist.

They can definitely play, but in the end it's like French Fries. The first one is all magical, the second one less so, and so on. There's nothing new here, but for fans of Nunchaku, I'd say this is probably the one to get if you're having a party and don't want to search through all your Nunchaku CDs looking for all the hits.
Mark Deutrom

UNITED
Distorted Vision
CD; Howling Bull; Details above

United is Japanese Crossover Metal. These are the bastard children of Metallica, DRI, Crumbsuckers, and others of that ilk. While this stuff ruled certain parts of the good ol' USA in

the mid-Eighties, it sounds a little long in the tooth now. How much bigger, tighter and faster can you get when everything big and fast and tight has been done? These kind of bands hinge on athletic oneupmanship instead of making any intrinsic artistic statement, no matter how banal.

United manages a couple of moments that are downright musical, such as on the track 'Colours', which contains the tender sentiment 'I pity children who are born into this piece of shit world'. Fortunately, all the lyrics are printed so we can sing right along! I havn't had so much fun since I sang 'Highway To Hell' at an AC/DC gig. United are somewhat diverse and certainly have their moments, but a little goes a long way so I'd have to recommend this only for the purist who likes his metal fast, loud, precise and in the company of other men, because no self respecting gal is gonna get within a hundred yards of you if you listen to this stuff. **Mark Deutrom**

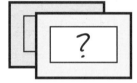

8 news

Outcry at Bible John comic

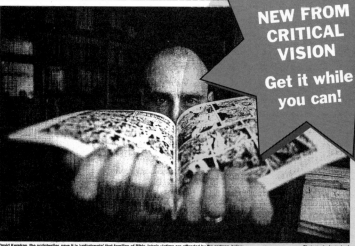

David Kerekes, the scriptwriter, says it is 'unfortunate' that families of Bible John's victims are offended by the cartoon, below

Photograph: Jason Lock

EXCLUSIVE
By **Neil Mackay**
Home Affairs Editor

THE infamous Bible John serial killings, which paralysed Glasgow with fear in 1969, have been turned into a grisly and sexually explicit comic book.

The family of Helen Puttock, the killer's last victim, have described the book as "disgusting", claiming it disgraces her memory and has unnecessarily forced them to revisit their painful past.

Bible John, who killed three women in Glasgow, was never caught. His victims were bound naked and strangled after being picked up by a well-dressed young man, who quoted Bible passages, at the Barrowland dancehall in Glasgow's east end.

The new comic strip, entitled The Tale Of Bible John: He Killed For Jesus, appears in Killer Komix, a collection of cartoon strips featuring murderers such as Fred West, the serial killer and rapist Ted Bundy and Peter Sutcliffe, the Yorkshire Ripper.

The book is published by Headpress, which specialises in printing disturbing books covering extreme sub-culture topics including bondage, fetishism, snuff movies and body modification.

Headpress director David Kerekes wrote the script for the Bible John comic strip together with infamous Italian cartoonist Antonio Ghura, who shocked Britain in the 1960s and 1970s with his sexually explicit comic strips.

The book opens with a graphic, full-frontal picture of Helen Puttock lying naked and dead

on grass. Her face is battered and bruised, there are ligature marks around her neck and blood is running from her mouth.

The comic strip action then moves to Glasgow's Barrowland dancehall, where the character of Bible John is seen walking among young dancers while quoting the gospels. The strip is filled with black humour mocking the conduct of the police during the failed murder hunt.

Each of the three murders is depicted by a sexually explicit drawing of a naked, beaten and strangled woman lying on waste ground. The comic also names each of the victims – Patricia Docker, Jemima McDonald and Helen Puttock.

In a grim in-joke, the name of David Kerekes appears in one drawing on the front page of a newspaper report about the murders. It reads: "David Kerekes arrested: I didn't [sic] do it, he said, as he was led away."

The comic strip ends with a frame featuring an aged Bible John wandering the streets of Glasgow in the present day.

Paul Carroll, a nephew of Helen Puttock, said: "This book sounds totally disgusting. To treat my aunt in this way is a disgrace to her memory. I can't understand why anyone would want to represent these events in this fashion, and make us revisit the past in such a painful and cruel way. It simply shouldn't be published."

Kerekes defended himself against accusations that he was representing violent, sexual murder in a salacious, titillating and insensitive manner. "I have always been fascinated by this case, primarily because the

killer was never caught," he said. "The killer remains mysterious and demonised. I think there will always be an exploitative element to any work dealing with serial murder, but I used a certain amount of humour to take away the mystery of the unknown killer. I

wanted to reduce him to what he was – a religious nut who killed women, not some mythical demon who we all live in fear of.

"It is unfortunate that the victims' families may be offended by this work. I am not making a joke of these women's deaths or trying to

make it sexually charged – I was trying to exorcise the demons of Bible John."

Kerekes, who also edited Killer Komix, had to censor one of the cartoon strips because of British obscenity laws. The story, called The Bondage Murderer! The True Twisted

Tale of Harvey Glatman, recounts the crimes of an American sexual sadist who killed a number of women during the 1950s.

It features scenes of extreme sexual sadism and hardcore bondage as well as graphic depictions of rape. One scene Kerekes censored – by simply placing a small black circle over the most explicit areas of the drawing – shows the rape of a crying and bound girl who begs for her life before being choked to death. Kerekes said: "I felt horrible about having to censor the book, but I had to abide by our obscenity laws."

The book also contains a short cartoon strip on the Cromwell Street killings, which ends with a frame showing Fred West lying laughing in a bath above the decomposed remains of his victims.

The book is interspersed with

mock-up movie posters for imaginary films about serial killers. One, called Grandpa Ghoul, relates to the murders of Albert Fish, a paedophile from the USA in the 1920s who was convicted of killing a seven-year-old girl and eating her. The cartoon poster says: "Gourmet Flesh Pictures Presents Grandpa Ghoul. Starring Albert Fish as the parents' sadistic nightmare. He doesn't care if the meat's well-done, medium or rare ... as long as it's human. For this old gentleman, your torture is his pleasure. When Albert invites you over for dinner, the main course is you. In Cannibalistic Colour."

A comic strip on Richard Speck, an American mass murderer who killed eight student nurses when he broke into their shared apartment, shows the killer surrounded by bound and gagged teenage

girls, either naked or dressed in lingerie, crying at his feet. One artist had prepared a comic strip on the crimes of Ian Brady and Myra Hindley, but Kerekes said he would not publish it, claiming it was too taboo.

"I am trying to be irreverent about the cult of the serial killer. I sympathise with the victims of these men, but their crimes are in the public domain and I have the right to deal with them. The Bible John artwork may be too sexual, but that was the artist's choice," said Kerekes.

The 37-year-old publisher added: "I realise this is going to cause a big furore, but I hope my critics see I've tried to balance things. Yes, it is exploitative, but I am trying to remove the glamour our culture attaches to killers. And yes, it may be shocking, but in our culture the only way to stop people being complacent is to shock them."

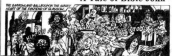

HE KILLED FOR JESUS!
A Tale of Bible John

THE BARROWLAND BALLROOM IN THE SUNNY HEART OF THE EASTEND OF GLASGOW...

KILLER KOMIX 2

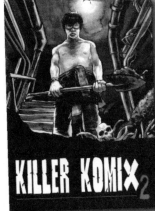

by
Sophie Cossette, Dogger, Steven Friel, Antonio Ghura, David Huxley, David Kerekes, Phil Liberbaum, Mike Matthews, Rik Rawling & Phil Tonge

AT LAST! The long-awaited follow-up to the critically acclaimed KILLER KOMIX! From a team of top artists comes **KILLER KOMIX**₂, a savage — and at times poignant — indictment of serial killer psychosis. Several notorious crime cases are represented in ADULT COMIC STRIP FORM, deconstructing the media circus surrounding the phenomenon of the serial killer, while at the same time recognising the impact these pariahs have had on (mis-)shaping the Twentieth Century.

Vile lust-murderers like Jack The Ripper and Bible John continue to be topical, with writers and filmmakers speculating on their real identities and motives. Faceless or known however, serial killers are omnipotent on the urban landscape — representing society's true life demons and bogeymen.

KILLER KOMIX₂ has a few tales of its own with regard to these murderous, almost mythical shadow-beings (featuring Ted Bundy, The Boston Strangler, The Yorkshire Ripper, Fred West, The Bondage Murderer and others). Not many of the tales have a happy ending, but — like life — not all of them have a sad one, either.

88 pages
ISBN 0 9523288 1 X
£9.95 plus p&p
(UK £1.35/Eur £1.85/Elsewhere £3.80)

NOTE: For mature readers only. Please confirm that you are 18 or over when ordering. Mail order address over page.

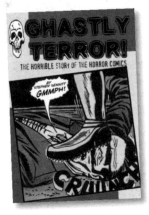
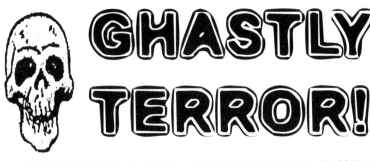